Downrange, the .338 Lapua round hit the assault team leader at 3000 feet per second. The armored figure lurched forward like he'd been kicked by a horse and slammed into the side of the warehouse before falling motionless to the ground. The gunner beside him spun just in time to take Manning's second shot in the chest. He staggered backward, tripping over his fallen companion.

The big Canadian rolled away and began to crawl to his next sniping position, as the enemy started to sweep the trees with automatic rifle fire.

Rotors whipped the treetops as someone sought him from above. Green tracers streaked down in vertical lines of smoking light as the door gunners did recon by fire.

"Phoenix One, I'm pinned down! If you're going to do something, you've got to do it fast!"

DON PENDLETON'S

STONY

AMERICA'S ULTRA-COVERT INTELLIGENCE AGENCY

MAN®

OCEANS OF FIRE

A GOLD EAGLE BOOK FROM

WORLDWIDE®

TORONTO • NEW YORK • LONDON
AMSTERDAM • PARIS • SYDNEY • HAMBURG
STOCKHOLM • ATHENS • TOKYO • MILAN
MADRID • WARSAW • BUDAPEST • AUCKLAND

First edition December 2006

ISBN-13: 978-0-373-61970-2
ISBN-10:   0-373-61970-7

OCEANS OF FIRE

Special thanks and acknowledgment to
Chuck Rogers for his contribution to this work.

OCEANS OF FIRE

To U.S. Special Forces

CHAPTER ONE

Tajikstan

"There's the bugger now." David McCarter scanned through his laser range-finder binoculars. His target led the front of a column of horsemen that wound its way through the mountain pass on ponies bred on the steppes of Asia. The shaggy little horses almost looked like overgrown dogs and the stirrups of their riders threatened to brush the ground.

"I make it an even forty." Gary Manning lay prone in the rocks beside McCarter and peered at their objective through the 3x10 variable-power optical sight of his .300 Magnum Dakota Longbow tactical rifle. "Man, is he ugly."

Gotron "The Goat" Khan was a little man with a head like a bowling ball and a body shaped like a pear. The sloping shelf of his brow, his wide, flattened nose and the sparse beard tufting his chin made him look like his nickname. The fact that he had a complexion that looked as if he had taken a fragmentation grenade to the face didn't help.

"He put the 'ugh' in ugly," Calvin James agreed over the com link.

The ex-Navy SEAL was right, but despite first impressions, Gotron Khan was the most feared man in the Zeravshan Mountains. He was a modern-day warlord with his own fief, a kingdom built on the profits of smuggling guns, opium and slaves, and he ruled with an iron fist. He carried a WWII Soviet-issue Cossack saber in his sash, which was the symbol of his rule. The law of Khan was simple. Minor offences required the removal of a hand; felonies called for a beheading. Khan liked to dispense justice personally whenever possible. His men were heavily armed with black market Russian military equipment of every description, from submachine guns to squad automatic weapons.

It was the suspected black market Russian military equipment wrapped in carpets on the pack mules that held the interest of Phoenix Force's leader. McCarter thumbed his throat mike. "I want the Goat, and what he's packing on those mules. Options?"

"Well, I make it a full platoon of light cavalry." Manning kept his crosshairs on Khan. "We can beat 'em easy, but securing them is another matter. When we start shooting, they can scatter and fast."

T.J. Hawkins chimed in from farther down the side of the gorge. He was the youngest member of the team but spoke with the hard-won experience of a Delta Force commando. "The next village is ten klicks east. We're ninety-nine percent certain that's where they're going. We can wait until nightfall, insert soft and make it a snatch rather than assault."

"Rafe?" McCarter queried.

"I don't know," Rafael Encizo replied. "We're in Khan's stomping grounds. We let him get into the village and who knows how many more men he'll have, and we'll have to worry about collateral damage if things go hot."

"Cal?"

"Rafe's right," Calvin James stated. "I say we take them here and now."

McCarter agreed with the assessment. "We take them here, in the narrow, and cork both sides of the bottle. T.J. you plug the back door. I'll take the front."

Manning frowned without taking his eye off his scope. "We'll need about a minute to get into position. How do you want to play it?"

"I guess I'll just go chat up the bastard." McCarter set down his binoculars. "All units. I'm heading down. Equip for Plan B. Be in position in two minutes."

Phoenix Force responded "Affirmative" from their various positions.

McCarter made his way swiftly down through the rocks. As he hit the mountain path, he could hear the clatter of the horses' hooves on the stones and smell the animals as they approached. The horsemen were in their own territory and at a low state of alert, laughing and smoking cigarettes. The Phoenix Force leader waited behind his chosen boulder until Manning spoke in his earpiece. "Ready on your go, Phoenix One."

The Briton stepped out onto the path. Horses reared and men shouted in alarm. McCarter smiled at the warlord in a friendly fashion. "Top of the morning, Khan."

Two dozen automatic weapons whirled in McCarter's direction. Gotron Khan sawed savagely on the reins. The horse rolled its eyes and stamped, but not in fear. McCarter had startled the stallion and now it wanted to attack him.

"Top of the morning?" The Goat slapped his thigh delightedly. "English! Goddamn it!"

McCarter smiled. "You got me."

"Hey!" Gotron took in McCarter's desert camouflage

fatigues, body armor and the scarf wrapped around his head. The warlord gazed appreciatively at the Barrett M-468 weapon system draped casually across McCarter's shoulder. The 6.8-caliber rifle looked like an M-16 on steroids. A SUSAT optical sight had been mounted on the receiver and a 40 mm M-203 grenade launcher hung beneath the barrel. Eight inches of United States Marine Corps OKC 3S bayonet hung conspicuously from the muzzle. The Goat stabbed a gleefully accusing finger at McCarter. "British SAS! Who Dares Wins!"

"Well…" McCarter shrugged. "Not exactly."

"Not exactly?" Khan leaned back in his saddle and scratched his goatee with the muzzle of a Russian A-91 compact assault rifle. "You lost?" He pointed south. "Afghanistan and NATO forces are eight hundred kilometers that way."

His horsemen, who spoke English, smiled unpleasantly.

"No." McCarter shook his head. "Not lost."

Khan cocked an eyebrow. "You are on a mission."

"As a matter of fact I am."

"Ah! Goddamn!" Khan leaned forward with almost childlike-curiosity. "A secret mission?"

"No, no secret." McCarter lifted his chin toward the baggage. "I'd just like to know what those mules are carrying."

Gotron Khan smiled to reveal a mouth that could only be described as dental armageddon. "Cucumbers!"

The horsemen laughed coarsely.

"Yeah, bloody great big ones." McCarter laughed. "Or so I hear."

The laughter of Khan's men became rougher and their eyes went hard. Manning spoke in McCarter's earpiece. "All units in position."

"The biggest!" Khan grinned.

"And where're you off to with your great big cucumbers, then?" McCarter shrugged innocently. "If I might ask."

"Mecca!" Khan roared. "We are on Haj!"

Khan's men laughed uproariously.

The leader of Phoenix Force smiled. Gotron Khan and his forty horsemen smiled back. It was all very congenial.

"I'd fancy a look," McCarter suggested.

The Goat sighed. "I fancy you give me your rifle now."

"I think I'll hold on to it." McCarter replied smiling. "But, tell you what, mate. Why don't you and the lads drop yours."

Gotron Khan stopped smiling. The muzzles of two dozen weapons pointed at McCarter in open hostility. The Briton spoke quietly into his mike. "Show of force, lads."

Horsemen shouted in alarm as Phoenix Force rose up out of the rocks. Khan craned around in the saddle and looked at Hawkins blocking the narrow path behind and James, Encizo and Manning in the rocks above.

"Well, English. You and your…four men?" Khan shook his head sadly. "Four men, have us surrounded, goddamn."

"Goddamn bloody right we do." McCarter nodded. "Now I'm going to count to five, and you and your men had better be dismounted and disarmed."

Khan stared incredulously.

"One," McCarter announced.

"Crazy Eng—"

There was no "Two." Phoenix Force cut loose.

Each man save McCarter held a South African 40 mm Milkor revolving grenade launcher. They hammered off three quick rounds into the horsemen. The grenades broke apart into multiple bomblets as they hit the ground, skipping and hissing beneath the horses' hooves. Khan's horsemen struggled to control their rearing mounts. McCarter fired his M-203 into the ground directly in front of Khan and stepped back behind his boulder as his grenade flipped apart. He stripped off his fringed scarf and prudently pulled his gas mask over his face.

Automatic weaponsfire erupted all along the mountain path, but Phoenix Force had already dropped back behind cover. McCarter jacked a rubber baton round into his M-203 as he stepped out from behind his boulder.

Yellow marking smoke flooded the gorge in thick clouds. In the saffron haze the rocky landscape looked like the surface of Venus. Had McCarter not been wearing a gas mask he would have found the atmosphere almost as hostile. Beneath the burning smell of the smoke element for a split second he might have detected the more subtle odor of pepper and apple blossoms as CN/DM gas mixture blossomed unseen in the yellow fog.

McCarter put Gotron Khan in his sights.

The Goat leaned forward and threw up on his horse's head.

CN/DM mixture was known colloquially as "Super Tear Gas." It had all the tearing and burning effect of military-strength CN with the fun and frolic of vomit gas. It temporarily blinded and burned the eyes and throat, and at the same time sent the gastrointestinal track and the colon into spasm.

Horses were happily immune to the effect.

They weren't immune to being regurgitated on by their riders, and they were instantly aware that their masters were no longer in control of them or themselves. Horsemen spilled to the ground as they were bucked spewing from their mounts. Phoenix Force had risen from cover. The 40 mm Milkors thudded in their hands as they emptied their remaining three chambers into the ambush.

CN/DM was rated as a nonlethal riot control agent, but

it was toxic in high enough concentrations, and a man who was choking and vomiting at the same time could drown as he swallowed his lunch into his lungs.

A few of Khan's men who were still mounted fired their guns blindly into the hillside. The sound of gunfire was enough for their horses to renew their bucking and send their riders to the ground. Gotron Khan remained in the saddle. He'd lost his rifle but his razor-sharp Cossack sword rasped from its sheath. He put spurs to his horse and charged, weeping and drooling to stab at McCarter where he stood.

McCarter triggered the M-203 and the grenade launcher thumped. The solid rubber baton round was the size of a shotglass and hit Khan in the chest at 85 meters per second. Remarkably the warlord remained in the saddle. He drunkenly raised his saber for the killing blow. Froth flew from the horse's mouth as it raced to trample McCarter.

The Briton stepped to starboard to avoid the saber and cracked the extruded aluminum butt of his carbine across the horse's muzzle. The stallion screamed as it sailed past shaking its head and bucking its hindquarters five feet in the air. Khan catapulted out of the saddle, flying, arms outstretched, until gravity brought him to the ground in a pinwheel of limbs.

McCarter put a knee in the warlord's back and hog-tied him with plastic riot-cuffs. "The Goat is secure. T.J.?"

Hawkins held up the lead rope to the string of mules. "I have the packages."

The Phoenix Force leader nodded. "Calvin, give me a head count and sitrep."

Khan's men were down in retching agony. Phoenix Force strode among them in their gasmasks and did a quick search. They kicked away weapons and buttstroked anyone who tried to rise with their Barrett rifles.

James was kneeling beside one of the prostrate horsemen. "All forty accounted for."

"Situation?"

"We hit them with twenty grenades. That's a high concentration. This one here had an allergic reaction to the gas and was going into anaphylactic shock. I hit him with epinephrine and he's stabilized." The ex-SEAL medic gazed upward. The clouds of yellow marking smoke were breaking up. "But the wind is around fifteen knots and we're getting rapid dispersal. Their bodies should detoxify the agent in thirty minutes, but they're going to be messed up with nausea, shortness of breath, physical weakness and possible mental depression for the next twenty-four hours. They won't be following us anytime soon. I'm willing to leave them as is."

"Aces." McCarter slung Khan over his shoulder. "Gary, what have we got?"

Manning was over by the mules. The big Canadian had unwrapped one of the carpets and was staring at the contents. "The Goat wasn't lying. He's got great big cucumbers all right."

McCarter approached and heaved Khan over a spare mule. Manning was the demolition expert of the team, but the Briton knew what he was staring at. The gray-green metal casing was roughly the size of a suitcase. Manning had flipped open a small control panel in one corner and he was examining the small bank of knobs and numeric dials.

Gotron Khan was transporting Russian nuclear demolition charges.

"You have a make and model?"

"It's hard to make out with these goggles on." Manning scanned the serial numbers along the side. "But this is definitely Soviet-era stuff. By the construction I'd say they were manufactured in the 1980s. They're dial-a-yield, anywhere from one to ten kilotons depending on the job."

"Right, let's wrap this up. Gather your weapons and grab your rucks. I want to be out of here in five minutes and at the primary extraction site in an hour." McCarter pulled his wandering-frequency satellite phone and deployed the chunky L-shaped black antenna. "Jack, we require extraction. We'll be at the primary extraction sight in sixty minutes."

Stony Man's ace pilot was stationed at the NATO coalition base in Kholm, Afghanistan. "I'll be there in forty-five."

"Roger that." McCarter hit a button on his phone. "Stony Base, this is Phoenix One. Over."

"Phoenix One, this is Stony Base." Mission controller Barbara Price was eight thousand miles away in the Stony Man War Room in Virginia, but her voice was as clear as a bell. "What is your mission status?"

"All four packages retrieved, and we have the Goat. We're moving to primary extraction site. Extraction estimate one hour."

There was a long pause on the other side of the line. "Please repeat, Phoenix One. Did you say four packages?"

David McCarter's stomach went cold. He knew it had been too easy. "Affirmative, Base. Four packages. One special guest."

Several moments passed before Barbara Price spoke again. "Phoenix One, we have a problem."

CHAPTER TWO

Oval Office, Washington, D.C.

"Six nukes?" The President of the United States wasn't pleased.

"Nuclear demolition charges, sir," Hal Brognola corrected. He wasn't happy, either.

"Demolition charges?" The President frowned. "You mean, backpack nukes."

"No, sir." General Jack Harper Hayes was the top military man on the President's cabinet. The wiry little man seemed almost too short to be a general, but he had started his military career as a combat engineer and he knew a few things about blowing stuff sky-high. "He means nuclear demolition charges. They're used to blowing things up."

The President raised a droll eyebrow. "So I gathered."

"What I mean is, sir, a nuclear demolition charge is not strictly a weapon. Its yield is low, generally between three to ten kilotons. No one has ever used one in combat but its typical purpose would be to destroy a very large or hard target, like a dam or an underground bunker or even to dig a giant hole if you needed one. We contemplated using them in Afghanistan to drop the tunnel complexes in Tora Bora, but the Joint Chiefs decided that although the nuclear fallout would have been nil, the political fallout of the United States being perceived to be using nukes would have been disastrous. So we went in the old-fashioned way."

General Hayes gazed off into the middle distance a moment. "The old-fashioned way" had changed over the years. In Vietnam the then Private Hayes had been the smallest man in his platoon and been "volunteered" to crawl down into the Vietcong tunnels and clear them out.

In Afghanistan they had lit up the tunnel entrances with fuel-air explosives that sent massive blast waves down the tunnels and then hit them from above with deep-penetrating guided bombs before heavily armed and armored Army Rangers had gone in wearing night-vision equipment and hurling tear gas ahead of them.

In Vietnam, Hayes had been sent down alone with a flashlight, a .45 and a knife.

The President nodded. "So you're saying it's a giant satchel charge."

"Indeed, sir," the general agreed. "An excellent metaphor."

"But a ten-kiloton satchel charge, nevertheless, and two of them seem to be missing."

"That does seem to be the situation." Hayes gazed at Brognola as he said it. The general clearly thought Delta Force could have wrapped things up quite nicely, and like a number of military men before him, he was extremely curious as to why there was a man from the Justice Department in the room, much less why the big Fed seemed to be one of the key people in control of the operation.

The President shrugged at Brognola. "Hal?"

"We got the word from British MI-6 two hours ago. They

have a contact in one of the Russian arsenals. He confirms the count is now six. We retrieved four of them in the Zerva-shan Mountains forty-five minutes ago. We have to assume the other two are taking a different route out of Tajikistan."

"And we have no idea as to that route?"

"No, sir, we don't. However, the team took a high-priority prisoner and they have hopes of getting some useful intelligence out of him."

The President scowled deeply. Both rightly and wrongly, the United States reputation for fair and humane treatment of prisoners had been tarnished in recent times. "That had better be done by the book or not all, Hal."

General Hayes chewed his lip. "I hate to suggest this, Mr. President, but we don't have time to ship this guy to Guantanamo and go through normal procedures."

The President stared at Hayes bluntly. "You're suggesting torture."

"I'm suggesting, sir, that while the yield is low and the fallout minimal, a nuclear demolition detonated above ground in an urban center would result in thousands of casualties." Hayes let out a heavy sigh. "And I'm suggesting we have contacts in that region. Allies with less scruples than ourselves."

"So…" The President steepled his fingers and looked into a very ugly place. "We wash our hands and let someone else do our dirty work."

Brognola met the President's gaze. "Sir, the team currently has the man in custody. They have been in this situation before and produced results in manners your predecessors found acceptable. Give them an hour."

"An hour?" Both the President and the general stared at Brognola in shock.

The Justice man nodded. "They have very…forceful personalities."

Dushanbe, Tajikistan

GOTRON KHAN WAS nervous. He had every right to be. The warlord was tied to a chair in a cellar, facing five of the most dangerous men on Earth. Khan sat beneath the single bare bulb and sweated while Phoenix Force stared at him, as silent as headstones. The criminal swallowed with difficulty and screwed up his courage. "I want a lawyer."

The men of Phoenix Force regarded him like a bug.

"I have been exposed to illegal war gas and wish medical treatment…and an interview with Red Cross representative."

Calvin James leaned against the wall with his arms folded. "You hungry, Khan?"

"I…" Gotron winced. His body had detoxified the CN/DM gas in his bloodstream, but he was still green around the gills and the violent stomach spasms he'd endured left him hunched and beaten as if he'd gone ten rounds out of his weight class. "I think n—"

"How about a nice, cold, greasy pork sandwich?" James suggested.

Khan paled.

"Mmm, tallowy." James Calvin sighed. "With a nice, tall, cool glass of olive oil with a butter floater to wash it down and—"

The sweat sheening Khan's brow began to run in bullets.

Hawkins shook his head at Calvin. "You are one sick dude."

Gotron Khan was the man who was sick. The warlord was as white as a sheet.

McCarter gazed down at Khan condemningly. "Where are the rest of the nukes?"

"I…don't…" Khan gasped.

McCarter pulled a spent grenade casing out of a ditty bag

and wafted it in front of Khan. A hint of apple blossom and pepper was discernable in the close confines of the cellar. Khan made a gobbling noise as his stomach spasmed in recognition of the scent. It was said that fatigue made cowards out of all men, but pain and fatigue could be endured through training, personal toughness and willpower.

Chemically induced nausea leveled the playing field, and Adamsite gas would bring Superman to his knees.

Gotron Khan shook like a man who had spent a bad eight days sailing the North Sea in winter and had been told he was going back out.

"No…" Khan gasped. "N-no, please, I…"

McCarter held the spent casing a little closer to Khan's nose. "Where."

"I…cannot tell you."

McCarter spun on his heel. "Gas him again."

Gary Manning slipped a grenade out of his jacket and pulled the pin.

Khan shrieked. "No!"

The big Canadian kept his thumb on the cotter lever and raised an eyebrow at McCarter. The Englishman turned and stared down at Khan implacably. "Where?"

"I do not know, but—"

"But you might know someone who does?" McCarter suggested helpfully.

Khan's eyes were riveted in horror at the cylindrical grenade in Manning's hand. "Perhaps."

"Perhaps you're about to puke so hard you're going to bring up your bloody shoes."

"No!" Khan's eyes rolled in revulsion and terror.

"Or perhaps not." McCarter shrugged noncommittally. "It's up to you."

"I—" Khan scuttled back as far as his restraints would let him as the Englishman loomed over him.

"Khan." McCarter peered deeply into the man eyes. "I really want you to get this right."

U.S. Embassy, Dushanbe

PHOENIX FORCE SAT in an arc around a titanium laptop attached to a satellite link. David McCarter checked his watch. "The lad's late."

T.J. Hawkins walked in on cue. He held an ice bucket loaded with drinks and set them on the table with a frown. "Explain to me how I became manservant for this chick-enshit outfit, again?"

"Because you're the youngest." Calvin James reached over and snagged a beer. The lanky black man grinned. "And it would be politically incorrect for me or Rafe to do it."

Hawkins considered for a half second suggesting Manning get up off his dead ass, but the big Canadian had put his feet up on the table and apparently was waiting for it with a smile on his face. Hawkins let that one die on the vine.

"T.J.?" McCarter pulled a bottle out of the bucket and frowned. "What is this?"

"Uh…a Coke?" Hawkins pointed at the wasp-waisted, fluted-glass bottle defiantly. "Look at that shape."

McCarter stared at Hawkins unblinkingly. "It's diet."

Hawkins stared at the bottle. Aside from the Coca-Cola logo it was covered with incomprehensible scrawl. "You read Tajikistani?"

"No, Tajikistan doesn't bottle Coke. They import from bottlers in Russia and the former Soviet states. This is Ukrainian, and diet. You can tell by the gold cap and the Cyrillic writing."

Hawkins blinked. "You need an intervention."

McCarter shoved the offending soft drink back into the bucket and pulled out a beer.

"Man…" Hawkins dropped into a chair and cracked himself a Russian brew. "How do I get transferred to Able Team?"

McCarter hit some keys on the computer. "Khan gave us two names." A picture of a bullet-headed man appeared. His shaved head and his face had uniform-length stubble. His flat black eyes lived up to his nickname. "Here we have Sharypa 'The Shark' Sharkov. He's Russian *mafiya,* and represents Moscow organized crime interests in Tajikistan. Interpol has a rap sheet on him as long as your arm. Standard provincial *mafyia* scumbag. He breaks legs, extorts, runs guns and prostitutes, and sends a piece to Moscow."

"First we get 'The Goat' and now 'The Shark'?" Rafe snorted in amusement. "All we need are Camelboy and the Limpet and we'll have our own bad-guy petting zoo."

McCarter hit another key. A disturbingly handsome man appeared on the screen. His black wavy hair was pulled into a short ponytail and his Vandyke made him look like Satan in an Armani suit. "This is Aidar Zhol, our local boy. He doesn't have an animal nickname. He is an animal. Name a law of nature and he's broken it. He likes the high life, likes gambling and spends a lot of time in Moscow. If you're a Russian general or high-ranking politician and you want a beautiful, virgin Tajik girl fresh from the hills for your rape room, Zhol's the man you see. He also owns a piece of any Afghani heroin that comes through the capital and owns the only casino in town. If you're transporting nukes through Tajikistan, it's a good bet Sharkov and Zhol at least know about it if they aren't actually extracting a safe-passage fee. We have two devices unaccounted for.

I'm betting either one or both of them have them or at least know which way they went."

James took a long pull on his beer. "Russian nukes don't just go missing. Someone has to deliberately misplace them."

McCarter nodded. "MI-6 has an informant who broke the news about the nukes. There's no doubt a Russian general had to be involved. The question is, which one? If these were actually nuclear warheads, we could narrow the selection down to officers of the Russian Strategic Rocket Forces, but these are nuclear demolition charges. They aren't governed by any treaty and several Russian military branches have their own small stockpiles, so tracking our wayward general is going to be tough on the Farm's end."

Hawkins leaned back in his chair. "So we're going to have to find him starting from the gutter up. Typical."

James echoed the sentiment. "Tell me we have some kind of in with these guys."

"We just might," McCarter stated.

James didn't like the smile on the Englishman's face. "Shit…"

"That's right. Our in just might be *you*." McCarter clicked more keys. A black man with a shaved head appeared on the screen. His powerful physique strained his immaculately tailored blue-silk suit. To the trained eye it was clear that he was wearing a pistol beneath his jacket. He sat at a table with a beautiful, grinning blonde under his left arm while a second leaned over his shoulder laughing. A massive diamond adorned one ear. Dozens more glittered on the gold rings on his fingers and the custom Rolex Submariner on his wrist.

Sitting next to him was Aidar Zhol. They both had their arms over each other's shoulders and were smiling happily into the camera.

"That is Clayborne Forbes." McCarter hit another button and the same man appeared staring forward, iron-jawed and stern, wearing the dress white cap and blue jacket of the United States Navy. Service ribbons adorned his chest. "Lieutenant Clayborne Forbes. Former United States Navy SEAL. A year ago he was on operations in Afghanistan. His tour was up and he declined to reenlist. Honorably discharged. The last that was heard of him was that he was an independent contractor in Afghanistan for one of the stateside security companies."

"And now the brother is dripping in blondes and bling in Tajikistan." James shook his head. "Bodyguard?"

"Ostensibly. The name Navy SEAL has a hell of a lot of cache. Having a man like Forbes for a bodyguard would certainly enhance Zhol's reputation," McCarter stated. "But the Farm figures he's probably a hell of a lot more than that. In the past year most of Zhol's competition has wound up dead. Now, I'll grant you, what with the civil wars, ethnic in-fighting, separatist movements, Russian *mafiya* and Muslim extremists, the former Soviet South Asian states are the wild, wild west. But Zhol's enemies aren't dying in the usual drive-by bloodbaths or car bombings, they're—"

"They're getting ghosted," James concluded. "SEAL style."

"That is the current conclusion we're working with."

"I don't like pulling the race card, David." James's eyes went hard. "But I don't like being sent to hunt my own, know what I'm saying?"

"I can understand that, but we're talking about a man aiding and abetting in heroin trafficking and selling little girls. There's also the matter of two loose nuclear demolition charges. And if his name was Nigel Ian Smythe and former SAS, I'd be the one going in."

James let out a long breath. "I hear you."

"Zhol's casino is called the Silk Road. When he's in town he lives in the penthouse. Intelligence says Zhol is in town. It's Friday night, so he'll probably be in the house and Forbes should be with him. We need to arrange a meet-and-greet."

McCarter gazed around the table. "Any suggestions?"

CHAPTER THREE

The game was Texas Hold'em. Calvin James was winning, and winning big. He stared coolly into the smoldering eyes of his remaining opponent. Everyone else had folded and it was James's deal. The man in front of him was heavy-shouldered and wore a poorly tailored suit of local manufacture, and a short turban.

The man was a maniac.

In poker a maniac was a hyperaggressive player who raised, bet and bluffed big pots whether he had a great hand or nothing at all. A genuine maniac wasn't a good player, though he or she could often dominate a timid table. Players who occasionally played maniac to confuse their opponents were quite dangerous.

James's opponent was positively psycho.

The game had attracted a crowd. The Silk Road mostly attracted Russian businessmen and local women who were ready to be relieved of their hard-earned currency. A smattering of diplomats and ex-patriots rounded out the clientele. Onlookers gasped as the man in the turban shoved chips forward to the tune of ten thousand dollars. He leaned in and thrust out his jaw, daring James to match it. It was a form of tell, or a habit that gave away the strength of another player's hand. The most amateur forms of tells involved leaning. People unconsciously leaned forward and projected aggressiveness when they were bluffing. By the same token they leaned back with unconscious relief when they were dealt a strong hand.

Psycho Boy might as well have put a neon sign over his head.

James's piles of chips tinkled and spilled as he shoved ten thousand dollars forward. "Call."

The maniac turned over his cards to reveal two pair, aces and eights, the Dead Man's Hand.

James turned over his cards. "Four ducks."

The man in the turban started stupidly at the four deuces on the table. James had cleaned him out, and reached for the pot. "Nice playing with y—"

"Cheat."

The immediate environment around the table went dead silent. The man looked up from the cards with murder in his eyes. "You cheat."

"Listen." James held up both hands in peace. "I—"

"Blackie…cheat." The man was literally vibrating with rage. "Every time you deal, you win."

James took a calming breath. "Friend, you—"

"Cheating negro," the man declared.

A mountainous pair of bouncers began moving toward the table.

James's fist closed around his drink. "You know, not my country, not my house, not my cards. I don't speak the language. Hell, I'm not even that good a player. I'm just lucky."

"Luck!" The man spit the word.

"Yeah." James leaned back in his chair and grinned. "Lucky to be sitting across from a loser like you."

The man froze.

James took a dainty sip of his gin and waggled his eyebrows over his glass insultingly.

"Bismillah!" The man erupted from his seat. He screamed incoherently and grabbed the edge of the table. The crowd screamed as he heaved the poker table upward, flipping it over and sending chips and cards flying. "I kill!" the man shrieked. "Kill you!"

The bouncers descended, trying to smother the irate gambler with shear weight. The man in the turban seemed awkward, but his fist flew into one bouncer's jaw and dropped him like he'd been shot. The other bouncer reached to grab the frothing man and was scooped up into a fireman's carry, airplane spun and sent flying across the craps table. Furniture shattered and patrons ran screaming in all directions.

The demented gambler advanced on James, his fingers curled into claws. "Kill you! K—!"

James rose from his chair and flicked his wrist, sending two ounces of gin into his attacker's eyes. Before the man could even react to the stinging liquor, the Phoenix Force commando's fist pistonned three times in chopping right-hand leads. The first blow snapped the man's head back. On the second, he turned his wrist over and jammed his thumb into the notch between the maniac's collarbones. The man had no time to gasp as his throat compressed because the third punch took him in the solar plexus.

The turbaned man made a sucking noise and went pale. James grabbed him by his shoulder and spun him, seizing him by his collar and the back of his pants. He marched the blinking and wheezing man past cringing patrons to the front of the building.

He whispered in the maniac's ear, "Sorry about this, Rafe."

Encizo's eyes rolled and drool came from one corner of his bloody mouth, but his voice was very quiet and lucid amid the chaos in casino. "No problem, amigo—"

James took two lunging steps for momentum and flung Encizo through the smoked-glass double doors. People outside the casino screamed as the Cuban flew to the pavement in a cascade of glass. He rolled to a stop and lay bleeding on the sidewalk.

"Punk," James announced as he made a show of wiping his hands.

The cocktail waitresses were still screaming and casino patrons shouted in consternation. A pair of Indian businessmen stood clapping their hands delightedly at the show.

James smiled and took a bow.

Shotguns racked behind him. He put up his hands and very slowly turned. Clayborne Forbes was pointing a stainless-steel Smith & Wesson .357 Magnum revolver at his face. The weapon was a custom job, a product of the Smith & Wesson Performance Center. Its frame was made of titanium while the barrel and cylinder were stainless steel. James could clearly see the extra pair of holes that turned the revolver into an eight-shooter and the ugly lead cavities of the hollowpoints it had been stuffed with. For the average human, firing a Magnum with a two-inch barrel would be problematic at best.

Forbes didn't look as though he'd have any problems.

He was even bigger in person, six-foot-four and built like an NFL tight end. His huge hand engulfed the grips of his pistol. Two more bloated, bearded bouncers flanked him, armed with enormous, 23 mm Russian KS-23, folding-stock shotguns.

"Well, goddamn." Forbes blinked at James in surprise.

Black men weren't exactly common in Tajikistan. He lowered his revolver slightly. "You African or American?"

"African American." James smiled. "Chicago, south-side born and raised."

"No shit?" Forbes jerked his head toward a steel security door at the far end of the casino. "Follow me, Chicago." He nodded at the bouncers. "Mukhtar, Askar, a round of drinks on the house and get this shit cleaned up, and find the brother's chips."

The two men lowered their shotguns and began shouting at the cocktail waitresses and the busboys. James followed Forbes into a standard casino security suite with banks of monitors watching the action at every table. Three security men stared up from their screens at James in open curiosity.

Forbes sighed. "Gonna have to relieve you of that piece."

James nodded and reached under his jacket. He drew his Heckler & Koch P-9 from the concealed small-of-the-back holster he wore and handed it over. Forbes took in the big .45's rakish lines appreciatively. "Nice."

Forbes's gleaming revolver rose to James's face and the cylinder full of gaping, 125-grain hollowpoints turned as Forbes cocked back the hammer. "Now, you want to tell me what you're doing in my crib? Or do I call in Mukhtar and Askar and have them squash it out of you?"

James leaned back slightly from the .357's muzzle and held up his hands. "Heard a rumor a brother was getting ahead up north and came to see for myself."

"Now that's the kind of rumor that can get your ass killed. You—" Forbes suddenly stared at the ring on James's finger. It was gold and carved with an eagle holding a trident and an anchor. It was the symbol of the United States Navy SEAL. Forbes's face went flat. "If that ain't for real, I'm going to cut it off you at the wrist."

James grinned delightedly at a similar ring on Forbes's gun hand. "Oh, man, you're shitting me!"

The security men stared uncomprehendingly as the two men began a sudden, rapid exchange of Navy SEAL–speak involving teams, operations, mutually known naval officers and the halcyon days of BUDS, or basic underwater demolitions/SEAL student training.

After about five minutes of family reunion, Forbes holstered his pistol. "Well, fuck me running. Calvin James, you know I think I might even have heard of you at a SEAL meet or two."

It was entirely possible. James and Forbes were two different generations of SEAL, but the United States Navy SEALs were a small, tightly knit community and African-Americans an even tinier minority within them. SEAL meets were get-togethers where SEALs past and present met to swap stories and gossip, engage in miniature SEAL-style Olympic events and down enormous quantities of alcohol.

"Man, they say you just up and disappeared one day, went all spooky. Got recruited by a special operations group or some other kind of top-secret black ops shit. Dropped off the Earth."

The best lies were told by omission and cradled in truth. "That is a fact."

Forbes handed James back his pistol. "And you came all the way here just to see my sweet ass? I mean, I know I'm pretty…" Forbes left his doubt hanging between them.

"I was retired for a while, and I really didn't care for it. Then the Man asked if I would like to reenlist for the War on Terror. I took a year contract, the coin was decent, but I heard the private work was better. Hired on with Knight Securities to help train their newbies."

"Heard of them," Forbes acknowledged.

"But I got all nostalgic and shit, and decided I wanted to see some action."

"Always a mistake."

"Don't I know it." James shrugged. "So I hit the dirt in Iraq. Hadn't been there in years. It was still 115 degrees in the shade, still infested with sand fleas and a brother still couldn't get a piece of ass to save his life, but the car bombings, private security boys being dragged and hung from bridges and the hostage beheading? That shit was new. I didn't dig it, so I went to Afghanistan. Lot of guys were making money in the private sector over there, double or more than what Uncle Sam was paying. Then one day in Kabul, I heard that rumor about a brother living large in Tajikistan. Sounded so crazy it had to be true." James opened his hands, taking in the cut of Forbes's suit and the diamonds and gold dripping from his hands. "And here you are."

Forbes frowned. "You sayin' you came here for a job?"

"You hiring?" James countered.

Forbes's laughter rumbled in his chest. "Well, now, I'll tell you. I got this town shit-scared. These Tajiks never seen a soul brother, much less soul brother SEAL. Shit, two of us? We could take this whole cracker-barrel country for every last somoni they got.

"Somoni?"

"Yeah, it's the currency they replaced the Russian ruble with around here." Forbes shook his head. "I wipe my ass with it." He dug into his pocket and held up a gold money clip thick with U.S. one-hundred-dollar bills. "The good news is this gig pays in long, cool green."

One of the security men nodded respectfully at the big man. "Mr. Forbes."

One of the monitors showed Encizo lurching to his feet. His turban was askew and his eyes rolled dazedly.

Forbes lifted his chin. "You want me to jack him up?"

"I already did." James flashed his smile. "And I took him for 10 K."

Encizo staggered away into downtown Dushanbe, bleeding and mumbling.

"Well, brother, I feel the love. I surely do." Forbes loomed forward. "But you are going to need references, and then you are going to have to meet the Man."

"CALVIN'S IN." McCarter confirmed.

"Excellent." Aaron "The Bear" Kurtzman said over the satellite link. "How did the initial insertion go?"

McCarter looked across the table to where Encizo sat holding a chemical ice pack against his lumped and purpled jaw. "Smoothly."

Kurtzman's brow furrowed at McCarter across the Web cam. "He's not wearing a wire, is he?"

"Calvin said to get the love he's got to show the love, and with a SEAL running security, wearing a wire would be suicide. I agreed with him. T.J. is watching the casino and will engage in a loose tail when he emerges. Rafe and I are ready to move on word go, and Jack has a helicopter hot on the pad with a full war load at the Dushanbe airport. Any other action is Calvin's call."

Kurtzman scratched his beard. "You know you've put that man out on a limb."

"The good news is that he has the best cover in the world, and that is his cover isn't a cover. He is who he says he is. The head honcho over at Knight Securities is a former SEAL, knows Calvin and was happy to back up his private contract story. Anything else Calvin can ad-lib as the situation warrants. Also, Special Forces groups are clannish, thick as thieves. Forbes is a United States Navy

SEAL, and he's got to be as giddy as a schoolboy to suddenly have a fellow SEAL as a partner in crime. On the criminal front, Forbes has done yeoman's work decimating Zhol's enemies, so Zhol has every reason to want to double his fun."

"I still don't like it."

"You get paid not to like it, Bear, and we appreciate that." Kurtzman sighed. "When does Calvin have his interview with Zhol?"

McCarter glanced at his watch. "He should be meeting the man as we speak."

"AN AMERICAN SEAL?" Aidar Zhol's eyes looked Calvin James up and down. The crime lord sat in the casino office. The walls were covered with crushed-red velvet. His thronelike chair was red leather, and the wood of his desk and the carpet matched. Zhol was dressed from head to toe in black. He sat in his blood-red room, draping himself elegantly across his chair, and looked positively satanic.

"Man, did you see the security tape of him whipping that deadbeat's ass?" Forbes waved a hand. "What else could he be? Besides, I've checked his references. He's who he says he is."

"Indeed, I do not doubt you." Zhol leaned back in his chair. His deep voice and accent made him sound like Dracula. "Though he seems a bit small to be a bouncer."

"I'm not suggesting you hire him as a bouncer, and you aren't thinking it." Forbes leaned his massive frame against the wall and folded his arms across his chest. "The brother has skills, know what I'm saying?"

Zhol lifted a sculpted eyebrow. "As good as yours?"

"Well, he is old-school SEAL," Forbes conceded with a grin. "But I can bring him up to speed."

Zhol's eyes were unreadable. "And you, Mr. James. What kind of employment are you looking for?"

"Well, like Clay said. I am old school. I gotta start thinking about my retirement. Now, I got some money squirreled away, and I can always sit my ass behind a desk at a security firm. For that matter I've got that Navy pension waiting for me. But you know?" James shook his head in disgust. "Fuck that shit. I'm thinking I want to shrivel up and die someplace warm, with a beach and a boat and a lot of willing señoritas as a comfort in my old age. That'll take some investment money. Honestly? I came up here looking for some fat paychecks."

A slinky cocktail waitress entered the office with a loaded tray. Her hair was so black and her skin so pale she looked like a vampire. Her lips were blood-red against her complexion. Her dark eyes slid up and down James in a very friendly fashion as she handed him a gin and tonic. Forbes lifted an immense snifter of brandy from the tray and a cigar from an open box. Zhol took mint tea from a gold cup and an unfiltered Turkish cigarette between his little and ring fingers. The girl lit their smokes. One corner of her lips quirked upward and she gave James a lingering look before swiftly disappearing.

Zhol let out a long stream of blue smoke toward the overhead lighting. "So, tell me, Mr. James, what are you willing to do for me?"

"Well, I'd rather not run drugs or pimp little girls. But I still have a few skills." He sipped his gin. "Tell me, Mr. Zhol. You have enemies?"

Zhol smiled at Forbes. "Significantly fewer than I once had."

"The law of business is to expand or be swallowed up. You strike me as an expansionist. I have no doubt you'll be making new enemies, and encountering new problems." James had kept his attitude relaxed, but he was a trained Special Forces soldier. Such men were a breed apart. Having joined Phoenix Force, he was now the elite of the elite, and one of the most dangerous men on Earth. He let that intensity show through as he stared deep into Zhol's eyes. "Both of which I can make disappear."

"Shee-it!" Forbes's smile lit up the room as he pointed at James, recognizing the eye of the tiger. "I told you, Mr. Zhol. I told you. Just look at that beautiful man. You put me and him together? We could take goddamn Moscow." Forbes became serious again. "And we have current projects, and we have run into problems. This man would be a fucking force-multiplier, guaranteed."

Zhol didn't blink as he stared into James's eyes. The Phoenix Force commando saw the sociopath behind the flat black eyes and knew the man was a killer. Zhol's eyes slit almost imperceptibly in decision.

"Mr. Forbes, give Mr. James ten thousand dollars. He will room with you in your suite until we find him his own place. We are on a swift timetable, and you will indeed need to bring him up to speed. However…" Zhol suddenly smiled disarmingly. "Bermet found you pleasing, Mr. James. Did you like her?"

"The Goth girl?" James sat up in his chair. "Oh, hell yes."

Zhol nodded at Forbes. "Tell Bermet Mr. James's door will be open to her tonight if she so desires. Tell her she might wish to bring along her friends Dariga and Tatiana." Zhol shrugged at Calvin. "They're twins."

James blinked. "Really."

Zhol rose and extended his hand. "Have a pleasant evening, Mr. James." He smiled as they shook hands. "I look forward to a profitable association."

"Man…" Forbes put a massive hand on James's shoulder and nodded as Zhol left the office. "I told you this was a good gig."

CHAPTER FOUR

"We have the Shark." David McCarter sat, apparently reading the paper, in the terminal. He watched the bullet-headed Russian mobster disembark with a pair of body-guards. Sharypa Sharkov was a big man, built like a rugby striker who had let himself go. His men weren't particularly large or imposing, but they scanned the crowd around their boss with hard and searching eyes. The men weren't mindless muscle. They were shooters, and their right hands never strayed far from the front of their black leather jackets. McCarter subvocalized into his throat mike. His signal was being picked up at the safehouse and bounced to Virginia through the sat link. "Two bodyguards. My instinct is they're ex-Special Forces. Packing heat."

"Affirmative, Phoenix One." Barbara Price confirmed. "Tail is go."

"Roger that." McCarter tossed down his paper and walked through the terminal slightly behind and parallel to Sharkov. They stepped out into the drizzly Tajikistani morning. Sharkov stepped into the back of a dilapidated

Toyota Land Cruiser. McCarter eyed the vehicle. "Base, according to intel, Sharkov likes to live large, correct?"

"Affirmative, Phoenix One. According to what we got from CIA Moscow Station, Sharkov tries to keep up with Zhol in the style department and usually fails."

"What's his usual ride?"

Price looked over the Sharkov report. "He keeps a Mercedes-Benz in every city he has a residence in."

"Right." McCarter threw a leg over his BMW F650 Dakar motorcycle. There was another nondescript SUV parked behind the one Sharkov had just gotten in. The vehicles had dents and scratched paint, and had apparently seen hard use over the years. Sharkov's had one headlight out. There was nothing strange about that. Toyota SUVs were one of the workhorses of the Third World. They were nothing if not reliable. If you just changed the oil every three thousand miles they could limp along for decades doing yeoman's work. Manning's eyes narrowed as he took in the tinted windows. He smiled as the SUVs' engines snarled into life and spit blue smoke into the misting rain. These weren't workhorses.

They were thoroughbreds.

The dirt and dings were cosmetic. Beneath the sheep's clothing their V-6 engines were supercharged. David McCarter was a connoisseur of motor vehicles. He took in the run-flat tires and recognized the work. The two Land Cruisers were the product of Asbeck Armoring Bonn. He suspected they were VIP 100 Models, and custom. They would be armored against massive attack, undoubtedly European "extreme protection" B6 category. They would be impervious to direct hits of up to .30-caliber. It would take a .50-caliber, crew-served machine gun or a shoulder-launched rocket to crack them.

McCarter's instincts spoke to him. Sharkov was going incognito and with maximum protection. The Briton followed the two-car caravan for a couple of blocks, and their destination was evident. "Base, targets are headed for the casino."

"Affirmative, Phoenix One. It's your call."

McCarter considered his options. If his suspicions were correct, he had just located the courier vehicles for the nukes. They needed to be marked. Once they went into the casino they'd be parked in Zhol's private garage. There were three options. James could go in and tag them, but that would risk his cover. Two, McCarter could send in a team to break into the garage and do it. It probably wouldn't be too difficult, but security would have to be overcome. There was a good chance that the enemy might know they had been breeched. They wouldn't know why or by whom, but the enemy security level would rise, and that threatened the entire mission.

Option three was for McCarter to do it himself, now.

"Base, I'm taking the shot."

"Affirmative, Phoenix One."

McCarter pulled up behind the Toyotas. He reached into his jacket. His hand brushed past the concealed Browning Hi-Power pistol and pulled out a slightly over-size cell phone. At a traffic light he came to stop beside Sharkov's vehicle. He could feel the gaze of the hardmen inside from behind the tinted windows. McCarter flipped open his phone as the light changed. The back passenger window of the Land Cruiser cracked slightly. McCarter passed the armored vehicle, apparently oblivious of scrutiny as he shouted into his phone in angry French.

The phone had no communications capability. Two stubby smooth-bore barrels and a pair of compressed air cylinders took up body of the phone. The flip-top acted as a simple see-through optical sight. McCarter slid open the muzzle cover and unlocked the safety while he blithered away about getting out of the goddamn country and delivery schedules. He let Sharkov's car pull slightly ahead.

"Merde!" McCarter took the phone away from his ear and held it forward, his thumb working the buttons as if he were dialing another number. He peered through the sight and put the crosshairs on the brake light above the cargo door of Sharkov's Toyota. He pressed zero on the keypad and the phone chuffed in his hand.

McCarter was rewarded as the .40-caliber paintball hit the bulge of the brake light and shattered, splattering across the top of the vehicle. He was slightly worried by the rain factor. He had only two shots, and one positive mark was better than two partials, and the window of opportunity was now. He pressed the button and fired his second barrel. He missed the brake light but luck was with him as the plastic sphere struck the luggage rack and broke apart.

"Marking complete, Base. Do you have the target acquired?"

"One moment, Phoenix One." Back in Virginia, Price turned to Kurtzman. "Aaron?"

The computer wizard was staring intently at a six-foot flat screen. The feed showed an overhead view of traffic. Cars and trucks moved through the grid of streets and buildings in high-contrast black-and-white. The paintballs McCarter had fired were filled with a liquid infrared luminescent material. Once it was exposed to air, it gelled and hardened, and the infrared chemical reaction began. The luminescent material was clear and, after it hardened, almost undetectable. Minute scrutiny would reveal it as a hardened film that would be difficult to scrub off. The infrared goo in the projectile was its own power source. Over the course of time it would fade. However, for the next three months, it would glow at a steady 300 candlepower in the infrared spectrum, invisible to the unaided human eye.

Three hundred miles above the surface of the Earth a distinctly nonhuman eye was peering intently at the traffic in downtown Dushanbe. The satellite's radio receiver was tracking McCarter by triangulation. Once he was acquired, it was child's play to keep him under observation. Kurtzman could make out McCarter on his motorcycle and he could see the truck he trailed. The infrared feed of the satellite was set to high-polarity white on black. Infrared light sources appeared in varying shades of white. McCarter's high-performance motorcycle had its own very distinctive infrared signature.

Kurtzman grinned as the top of Sharkov's armored SUV suddenly began to glow in brilliant bright white. The satellite instantly noted the candlepower and frequency of the infrared light source and transmitted them to the net of satellites that the NSA had programmed to observe Tajikistan. Day or night, rain or shine, anytime Sharkov's vehicle was above ground, Kurtzman and his team would be watching it.

Kurtzman nodded at Price. "The Shark is marked."

"Good work, Phoenix One. Target has been acquired."

"Affirmative, Base." McCarter's motorcycle peeled down a side street. "Breaking contact."

The Stony Man computer wizard watched Sharkov's armored convoy as it wound its way through traffic and disappeared into the casino's rear garage. He leaned back in his wheelchair and typed a few keys. The giant screen split between the real-time feed of the satellite watching the Silk Road casino and a geopolitical map of Southern Asia. "The question is, Sharkman," Kurtzman mused, "if you have the packages, where are you planning on taking them?"

"Now, I don't normally dig nines." Clayborne Forbes held up an SR-3 Vikhr short assault rifle. "But this baby puts them out at a thousand feet per second with a bullet twice the weight of a normal 9 mm. Throw in the tungsten steel penetrator? This shit sings. Kevlar? Car doors? Titanium? If you aren't wearing ceramic when this hits you—" Forbes's smile was ugly as he handed it to Calvin James "—Jack, you are dead."

Sharkov laughed harshly and took another weapon from the crate.

James examined the weapon. It had a stubby barrel and a folding sheet-metal stock. The super-heavy 9 mm bullet was fired from a cut-down AK-47 rifle shell. The weapon's light weight produced heavy recoil and a cyclic rate of 900 rounds a minute that was almost impossible to control on full-auto, and ate up the 20-round magazine in a matter of heartbeats.

However, in the Vikhr's favor, the design bureau of the Russian Central Institute of Precision Machinery Construction had been asked to create a compact, concealable weapon that could penetrate most known forms of body armor and semihardened vehicles for Russian Special Forces. That was all metaphor. The real specification was in fact for a short-range weapon that would penetrate armored limousines, body armor, the bodyguards wearing it and the VIP they were trying to protect. The Vikhr had been designed as an assassination weapon, pure and simple, and it had met the specification with wild success.

James snapped the folding stock into place and shouldered the Vikhr. The weapon's inaccuracy was somewhat mitigated by the laser-designator mounted beneath the barrel and the optical sight above. He wouldn't care to go into open battle with it, but for slaughtering someone in a phone booth or defoliating the occupants of a limousine during a drive-by, he was hard-pressed to think of a better weapon.

Forbes seemed intimately familiar with it.

"Fact is, Cal. This town? Hell, this whole country, is wide open. Zhol's got the local juice." Forbes grinned at Sharkov. "And the Shark has Moscow backing him."

"*Da.*" Sharkov nodded. "That is correct."

"Hell." Forbes checked the fit of the Vikhr's shoulder rig. "As long as we don't assassinate the president or blow up a mosque, we can do anything we want, kill anyone we want, hell, take anything we want." He racked the action of his weapon and chambered an armor-piercing round. "This place is a goddamn gold mine."

"You Navy SEAL, huh?" Sharkov turned his black eyes on Calvin James. "Like Forbes."

"Yeah." James tried his shoulder rig and found he could draw the weapon smoothly from under his leather jacket. "Back in the day."

"Back in day." The Russian savored the American slang. "So what's the plan?"

"Baby-sitting from Point A to Point B. Nothing could be simpler."

James knew too much eagerness on his part would get him killed. They were both Special Forces operators, and from long, hard experience, hated being kept in the dark. He put some doubt into his voice. "Uh-huh."

"Listen, man, I know you don't like being out of the loop, but this shit is on a need-to-know basis."

"Need to know." Sharkov nodded.

James let his frown speak for him.

Forbes nodded in empathy. "We aren't pimpin', and we aren't pushin' drugs. I can tell you that."

Sharkov scowled at the admission.

"No, man, I told you, the brother's cool." He looked at James frankly. "We're transporting technology that some people with the right kind of money want to acquire. That's really all you need to know. Consider yourself a caravan guard. You guard the boss and the goods with your life. You do that and you're gonna see the fattest paycheck of your life, with more to follow."

Sharkov grunted. "Exactly so."

Forbes cocked his head. "You down with this?"

James racked his Vikhr and flicked on the safety. "I'm down with it."

"Good, that's real good." Forbes handed him a bandolier with eight spare 20-round magazines. James checked each one out of habit, noting the blue-gray needle points of the tungsten carbide cobalt penetrators protruding from the tips.

"Point A to Point B, huh?"

"That's right."

"Does a brother get to know where Point B is?"

Forbes looked to Sharkov. The ugly Russian shrugged dismissively. "He is SEAL. He will figure it out soon enough anyway."

James looked back and forth between the two men. "And?"

"Afghanistan, man. Kabul." Forbes tossed his weapon and ammo on the bed. "Our old stomping ground."

"We're driving from Dushanbe to Kabul?"

"That's right."

"That's a long-ass drive."

"Right again." Forbes leaned in and spoke in a conspiratorial tone. "But, strangely enough, the safest. Like I told you. We got the juice."

"So when do we ship out?"

"Tomorrow, at dawn." Forbes leered. "So tonight I'd go with Bermet or the twins, but not all three. You're going to need your beauty sleep for this one."

CHAPTER FIVE

"Wake up, Sunshine."

Calvin James was already awake. He had sensed the door of his room opening and without opening his eyes had known it was Forbes by the big man's footfalls and the power of his aftershave. Some of James's limbs were pinned by the sleeping Bermet, but beneath his pillow his right hand was curled around his Heckler & Koch .45. "Morning."

"Look at you." Forbes stared down in mock disapproval at the tangle of bodies on the bed and the champagne bottles strewed about. The big man tsked and shook his head. "You're a disgrace to the race."

James began to disentangle himself from Bermet. "When you see a sister here in Tajikistan, you let me know. Until then…"

"When in Rome." Forbes grinned and handed him a mug. The coffee was Turkish, strong enough to strip paint and heavily laced with sugar and cardamom. James sighed as he sipped the coffee. "This place does have amenities."

"It's good to a big fish in a small pond," Forbes agreed.

"Yeah." James stood. "But I want to be a big fish in a big pond."

"Oh, yeah?" Forbes looked at him measuringly. "Well, first things first. We got a job to do. Get dressed. Bring your bag. Follow me."

"How soon till we leave?"

"You have twenty minutes."

James got up and went to the bathroom. He ran water and then pressed his ear to the door. He could hear Forbes speaking very quietly and Bermet answering. She was being debriefed. She had gone through his bag and dresser drawers the first night. One look at his shaving kit told him that her nocturnal trip to the bathroom had included riffling his few belongings by the sink. Forbes had already checked James and his belongings for bugs, telling him he was on "probation," but the big man was taking no chances. James suspected his room was bugged. He couldn't afford to be caught on the phone or sending smoke signals from the roof.

But he had the collected minds of Stony Man Farm on his side.

James took out his toothpaste and squeezed. About five inches of minty-fresh, tartar-control dentifrice squeezed out and suddenly the tube ribboned forth clear gel. He stuck his arm out of the small bathroom window and began crudely writing on the side of the casino with infrared luminescent gel.

NUKES HERE

DPT 2O MIN

DST KABUL

James shucked himself into the clothes hanging on the door hanger. He took the gel and drew an invisible circle on the back of his leather jacket, then brushed his teeth and shaved. When he came, Bermet was gone. His bag was already packed and a second gym bag contained the Vikhr compact assault rifle and ammo. Forbes sat on the bed smoking a cigar and watching news on the casino cable. James strapped on his pistol and his knife. "Let's do it."

Forbes rolled to his feet. "Follow me."

They took a private elevator down to a private garage. Sitting incongruously among the limousines, sports cars and luxury sedans were three battered-looking Land Cruisers, their engines running. Zhol and Sharkov stood waiting, surrounded by a full squad of hardmen. It was bitterly cold. You could see the men's breath in the unheated garage. Beneath their bulky jackets the hardguys were clearly wearing armor and each had a gym bag like James's by his feet. Zhol smiled and rolled back a calfskin glove to glance at his Rolex watch. One satanic eyebrow rose in question.

"Sorry we're late, Mr. Zhol."

Zhol beckoned James over. "Mr. James." He nodded at one of his men, who raised the hatchback of the center vehicle. The Phoenix Force commando gazed at the cargo. In the back bed of the SUV were two suitcase-size metal casings painted in Russian military gray-green. Each was wrapped in military webbing with a pair of padded straps so that the device could be carried like a backpack. "Do you know what those are?"

James scrutinized the casings. "Clay told me we were transporting technology. Never saw a security case like that before, but it looks like military security and tamper-proofed."

"Indeed. And?"

"In the U.S. we liked to use thermite in security cases to burn the contents if someone messed with them. Russian military always preferred high-explosive charges. They like to kill the thief as well as destroy the contents." James eyed the case warily. "My bet is if someone tries to get inside that case it'll blow.

An enigmatic smile passed across Zhol's face. "Yes, Mr. James. If someone tampers with those cases, they will blow."

Sharkov nodded, smiling at the joke. "We do not want those falling into wrong hands, Mr. James."

"No," James agreed earnestly, "we don't."

Forbes's cell phone rang. He listened for a moment, then nodded. *"Guten morgen."* Forbes shook his head. *"Nien, keine Probleme, kein Problem an allen."*

James yawned and looked at his watch. Forbes was speaking German. There were no problems, no problems at all.

"Alles ist auf Zeitplan." Forbes smiled. *"Ja danke. Auf wiedersehen, meine Herr."*

All was going according to plan.

Forbes clicked his phone shut. He put a hand on James's shoulder and pointed at the two devices in the back of the truck. "Cal, you gotta guard that shit with your life."

James spoke with utmost sincerity. "I will."

Stony Man Farm

"THE PACKAGE IS MOVING." McCarter's voice spoke calmly over the sat link. "On schedule, just like Calvin said."

On the giant screen the satellite image of the Silk Road Casino showed three vehicles pulling out of the private rear garage. It was a misty morning, not ideal for infrared viewing, but the vehicle in the middle was still glowing bright white where McCarter had marked it the day before. "Roger that, Phoenix One." Barbara Price swung into her chair and adjusted her headset. "Showtime, people. Phoenix Flight, you are go."

The pilot's voice came back over the sound of rotors. "Gary and I are airborne. ETA downtown Dushanbe five minutes."

"I've established the tail." McCarter spoke over the sound of his motorcycle. A circle of bright white infrared luminescent paint marked his helmet like a halo. "They're heading due south, as predicted. Looks like they're going to take route A377 all the way down to the Afghan border."

Aaron Kurtzman shook his head. "I'm just not buying a road trip all the way to Kabul, despite the vehicles David reported. The route is too long, too mountainous and there are far too many curious and unfriendly people with AK-47's up in those hills. Zhol and Sharkov know they got hit up in the mountains once already, and by now they know Gotron Khan's gone missing. They're driving now to avoid the airport and any possible surprise inspection or ambush, but I'm betting after they leave the city they're getting off the main route ASAP. For that matter, those are off-road vehicles. I think they're going to go cross-country where a helicopter is going to pick them up."

Price's brow knitted. "These are Russian gangsters. They're known for their sticky fingers. I doubt they'd leave behind three custom-made, Asbeck-armored VIP specials. You're looking at over half a million dollars' worth of rides."

"You know, you're both right." Everyone in the War Room could almost hear Jack Grimaldi grinning behind the stick of his helicopter as things fell into his area of expertise. "Zhol owns construction companies, and this is Tajikistan. Ninety-nine percent of the country is mountain or desert, and the roads are so bad that almost any company that can afford it does their major hauling with helicopters rather than trucks. I'm betting Zhol has one or more Mi-26 Halos hot on the pad in some clearing outside the capital. The Halo's the most powerful helicopter on Earth. It's like a C-130 Hercules except with rotors. We're talking large-cargo clamshell loading doors in the back and a maximum payload of 44,000 pounds plus."

"Damn it." Price watched the three-car caravan wend its way south through the early morning traffic. "They'll just drive their SUVs inside the chopper and take off."

"It's worse than that." Kurtzman stared into middle distance as he began to crunch all the angles. "Jack's right. Zhol owns construction companies, so he probably has access to a fleet of helicopters. He knows he's been hit already. He'll be taking every precaution. If Zhol hasn't factored in possible satellite surveillance, Forbes has. They'll have multiple helicopters."

"A shell game." Price watched the satellite feed as Rafael Encizo and T. J. Hawkins pulled into traffic in a Russian Tarantula off-road vehicle marked with a broad circle of infrared luminescent paint on the hood. "And we can't be sure which vehicle the nukes are in, or if they've been split up."

"That's right," Kurtzman said. "We're playing nuclear poker with a Navy SEAL. The best of the best."

"Base, this is Phoenix Two," Encizo reported. "We have the caravan in sight. Paralleling."

"Affirmative, Phoenix Two," Price said. "Bear?"

"We can't afford to let these guys get out of the city, or even into a park or city square wide enough to land a helicopter." Kurtzman nodded and hit his comm switch. "Phoenix One, this is Bear. Take them down. Take them down now."

"AFFIRMATIVE, BASE." McCarter was a hundred yards behind the convoy. He wore infrared goggles beneath the visor of his helmet and he could see the white light shining off the back of the middle car. "Phoenix Flight, what is your ETA?"

"I have you in sight, Phoenix One."

"Phoenix Two?"

"We're parallel on Western Avenue, Phoenix One," Encizo replied.

"All units, I'm assuming the middle car has the VIPs and the packages. I want to avoid directly attacking it if possible. We take out the guard vehicles first then try to force the main target to stop. With luck, Calvin can work some magic from the inside. Phoenix Two and Three, come from behind. Phoenix Flight, drop Phoenix Four to plug any holes."

All units came back "Affirmative."

McCarter slid a Farm-modified RKJ-3M grenade from his jacket and pulled the pin. "Phoenix One, beginning attack run." The Dakar 650 snarled and spit blue smoke as the Englishman gunned the engine. McCarter's visor beaded with mist as he shot forward through traffic like an arrow.

The RKG-3M antitank grenade was a forty-year-old design, though still a clever one. The operator threw the grenade above the tank. A small parachute deployed from the handle so that the warhead deployed nosedown against the tank's thin upper armor. It had been used effectively in the 1973 Arab Israeli War, but its main drawback then and now was that the operator had to run up and throw the grenade at the tank. Tanks and armored vehicles generally bristled with cannons and machine guns, and their crews tended to take a very dim view of anyone running toward them with cylindrical metal objects in their hands. Antitank grenades were considered at best a last-ditch defense if not open suicide. In the twenty-first century there were few modern tanks or APCs against which the RKG-3M would still be effective even if the operator could survive to get close enough.

An unsuspecting Toyota Land Cruiser in misty morning traffic was another kettle of fish.

McCarter flew past the rear and middle cars of the convoy. He lifted his thumb and the cotter lever pinged away in his wake. He whipped in front of the lead vehicle, took a moment to match its speed and tossed the grenade back over his shoulder.

Tires screamed on the wet asphalt as the lead driver stood on his brakes. McCarter had counted on that. The grenade bounced off the windshield and landed nosedown on the hood of the vehicle.

The magnetic ring that had been welded around the edge of the cylinder-shaped grenade clacked onto the metal hood, and the parachute collapsed around the throwing handle as the grenade locked in place.

McCarter had five seconds of fuse time to get out of the ten-meter secondary fragmentation radius. The BMW Dakar screamed into the red line as the grenade detonated behind it. The copper forcing cone inside the grenade shaped the detonating 567 grams of TNT and RDX high explosive into a highly condensed jet of superheated gas and fire.

The fire shot out the wheel wells like a rocket in takeoff, and the SUV lifted off its front tires. German engineering was nothing if not efficient. The designers at Asbeck knew they couldn't make an SUV that could withstand shaped-charge attacks, but they had worked to minimize the damage and injury to passengers. The armored box around the engine channeled the blast up and down, and kept grenade and engine fragments from ripping through the passenger compartment. Halon fire-suppression units blasted out the burning oil and fuel, and hissed against the molten metal.

The stricken SUV slammed down on the molten remains of its run-flat tires.

McCarter whipped his motorcycle around in a screaming 180-degree halt. His 10 mm Parker-Hale Personal Defensive Weapon ripped free of the Velcro holding it in its shoulder holster. He snapped the folding stock into position and shouldered the weapon as all four doors of the armored Land Cruiser flung open at once.

The red dot of McCarter's reflex sight was a glowing white blob through his infrared goggles. The white blob coincided with the forehead of the driver, and McCarter squeezed the PDW's trigger. Three 10 mm armor-piercing slugs opened the smuggler's skull to the sky in a spray of brain and bone. McCarter raised his sights slightly as the driver collapsed and gunned for the man coming out of the driver's side passenger door. The Briton's first burst clipped the killer's shoulder and spun him, the second took him in the side of the face and rippled his head into ruins.

McCarter stood and shot. The men who leaped out of the passenger doors died even as they tried to level their automatic weapons. "Lead vehicle down! Hostiles down! Phoenix Two, attack—!"

The Phoenix Force leader swung his weapon back to the driver's door and exchanged fire with a fifth man who popped out spraying lead from a compact assault rifle. Sparks sprayed as McCarter's weapon mangled in his hands and his head snapped back like he'd taken a punch from a heavyweight. The Russian shooter fell with a crushed skull.

"Phoenix One!" Grimaldi shouted across the radio.

The PDW had taken two hits, and its action was dented and held open in a permanent jam. It fell from McCarter's nerveless fingers as he toppled back across his bike.

The Briton tasted blood in the back of his throat. He ripped his helmet free and drew his Browning Hi-Power pistol. The world spun as he tried to sit up, and he fell back again. The front of his motorcycle helmet had an inch-deep crater blasted in the forehead. The copper base of a bullet gleamed from the middle of the hole. Only the ballistic ceramic insert had saved his life from the armor-piercing round.

"Move!" Grimaldi roared.

McCarter rolled to his feet as the other two SUVs pulled around the smoldering lead vehicle. Their tires screamed on the wet asphalt as they caught sight of him and swerved inward. The rest of the caravan was swerving to crush McCarter beneath its wheels.

The Briton began to empty his Browning Hi-Power into the windshield of the left-hand vehicle. His pistol stood no chance of piercing the armored glass, but the bullets did spall and create spiderwebs of cracking in the upper glass layer. McCarter ran for the curb and his opponent swerved to take him. He leaped, arms outstretched, for the top of a parked ZIL sedan. His hands closed around the luggage rack as he heaved himself onto the roof. Metal screamed as the Land Cruiser sideswiped the ZIL. McCarter's foot went numb as the SUV's passenger window clipped his boot heel in passing and he was flung from his perch. He hit the sidewalk with bone-jarring force and rolled. He got to his feet and emptied the last four rounds of his pistol into the back of the second armored SUV in parting.

The driver spitefully ran over McCarter's Dakar, crushing one of the motorcycle's wheels and crumpling the front fork.

The Briton snarled in anger and limped back to the vehicle he had disabled. He took a compact assault rifle and a bandolier of ammo from one of the fallen gunmen as he roared into his mike, "Phoenix Flight! Cut them off!"

"Phoenix Flight in position!" Grimaldi replied. "Deploying Phoenix Four!"

Rotors beat the air as the pilot dropped his helicopter like a stone three blocks up the street. The little Russian Mi-34 Hermit was a civil aircraft Phoenix Force had acquired locally. Grimaldi held the Hermit a hundred feet over the intersection. Gary Manning fast-roped out of the cabin, falling toward oncoming traffic like a spider. Horns blared and brakes shrieked as Manning's boots hit pavement and traffic parted like the Red Sea around the heavily armed man. Manning spun his weapon on its sling as his two targets screamed through the intersection one block down.

"Phoenix Four in position. Targets acquired." The big Canadian shouldered his Barrett M-82 A-2 rifle. It was a huge rifle, more than five and a half feet long and weighing twenty-seven pounds. It used the same action as the Barrett "Light Fifty" heavy sniper rifle, but had been redesigned in bullpup configuration. Most of the weapon's massive action was situated in the back of the gun rather than the middle, and passed over the operator's shoulder.

McCarter dropped to one knee, holding the big Barrett over his shoulder like a rocket launcher. The two armored SUVs came on. One pulled ahead as Manning peered through the 3x infrared sight. He saw the halo of light eclipsed as the lead Land Cruiser pulled directly in front as a shield.

"This is Phoenix Four. I'm taking out lead vehicle." Manning put his crosshairs on the grille of the oncoming SUV. The .50-caliber round had been designed in the latter days of WWI with the specification of being able to attack observation balloons, aircraft and the tanks of the day. It had defeated such targets with grotesque ease, and a hundred years later it was still the most powerful round that one man could reasonably operate in a weapon.

The Canadian master rifleman squeezed the trigger.

The huge .50-caliber round shot forth a four-foot blast of flame from the muzzle and Manning grimaced as the rubber recoil pad behind the magazine kicked him like a mule. Steam blasted out of the lead vehicle's grille as the .50-caliber armor-piercing round punched through the armored box surrounding the engine. Manning yanked his muzzle down and fired again. The engine shrieked and clanked as the engine block cracked and the vehicle lost power.

Manning put his third shot through the driver's side of the windshield.

The armored windshield cratered around the .50-caliber hole and the interior went red in a spray of arterial blood. The SUV fishtailed out of control as the dead driver collapsed against the wheel. The vehicle veered onto the wrong side of the road and rammed into a parked bread truck at forty miles per hour. The side of the panel van folded around the front of the armored car.

The bumper of the last SUV was aimed straight at Manning and appeared to have no intention of stopping. Shooting into the last vehicle wasn't the preferred action. Calvin James was inside, along with two, ten-kiloton nuclear demolition charges. Sending armor-piercing bullets sailing through the car body or shaped charges sheeting the interior with superheated gas and molten metal was a last option.

The driver had no such reservations.

He accelerated straight for Manning where he knelt in the middle of the intersection. Manning dropped the big Barrett on its sling and clicked the brake on his repelling harness. "Phoenix Four requesting immediate extraction!"

"Extracting!" Grimaldi said.

The radial engine in the helicopter overhead roared into emergency war power. Manning's harness cinched against him as the helicopter's rotors hammered the sky and clawed for altitude. The Land Cruiser bore down on him like a juggernaut. Manning's feet left the ground as the helicopter pounded straight up into the sky like an elevator.

The vehicle tore past less than a yard beneath Manning's boots. "Phoenix Flight, Phoenix Four redeploying!"

"Affirmative, Phoenix Four!"

Manning released the brake and repelled to the ground, releasing the rope from his harness. "Phoenix Four deployed and clear!"

"Roger, Phoenix Four." Grimaldi took his helicopter back above the rooftops and resumed the chase.

The doors of the crashed Land Cruiser flew open.

The big Barrett was too unwieldy for a close-range fire-fight. Manning shrugged out of the sling and drew his pistol. The Para-Ordinance P16-40 barked in his hands as he began double-tapping the enemy. The range was twenty-five yards and the big Canadian could see the bulge of body armor beneath their jackets. At that distance he could reliably put every shot into a dinner plate in rapid fire. His first double-tap shot away one hardguy's jaw, and his second neatly put out another man's eye and brain as he went for head shots.

Manning moved toward cover as men deployed from the opposite side of the Land Cruiser. He dived behind a white Sputnik 4x4 sedan and rolled up, slamming his pistol across the hood. The .40-caliber weapon barked twice, cracking the skull of one of the Russian hardmen behind the SUV. Manning dropped low as the other two men opened up, their compact assault rifles spewing flame like buzz saws in their hands.

"Shit!" The Phoenix Force commando flinched as bullets zinged straight through the car he was using for cover. He jammed himself as low as possible between the curb and the tires. The Sputnik shuddered above him as it was riddled by automatic fire. The bullets zipped through and blasted on into the hairdresser's shop behind him. A bullet plucked at the shoulder of his jacket and sparks flashed inches over his eyes as the car body tore like cheesecloth. "Phoenix Four requesting immediate backup!"

"Phoenix Four, this is Phoenix One, I'm on your twelve!"

A man screamed as McCarter opened up from behind. Manning leaped to his feet as the remaining Russian dived over the hood of the Land Cruiser to avoid McCarter. Manning whipped up his pistol. His first two rounds hit the killer in the chest, standing him up and pushing him back against the vehicle's fender. The Russian raised his rifle even as he took hits.

His forehead geysered jellied brain as McCarter's bullet transversed his skull from behind. Manning holstered his pistol and sprinted forward, confiscating the dead man's rifle and his bandolier of spare magazines.

McCarter came up at the run. "Phoenix Flight, sitrep!"

"We have third vehicle directly beneath us," Grimaldi reported.

"Phoenix Two, what's your position?"

"Parallel course," Encizo replied.

"Step on it! Pull ahead three blocks and Phoenix Flight will vector you in." Manning fell into step with McCarter, scooping up his Barrett .50 as they charged up the street. McCarter broke into a dead run. "Take them out."

"Affirmative, Phoenix One." McCarter could hear the roar of Encizo's engine over the link as he accelerated. "Taking them down now."

CHAPTER SIX

"We're getting goddamn hammered!" Forbes thrust his finger angrily over the driver's shoulder and pointed at Manning where he knelt in the middle of the intersection. "Run his ass down, Gurza! Do you hear me? Run his ass down!"

Gurza stood on the accelerator. Manning made no attempt to move. Calvin James cradled his rifle, prepared to blow out Gurza's brains. Zhol rode shotgun next to Gurza, and Forbes was next to James on the seat. Sharkov and one of his hardmen were in the back, sitting on the nuclear devices. James doubted he could get all six, but that was his last option. Ideally, Phoenix Force would force the vehicle to a halt and convince Sharkov and Zhol to surrender. If that succeeded, then James would go along and surrender, also, continuing his cover and hopefully getting Forbes to drop information about the who and the where the nuclear demolition charges were headed.

If Sharkov and Zhol decided to go down fighting, James would be the Trojan horse and blindside their attack. His other duty was to make sure no one in the vehicle decided to go down in a blaze of glory and detonate the devices in downtown Dushanbe.

However, James wasn't about to let Gary Manning get turned into applesauce across the armored car's grille. The muzzle of his weapon drifted to the back of the driver's head.

Gurza swore. James watched through the armored glass as Manning was sky-craned into the air like a jumping jack up and over their vehicle. Forbes flipped his assault rifle to automatic fire as he swiveled. Manning had already repelled back down and was engaging the crashed car.

"God...damn it!" Forbes's face was a mask of rage. "Who are these guys!"

"Clay, that mother had a Barrett .50. These guys, they aren't *mafiya*. They're operators." James stared at Forbes grimly. "Brother, we're in trouble."

Sharkov snarled from the back of the truck. "Gotron! He was captured! Compromised! He betrayed us! I told you not to trust that goddamn hill bandit!"

"Gotron Khan did not know enough to betray us." Zhol produced a Russian R-92 revolver like a magic trick. The muzzle of the snubnose gaped only inches from James's eyebrows. "But he did."

Forbes spoke in a very low, very professional voice. "Mr. Zhol, we checked the man. His bonafides are real. We checked his room and everything he owns for bugs. I was with him every minute of the day and Bermet was with him at night. He had no way to communicate."

"Nevertheless." Zhol thumbed back the shrouded hammer of the revolver. He and James locked gazes. "He betrayed us."

Sharkov's carbine pressed into the back of James's head. "Bastard..."

James wasn't entirely certain his weapon would cut

through the armored panel in Zhol's seat back, but he wouldn't live to raise it, and regardless, it would be the last thing he ever did. He spoke without taking his eyes off Zhol. "Clay…"

Forbes's voice went cold. "Mr. Zhol…"

Zhol ignored Forbes as he and James continued their staring contest. "Will your friends negotiate for your release?" He smiled slightly as he answered his own question. "No, but they will pretend to, to buy time and set us up for another ambush. Mr. Forbes, take his weapon. Sharkov, radio the helicopter. Tell them to come into the city. We are extracting from the square in Pamir Park, but first, tell them to shoot down the enemy helicopter."

Sharkov began to shout in his radio.

Zhol still hadn't blinked. "Mr. Forbes, take Mr. James's weapon." He spoke to Sharkov's man in the back. "Levchenko, if Mr. Forbes does not take Mr. James's weapon, shoot him in the head."

Levchenko pointed his rifle at the back of Forbes's gleaming skull.

Forbes's weapon was pointed at the driver. "I'll blow Gurza's head off. This car will crash, and we all go down."

"Mr. Forbes, you know I respect you, but right now our priority is extraction. We can settle this situation later." Zhol's eyes and the muzzle of his pistol stayed trained on Calvin James. "But I am not going to ask you again. Take his weapon."

Forbes grimaced. "Cal, give me the goddamn gun. I got your back. Once we're out of here I'll straighten this shit out."

James shrugged. "Fuck it."

The compact assault rifle clattered to the floorboards. Everyone except Zhol sighed with palpable relief. Zhol's one concession was that he uncocked his revolver. "Good."

"I got your back, Cal." Forbes leaned down and picked up the rifle. "We'll straighten this shit out. I promise you."

Zhol jerked the muzzle of his pistol at James's waist. "The pistol, if you please."

Everyone's attention was on James. Even the driver had been keeping his attention on the rearview mirror, flicking his gaze back and forth between James and Forbes and the assault rifle aimed at his head.

They hadn't seen what the Phoenix Force warrior saw over Zhol's shoulder. James lifted his chin. "What's that?"

Everyone in the armored car looked out the passenger-side windows.

"Shit!" Forbes roared.

Calvin James braced himself as Gurza desperately cranked the wheel.

The last thing anyone saw before the world ended was Rafael Encizo grinning out of the roll cage of the Tarantula 4x4. The off-road vehicle T-boned the Land Cruiser broadside at fifty miles per hour. The armored SUV whipped into a violent 360-degree spin. Gurza lost control of the vehicle and rolled it. The world tumbled end-over-end as metal buckled, tearing and screaming into ruin. Sharkov and his man in the back weren't strapped in, and one of them bounced into the passenger area and landed on top of James and Forbes. The Phoenix Force commando grunted as the big man crushed him and was instantly flipped away as the Toyota rolled again. James tried to brace himself, but a ten-kiloton nuclear demolition charge bounced squarely into his face. He saw stars and tumbled with everyone else like the contents of an armored cocktail shaker. The Land Cruiser hit something and bounced. Everyone and everything collapsed to the roof as the SUV came to a rest on its back like a turned-over turtle.

The world was still spinning and James viewed it upside down and through a very long and dark tunnel. His mouth was full of blood and he couldn't clear his head. Battle instincts took over. He clawed for the door handle and shoved. The armored door was heavy, but James pushed it open with a groan. He reached back and his hand closed around pack straps. He crawled out of the Land Cruiser dragging the nuke onto the pavement with him.

It was early morning, but people were leaning out of windows and gathering on the street, shouting. James pushed himself to his hands and knees to retrieve the other device.

He threw up instead.

A large hand clamped down on his shoulder. "C'mon, Cal." Forbes heaved the man to his feet. The other nuke was already strapped to his back "Gurza's neck is broke. Suck it up. Help me with Zhol and Sharkov. We gotta steal a car and go." He turned back to the stricken SUV.

"Clay."

Forbes turned to find James's pistol pointed at his forehead.

"Don't move."

Forbes's eyebrows dropped dangerously as he stared down the barrel of the .45. "You Judas bastard."

"Calvin!" Manning and McCarter were shouting his name from somewhere along the street. "Calvin!"

Ten yards down the street the Tarantula lay on its side. Hawkins hung in his harness. Encizo was climbing out of the roll cage shakily.

"Judas bastard," Forbes repeated.

James didn't bother to respond. He saw three Clay Forbeses in front of him. He kept his front sight on the one in the middle.

Zhol's door was crumpled, but remarkably his power

window whined upward. The Tajik gangster wormed his way out onto the street. His face was a mask of blood. James kept his pistol on Forbes. He stepped to his left and slammed his boot into the side of Zhol's jaw. Zhol's eyes rolled back in his head as he rolled belly-up with the blow.

"Forbes. Shrug out of that nuke."

Encizo limped forward with his SIG-Sauer P-226 leveled. "And lose the piece. Real slow."

Out of the corner of his eye James noticed Sharkov lying in the back of the Toyota. He was speaking rapidly into his radio.

McCarter and Manning pounded down the street, shouting at the top of their lungs. "Calvin! Get out of there!"

Grimaldi suddenly veered his helicopter off.

An aluminum cloud came hammering out of the sky. The Russian Halo was the second largest helicopter on Earth, and the giant machine roared over the rooftops. It was a dedicated transport, but the Russians never designed a helicopter without some kind of armament option. The DShK-38 heavy machine gun mounted in the Halo's nose ripped a line of smoking holes through the tail boom of Grimaldi's little Hermit helicopter. The Halo came on and dipped its nose.

Tracers screamed down, ripping asphalt in a line that ran straight at Calvin James, who hurled himself aside. He was sprayed by chunks of road as the line of the death passed him by. He rolled back up into a gunfight.

"Hey, Cal!" Forbes's gleaming Magnum revolver boomed in his hand. James staggered as a .357 hollowpoint round hit his armor at the top of his sternum. He felt the supersonic crack like a knife through his eardrum as a second bullet passed inches from his ear. James's .45 thudded in his hand as he returned fire. Forbes jerked as the heavy slugs hit him and sat him down hard against the Land Cruiser.

Encizo dived for his life out of the line of the Halo's fire.

McCarter was spraying his rifle up into the air. "Calvin!"

The giant Halo's rotors beat the air like thunder and whipped the air between the city buildings into a hurricane. The mighty machine spun on its axis to bring its gun to bear on James again. The Phoenix Force pro took six running steps onto the sidewalk and hurled himself through the window of a tea shop.

Shattered glass fell in a cascade around him.

Armageddon erupted as the Halo opened up and fired its heavy machine gun into the shop at six hundred rounds a minute. The brick walls of the building were no cover but they took James out of sight. He rolled back directly against the wall to try and get under the helicopter's angle of fire. Glass, brick and mortar rained down as a thousand rounds of armor-piercing ammunition tore the tea shop apart.

James popped up as the fusillade suddenly ended. He ignored his cuts as he leaped back out. Manning was in the middle of the street with the big Barrett over his shoulder. He was firing nearly straight up. The heavy sniper rifle recoiled like a jackhammer in his hands as he pumped his own armor-piercing rounds into the chin of the Halo. The giant helicopter broke off, dipping to one side and disappearing back over the rooftops.

Clayborne Forbes was swiftly disappearing down the street with the nuke strapped to his back.

James broke into a dead sprint after him. His head throbbed with every footfall but he doggedly pursued. Forbes ran like the fullback he'd been at the Naval Academy. James staggered as a bullet struck him like a hammer between the shoulder blades. He turned to find Sharkov leaning against the Land Cruiser firing a pistol. James's .45 thudded and Sharkov staggered. Then he shuddered as McCarter ripped a 20-round magazine through him from his Vikhr rifle. Sharkov's man, Levenchko, dropped his rifle and dropped to his knees with his hands up.

McCarter waved James forward. "Get the nuke! Go! Go! Go!"

James slammed in a fresh magazine and sprinted on. The fact was, Forbes was younger and faster and had the lead. Forbes hit an intersection and turned left. The Halo suddenly thundered into view and followed him. James tasted the lactic acid in the back of his throat as he called on every last ounce of his flagging strength.

He rounded the corner and saw Forbes rising up into the air on the end of a rope. James took his pistol in both hands. The pistol cycled seven times in rapid semiauto and clacked open on empty. McCarter and Manning ran up behind him, weapons leveled, but the Halo was already receding from sight with Forbes strung beneath it.

James sank to one knee and tried to get air into his lungs. "What's...the situation?"

"Rafe has the other nuke. T.J.'s unconscious. Jack was losing power to his tail rotor and had to set her down. He crashed it in a soccer field three blocks from here. He's okay and heading our way. The good news is that we have Zhol. The bad news is..." McCarter trailed off as he watched the helicopter disappear into the rising sun.

"Bad news is we have a Broken Arrow," James finished. "Loose nuke."

CHAPTER SEVEN

Panji Poyan, Tajikistan

"Forbes." The voice on the secure phone was cold, clipped and spoke with a heavy, non-Russian accent. Forbes was fluent in four languages, but the man on the other end of the line chose to speak English. "Report."

"Sharkov's dead." Forbes sat in a safehouse on the Tajikistan-Afghan border and held an ice pack to his head. "Zhol's in custody."

"And the packages?"

Forbes's finger absently tapped the suitcase-size device next to him on the bed. "I have one."

The voice on the other end waited for moment. "And the other?"

Forbes glanced at his lumped face in the mirror and shook his head. "I have one," he repeated.

"And who has the other one?"

"I don't know."

"You do not...know?" the voice repeated.

Forbes scowled. "These guys who hit us, they were—"

"Were what?"

The ex-SEAL thought back on the battle. "Unorthodox. Throwing antitank grenades from motorcycles, ramming attacks, and their equipment was like they had their own candy store, whatever the job required. No budget constraints."

"So who are they?"

"They ain't SOCOM, that's for damn sure. All I know is one of them—"

"Used to be a Navy SEAL, like yourself, Mr. Forbes." The man on the other end of the line paused significantly. "This man you hired."

"Mr. Zhol hired him."

"On your glowing recommendation, as I recall."

"Yeah."

"I want the device back."

"Yeah."

"You wish payback."

"Yeah."

"What do you intend to do about this?"

"The only possible connection they have left is Sharkov. They'll have to go after the boys in Moscow, and they'll get information on them out of Zhol." Forbes began jacking truncated-cone, Teflon-coated, armor-piercing bullets into his .357 Magnum.

"What do you intend?"

"I intend go north." Forbes continued to feed slugs into his pistol. "And kill Calvin James's Judas ass."

"They will indeed most likely head to Moscow, but I think I have a better idea."

Forbes slid in the sixth round. "I'm listening."

The man on the other end spent several moments outlining his plan. "You concur, Mr. Forbes?"

"Yeah." Forbes grinned from ear to ear as he snapped shut the cylinder of the Smith & Wesson N-Frame. "Oh, hell, yeah."

U.S. Embassy, Moscow

"WE'RE LOOKING for a Russian general in bed with the Russian *mafiya*," Kurztman said.

The question would be finding the right one, and the team was pretty banged up. It had been a hard flight north with little time for rest or medical attention.

"One thing's been bugging me," James said. "Down in the garage, Forbes was talking to some guy on his cell, and he was speaking German."

"German?" Hawkin's eyes widened out of the purple raccoon mask of bruising. "You sure?"

"Oh, yeah. And he was talking respectful, like he was talking to his superior."

"I don't see the German angle, particularly if Forbes was muscle for a Tajik gangster." Encizo shook his head. "But then again I think there's a lot of things on this one we don't see yet."

"Let's stick with what we can see." McCarter turned to Calvin James. "What about Zhol?"

James leaned back in his chair. "We have him illegally detained downstairs. I spent the morning with him, and he isn't responding to interrogation." He looked pointedly at McCarter. "Question is, do we hit him with chemicals, or cut him loose and see where he goes?"

McCarter steepled his fingers in thought. "I say we cut him loose here in Moscow and see who comes to claim him."

"Or see who comes to kill him." Manning frowned. "Aidar Zhol is flesh-peddling scum, but right now he's scum under our protection and he's damaged goods. We cut him loose and someone is more than likely going to come and punch his ticket."

"Good." Hawkins had a light concussion and wasn't in a particularly merciful mood. "I say he cooperates with us or we let him and his damaged-goods-status ass go play with the Moscow boys."

"All right." McCarter nodded. "Cal, give him the choice, flat-out."

"I did."

"And?"

Calvin James sighed. "He used a number of politically incorrect words, but the gist of it was f— off."

Hawkins grunted. "Then he's made his choice."

McCarter had to agree. "Jack, we're going to need a chopper and permission to fly over Moscow airspace. Work it out with the CIA station chief."

"You got it."

"Cal, I want Zhol bugged so deep that even he doesn't know he's wearing a wire."

James scratched his chin. "Then let's set him free in the morning. I'll put something in his food tonight so he sleeps soundly and we'll rig him for sound and trace."

"All right, then." McCarter stood. "We set our pigeon free at dawn and see which way he flies."

Kremlin Square

"GET OUT." Aidar Zhol blinked as the hood was pulled off his head. He had never seen Jack Grimaldi before. Grimaldi popped the lock on the passenger door of the still-moving Mercedes 350SL. He grinned maniacally as he leaned across Zhol's bound wrists and opened the door for him. "I said out."

The gangster gaped around in himself in disorientation. "But—"

"See ya!" Grimaldi shoved Zhol out the door without coming to a complete stop. The gangster hit the paving stones, and the Stony Man pilot threw the key to his handcuffs after him. The pilot closed the door and pulled back into traffic. "Houston, the pigeon has landed."

"I have target in sight." Hawkins sat ten yards away on a motorcycle eating a sausage he'd bought from a vendor. He was dressed as a business messenger with a bag across his shoulder and a box bungee-corded to the luggage rack. "He's heading straight for the pay phone."

Zhol limped toward a pay phone, shoved in some change and began to speak immediately.

Gary Manning was deployed across the square on a second motorcycle. The rest of Phoenix was in a ZIL panel van loaded with surveillance gear courtesy of the CIA Moscow station chief. Encizo sat in the back of the van listening intently into a pair of earphones. He was connected with a translator in the U.S. Embassy's secure communications room. "Translator, do you read?"

The night before Aidor Zhol had slept extremely soundly. During that time they had put a tracer in the stacked leather heal of his Italian dress shoe and a second one in his watch. A microphone had been emplaced in the tooled silver gather that held his shoulder-length black hair in a ponytail. The cape of his leather duster had been broadly painted with infrared luminescent paint.

CIA Linguist Judith Tarko responded. "Target has not mentioned any names. He has identified himself, his location and demanded pickup. Your audio picked up the key tones of the phone. I have a man here running the tone tape to establish the number." Tarko paused as another voice spoke in Russian. "They have told him to sit tight where he is and they will bring him in."

The line suddenly clicked dead. Zhol hung up the phone and glanced around himself suspiciously.

Tarko sighed. "That's it, sorry we couldn't be more help. Give us thirty seconds to establish his destination number."

"Excellent work, Translator." McCarter watched Zhol through his binoculars. "Let us know when you have the number."

Tarko came back almost instantly. "I hate to say this, but it's a cell phone, belonging to one Zoya Krinkova, fifty-two-year-old housewife, and that isn't Zoya on the other end with Zhol."

It was a cutout phone. Either stolen or else some street level thug had given Mrs. Krinkova a small sum of money to start the account under her own name and keep it up while the phone itself had been distributed to parties unknown. The phone would be used once, in an emergency, and thrown away. Tracking the end user through her would be a monumental if not impossible task without the aid of half the Moscow police, and the Russian *mafiya* owned well over half of them.

"Thanks, Translator. We'll keep you posted." McCarter addressed his team. "It's a waiting game now. We wear Zhol like underwear and see where he goes. If he gets capped, we go in hard for the gunmen."

Phoenix Force came back in the affirmative.

Zhol sat on a bench and checked his watch. Hawkins leisurely strode by him and bought another sausage. McCarter drank three bottles of Coca-Cola while Enzizo and James went through a thermos of coffee.

After forty-five minutes, a bottle-green panel van pulled up to the curb near Zhol.

"Phoenix, we are go!"

Hawkins and Manning both threw a leg over their bikes.

Zhol rose and looked around himself. The sliding door of the van opened, and a black-gloved hand reached out to Zhol to help him inside. Zhol took the hand and put a foot into the van.

"Shit!" Hawkins warned. "We have trouble!"

The twin barrels of a sawed-off shotgun extended out the door at Aidar Zhol's face. The Tajikistani mobster's satanic eyebrows rose in horror and his eyes went wide. He jerked at the hand holding his, but he wasn't going anywhere.

"All units converge!" McCarter commanded.

Manning's bike burned rubber across the square as he tore toward the green van. The tires on the surveillance van screamed as James peeled out. Hawkins's SIG-Sauer P-226 pistol ripped free of its holster. Flame blasted from both barrels of the shotgun. Tourists and sightseers screamed at the twin detonations. Zhol's face disappeared in a red haze. His assassin let go of his hand and Zhol collapsed to the curb like a puppet with its strings cut.

The sliding door of the van slammed shut, and the vehicle roared away from the curb.

Hawkins's pistol trip-hammered in his hands. The rear tires of the old van exploded as he pumped a double tap into each one, and its back end dropped as it sank onto its wheels. The bumper showered sparks as it dragged along the pavement. Hawkins raised his aim and fired the remaining twelve rounds in his magazine into the back of the vehicle. Brakes screeched and horns blared as the stricken vehicle fishtailed crazily into traffic.

Hawk slammed a fresh mag into his SIG and gunned the engine of his Ural. "What about Zhol!"

"Forget him!" McCarter ordered. "Let Moscow police take him! We have a contact! Take the van!"

Hawkins shot into traffic. Manning had already crossed the square and was weaving between cars in pursuit. The van wasn't hard to spot. It had ripped away the shreds of its tires and was showering sparks off the back bumper and out of both wheel wells.

Traffic parted around it like it had the plague.

The driver of the van leaned out of his window. The small blue-steel shape of a Makarov pistol began popping off rounds at Manning in rapid fire. Manning's .40-caliber weapon filled his hand and boomed back. The driver jerked back inside as his side mirror exploded inches from his abdomen.

Sirens began wailing in the distance.

McCarter's voice came across the radio. "We have to wrap this up fast. It's broad daylight and we don't have a hunting license."

"Affirmative, Phoenix One." Manning pointed as Hawkins pulled up into the wingman position. "Front tires! I'll take the passenger side!"

"Affirmative!" Hawkins split off into the left lane as Manning went right. The former Ranger pulled in a few yards back from the driver's door and extended his pistol. The Swiss pistol barked three times and the van slumped into a left-leaning tilt. The driver nearly lost control as he overcorrected the wheel.

Manning raised his .40 to take the van's last leg from underneath it.

The driver violently spun his wheel to the right. Manning went full-throttle and leaped his bike up onto the sidewalk to avoid being crushed. Civilians screamed and dived out of the way as the big Canadian roared down the pavement. Manning jammed on his brakes to avoid running over an immense woman walking her dog. The woman stood screaming in place and the little dog jumped and barked between her legs. Between the cars parked on the curb and the storefronts girding the narrow sidewalk there was nowhere to go but through the woman and her dog.

Manning yanked his bike to the right, popped a wheelie and went through the display window of a flower shop instead.

His front tire erupted through the window; his rear tire hit the brick beneath it. The rear end of the bike bucked Manning off like a mechanical mule as it flipped nosedown through the display case. He flew through space in a cloud of sunflowers, daisies, marigolds and broken vases.

He came to a violent halt as he flew headfirst through double glass doors of the cold case. Manning smashed the shelving holding the displays and bounced off the solid wall behind them, then collapsed with the upper half of his body in the refrigerated case and his legs sprawled out on the floor. He lay stunned for a moment with sprays of roses and shattered arrangements heaped upon him like accolades upon the body of a fallen hero.

Manning pushed himself out of the case and fell back on the sea of broken glass covering the floor. His helmet and riding leathers had prevented him from being sliced to pieces. He waited for the telltale nausea that signaled broken bones.

"Phoenix Four!" McCarter yelled across the radio. "Phoenix Four!"

"Phoenix Four...down." Manning groaned. "I need extraction."

"Sit tight! We're on our way! Phoenix Five! What is your status?"

Hawkins had continued to follow the van. After trying to crush Manning it had gone one more block and come to a halt behind a parked truck in a space marked off by orange traffic cones.

"Target has stopped. No movement." Hawkins dismounted but his muzzle never left the vehicle. He ripped off his helmet and shouted in Russian, "Police!" He waved his hand violently and the few bystanders on the side street scattered. He stared at the parked truck and cones framing the van in the parking spot.

"I don't like it," Hawkins said as his instincts spoke to him. "I think this is their final destination— Shit!"

He dived over the hood of a parked sedan as a grenade spiraled out of the shattered back window of the van and bounced near him and his bike. The grenade detonated with a whip-cracking yellow flash and shrapnel rattled against Hawkins's cover like hail. He rose over the hood of the sedan and emptied his pistol into the van, firing low to catch anyone hugging the floorboards. He reloaded and ran to the passenger window. Hawkins snaked his pistol inside and emptied eight rounds into the interior before ripping the door open.

James brought the surveillance van to a screeching halt at the top of the street and Encizo and McCarter leaped out. Hawkins glared at the interior of the bullet-riddled van. A trapdoor had been cut in the floor. In the street beneath a gaping circular hole emptied into blackness below. The heavy iron disk of the manhole cover lay in the back of the van. McCarter ran up beside Hawkins while Encizo stayed back to cover. "What have you got?"

"They've extracted into the sewer sys—" Hawkins jumped back as something metallic rattled against concrete below. He grabbed McCarter's jacket and yanked him back with him. "Fire in the hole!"

Streamers of winking yellow fireflies fountained up out of the manhole borne on a geyser of superheated smoke. McCarter and Hawkins sprinted down the street as the smoke blasted out of the broken windows, sending its streamers of molten phosphorous in all directions. Seconds later the van's gas tank caught and van went up like a metal balloon.

McCarter watched the van burn out of control. Besides Zhol's body back in Kremlin Square there wasn't going to be much in the way of forensic evidence. The Briton felt his temper begin to boil. It wasn't that the mission had gone FUBAR. That was part of the game.

What galled him was that he and Phoenix Force had gotten played.

Payback was owed.

"We're out of here."

CHAPTER EIGHT

"I'm thinking closed casket," Calvin James suggested.

McCarter had to agree. Aidar Zhol's corpse had been cleaned up but his head and face were still horrible to behold. McCarter had seen a lot of shotgun wounds, but the Tajik gangster looked as though someone had teed off on his face with a claw hammer. "What the bloody hell did that, then? Not buckshot."

"Nyet." Forensic Pathologist Sirpa Sokolova sighed in recognition. "Kopeck do this."

"Kopeck?" James cocked his head, reexamining the wounds again with a combat medic's eye. "You mean, the money or a man?"

"Both." Aside from being the deputy assistant coroner, Dr. Sokolova was also a CIA intelligence asset. Barbara Price had arranged for the woman to extend McCarter and Calvin James every professional courtesy. The forensic pathologist was six feet tall and built like a ballet dancer. She'd put a wiggle in her walk for her two American guests that hadn't gone unnoticed or unappreciated on the walk to the basement morgue.

The carnage inflicted on Aidar Zhol's corpse held everyone's attention now.

"Both?" McCarter gazed down at the carnage once more. "What do you mean, both?"

"Mean both." Sokolova's accent was thick enough to cut with a knife. "You ask what do such damage?" She opened a tray beneath the metal gurney and pulled out a plastic bag. The contents tinkled onto the stainless-steel tool tray as she emptied them into a glittering pile. "Twenty-five silver, Csar Nicholas, ten-kopeck pieces. Twenty-five more pulled from body armor in chest."

"Bloody hell." McCarter shook his head. "Shot him full of silver."

"*Da*," the doctor agreed. "Shotgun loaded with silver kopeck do such damage."

James ran his hands through the coins. They were pitted from being fired from a gun and many had deformed when they'd hit bone, but each was genuine minted silver with Csar Nicholas on the face. They were about the diameter of a dime but twice as thick, and by James's estimation twenty-five of them would fit just about perfectly into a 12-gauge shotgun shell. "You know, the Italian Mafia used to do this kind of shit in Sicily, back in the day. They killed you with enough money to pay for your funeral. Some kind of messed-up, old-school respect thing."

McCarter stared at the pile of coins that had been pulled from Aidar Zhol's skull. "Dr., you said kopeck was the method and a man's name."

"*Da*, every cop in Moscow know Kopeck. Kopeck is assassin. Double-barrel shotgun loaded with silver kopeck is his MO. One barrel in chest. One in face." Dr. Sokolova tossed her head. "Kopeck is bad man."

"What else do you know about him?" McCarter asked.

Dr. Sokolova went to a filing cabinet and pulled out a thick folder. File after file had pictures of horribly, unmistakably, coin-mutilated corpses. Sokolova pulled out a separate file. It was written in Cyrillic, but it was clearly a police rap sheet. McCarter gazed at the mug shot at the top. Kopeck's face was all brutal bulges of brow and cheekbones and jaw with cauliflowered ears, and his hair was clipped close to his skull. He had bad teeth. McCarter could tell because Kopeck was grinning shamelessly into the police camera.

"Name, Pietor Shulin, alias 'Kopeck.' Was wrestler in ninety kilogram weight class but failed to make Olympic team. He lose sports dispensation and do army service in Chechnya. Implicated in atrocities against civilians but not prosecuted. Honorably discharged. Shulin became doorman at Moscow club where it is assumed he made *mafiya* connections. First 'kopeck killing' in Moscow occur two years ago. Victim was witness to alleged *mafiya* slaying. There have been eleven kopeck killings within last twenty-four months. Shulin has been arrested in conjunction with three but unsuccessfully prosecuted. Once before, murderer with this same MO escape police pursuit by using manhole trick you describe."

McCarter shook his head at how they'd been eluded. He'd been in the bowels of Moscow before. The modern sewers connected with the ancient sewers built during the time of Peter the Great as well several extensive systems of catacombs that were even older. A mind-numbing labyrinth existed below the streets of Moscow and Russian criminals had been making use of it for centuries.

"Dr. do you have any idea which syndicate he's with?" James asked.

"Kopeck is thought to be freelancer. You wish man

dead? You have money? Kopeck kill. You wish woman or child dead? Kopeck kill them, too."

McCarter had seen the type before. In the old days hit men had been the soldiers of their syndicate. They were trusted members of their families who did the dirty work of defending them. The family system in organized crime had steadily eroded since the 1960s with the rise of the narcotics trade. Kopeck was part of the new breed of killer. He wasn't a hit man so much as an assassin, and aside from his colorful MO, he was true to type.

Kopeck was a sociopath with no loyalties to speak of. He killed for money and because he liked it.

"Kopeck's a bad man," James stated.

"Yeah, and if he's freelance, that means he doesn't have a syndicate backing him," McCarter stated.

James grinned. "Maybe we should go and have ourselves a Come to Jesus with this boy Kopeck."

"I wish you would." Dr. Sokolova favored them with a predatory smile. "I weary of pulling coins from faces."

"We need to put together a snatch, then." McCarter turned to James. "Get on the horn to the Bear, we—"

A pair of orderlies entered the room pushing a gurney laden with a sheet-covered corpse. Dr. Sokolova gave the two orderlies a withering look and spoke in Russian. "I specifically gave orders not to be disturbed."

McCarter cleared leather. James shoved Sokolova to the floor and drew his weapon. The orderlies withdrew PP-2000 machine pistols from beneath their smocks as McCarter and James opened up. McCarter's Browning Hi-Power "Detective" model was an Argentine weapon with a three-and-a-half-inch barrel for concealed carry. The 13-round magazine was "Dutch-Loaded" with 9 mm +P+ hollowpoints and Teflon-coated, armor-piercing ammunition. The high-performance ammo screamed from the shortened barrel in ear-splitting blasts of fire. An armor-piercing round punched a neat hole through the first assassin's heart. A hollowpoint round exploded his throat and dropped him to the floor.

James's Heckler & Koch boomed four times in rapid succession. The big .45 smashed the second killer across the room and dropped him flapping to the floor. The man on the gurney sat up out of his shroud like the living dead, a sawed-off double barrel shotgun in each hand.

McCarter and James emptied their pistols into him.

The assassin jerked and shuddered under the fusillade. His right-hand shotgun boomed out of both barrels, and McCarter felt the sting of the hit in his left arm. He dropped his left arm and fired one-handed until his pistol racked open on an empty, smoke-oozing chamber. The killer lay back on the gurney in final rest with fifteen holes in his chest.

James slapped in a fresh magazine and shot his slide home on a fresh round. McCarter ignored the burning in his arm and reloaded, as well. Out in other areas of the morgue people had begun to scream. Dr. Sokolova started to push herself up and McCarter put a hand on her shoulder to keep her down. "Wait."

James went to the double swinging door and kicked it open. He led with his pistol as he quickly scanned the corridor. "Clear."

Sokolova rose and touched McCarter's arm. "You are hit."

James stayed in the doorway. "You all right?"

The doctor took a scalpel and cut away the sleeve of McCarter's jacket and shirt. Blood ran in a river down McCarter's arm from a pair of ragged but shallow wounds. She took a pair of forceps from the tool tray and stopped. "My God."

McCarter took the forceps from her hand and grimaced as he pulled a projectile from his arm by its edge and held it up to the light. "Bloody hell." He held a silver kopeck. "Cal, check the bloke on the gurney. Is he our man?"

James eased back from the door and scanned the corpse. "Nah, man. He's ugly, but there's no resemblance."

McCarter pulled a second coin out of his bicep and dropped it to clink onto the stainless-steel tray. "Sent his bloody errand boys, then."

"Looks like it." James eyed the hallway. "There had to be a lookout. Kopeck's going to know he failed. You still want to go for the snatch?"

Dr. Sokolova began to swab and stitch McCarter's wounds.

McCarter's glare stayed fixed on the ragged holes in the sleeve of his jacket lying on the table. "Seven hundred dollars of Italian leather. Kopeck owes me." The Briton scooped up the two scarlet-stained silver coins and jingled them in his palm. "And he's bloody short."

IT WASN'T A NICE PART of Moscow, but it appeared Kopeck could afford to take the entire upper floor of a warehouse by the river for his base of operations. McCarter watched the old building through the gray-green filter of his night-vision equipment. Nothing was moving. "What have you got, Phoenix Four?"

Hawkins responded from the other side of the warehouse. "No activity. Grounds are secure to the east."

McCarter nodded. "Phoenix Two?"

"No activity on the river," James reported. "The pier is deserted."

"Phoenix Three, what do you see?"

"Dog crap," Manning answered. "But no dogs. I'm willing to assume they're inside."

McCarter turned to Encizo. "Anything?"

Encizo wore earphones and directed the black plastic dish of a Bionic Ear and sound booster at the warehouse. "The lights are on, and someone's home. I detect two distinct voices, one male, and one female, both speaking Russian. There are other voices and sounds, but I'm attributing them to television noise."

"That's it?"

"That's it."

McCarter considered. "I don't like it."

"Me neither," Encizo agreed. "For a guy who dropped a punk card on you at the Moscow morgue, he's pretty goddamn lax on security. He's got to expect some payback."

McCarter liked it less and less by the second. "Phoenix Two?"

James sighed. "I don't know. You think he's so stupid that he assumed he got us?"

"No, bonkers maybe, but not stupid," McCarter responded. "Stupid assassins don't last this long."

Rafe let out a long breath. "So it's a trap."

McCarter nodded slowly, not taking his gaze from his binoculars. "Too right, it is."

"And...?" Encizo prompted.

"And we're going to trip it, then, aren't we?" McCarter began to move forward. "All units converge."

Phoenix Force loped through the river district like wolves, little more than shadows in darkness. They were armed with sound-suppressed 10 mm Heckler & Koch MP-5/10 submachine guns. Manning held his position in the trees, his T-76 Dakota Longbow sniper rifle covering the team's assault. "No movement. You're still clear."

McCarter came to the side of the warehouse with Encizo beside him. "Phoenix One and Four are on the east side."

James and Hawkins responded from the other side of the building. "In position."

"Watch out for the dogs." Manning advised them.

McCarter loosened the can of pepper spray in his web gear. Police strength pepper spray was 10% Oleo-Resin Capsicum. McCarter and his team were carrying Alaska Guard 20% bear strength, rated against Alaskan grizzlies. The Phoenix Force leader put a hand on a galvanized pipe bolted to the wall that ran to the roof. He pulled against it and grinned as he determined it would bear his weight. "All units hold position. I'm heading up top for a look-see."

McCarter winced as the stitches in his arm pulled, but he clambered up the two-story pipe like a spider. He peered over the eaves but the roof was deserted. He smiled at the glow of light coming up out of the skylight. McCarter crept to the skylight and peered down.

Pietor "Kopeck" Shulin sat in a leather chair in his boxer shorts and a sleeveless T-shirt, drinking vodka and watching a gigantic flat-screen television. A voluptuous redhead wearing one of his T-shirts and not much else sprawled on the couch reading a magazine. "Target acquired. Move in."

"We have a video camera watching the front door," Encizo responded.

"Take the building. Fast approach."

The Cuban nodded to Hawkins, who drew a Mark 23 silenced SOCOM pistol from his thigh holster. The .45 was loaded with ultraheavy .300 grain steel-jacketed subsonic flat-headed bullets whose main purpose in life was to smash locks quietly. Hawkins stepped to the front of the steel double door of the warehouse and put a bullet into the camera and two more into the door latch and each of the hinges. He stepped forward and put his boot in the middle of the two doors and smashed them inward on their sagging hinges. The three men entered the cavernous interior of the warehouse. There was very little inside save a Porsche Boxster, a Harley-Davidson motorcycle and a Jeep Cherokee whose oversize wheels jacked it up nearly six feet in the air.

Calvin James scanned the interior. "Phoenix One, we're in. Any response upstairs?"

McCarter crouched over the skylight. Below him Kopeck poured himself another shot of vodka. The assassin seemed oblivious to the invasion. "Target hasn't moved a muscle—wait."

Kopeck stood out of his chair and stared blearily at something out of McCarter's view. He picked up his remote, clicked it several times and stared in shock at what he saw.

McCarter nodded. "Entry team, you are made."

"Advise," Encizo asked.

McCarter was affixing a rope to his harness and a ventilator housing. "Phoenix Four, any movement?"

"Nothing's moving out here," Manning responded.

The Briton tested his rope. He slung his HK and drew his pistol. "Entry team, you are go."

Inside the warehouse a freight elevator and a flight of wooden stairs led to the second level. Encizo motioned Hawkins to take the elevator while he and James moved to the stairs. At the top of the landing a gleaming steel security door barred their way. "Phoenix One, what's happening?"

"The bugger's loading his shotgun." McCarter scowled down the skylight as Kopeck jacked shells into the breech of a sawed-off double barrel. The woman was hiding behind the couch. "Hit the door, but don't go in. Let him fire both barrels."

"Affirmative, Phoenix One." Encizo nodded, and James

blew away the lock. The Cuban put his foot to the door and it smashed off its hinges. He and James pressed themselves to either side of the landing as a shotgun roared from inside and a woman screamed. Encizo snarled in Russian. "Police!"

Kopeck answered with his second barrel.

"Phoenix One inserting." McCarter took a hop out into space and rammed both feet through the skylight. The woman screamed like a banshee. Kopeck looked up and screamed, as well. McCarter came down in a shower of glass. He pumped the break on his harness and punched both boots into Kopeck's chest. The Russian flew back and bounced against the couch as the woman continued to scream. Encizo and James charged into the room.

Kopeck shouted in Russian, *"Sasha! Raisa! Attack!"*

A pair of one-hundred-pound mastiffs bounded into the room. Muscle rippled across their barrel-shaped bodies beneath their short golden fur. Their faces were black masks of rage as they bared their fangs. Encizo and James drew their pepper-gas canisters and fired. Twin high-pressure cones of mist hit the attack animals head-on. The mastiffs shrieked as their eyes and olfactory organs were instantly overcome. Their claws scrabbled on the hardwood as they lost their equilibrium and spun out. They rolled to the floor yipping and pawing frantically at their muzzles.

The chubby redhead came out from behind the couch with a broom and advanced on McCarter as if he were a piñata. He drew his own pepper-gas canister and pointed it at her face. The redhead paled and dropped the broom. McCarter jerked his head and she sat on the couch.

Kopeck sat on the floor, cradling a left arm that hung ugly from a broken clavicle.

McCarter unhooked from his rope. He scooped up

Kopeck's shotgun and closed the breech on two fresh loads. "Phoenix Four?"

"Still clear," Manning replied.

"Phoenix Three, come on in." The elevator shaft rattled as Hawkins ascended. "One, Two, clear the rest of the floor."

Encizo and James swept the interior. The top floor was simply an open space with designated bedroom, kitchen and dining-entertainment areas. The only part that was enclosed was the bathroom. James kicked the door to the commode. "Clear."

McCarter shoved the sawed-off shotgun under his belt. "Phoenix Flight, this is Phoenix One requesting extraction."

Grimaldi's voice came over the hammering of rotors. "ETA two minutes, Phoenix One."

McCarter turned his attention to Kopeck. "You and I need to talk. Who hired you to kill Aidar Zhol?"

Kopeck glared. "You not police."

"No, Sunshine." McCarter agreed, "I'm not."

"You not even Russian." Kopeck's brow furrowed through his pain. "What I do to you?"

McCarter reached into his pocket and pulled out two silver kopecks. Shulin flinched as the leader of Phoenix Force flipped them into his face. He turned his arm over to show Kopeck where his pulled stitches were bleeding through his raid suit. "I owe you, Kopeck. Twenty, plus interest."

Kopeck blinked in confusion.

McCarter's eyes narrowed. He had expected fear or bluster or denial.

Kopeck was staring at McCarter as if he were trying to place him. "Who you?"

McCarter closed his eyes in self-disgust. "Bloody hell."

"You're right." Encizo nodded. "It's a trap, but Kopek didn't set it."

"No, he's the bait and doesn't even know it." McCarter snarled into his mike. "Phoenix Flight! We need extraction ASAP!"

"ETA ninety seconds!"

Manning's voice roared over the radio. "Choppers in the sky! Inbound across the river! They are— Missiles away! Get down!"

Kopeck screamed as McCarter grabbed him up and hurled him bodily into the stairwell. Encizo grabbed the girl and Phoenix Force threw themselves after him. Hawkins hit the emergency stop on the elevator.

James scooped up a ring of keys, crashed through the wooden grate guarding the elevator shaft, and plummeted to the top of the car.

Four Spandrel-guided antitank missiles hit the warehouse simultaneously. The first warhead was a long-rod penetrator that punched through the thin metal walls of the warehouse as if they didn't exist. After the millisecond it took to breech the corrugated iron barrier, the tank-defeating secondary warheads detonated. Superheated gas and fire expanded across the second floor. The secondary shrapnel effect that ripped through everything like buzz saws was almost unnoticeable in the inferno.

McCarter dragged Kopeck down the stairs.

The thunder of rotors rattled the walls and windows of the warehouse.

"Two choppers!" Manning advised. "One team is repelling into the upstairs! Six men! Second chopper is fast-roping a team to the ground outside. I make it a full squad! They are deploying outside the front door and the loading dock!"

McCarter holstered his pistol and unslung his subgun. "Phoenix Four, keep them busy at the front door."

"Affirmative, Phoenix One." Manning sighted through

his Longbow rifle. It was chambered in .338 Lapua, a round that had been designed from the ground up as the ultimate tool for a sniper. The 250-grain, full-metal-jacketed, boattail locked-base bullet was designed to arrive at the 1000-meter mark with enough energy to penetrate five layers of military body armor and still make the kill. The Lapua's range was one mile, and in the right conditions and with the right man behind the rifle, it could come very close to the 2000-meter mark.

Manning lay prone in the trees peering through his laser range-finding, 3x10 variable night-vision sniper scope and made the range to be eighty meters. He watched the six-man team warily approach the sagging front door. They were dressed from head to toe in black, night-vision goggles made them look like invaders from Mars, and they bristled with weapons. Manning picked out the leader as he sent his men toward the doorway with hand signals. He was also the man whispering into his throat mike.

The big Canadian put his crosshairs between the man's shoulder blades and fired.

The Longbow hammered back against Manning's shoulder as he flicked the bolt to chamber a fresh round. Downrange the .338 Lapua round hit the assault team leader at 3000 feet per second and dumped two and a half tons of energy into him. The armored figure lurched forward like he'd been kicked by a horse and slammed into the side of the warehouse before falling motionless to the ground.

The man beside him spun just in time to take Manning's second shot in the chest. He staggered backward and tripped over his fallen companion. Manning rolled away and began belly-crawling to his second shooting position as the men began to sweep the trees with automatic rifle fire.

Rotors whipped the treetops as someone came seeking him from above. "Shit!"

Green tracers streaked down in vertical lines of smoking light as the door gunners in one of the choppers did reconnaissance by fire through the small copse of trees. "Phoenix One, I'm pinned down! If you're going to do something, do it fast!"

CHAPTER NINE

"Jack, I need you."

"I can see that, Phoenix One." Grimaldi tore along the Yauza River behind the stick of a civilian model Mi-8 Hip helicopter. The bad guys had gotten a piece of his little Hermit helicopter over the streets of Dushanbe and Mrs. Grimaldi's boy wasn't going to get caught flatfooted by the same shitheels twice. The U.S. had assets in Moscow, and his Hip was an on-loan CIA special. Pontoons were mounted on either side of the fuselage and each oblong flotation device concealed a sterile PKT 7.62 coaxial machine gun that had once belonged to the Serbian side of the former Yugoslavian Republic.

A civilian Hip helicopter much like Grimaldi's own was orbiting the warehouse. A second aircraft hovered over the copse of trees where Manning had been doing his sniping. A door gunner hung out of each side of the cabin on chicken straps and they were pounding the holy hell out of Manning's position.

"Phoenix Four, what is your situation?"

"Little help!" Manning snarled.

"Sit tight, Phoenix Four."

Neither of the enemy aircraft had radar and neither saw Grimaldi come swooping down out of the sky like a bird of prey. The Stony Man pilot flipped up the simple, concealed cross-hair sight out of his instrument board and aimed the nose of his chopper at the aircraft offending Manning. He hit his trigger and twin lines of tracers burned into the enemy broadside at 700 rounds per minute.

The door guns fell silent as the gunners jerked and shuddered and fell limp in their straps. Grimaldi swept the cabin. He kicked his collective pedal and his helicopter rotated to train his twin guns on the unarmored cockpit. The enemy chopper tilted crazily and suddenly began spinning in violent 360s on its axis. Grimaldi held his trigger down as the aircraft spun itself through his sights stem to stern.

The enemy craft yawed and spewed smoke from the engine compartment and began autorotating toward the ground as the dead pilot relinquished control and the besieged engines lost power.

"Phoenix Four, this is Phoenix Flight, suggest you get out of the trees ASAP."

"Affirmative!" Manning burst from the trees at a dead sprint. Behind him the stricken Hip hit the trees. Its rotors snapped off and flew through the air like giant scythes as the fuselage crashed down through the canopy and broke its back as it hit the ground.

Bullets rattled against Grimaldi's windscreen as he took ground fire but the short .22-caliber assault rifles of the enemy didn't have the power to penetrate the Hip's crash-resistant cockpit glass. Grimaldi dipped his nose and returned fire. His machine guns stitched the ground in twin tracks of geysering turf as he swept the team in front of the warehouse. Two of the six men fell as the rest scattered.

Grimaldi banked hard as the second enemy aircraft turned its attention on him. His engines roared as he red-lined into emergency war power to climb above the enemy and get above the elevation of the door guns.

"Phoenix One, this is Phoenix Flight! One aircraft down and engaging second! Four hostiles still active outside! West side of warehouse! More on the river side! Make your move!"

"Roger that, Phoenix Flight!" McCarter responded. "We are extracting!"

THE PORSCHE SCREAMED like a leopard as McCarter revved the 24-valve, 228 horsepower engine. "T.J.! Send them a Christmas present!"

Hawkins spun the timer on the satchel charge for ten seconds and slid the sack into the elevator. He released the emergency stop button and the wooden gate rattled closed. "Fire in the hole!"

"Get in!"

Hawkins vaulted the Porsche's passenger door and slid down into the seat.

Encizo and James exchanged bursts up and down the stairs with the entry team lurking in the landing doorway.

"Break contact!" McCarter ordered.

The Cuban and James pulled pins on a white phosphorous and a fragmentation grenade and lobbed them up on to the landing. Jagged bits of metal rattled the walls of the warehouse and smashed light fixtures. A second later the landing was enveloped in a hellstorm of burning white phosphorous and choking smoke.

The freight elevator reached the second floor and twenty pounds of C-4 detonated in the already burning upstairs.

McCarter whipped his hand in a circle. "We're out of here!"

Encizo punched the button for the dock doors. James threw a leg over the Harley and the hog roared to life. He gunned the motorcycle and thundered out the front door. The dock door rattled upward and the second he had clearance McCarter shoved the Porsche into gear and screamed forward.

Six bad guys were waiting outside. Their AKSU carbines strobed into the warehouse on full-auto. The bad guys were expecting a breakout. They weren't expecting David McCarter behind the wheel of a high-performance automobile. The Porsche howled forward. The Russian carbines fired very light bullets and had sacrificed vast amounts of velocity for the convenience of their short barrels. The bullets hit the hood of the Porsche and yawed as they penetrated to ricochet around in the front trunk of the mid-engine car. They failed to penetrate the sloped windshield all together. The Porsche Boxster did 0 to 60 in 5.7 seconds. At 2.5 McCarter hit the enemy point man at 47 miles per hour. The windshield buckled in its frame as the assassin bounced up the hood and flew over the back of the car.

Hawkins spun in his seat spraying bursts from his submachine gun. Another assassin fell as five 10 mm rounds walked up his chest. McCarter yanked his parking brake and spun the Porsche into a shrieking bootlegger's turn to acquire another target. The remaining four gunmen swiveled to track him.

Encizo rumbled out of the warehouse behind the wheel of the monster 4x4. Kopeck and his woman were hog-tied in the back bed. The assassins wheeled to meet the new threat. The screams of the closest killer were lost as he went beneath the giant wheels of the Jeep. Hawkins fired over the cracked windshield of the Porsche as McCarter aimed his bumper at another assassin. The remaining four gunmen found themselves between a Porsche and a hard place.

They broke and ran.

One didn't make it as he fell under a hail of 10 mm rounds from Hawkins's gun. The Porsche lurched as McCarter ran over the human speed bump and chased the last three with Encizo thundering in from behind. The three killers ran for the river. They tossed aside their carbines and leaped straight off the loading dock and into the river. McCarter brought the Porsche to a screaming halt. Hawkins leaped out and raced to the dock, burning the rest of his magazine into the water. McCarter jogged to his side. "What have you got?"

Hawkins slapped in a fresh magazine and racked his bolt on a fresh round. "They aren't coming up."

"You get all three?"

"I doubt I got any of them."

McCarter looked back at the warehouse. The building was burning out of control and he recognized the stench of burning flesh. Between the white phosphorous and the C-4, he doubted any of the enemy entry team was still alive. He thumbed his throat mike. "Phoenix Two, status."

James came rumbling around the side of the warehouse on his hog. Manning sat behind him with his sniper rifle slung and a pistol in each hand. James cut his engine. "Six KIAs in front. Jack got two, Gary got three, and I caught up with one trying to extract onto the street."

McCarter scanned the shot, mangled and run-over bodies around the loading area. They just weren't going to get many prisoners today. But they had Kopeck, and that had been the primary objective. McCarter looked up at Grimaldi's helicopter as it swooped back onto the scene. "Phoenix Flight, what is your status?"

"Enemy aircraft broke contact. Came back to give ground support and extraction rather than give chase."

"Good call," McCarter acknowledged. "Get us out of here."

Grimaldi dropped the Hip to the ground outside the warehouse and Phoenix Force embarked with their prisoners. The pilot took the chopper out over the Yauza and hit a button on his console. The explosive bolts holding his pontoons fired and his two machine guns dropped to the river below. There was nothing seaworthy about the pontoons. In fact they had been designed for just such disposal. They hit the river and swiftly sank beneath the dark waters.

McCarter looked south and saw the flashing lights of emergency vehicles as Moscow fire and police responded. The leader of Phoenix Force turned to Kopeck. The hired killer flinched under McCarter's gaze.

"Now, what were we talking about again?"

Baden Wurttemberg, The Black Forest

THE BOAR WAS BLOODIED and cornered. The hunter had called off the hounds. The hunter's rifle was a Merkel Drilling. One barrel was bored for 16-gauge shot shells. The one beside it was chambered for the powerful European 9.3x74 big game cartridge. The third barrel beneath them was a .22 Hornet for small game. One of the joys of hunting the Black Forest was that one could hunt deer, wild boar, pigeons and fox simultaneously. This day the hunter wanted a trophy boar, and he'd found one.

The $40,000 dollar combination rifle rested in its saddle scabbard. He reached back with one hand and one of his huntsmen pressed the eight-foot, ash shaft of the boar spear into the hunter's hand. It was a three-hundred-pound boar, with curving, two and a half inch tusks that would hamstring a man or horse and shred them when they fell. The snow-white Arabian the hunter rode was trained for the hunt.

The hunter spurred the horse forward.

The boar squealed and leaf duff flew beneath its hooves as it charged its tormentor. The boar's body was pyramidal, built low to the ground and tapering toward the spinal crest with thick layers of gristle armoring its shoulders. One had to get dangerously low to reach the vital organs.

The hunter leaned completely out of the saddle, his head hanging a bare two feet over the ground as the enraged boar came on. Horse, rider and pig flew at one another in a terminal collision course. At the last second the hunter slung his spear forward, putting the combined weight of him and his horse behind the blow. The pig's squeal rose to a scream as the diamond point sank between its throat and collarbone. The blade slid its eighteen inches into the pig's vitals, only stopping on the stainless-steel crossbar behind the blade. The hunter released the spear and yanked himself back up in the saddle as the pig passed. The boar's snout punched down into the ground as it went limp. The spear haft snapped as the boar's momentum sent its entire three-hundred-pound frame into a somersault to fall in an explosion of leaves to the forest floor.

The hunter expertly wheeled his horse and leaped from the saddle. The twenty-two-inch blade of his hunting sword rasped free from the sheath on his hip. There was no need for the coup de grâce. The spear's massive, leaf-shaped blade had sheared the boar's heart in two.

The ring of mounted huntsmen and assistants clapped politely.

Laurentius Deyn sheathed his sword and lifted his head as he heard the sound of rotors. He stepped to his boar and pulled the shattered spear shaft from the pig's breast. His huntsmen swarmed the pig to behead it, skin it and butcher it. A red-and-white Hughes 500 helicopter swept over the treetops and landed in a glade fifty yards away. A huge black man lowered his massive head beneath the rotors as he disembarked to stroll toward the hunt. He nodded curtly to the hunter.

"Mr. Forbes."

Clayborne Forbes regarded his employer. The man was sixty-eight years old but held himself erect with casual ease. He wore the traditional loden-green hunting garb and feathered cap of a German *jager*. Forbes would have considered the archaic clothing ridiculous save for the arterial spray staining the waistcoat, the bloody, broken spear held casually in the man's hand and the penetrating gaze of the man's eyes. The man had been a hunter all his life, and he had hunted and killed far more men than beasts. Deyn jerked his head and his huntsmen moved away.

Forbes grinned. "Pork for dinner, Larry?"

"Clay." Laurentius Deyn smiled. "It is good to see you. Thank you for flying out on such short notice, but I must know what is happening in Moscow."

"We got troubles," the big man conceded.

"This Navy SEAL of yours? Calvin James?"

"And his friends."

"They are related?"

"Most definitely. I positively ID'd Calvin James's ass at the warehouse, and another son of a bitch was shouting with an English accent. Just like Dushanbe, and the English son of a bitch seemed to be in command."

"English?" Deyn scowled. "I have a difficult time believing the United States and the British are running combined Special Forces operations on the streets of Moscow."

"No, not a combined op. These guys were tight. They were a team."

"Yes, they killed fifteen of my men, and forced the survivors to extract, leaving weapons and evidence all over the scene."

Forbes shook his head as he remembered the battle. "They still don't have shit. The Russian authorities have the bodies and money has been put in place to have them cremated."

"They have this coroner, Dr. Sokolova. They also have Kopeck."

Forbes rolled his massive shoulders. "What does that give them?"

"Kopeck can lead them to the Rurikid brothers, who could conceivably lead them to our Russian friend, and from there…" Deyn let the implication hang.

"That's a pretty goddamn Byzantine path to the top if you ask me."

Deyn spiked the broken spear into the ground like a giant lawn dart. "They have you, Clay."

"Yeah, I hear you." Forbes let out a long breath. "How do you want to play it?"

"Extract our Russian friend, but you have my permission to kill him if it becomes expedient. Kill Sokolova. Have the Rurikid brothers send some of their men to do it, and then kill them, as well."

"You got it." Deyn hunted and killed men the way some men played chess. Forbes kept the nervousness off his face. "What about me?"

"Pig for dinner?" Deyn's face suddenly broke into a smile. The killer could turn congenial without warning. "I have a Gewurztraminer from Alsace I believe you will appreciate. Will you join me?"

Forbes turned to watch the huntsmen. They had hung

the boar from an elm and were cutting huge slabs of steaming meat from the carcass. He had a lot of killing to arrange in the next twenty-four hours. He could use a sit-down dinner under his belt. "Damn straight."

CHAPTER TEN

Krylatskoe suburb, Moscow

Dr. Sirpa Sokolova awoke with a scream. A hard, calloused hand clamped implacably over her mouth and smothered her cry. She had been dreaming of the killers that had come after her in the morgue, and now the assassins were in her home. Sokolova fought, clawing for her assailant's eyes, but suddenly both of her wrists were expertly pinned in a cross over her breasts. She had put her father's Tokarev pistol beneath her pillow, but it had been of no avail. She was silenced, pinned and at the mercy of her enemies.

David McCarter spoke very low into her ear. "Someone's in the house."

Sokolova sagged and McCarter eased his hand from her mouth. "Get your gun, get out of the bed and get low." The naked Englishman rolled out of her bed with his Hi-Power pistol in his hand. Sokolova reached back and curled her fingers around the worn, hard rubber grips of the Tokarev.

McCarter reached down into his ditty bag, and pulled a pair of night-vision goggles on over his eyes and extracted his cell phone. The interior of the doctor's bedroom lit up in grainy greens and grays. Sokolova's house was small and old. It was nicely furnished but size wise it was little more than a cottage. McCarter catfooted to the far side of the bedroom door as he heard a floorboard gently squeak in the narrow hall outside. He punched in a number on his phone and rapidly thumbed a text message.

"Pheonix One. At Docs. About to get hit."

The bedroom door smashed back as someone put his boot to it. A fat man in a coverall stood in the doorway holding a gigantic revolver in each hand like a gunfighter. He leveled the immense 12.3 mm UDAR revolvers at the bed. The pistols rolled in his hands with recoil, booming like cannons as he emptied them into the bed as fast as he could pull the triggers.

McCarter's Hi-Power barked once in short, sharp response to the thundering fury of the assassin's firearms. The 9 mm +P+ hollowpoint round stove in the killer's mandible and transversed his skull. The hollowpoint expanded as it traveled to carve a channel that skimmed the man's hard palate and the bottom of his brain before blasting out the other side of his jaw.

The killer collapsed bonelessly to the floor.

McCarter jerked back from the door as a submachine gun ripped wood from the frame. His pistol barked twice and the man fell back against the wall with a thud, but the assassin's weapon kept ripping the space where McCarter had been a moment before.

Sokolova snarled something that sizzled in Russian and her antique Tokarev blasted at the wall. McCarter smiled harshly as he heard the thump and clatter of a body and gun hitting the hardwood floor in the hallway.

Everything was suddenly silent.

McCarter crouched, listening for long seconds. "Wait here."

Sokolova let out a breath that shuddered with adrenaline reaction. "I will wait."

McCarter knelt by the first shooter. He was still gurgling but his jaw hung from his head by threads of tendon and his limbic region was jelly. McCarter risked a look out the door. The second shooter lay facedown on the floor, blood spreading around his head in a pool. A Stetchkin machine pistol with the wooden shoulder stock attached lay a foot away from his limp hand.

Sokolova whispered from her crouch by the dresser. "They are dead?"

McCarter put a finger to his lips. "Shh…"

Instincts won the hard way told McCarter there was another killer in the house. He willed his heart to slow, and he breathed silently in and out through his mouth. The leader of Phoenix Force waited. Dogs were barking up and down the street from the sound of the guns. Five minutes passed.

An urgent voice whispered from the kitchen. "Dimochka! Feydor!"

McCarter's smile was ugly.

Bloody amateurs.

He could see everything in his night-vision goggles, but the light from the streetlights came in through the window and the gloom was enough for Sokolova's night-adapted eyes to see by. McCarter waved his arm in a circle until he had her attention, then pointed at the holes she'd punched in the wall with her pistol. He made a gun out of his thumb and forefinger meaningfully.

Sokolova nodded and took a shooting rest on the top of the dresser, pointing her pistol where he'd indicated.

"Dimochka!" The voice hissed again. "Feydor!"

McCarter only spoke a few phrases in Russian, but like any soldier who'd fought in a foreign land he knew the choice ones. "Dimochka and Feydor are dead."

The other assassin roared in rage and fear. Guns began detonating from the kitchen and feet thudded on the floor as the enemy charged the bedroom with guns blazing. There were two of them. McCarter dropped prone as bullets ripped overhead. He waited until he could see both men clearly and they closed on the body of the man in the hall.

"Shoot!" McCarter shouted.

Sokolova began to shoot. Tokarevs shot small bullets at very high velocity, and with full-metal-jacketed rounds they had a well-warranted reputation as drillers. They passed through the interior wall of the house with ease. McCarter's pistol spoke out loud in brutal accompaniment.

The would-be assassins in the hallway jerked and fell in the withering cross fire.

"Empty!" Sokolova whispered.

By his own count McCarter had three rounds left. "Don't move."

He rose from the floor.

Sokolova screamed as the bedroom window smashed in and the twin barrels of a 12-gauge shoved through the broken pane and blasted blindly. McCarter spun like a turret and fired. The man outside screamed as the 9 mm bullet expanded violently into his right hand and broke apart in all directions as it hit the stock of his weapon. The shotgun fell to the floor and McCarter's second shot punched into the man's shoulder and spun him back out of the shattered window.

The Briton leaped on top of the bed to avoid the broken glass all over the floor. Out the window a man was staggering toward the sidewalk clutching his right arm and hand.

The Hi-Power barked and the man screamed as the

bullet hit the back of his thigh and smashed his leg out from under him. McCarter punched a button on his phone and Calvin James instantly answered. "What is your situation, Phoenix One?"

"We got hit. Three suspects down. One prisoner. The doctor is alive. We're extracting."

Secure communications room, U.S. Embassy, Moscow

"THEY WERE AMATEURS." McCarter scowled. "Bloody cornershop killers. Not the same caliber of lads who came for us at Kopeck's warehouse at all."

T.J. Hawkins flipped through a file. "Yeah, intelligence confirms that. You brought down Dimochka Vishnenov, Feydor Ulanov and Vasily Shulko. The guy you brought in is one Constantine Markakov. All have impressive rap sheets with Moscow P.D., but they're street soldiers, not much more than thugs and leg-breakers, and known associates of the Rurikid *mafiya* group here in Moscow."

There was a knock at the door and Dr. Sokolova entered. The leggy Russian took a seat at the table. She looked shaky, but her jaw was set determinedly. "Good morning."

"Thank you for joining us." McCarter glanced at the thick sheaf of files the doctor held. "Did you get anything useful from Kopeck's warehouse?"

"The assault team was armed with Russian AKSU carbines loaded with RPK, 45-round light machine magazines. Each individual had Gurza semiautomatic pistol and Spetsnaz combat knife. Several had silenced pistols as well, two men carried handcuff and plastic restraints."

It was typical Russian raid equipment. "How about the bodies? Did you get any IDs?"

Sokolova shook her head. "Fingerprints and dental

records of assailants are in no Russian military or police database that I have access to."

McCarter leaned back in his chair. Their mystery assailants were remaining a puzzle.

Sokolova chewed her pencil for a moment and then tapped it on the pile of files in front of her. "However, while it is only hunch, I do not believe your opponents at warehouse were Russian."

Calvin James had been thinking the same thing. "What makes you think that?"

"We had no dental records of victims, but some cadavers had signs of dental work. Most Russians with bad teeth simply get gold ones or dentures or do nothing. Several victims had dental work not typical of Russian dentists. Higher quality and more expensive than Russian soldier can afford. More typical of Western European medicine. Other small things, such as vaccination scars. Russian Special Forces receive them like assembly line. These men had none or atypical. Another man had tattoo on biceps. It was, how do you say, a broken heart, with word 'Mother' written across, but not in Cyrillic, it was spelled m-u-t-t-e-r."

Manning perked an eyebrow. His mother had been born in Munich. "That's 'mother' in German."

James nodded. "This German connection keeps coming up."

"That's another thing." Encizo raised a finger pointedly. "The guys who hit us at Kopeck's place, they didn't act like ex-Russian military. They were tip-top."

McCarter'd had the same feeling. Russian Special Forces were good, but since the Soviet Union had collapsed they had become something less than the clandestine special operations force they had once been. Their mission had shifted from infiltrating NATO targets on the eve of Armageddon to dealing with bloody civil wars and internal Russian conflicts. Special Forces funding in the former Soviet Union had also dried up. Russian Special Forces were still better armed, equipped and trained than their regular Russian army counterparts, but the decade-long war in Chechnya with the endless street fighting and suppression of the civilian population had turned them into door kickers and shock troops rather than real operators in the Western sense.

McCarter smiled sardonically. The lads at Kopeck's place had been operators, and crackerjack ones at that. "Let's call them bloody German Special Forces and be done with it, then."

Manning shook his head unhappily. German commandoes were neck and neck with the U.S. and UK for best in the world. "That ups the ante."

"That's right," McCarter agreed. "Our boys came in with overwhelming force and firepower. Their only problem was they weren't ready for what Phoenix brought to the table. They surprised us and we surprised them right back."

"Okay, I'll buy it." Encizo considered the competition. "But why? What are German operators doing in Moscow, much less operating against us?"

"Let's call them *former* German operators for the moment, private contractors, and they're here to get the nukes and suppress resistance. The question is, who are they working for?"

The answer was obvious but still left a gaping mystery.

"Whoever Forbes was talking to in Dushanbe would be my bet." James snorted. "Figuring that out is going to be the fun one."

Encizo reviewed the battle in his mind once more. "You know we were in place outside Kopeck's three hours before we hit the place. We did a full recon. The warehouse was isolated. We would have detected a surveillance team anywhere within range. We had good hides and we would have detected anyone coming to the party late, but they were on us, instantly, the moment we moved in."

McCarter frowned. "What are you saying?"

"I'm saying they had to be several miles away but they still hit us like lightning." Encizo grimaced. "I'm saying they were watching Kopeck's place by satellite."

Hawkins grunted. "You're assigning them some pretty big assets."

McCarter agreed with Encizo's assessment. "But it makes sense. Put Bear on it. We need to know every satellite in the sky last night that could have been watching Kopeck's place, and I want to know who owns it." McCarter turned back to Sokolova. "What do you know about the Rurikid *mafiya* family."

Sokolova's eyebrows rose over her glasses. "You did not hear?"

"We've been in conference for the past hour. What have you heard?"

"Ivan and Andrej Rurikid were found dead forty-five minutes ago. Shot to death, in their beds. Their families were killed too. It is all over television. It is being called the worst gangland hit in Moscow in ten years. Moscow P.D. fears there will be war in the streets."

Hawkins shoved his Rurikid file away in disgust. "Well, that's awfully damn convenient."

"No, it's good." James raised a finger. "Last night they tried to hit the doctor. At the same time they hit the Rurikid family and cut its head off. They're cleaning up loose ends."

"And?" Hawkins inquired.

"Well, we've been trying to figure out which Russian general might have been involved in stealing the nukes."

"And?" Hawkins prompted again.

"And my bet is a Russian army general with access or oversight over tactical nuclear weapons is going to be found dead or AWOL within the next forty-eight hours."

CHAPTER ELEVEN

Computer Room, Stony Man Farm, Virginia

"So." Aaron Kurtzman sat at the head of the conference table. "You're saying we have no missing Russian generals?"

Carmen Delahunt blew a lock of blazing red hair from her brow. It had been a very long day of searching databases and calling in markers. "We've been in contact with the CIA, the NSA, M-I6, French Action Direct, as well as every Russian contact we've got. Every Russian general, active and retired is accounted for."

Kurtzman steepled his fingers. He didn't look forward to telling David McCarter that they'd come up goose eggs. "How about someone lower level, a major-general or a colonel?"

Delahunt had already considered that. "From everything I've been able to gather, it would take a general's clout to steal the devices and then cover it up."

Hal Brognola had flown from D.C. to take in this meeting and the big Fed didn't like what he was hearing. "Maybe our boy has big brass balls and he's sitting tight."

"That's one possibility," Delahunt conceded. "But Phoenix Force seems fairly certain that these alleged German bad guys are doing a full clean-up. That means they can't let the guy who stole the nuke be captured and compromised. David believes whoever the military contact is, that man is either at the bottom of the Black Sea or in bed in Berlin. Frankly I agree with him."

"I would, too," Kurtzman concurred. "But your intelligence sweep says no Russian general is AWOL. So who's got the juice?"

Akira Tokaido had one earbud of his MP3 player screwed into one ear while he listened to the conversation with the other. "What if he's not a Russian army general?"

Hal Brognola's brow furrowed. The man from Justice had never quite understood how the young man could blast his brains into jelly with heavy-metal music 24/7 while at the same time be one of the greatest living cybernetic hackers on the planet. The words "idiot savant" had crossed his mind more than once. "What do you mean?"

Tokaido shrugged. "What if he's an Air Marshal? They have nukes."

Delahunt shook her head. "I'll check. The bomber force of course will have nuclear weapons, but I don't believe nuclear demolition charges fall under their purview. It's the Russian Army Engineers that digs holes and blow things sky-high on the ground."

Tokaido wasn't fazed. "Okay, how about an admiral?"

"Hmm." Kurtzman considered it. "Their submarine force has nuclear missiles. Some of their ships carry nuclear armed cruise missiles, as well, but again, we're talking about missing nuclear demolition charges. That's a very odd and mission-specific piece of ordnance."

"Yeah, but they have frogmen, don't they?" Tokaido

leaned forward as he warmed to the subject. "I have a game on my computer where in the year 2015 the Soviet Union and the Nazis rule Earth. One of your attacks is to send your combat swimmers with backpack nukes to blow damns and bridges across Europe. The graphics are incredible. Last night I nuked the Danube and they have a new, optional 3-D effects card where you can actually see the flesh melting off the victims' bones during the detonations and their shadows being flash-photographed into the concrete. Then the coolest thing is that—"

"That's an excellent idea." Kurtzman interrupted. Once Tokaido got on the topic of music or computer games it almost took a bullet in the cerebellum to stop him.

"Carmen, get me a list of every living Russian admiral, active or retired, and cross-reference it with every contact we have." Kurtzman smiled. Tokaido was on to something. "Find me an admiral with access to nukes who's gone missing."

Berlin, Germany

"ADMIRAL." Laurentius Deyn extended his hand as Admiral Sergei Beniaminov and his bodyguard stepped off the helicopter. "It is good to finally meet you."

"Indeed." The admiral shook Deyn's hand. "I am glad to be out of Russia. It seems things are getting hot."

"Yes, we have had some setbacks." Deyn ushered them in to the penthouse suite of the soaring high-rise. The sun was setting over the vast metropolis of Berlin and they were standing at the highest peak of the city. The admiral was clearly impressed. Clayborne Forbes rose from the couch. Admiral Beniaminov gestured at his guard. "Allow me to introduce you to my best man, Alexsandr Zabyshny. He has been instrumental in many of our projects."

Deyn knew Zabyshny's history. The man was six foot three, dark and rangy, and constantly wore a long black coat underneath which he was festooned with weapons. He had been a combat swimmer in the Russian navy and gone on to join Spetsnaz, Russia's combat elite.

Forbes grinned. "Hey, Alex."

The Russian operative grinned back. "Clay."

"Alexsandr?" The admiral looked back and forth between the two men. "You two know each other?"

"We've taken some meetings," Forbes admitted. He kept his eyes on the Russian operative. "You thought about what we discussed, Alex?"

"Yes." Zabyshny nodded once. "I accept your proposition."

"Good." Forbes nodded toward some plastic sheeting in the corner. "But not on the carpet."

The admiral blinked in confusion. "What is—"

Zabyshny grabbed the admiral by his necktie and spun him, slamming him into the wall and standing him on the plastic tarp.

"Al-!" The admiral's words choked off as Zabyshny pinned him to the wall by the throat with one hand and drew a Pernach machine pistol from beneath his coat. He rammed the muzzle into the admiral's paunch and squeezed the trigger. The pistol cycled like a buzz saw in his hand, ripping eighteen 9 mm Makarov rounds into the admiral's vitals in two seconds.

Zabyshny released the dead naval officer and let him fall to the tarp. The wall behind him was a modern art masterpiece of murder in scarlet arterial sprays and gobbets of masticated human meat. Deyn was almost tempted to have it lacquered in place and leave it, but the eighteen bullet holes left little doubt of its origin.

Forbes clicked open his phone and spoke in German. "Security, we need cleaning and disposal in the penthouse."

The reply was instant. "Yes, Herr Forbes, at once."

Deyn shook Zabyshny's hand. "Congratulations, Alex. You are now head of Russian Operations."

Computer Room, Stony Man Farm, Virginia

BARBARA PRICE WAS SMILING. "What do we have?"

Carmen Delahunt clicked keys on her laptop and a photo appeared on the six-foot wall screen. A middle-aged man in full Russian navy dress uniform dominated the monitor. He was wearing enough ribbons and medals to sink a battleship. "Admiral Sergei Beniaminov."

"Is he missing?"

"The CIA really came through for us on this one. Beniaminov was scheduled to deliver a paper at the Naval Academy on Friday, but he called in sick with the flu forty-eight hours ago and canceled. The CIA sent a team by his town house in Moscow and to his dacha outside the city. No one is home and it doesn't look as though anyone has been for over a week. We know he has a summer home on the Black Sea and we have local assets on their way to check it out now, but I'm thinking he's not there, either. I'm going with David. Our boy the admiral is either drinking beer in a safehouse in Berlin or he's been buried."

Price nodded. "Bear?"

"I think David is right. These guys are very tidy, very anal." Kurtzman grunted to himself. "Very…German. Let's assume Sergei's dead, but let's assume they paid the admiral big money for his help. So, where is the money now, and maybe they want to recover those assets. Akira, do you think you can break into the admiral's financial records from here?"

"Yeah, we have some good encryption guys in Moscow. They should be able to set up a link and I should be able to find the money trail from there no problemo."

Things were rolling. Price checked her notes. "Carmen, how about the satellite situation over Moscow? Was the NSA able to give us a list?"

"Yeah, but it's a big one. Even eliminating our own birds, we're talking eighty satellites with known high-definition, ground-imaging capability. NSA is estimating a possible thirty more that may have the ability but are disguised as communication satellites. We're talking Russian, Chinese, English, French, Japanese, you name it. It's a regular UN mile-high club over Moscow 24/7."

"How many German satellites are known to be high-imaging or possibly disguised?"

Delahunt already had that answer circled. "Seven of known German origin. Four known to be high-imaging, three are big enough to be disguised as something else."

"How many are military?"

"Three, and those are out of the known imaging satellites. Four are civilian owned."

"I want a full dossier on the owners of all four civilian jobs, as well as who has had access to them in the past seventy-two hours."

"I'm on it."

"Tell Phoenix to be ready to move. And I want to be able to give Phoenix something on the satellite and the money trail ASAP."

Delahunt expertly slid her notes together. It was going to be a long night. "Anything else?"

"Tell Hal I want Able Team assembled here at the Farm, armed and ready to be anyplace on the planet within twelve hours."

Berlin, Germany

LAURENTIUS DEYN LOOKED down over the city. His balcony office hung out from the skyscraper in an arc overlooking the Spree River. His desk was a matching arc of lustrous teak. Deyn thought of his sons. He often did. He looked at the picture of them on his desk. The two young men stood on a boat in the blue waters of Hawaii, bronzed and as fit as gladiators. They stood arm-in-arm, smiling into the camera with scuba gear all around them. It had been a long time since Deyn had wept or felt the sting of tears, but a very old, cold, bitter wind blew through his bones. His sons, Steffan and Karl, lost to him all these years.

Not lost.

Taken.

They had followed in his footsteps, been destined for greatness, and their lives had been taken. Taken by cowardice, stupidity and incompetence. Deyn's bitterness kindled to anger. Deyn's still powerful hands clenched into white-knuckled rage.

The earth would tremble when they were avenged.

Deyn's personal secretary buzzed him on the intercom. "Mr. Deyn. Miss Marx is here with her report."

"Send her in."

The door to Deyn's private office slid open silently and Franka Marx entered. She was a beautiful woman, but she dressed as if she were ashamed of it, keeping the lush curves of her body covered in stark and functional business suits and keeping her red hair severely restrained. Her eyebrows were almost permanently drawn down with intensity and her sensuous lips kept in a hard line. She had been an ugly duckling who had never quite recovered even after she had blossomed. She immersed herself in her work and had almost no social life to speak of. Deyn encouraged the situation with subtle manipulations. Marx lived to serve, and shuddered like a puppy at a single word of praise from him.

Deyn shoved his rage down into a very deep, dark part of his soul where it had been growing for years and favored Marx with a smile. "Ah, Franka, you have a report?"

"Yes, sir." Marx blushed despite herself. "The computer systems you requested for the Atlantic and Pacific stations are in place and uplinked to the satellite. All is in readiness."

Deyn could read the woman like a book. "But you have questions."

Marx stumbled over her words. "Yes. I mean, no. I mean..."

"Franka, you are one of my most valued employees."

Franka Marx blushed furiously and looked at her feet.

"You do not understand why such systems are needed, much less in such locations."

Marx nodded, ashamed at her temerity in questioning him.

Deyn chose his words very carefully. "Very soon, I am going to move, aggressively, against some of my enemies. Once I set things in motion, you will be my right hand, but for the moment, what you do not know cannot hurt you. Do you understand?"

Deyn watched Marx's reaction. She was aware that not all of his business dealings were strictly legal, but by the time she'd learned of this, she had already worked for Deyn for years, seen rapid promotion and her talents appreciated. Her loyalty to him and his designs had become as utter as one of his hounds, and she had willingly become an accomplice in numerous acts of industrial and economic warfare. Of course, she had absolutely no idea how far some of his plans had gone, but moral compromise was best taken one step at a time.

Marx squared her shoulders. "Yes, sir. I understand."

"Excellent, leave your report. I have some things to attend to now, perhaps you and I can discuss it over a cup of coffee later."

"Yes, sir." Marx had to restrain herself from skipping as she left the office.

Laurentius Deyn smiled like a shark. He had many weapons at his disposal, financial, military and political, but the brain of Franka Marx was one of his best and most lethal. Somewhere in the United States there might be cybernetic intelligence operative who could challenge Franka, but Deyn doubted it and he would pay good money to see him match his brain against Franka's.

CHAPTER TWELVE

Computer Room, Stony Man Farm, Virginia

"Got it!" Akira Tokaido leaned back in his computer chair, elated.

Carmen Delahunt peered up from her workstation. "You got the money?"

"Oh, I got the money, all right."

Kurtzman spun his chair away from his bank of terminals and rolled Tokaido's way. He peered over the young genius's shoulder and perked an eyebrow. "Well, now, Sergei was a socially secure Russian admiral, wasn't he?"

Sergei Beniaminov was ten million euros richer than the average Russian admiral approaching his pension. "Whom is he banking with?"

Tokaido scrolled upward. "An outfit called Infinite Financial Antilles."

"Offshore in the Caribbean." Kurtzman nodded. "Should have guessed."

"You know Russians," Carmen chimed in. "They love to put their money someplace warm."

Kurtzman peered at a map of the Caribbean inset in Tokaido's screen. "What island?"

The young hacker punched a key and the Caribbean Sea zoomed into focus. He clicked a few more and a small dot near the northern coast of Venezuela zoomed up into a geopolitical map of a small island. "The island of Bonaire, its part of the Netherlands Antilles chain. It's a Dutch dependency."

"So what can you tell me about the admiral's financial transactions?"

Tokaido frowned. "Not much."

Kurtzman scowled. "What do you mean, not much?"

"Admiral Beniaminov made some major mistakes on his end. I was able to access a lot of his records." He tapped his finger on the screen. "But Infinite Finances Antilles is an offshore banking facility. Discretion and secrecy are their middle names. They get paid the huge bucks not to get hacked."

Kurtzman folded his arms unbelievingly. "You're saying you can't hack it?"

"Oh, I can hack it. But I can't guarantee we won't be discovered."

Kurtzman preferred to do it sneaky. "We have Able Team in residence and on one hour standby. What if they can put someone in place?"

"You mean, actually onsite?" Tokaido shrugged. "Yeah, if you can actually get someone good inside the Infinite Financial building and give them physical access to the company's mainframe, that would simplify things. They could probably break in without being detected."

A plan began forming in Kurtzman's mind. "All right, I'll go have a talk with Carl and we'll brainstorm this thing. Meanwhile, get me a list of people from NSA and the FBI who you think could pull it off." Kurtzman rolled up out of the War Room to go find Carl Lyons.

"THE FIELD!" Kurtzman was outraged. "You want to take Akira out in the field!"

Carl "Ironman" Lyons raised an eyebrow. It was unusual to see the Bear turn purple.

"You remember what happened the last time one of you Einsteins took Akira out into the field!"

Lyons cocked his head slightly. To his knowledge, he couldn't remember the Bear calling anyone, much less himself, Einstein.

"What the hell are you thinking, Carl!"

Lyons stood like the blue-eyed blond embodiment of his nickname, unphased by Kurtzman's outburst. "We have to get into the bank records and leave no trace. That means we have to break into the bank and put the hacker on-site. Breaking into the bank and then breaking into the database is asking a lot. I think we should cover one with the other. Able and I are going to rob the bank. Meanwhile Akira sneaks in during the diversion and hacks the database. It's a small island in the Caribbean. It shouldn't be that tough."

"You remember what happened the last time I let Akira out in the field, Carl?"

"Yeah, he got stomped. As a matter of fact he gets stomped every time he leaves the nest." Lyons shrugged. "So? There's no one better for the job, and you know it. Akira is here with us already and doesn't need briefing. We can be there in four hours and do the job in eight."

"Well, I don't like it!"

The Ironman stood impassive as stone. "You don't have to like it, Bear, but you have to okay it. I won't take Akira out without your blessing. If I don't have it, then we'll have to find someone else to take into the bank. No one's better than the kid." Lyons checked his watch. "We got nukes loose, and the clock is ticking. Decide."

"Damn it!"

"I'll take that as a yes."

"All right! But you tell me this. Who's baby-sitting Akira while you yahoos are robbing the bank? Who's extracting him if things get hot? Phoenix touched down in Berlin half an hour ago and can't spare anyone. Mack's busy."

"I don't know, pick an asset, pick anybody. Just do it in the next ten minutes."

"Ten min—" Kurtzman glowered. He sat back in his wheelchair while he frowned mightily. "All right, Carl. I guess it will have to be a blacksuit."

That was the way Carl had figured it. "Who do you want?"

"I want Tino."

"Tino?" Lyons rolled his eyes. "Yeah, he's not going to stick out in the Caribbean."

"Like you're not, Blondie, and Tino can pick up Akira and swim him home if it comes to it."

"Well, there is that. Okay, Bear, you got it. Call Tino and tell him you got a job for him. Then send Akira to the Cowboy."

"Why?"

"'Cause Akira always gets stomped. Let's see if we can prevent that from happening again."

Bonaire, Netherlands Antilles

"A THOROUGHLY MODERN FACILITY." Hermann "Gadgets" Schwarz took in the blazing white building overlooking the town and beach. Infinite Financial Antilles looked more like a flying wing than a traditional bank. It hung from the tropical hillside like a bird of prey about to take off. "Just like the brochure said." He grinned at Tokaido. "Think you can crack it, tough guy?"

The young computer genius had hacked undetected into the top-secret databases of most of the major military powers on the planet, both friend and foe of the United States. He had been clandestinely privy to secrets of state that would get him killed in most corners of the world. In his experience, the cybernetic defenses of governments and militaries were monolithic and mind-numbingly, militaristically predictable. All they took was time. Tokaido stood on the hotel balcony and gazed upon the sweeping structure that was his enemy. The problem as he saw it was that his opponents weren't guarding nuclear secrets or Byzantine strategic plans for world domination. That would have been relatively simple.

These guys were Dutch financiers and they were guarding money.

Their defenses would be state-of-the-art, as slick as grease, and their counterattacks across the datum plane lighting-fast.

And they would have hired someone like himself to design them.

"No problem."

Tino Nathaniel Tenari tossed back a Red Stripe beer almost without swallowing. "Check out the big brass balls on hacker boy."

Tenari was 280 pounds of American Samoan jammed into a blue Guayabera shirt and khaki shorts. He was also a former Air Police sergeant. His nickname was TNT, and he qualified as a one-man brute squad. He had accepted the bank job without a second thought.

Tokaido was looking up at the bank as if he could see through the walls and was staring at their computer network. His concentration was so total he spoke to no one in particular. "No, all you have to do is get me in. Hook me up directly into their system, and I can defeat it." He nodded slowly. "They'll never know I was there. They'll never know what data they're missing."

Tenari waved his empty beer bottle in a vaguely appalled fashion. "I hate it when he gets like that. Creeps me out."

"Yeah, well, you're baby-sitting him." Carl Lyons stared up at the architectural wonder and contemplated an entirely different set of defenses that needed to be overcome. "We'll be busy."

"Just as long as I don't have to listen to his music."

"The plan is pretty straightforward. We don't want anyone to know we were in the computers, so we're going to make it look like a heist. Able robs the bank. Akira, you and Tino heist the data." Lyons opened up a bag and pulled out three rubber masks.

Blancanales opened a suitcase full of weapons. "So, we go in like Butch Cassidy and the Sundance Kid?"

"We go in like the Mongol horde," Lyons corrected him. "Gadgets blows the security suite, then we steal everything that isn't nailed down, set fire to the place and leave slogans about multinationals, stolen money in offshore accounts and indigenous islanders' rights."

Blancanales pulled out a rather beat-up looking ex-Venezuelan navy Walther MPK submachine gun. "Jesus, Carl. *Muy primitivo.*"

"We're just shooting the place up." Lyons pointed to some canisters of ancient-looking British police riot gas. "If we face local opposition, we use the gas to break contact. Regardless, we head for the southern side of the island. There's a speedboat waiting, and a mile and a half out, the submarine *City of Corpus Christi* will be waiting for us. Any questions?"

Infinite Financial Antilles

"OH COME ON, Rita." Sybo Dykstra leaned over the reception table. It was Sunday morning, things were slow, and even at the firm's busiest on Monday mornings when the markets opened, Rita Mannlicher held at least half of the young man's attention. Rita was half Dutch half and half islander, and her hair skin and eyes were all the same startling shade of cinnamon. The effect only enhanced the tropical-weight white skirt and jacket she wore. "Come with me to Florida."

Mannlicher sighed. "Oh, I don't know, Sybo, I…" The woman cocked her head and looked out the front door. "What is that?"

Dykstra turned to look out the vast glass doors. "What?"

A dilapidated Land Rover was barreling down the road toward the bank. Infinite Financial Antilles engaged in a number of forms of business on Sundays but walk-in banking wasn't one of them. "Maybe some kids joyriding, the road forms a loop…"

"Sybo!"

Mannlicher screamed as the vehicle plowed right through the glass doors. The tires shrieked to a halt on the Italian pink marble floor. A rubber-faced facsimile of former President Richard Nixon leaped from the passenger seat. He raised a German submachine gun in each hand and fired them in a blazing arcs into the ceiling. "Peace and freedom! Blood and fire!" Nixon screamed.

Senator Ted Kennedy leaped from behind the wheel of the Land Rover, his weapon ripping nameplates, pens and stacked forms along the teller windows. "Death to the running dogs!"

A third masked man, former president Jimmy Carter,

jumped from the back and pointed his submachine gun into the bank employees' face. "Down! Down! Down!"

The employees complied instantly.

"Up! Up! Up!" Kennedy yanked Dystra back up by the arm. "Where's the money!"

"Money? We don't have any money!"

"You're a bank!" Carter screamed. "You got to have money!"

IFA often did receive very large sums of money in cash, bearer bonds, gold and gems, but they were met by appointment, swarmed by guards, placed in the vault and then swiftly converted into less tangible assets for their clients who wished to keep their money secret. Part of the offshore bank's lease required them to give the local Bonaire island population banking services at very favorable rates of interest, which accounted for the row of teller windows, but the vast majority of those accounts were small and hardly worth the bank's time.

"I mean, we do! But we don't!"

"Are you being indecisive!" Carter screamed.

"No! I mean, we're not like a local bank! It's Sunday! The teller tills were all emptied on Friday! Anything in the bank is in the vault! No one here has access to it!"

Kennedy walked over and shoved the hot muzzle of his submachine gun into the financier's temple. "Open the vault!"

"I can't!" Dykstra shrieked.

"Open it, Nixon!" Kennedy howled. "Let them feel the fire of freedom!"

Nixon and Kennedy blasted their submachine guns in all directions. In their random orgy of destruction they just happened to take out the lobby security cameras, and Nixon put a full magazine of armor-piercing ammo into a section of wall that happened to be a nexus of the building's security suite.

"The vault!" Nixon pulled a satchel out of the Land Rover and dragged Dykstra across the floor. "Show me the vault!"

The young man shuddered as he led the Republican President down a wide arc of marble steps. The door to the vault was a gleaming, six-foot circle of massively thick steel with a gate of steel bars in front of it. Nixon opened a satchel full dynamite.

"For God's sake!" Dykstra howled. "You can't blow it open with that! You'll kill us all!"

"Blood and fire!" Nixon screamed. He pulled out a butane lighter and lit the fuse.

"Oh, my God!" Dykstra ran for his life and Nixon let him. Rosario "Pol" Blancanales subvocalized behind his mask as he shoved the satchel through the bars. "Hostage on his way upstairs. Intercept. Detonation in ten seconds. T, be ready to move." Blancanales raised his voice to the heavens in a mad scream. "Behold His rod of correction!"

Upstairs, Dykstra screamed in sudden terror.

"Hostage acquired," Lyons came back.

"Ready to move on your signal," Tenari responded.

Blancanales took the stairs three at a time. He reached the main landing and dived over the teller windows. "Blood and fire!"

Downstairs the dynamite detonated. The sticks had been neutered and the actual explosive charge was fairly minimal, however the blast, smoke and wave of heat that rolled up the steps felt like the end of the world. The bank employees were curled into fetal shuddering balls on the floor as black smoke rolled through the lobby.

Carl Lyons thumbed his throat mike. "Move, T."

"LET'S DO IT."

Akira Tokaido followed Tino Tenari as the big man burst out of the foliage and sprinted into the smoke-filled lobby of the bank. Tokaido's bag of tricks thumped against his back and he held his hand to his face against the choking smoke and the overpowering acrid scent of high explosive. The fire alarms were ringing and the fire-suppression sprinklers were dousing everything. Glass broke beneath his sandals. A pair of bank employees lay shuddering and clutching each other as Kennedy and Nixon danced around them screaming political slogans and firing their weapons into the air.

Jimmy Carter looked over from spray-painting graffiti and jerked his head toward the back. The two men raced to the stairs and went up. While they hadn't been able to covertly break into Infinite Financial Antilles secure banking records, acquiring blueprints and wiring schematics of the building had been a much simpler prospect.

Physical security was Tenari's provenance. It was something he was already good at and he had all of Gadget's Schwarz's coaching and know-how backing him up. He overcame the lock on the financial office door like a ghost. "We're in."

Tokaido sat in front of the main computer terminal. The computer, actually the Local Area Network, was on. The worst possible thing you could do to a computer was to turn it on or off. He smiled at his prey and pulled a highly modified laptop out of its carry case.

Tenari crouched with his bulk filling the door frame. A silenced .45 SOCOM pistol filled his hands. He peered over at Tokaido as he began connecting his laptop to the central LAN terminal. "I'm an Apple man, myself."

Tokaido gazed heavenward for patience. Then his fingers began to fly like birds across his keyboard.

Moments later he punched Control-Alt-Delete on his computer and financial records began scrolling down his screen. "We're in."

"That fast?"

Tokaido leaned back smugly. "That fast."

Sirens began howling in the distance.

CHAPTER THIRTEEN

Stony Man Farm, Virginia

"Saudi Arabia." Hal Brognola shoved his cigar around in his mouth and stared long and hard at the data Tokaido had sent from the Antilles. "We're sure this is good intel?"

"Good as gold, I'm calling it." Though Barbara Price wasn't entirely pleased. "Did you check the name that Akira earmarked as the money end source?"

"Sheikh Harith Jaspari. It almost sounds familiar but—" The shoulders of the man from Justice sank. "No, no, no…"

"Sorry, but I'm afraid so." Price brought up a photo on the monitor of a middle-aged Arab in a jibbah and burnoose on a brilliant green golf course surrounded by sand dunes. "He's Saudi royal family."

"Damn it…"

Kurtzman spoke up. "Could be worse. Our boy Harith isn't part of the royal line with any kind of claim on the throne. He's one of the nonroyal branches of the family.

"Are you saying we can reach out and touch this Harith guy without pissing off the royals?"

Kurtzman scratched his beard. "Members of the Jaspari family branch have always been outsiders. They're desert dwellers and have stayed that way. They've been on the wrong side of succession struggles more than once. In their favor, they are very orthodox Sunni Muslims, and are known for their piety and the number of highly respected clerics in the family. They've also been known to support terrorist causes in the Middle East. They're fanatically anti-Israel and anti-American. There was a stink two years ago when some of the Jaspari young men were captured fighting in Afghanistan and Iraq and had to be quietly handed back."

"Let me ask you a different question. Could Harith drop thirty million into an Antilles offshore bank account?"

"Well, they're not Saudi powerhouses but they marry well, and have some pretty vast personal fortunes, I would suspect—"

"Yes or no?"

"Without blinking," Kurtzman replied.

Brognola grunted. "Barbara, have Phoenix get ready to head to Saudi Arabia."

"What about Able?" Barbara asked. "They're still in the Antilles."

"Leave them there. Tell them to keep their jet hot on the pad, be ready to go to point anywhere on the planet within twenty-four hours." Brognola raised his bulk from the conference table. "I've got to go talk to the man."

Berlin, Germany

"MR. DEYN?"

Laurentius Deyn clicked a button on his intercom. "Yes, Franka. What is it?"

Deyn's cyberneticist-security agent had a strange tone in her voice. "I am not sure, but I know you wished to be kept abreast of any anomalies…"

Deyn sat up in his chair. "What kind of anomalies?"

"It is strange, but I have a report that Infinite Financial Antilles was robbed."

"Robbed?" Deyn frowned. Robbing an offshore banking facility was nearly impossible. "How? Was the system hacked? In what amount were assets transferred?"

"It did not appear to be that kind of robbery. I am transferring you the report and file footage."

Deyn watched the security camera tape of two employees talking at a desk when a Land Rover came smashing through the glass doors. He noted the Walther MPK submachine guns as they sprayed in the air and remembered that the Venezuelan navy had issued such weapons at one time. He found the rubber masks to be in extremely poor taste. The tape ended abruptly as bullets smashed the cameras.

"They tried to breech the vault with dynamite. Naturally they failed."

A picture flashed on the screen of the massive vault door. The walls around it were blackened but the gleaming steel remained unscratched.

"Fools."

Pictures from the police report flashed across the screen, showing the smoke-damaged and bullet-raddled interior of the lobby and the political slogans crudely spray painted onto the walls and artwork. "Death to the Imperialists!" "Power to the People!" "End the Multinational Monarchy!" Laurentius Deyn was the defacto head of one of the most powerful multinationals on Earth, and like most of his kind, he found the local people in the Third World countries where he made his greatest profits revolting.

"Goddamn savages." Deyn was completely disgusted. "Did they get away with anything?"

"The tills had been emptied previously and put into the vault. Naturally, neither of the employees could access the vault. Indeed no one save the president, the chairman and the bank director could access the vault until Monday. The two employees were robbed of their watches and the money they had on them." Marx sighed. "All of the ball-point pens in the teller's windows were stolen."

Deyn shook his head slowly. There was nothing on Earth more unforgivable than stupidity. "And what became of them?"

"They escaped, sir."

The second thing Laurentius Deyn couldn't abide was incompetence. Deyn's voice grew cold. "Why have you brought this to my attention?"

Deyn could almost hear Franka flinch on the other side of the line. It took her several moments to regain her courage in the face of her mentor's wrath.

"Mr. Deyn, we have no assets currently in play with Infinite Financial Antilles, but we did arrange the routing of certain funds through it…"

Deyn's demeanor changed in an eyeblink. There was nothing at Infinite Financial Antilles that could lead to him or his activities, but there were possible loose ends. "Franka, I want this to be considered a Level 4 security breach."

Marx gasped.

Deyn continued. "I want a cybernetic team sent to the island of Bonaire. You will lead them. I want the computers and data within them thoroughly examined. Take your best people. I also want a full crime scene investigation of the upper offices. I will route a double strength security team from our South American headquarters to meet you there. Pack your bags, you leave within the hour."

Deyn punched a button for his personal secretary. "I need a secure satellite line to Saudi Arabia immediately. Then get me the head of Middle East security."

Saudi Arabia

THE CAMEL GROANED and spit green froth into the sand. The Bedouin and his band sat on their camels by the side of the road, placidly swatting at flies with his switch and waiting for the herd of goats to pass. The goats bleated and clip-clopped over the dusty single-lane road with the bells around their necks tinkling. The old goatherd wore a faded T-shirt with Saddam Hussein's smiling face on it. He nodded at the Bedouins and smiled to reveal a nearly tooth-less mouth. *"Asalaam aleiku."*

The Bedouin stared down, his face hidden by dark sun-glasses and a headscarf. *"Aleiku salaam."*

The old man jammed a thumb against the face of the former dictator emblazoned on his T-shirt and held up his forefinger in a "He's number one!" gesture. The Bedouins nodded as the man and his flock of goats moved down the road.

McCarter muttered beneath the folds of his scarf. "Bloody, goat-shagging..." He tapped his camel on the withers with his switch. "Hut! Hut! Hut!"

The camel groaned and lurched into motion. The men of Phoenix Force spread out and back to either side in a five camel arrow formation. Dust devils danced as the late-morning wind whipped the fringe of the Nafud Desert. The Hijaz Mountains loomed off to the west. Phoenix Force wove its way through the low hills and rock formations and plodded sedately toward its target. The land here wasn't quite desert, but it was too far from the mountains to receive their water. There was water here, but it was underground. The sudden burst of green palm trees shimmering in the distance identified the oasis.

The Jaspari clan controlled this oasis and a string of five more in this corridor between the mountains and the desert. This was one of their smaller holdings. For centuries it had been little more than a watering stop for caravans skirting the Nafud. There were three wells and a little small-scale date farming, mostly for local consumption. At any given time about three to four hundred men, women and children of the Jaspari clan occupied the small brown compounds of clay and brick huddled among the palm trees.

Rafael Encizo grinned under his scarf as they approached. "Looks quiet."

The rest of Phoenix Force groaned. Special Forces operators were surprisingly superstitious. In any language there were no worse jinx words in the Special Forces lexicon than "Looks quiet."

McCarter spoke into the mike strapped to his throat. "Phoenix One to Stony Base, what do you have on the oasis?"

Barbara Price came back. "No movement, Phoenix One."

"Repeat, Stony Base. No movement?"

In the War Room in Virginia, Barbara and the entire Farm team were watching the proceedings from a powerful imaging satellite. "Phoenix One, I have approximately fifty camels in the corral. Six parked civilian vehicles. Some goats and chickens wandering around underneath the trees. No human movement. No hostiles visible."

"Well." Manning loosened the ropes that bound his weapons and gear into rolled carpets. "It's getting close to noon and its a hundred degrees and climbing. Traditional

desert tribesmen take a siesta right about now and wait for
the noon prayer. Then they take another siesta and wait for
the heat to die down in late afternoon."

Encizo was grinning from ear to ear. He could smell the
ambush on the wind. "Looks quiet."

Price spoke quickly across the link. "Phoenix One, I
have movement."

"What kind of movement, Base?"

"West side of the compound. Two men are removing
some kind of awning from a small courtyard. It looks
like— Phoenix! Mortars in the courtyard! Two of them!
Hostiles are deploying inside the compound!"

"Hut! Hut! Hut!" McCarter whipped his switch across
his camel's haunch and the beast burst into a sprint. He
heard the double thud of tube noise as the mortars lobbed
their shells high into the air. The men of Phoenix Force
spread apart, looking for shelter among the rocks.
McCarter threw himself off his mount and jammed himself
behind a tombstone-size rock as a high-explosive shell
detonated thirty yards behind him. He instantly rose and
yanked his weapon roll from his mount. The camel honked
and bolted away. McCarter threw off his robes and drew
his Barrett M-468 rifle.

Hawkins spoke across the battle link. "I make it 81s."

McCarter had been fired at by mortars on every conti-
nent and had learned their tube noise well. "No, mate.
Those are ComBloc 82s." Not that one millimeter of tube
girth was going to make much difference. "Stony Base, this
is Phoenix One. I need an estimate of enemy strength."

The two mortars in the compound thudded again in unison.

Price didn't sound pleased by what she was looking at.
"Two hundred to two hundred and fifty estimated, Phoenix
One. Do you want extraction?"

Calvin James spoke across the line. "We're looking at reinforced company strength."

"Base, can you give me a civilian count?"

"No civilians visible, Phoenix One."

The mortar rounds pounded into the rocks and filled the air with black smoke. Another double thud told McCarter two more had taken flight from the compound. McCarter flicked up the ladder sight on his grenade launcher. "Phoenix Flight! What is your ETA?"

"I'm airborne, twenty minutes from your position. Do you want extraction?"

They were in the middle of nowhere. The enemy had vehicles and could quickly ride them down in the open terrain. They were twenty minutes from extraction, and Phoenix Force was outnumbered fifty to one. McCarter was ex-SAS. There was only one thing to do.

"Base, we are counterattacking. Phoenix Flight, request shock and awe on arrival. Will pop blue smoke."

Jack Grimaldi's voice came over the thud of rotors. "Affirmative, Phoenix One. Phoenix Flight inbound."

McCarter rose from his rock. "Gary, give us covering fire! Phoenix, by twos! Go! Go! Go!"

McCarter and James began to fire short bursts toward the compound as Encizo and Hawkins raced forward. McCarter tracked men through the 4x magnification of his SUSAT optical sight. Men in khaki uniforms were spilling out of the compound like a kicked-over anthill. A volley of brass shells tinkled on the rocky ground as McCarter bowled men down as fast as he could swing his sights from target to target. Off on the right Gary Manning's Dakota Longbow rifle fired with slow, methodical precision.

"Empty!" McCarter roared.

"Go!" Encizo shouted.

McCarter rose, clawing for a magazine as James fired his rifle dry. The two men charged forward. Encizo and Hawkins dropped into rifleman's crouches and began popping off shots. The Phoenix Force leader slammed in a fresh magazine and shot the bolt home. The sheikh's men had matching uniforms and AK-47s, but they were clearly street fighters and insurgents rather than soldiers. Three hundred yards was the practical limit for most men armed with a Kalashnikov rifle. The range was five hundred and most of the enemy gunners weren't using the sights of their rifles. All fired long bursts that sent most of their shots high and wide of their targets. Encizo and Hawkins could see their enemies' eyes through their optical sights. Nearly every shot was a kill. Many of the sheikh's men were trying to use the trees of the oasis for cover. They very quickly learned that the pulpy trunk of a palm was no defense at all against a full-metal-jacketed 6.8 mm rifle bullet.

Tree pulp flew as did the torn and pulped tissues of the men behind them.

McCarter and James ran past their teammates.

The Cuban rose with his rifle smoking. "Empty!"

"Go!" McCarter and James dropped, firing as Encizo and Hawkins leapfrogged their position and reloaded. Mortar rounds detonated behind them as they charged underneath the tube artillery's deadly arc. The problem was, now that they were in the dead open, they had to depend on their armor and accuracy to save them. The enemy still had hundreds of men firing a hailstorm of lead in their direction.

"Empty!"

"Go!"

McCarter and James ran forward reloading. The two, two-man fire teams took turns firing and charging as they plunged straight into the jaws of the serpent. The serpent began spitting fire. RPG-7 rocket teams rose up from cover and rocket-propelled grenades hissed from their launchers. The football-shaped grenades shrieked past, trailing smoke from their rocket motors. Phoenix Force was well within their five hundred meter range, but they were four men out in the open. They could literally step out of the incoming antitank weapons' path and let them pass by to detonate in the rocks a hundred meters behind them.

"Empty!" Hawkins shouted.

"Go!" McCarter crouched. The enemy was now in range of their M-203 grenade launchers. Enemy riflemen were crouched around the low, stone-pile wall surrounding one of the wells, and they were taking time to aim their rifles. McCarter flicked his sight to three hundred meters and pulled the M-203's trigger. The weapon belched pale yellow flame in the sunlight. The fragmentation grenade landed within the stone ring a second later and detonated like a whip cracking. Men screamed as shrapnel shredded them. The Briton lowered his muzzle and began rapidly firing his rifle. He expended his twenty-eight rounds into human flesh and rose.

"Empty!"

"Go!" Hawkins knelt and his grenade launcher thumped. Jagged bits of metal borne on wings of high explosive hissed through the palm trees, killing and maiming as the grenade detonated. Encizo's rifle fired burst after burst into the enemy positions. By the second well a weapon spit fire in the long sustained fire of a light machine gun. Hawkins could tell by the firing signature it was a Russian-made PK, firing the 7.62 mm Russian high-powered rifle round.

"Empty!" Encizo broke into a run.

James dropped into a firing crouch. "G—!"

He rocked back as he took three trip-hammer blows to the chest. He reeled on his heels a moment trying to bring his weapon to bear, and a second burst knocked him flat on his back.

"Phoenix Two down!" McCarter snarled. The Briton lifted his grenade sight for the light machine gun by the well. Manning's sniper rifle boomed from two hundred meters back and the machine gunner slumped over his smoking PK with his skull cracked open like an egg. McCarter swung his weapon onto the third well and looped his grenade for the gunmen huddling in its cover.

Encizo pounded up to James, who lay on his back gaping, stunned, into the desert sky. He'd taken five rounds into his solar plexus, but the ceramic trauma plate of his armor appeared to have survived the high-power rifle hits of the machine gun. And so, subsequently, had Calvin. Encizo had taken hits on his own armor more times than he cared to remember, and it still felt like being kicked by a mule.

He rolled James prone and shoved his rifle back into his hands. "Shoot!"

He ran on as James began to fire.

McCarter knelt, shouting into his mike and firing his rifle at the same time. "Stony Base! Enemy Sitrep!"

"Enemy forces taking massive casualties, Phoenix One! Reduced by estimate one-third!"

That still left well over a hundred enemy fighters, and Phoenix Force was running out of ammo. "Empty!"

McCarter rose and reached for his second-to-last magazine.

Hawkins jumped to join him as Encizo and James kept firing prone. James's voice was hoarse across the link. "What now? Fix bayonets?"

McCarter ignored the remark while a part of him knew it just might come to that.

"Empty!" Encizo shouted.

McCarter hurled himself prone. AK bullets were kicking up sand and dirt all around him. "Down! Pop blue smoke!"

CHAPTER FOURTEEN

"Five men!" Sheikh Harith Jaspari was incensed. He waved a gigantic dagger in one hand and an AKSU automatic carbine in the other. "You retreat before five men!"

Thamud Fazran cringed before the sheikh's wrath. He had been a volunteer fighter against the U.S. occupation of Iraq. Fazran had survived the intense street fighting in the battles for Fallujah and Mosul. He had followed the black banner against the Christian crusaders. He was a veteran ambusher, and the ambush they had planned seemed like a very good idea. They had every advantage. Two days ago they had been warned that a small group of western special operatives might try to infiltrate the oasis or set up an observation post. They'd been warned it was very possible they might try to kidnap the sheikh. Fazran didn't know who the sheikh's secret benefactor was but the information they had provided was priceless. Just six hours ago they had been warned of a five-man camel caravan that seemed to have sprouted from the desert itself.

Fazran knew such information could only have come from a satellite.

He had been well pleased. Too many times as a foreign fighter in Iraq he'd been forced to fall back and flee before the superior firepower of the American and British soldiers. This time the numbers and firepower were on his side. The sheikh had given with an open hand and supplied Fazran and his men with everything they needed. He'd bought brand-new Russian rifles and the latest generation of RPG rocket launchers. A pair of 82 mm mortars had been flown in along with a trained Syrian mortar team. Above all they had the priceless gift of surprise. The plan was perfect. Overwhelming such a small enemy force in the open would be easy. Prisoners would be taken. Fazran had flushed with pleasure at the thought.

It had been two years since he had cut off a westerner's head with a knife. The room was set and the video camera ready.

But now...

"Sir, I think it best if we evacuate you from here and—"

"Go!" the sheikh cried. "Kill the nonbelievers! Separate their heads from their bodies and let their entrails be the feast of hawks!"

Fazran ran from the sheikh's parlor. Outside everything was screaming and confusion. Men were plastered behind the walls or in doorways of the compound. Other men hid behind the vehicles or lay cringing behind palm trees. The slaughter was appalling. The dead lay everywhere. Even in the confusion Fazran was horrified to see that well over two-thirds of the casualties seemed to have been taken with a single shot. The mortars were firing way off target, more than a hundred meters behind the enemy. The mortar team was safely ensconced in the courtyard. Fazran looked around for the mortar forward observers and saw both two-man teams lying dead. The observers's binoculars were shattered as were the heads of the observers who had looked through them. The men on the cell phones who had directed fire lay dead beside them.

Fazran crouched in the doorway and took stock of the enemy. He saw four fighters out in the scrub approximately three hundred meters away. They had dropped prone and were using the optics on their weapons to maximum effect.

Dropping prone would be their downfall.

"Sadiq!" Fazran sought out his right-hand man and found the burly Bedouin huddled beneath a low wall of piled stone firing his AK blindly over the top. Fazran dived behind the wall as a bullet whined off the lip. "Sadiq! The enemy has halted! They are prone in the open! I will direct the mortars and then lead the counterattack! Take twenty men and put them in the vehicles. Flank the enemy!"

"Yes!" Sadiq rolled up to his feet. "It will work!"

"Good, take two of the RPG teams and…" Fazran trailed off as plumes of blue smoke began to drift into the sky around the four enemy fighters and from a point two hundred meters behind them in the rocks. He couldn't understand why they would announce their locations, clearly marking themselves….

"Sadiq!"

The men turned and looked. "Marking smoke! Commander I—" Sadiq's head burst apart as a .338 Lapua Magnum rifle round took him from the rocks six hundred meters west.

Fazran threw himself behind the wall and a second sniper shot cracked stone an inch above his head. He became aware of the sound of rotors and looked around wildly for the aircraft. To the north he saw a rapidly moving rooster tail of dust and sand tearing toward the oasis. Sheikh Jaspari stepped into the doorway shouting and waving his weapons. "What are you doing, Thamud! Must I kill the Americans myself! I—"

The sheikh's jaw dropped in horror as death rose up from where it had been hugging the deck and came screaming scant feet above the palm trees. Across the globe it was every insurgent fighter's worst nightmare made manifest.

The gunships had come.

Fazran tackled the sheikh through the door as hell erupted.

No SAUDI OFFICIAL would allow a combat flight from Israel over Arabian airspace. Nor would any Saudi general order an attack on a member of the Saudi royal family, however distant or embarrassing that member of the family might be. Allowing foreigners to use Saudi military assets would be equally unthinkable.

However, the Farm had a few friends and a card or two they could play.

At the same time Phoenix Force had been rerouted to Saudi Arabia, a civilian C-130 freighter had flown nonstop from Virginia to the Saudi Red Sea port of Al Wajh. Its cargo manifest declared it was carrying a civilian "pleasure helicopter." Markers had been called in and there had been no problem with customs inspections. At 4:00 a.m. that morning, in the dead of night, a helicopter had emerged from the fat belly of the C-130 like a dragonfly emerging from the ponderous round husk of its larval stage.

There was nothing civil about its appearance, and pleasure was not its business.

Dragonslayer unfolded its rotors, spread its stub wings and thundered into the purple predawn desert sky searching for prey.

It was helicopter like no other. It had been built up from a civilian airframe but it had been optimized for exactly such missions as it flew this morning. Its avionics and electronics were of the very latest generation but were a hodgepodge of both U.S. and European suites. With its stub wings attached it could carry any NATO weapons fit. With a different set of wings and a modular fire control refit it could carry Russian or Chinese weapons systems with equal facility.

Dragonslayer was Stony Man Farm's ugly surprise for those who thought they were untouchable in their own territory.

It was a beautiful morning for flying.

Jack Grimaldi burned across the sere scrub a mere ten feet off the deck. He noted the plumes of blue smoke and prone forms of Phoenix Force to the west as they fired into the oasis. He swung wide and approached from the north. His first priority was the mortars. Phoenix Force was stopped in the open and if the gunmen behind the tubes could get their fire coordination correct, Phoenix Force was going to be lunch meat in another few seconds. The Stony Man pilot popped up off the deck and palm trees whipped about in his rotor wash as he rose over Sheikh Jaspari's compound.

Dragonslayer's weapons this day were French. An Egyptian arms dealer in Qus had been convinced to ship them across the Red Sea to Al Wajh in crates marked Auto Parts. Jack Grimaldi was a red-blooded American boy and he really didn't care that much for French politics in recent years. That didn't stop him from kissing their women, drinking their wine or eating their cheese. He had no complaints whatsoever about using their weapon fits. The French had invented the helicopter gunship concept during their colonial war in Algeria. U.S. gunship design had long ago outstripped theirs, but French aircraft weapon systems continued to be well thoughtout.

He flipped his selector switch to Missile.

The AS.11 was a stubby little guided antitank missile with big square fins nearly as wide as the missile was long and had been soldiering on with innumerable product improvements since 1953. It was long obsolescent, but the sky-blue, bullet-shaped, wire-guided weapon was equal to the day's task.

Dragonslayer rose over the low, rambling, castle-like oasis compound. Her nose dipped accusingly at the two horrified mortar teams. Mortar men scattered in all directions. Grimaldi pressed the trigger on his joystick and the happy little blue missile hissed off of its launch rail trailing its guide wires.

In a fit of good sense the French had designed their air-to-ground missiles with the option of antiarmor or antipersonnel rounds, depending on the situational requirements. Grimaldi aligned the stabilized, image-intensifying sight over his right eye with the missile's spotting flare. He ignored the pop and rattle of rifle fire against his fuselage and kept his crosshairs squarely on the missile, guiding it to the pallet of 82 mm mortar rounds sitting between the two mortar tubes. The AS.11 slammed into the thirty projectile pyramid of mortar rounds and its 5.72lb Type 140AP59 contact-fuzed fragmentation warhead detonated.

Grimaldi veered *Dragonslayer* away as the pile of mortar rounds went up like a monstrous string of firecrackers and the center of the compound began disappearing in orange fire. He slid south where the vehicles were parked. Armed men were running to the vehicles. The Stony Man pilot flicked his trigger to Guns. Beneath the gunship's right stub wing a GIAT 554 30 mm cannon locked and loaded a round. The oasis had a small clearing that served as a vehicle park. Within were parked a gold Mercedes armored limousine, two Toyota Land Cruisers, a Jeep and a Unimog truck. The cannon was on a fixed mount so Grimaldi simply pointed his helicopter. Two men had leaped into the Jeep and were starting to pull away. He gave his trigger a short squeeze and *Dragonslayer* shook as five 30 mm rounds streamed from the muzzle of the cannon. The Jeep flew apart in satisfyingly small smoking parts. The pilot slowly rotated his aircraft on its axis, methodically putting bursts into each of the parked vehicles, none of which was up to the task of surviving multiple hits from 30 mm HE shells.

The Mercedes spit gravel and surged in reverse for the dubious cover of the palm trees. Grimaldi flicked his selector to Missile and a second AS.11 shrieked from its rail trailing smoke from its rocket engine and red fire from its aiming flare. The Mercedes slid beneath the shelter of the palm plantation. The pilot eyeballed the twin tire ruts the limousine left behind and sent his missile beneath the palm fronds. A fireball blossomed below and the golden hood of the Mercedes scythed skyward.

The helicopter spun back on the oasis. The majority of the bad guys had very conveniently taken firing positions along the western wall to fire at Phoenix Force. He aimed *Dragonslayer* along the wall's axis and held his trigger down. The western wall and the men manning it were blasted apart as Grimaldi walked the jack-hammering aircraft cannon along its length.

He spoke into his mike. "Phoenix One, this is Phoenix Flight. You are clear to advance. Do you wish the compound demolished?"

"Negative," McCarter responded. "We want to try to take the sheikh alive and retrieve data. Phoenix Force advancing. Commence mop-up and be prepared to bring up supporting fire."

"Roger that, Phoenix One. Beginning mop-up."

Scores of armed men were streaming away from the compound and beating it for the trees. Phoenix Force couldn't survive if the enemy regrouped and made a suicide charge across the open, and Grimaldi wasn't about to let them mass their ground fire up in his direction.

Grimaldi flicked his selector to Rockets. He had the further choice of single shot, rippling fire or all-at-once salvo. He elected for ripple fire and squeezed the trigger. A volley of 68 mm SNEB rockets began flashing from the Brandt 36 tube double-rocket box beneath the chopper's left wing. Grimaldi kicked his collective and lazily tilted *Dragonslayer* from side to side like a porch swing as the rockets whooshed away, delighted with the graceful arc of rocket dispersal the maneuver produced.

The palm plantation bore fruit to fragmentation and fire as the thirty-six French general-purpose aerial rockets exploded beneath the trees and harvested human targets.

Dragonslayer rose a hundred feet. Smoke oozed from the crater that used to be the compound courtyard. It was summer and most of the palms had a thick underlayer of dried fronds. In the plantation well over half of the trees were burning like torches. Very little moved in the oasis.

"Ready for fire support as needed, Phoenix One."

"Affirmative, Phoenix Flight, we are moving in."

McCARTER SURVEYED the carnage. Phoenix Force approached in two loose pairs, McCarter and James from the front while Encizo and Hawkins moved in through the burning palm trees. The oasis was a hellzone. Bodies lay everywhere. Nearly every man with a bullet wound was dead. Those burned and torn by shrapnel moaned and choked on the black smoke billowing through the trees.

"Fix bayonets, lads."

Phoenix Force hung razor-sharp steel from the ends of their rifles. McCarter held up a fist and they all halted and took a knee. "Phoenix Flight, what have you got?"

Dragonslayer made slow circles of the oasis one hundred feet above. "No movement, Phoenix One."

"Gary?" McCarter asked.

Five hundred yards back Gary Manning scanned with the ten power telescope of his Longbow sniper rifle. "Nothing's moving."

Phoenix Force moved in on the compound. The gate was blasted apart, and the front door was open. McCarter pulled the pin on a frag grenade and the cotter pin pinged away. "Fire in the hole!" He lobbed the grenade through the open door and stepped aside. Yellow fire flashed as the grenade detonated and the expanding sphere of shrapnel sent razor-sharp bits of steel hissing back out the door.

McCarter entered the compound. The power was off and smoke and dust filled the interior. He flicked on the tactical light attached to his weapon and played it around the foyer. It was typical Middle East architecture and formed a series of squares. The outside was very plain with few or no windows. Within, the rooms were very open and tall, and turned inward to face the courtyards. Narrow halls connected them. The oasis had been a stopping point on the trade routes through the desert since Medieval times. Parts of the compound were undoubtedly hundreds of years old. McCarter scanned the room. "Clear."

James came in, followed by Encizo and Hawkins.

Grimaldi spoke over the tactical channel. "I'd say at least a dozen men ran back inside when I began my attack run."

"Thank you, Phoenix Flight. Roger that." McCarter moved forward. Part of the room's back wall was missing.

The room beyond it was nothing but rubble, and the courtyard opened onto a smoking crater. He had seen the secondary explosions when *Dragonslayer* had unleashed on the mortar teams and the conflagration had sent fire forty feet up into the sky. The four walls surrounding the courtyard were demolished. Clay and brick construction were remarkably unresistant to high explosive.

"Movement!" Hawkins shouted.

Across the crater a man appeared in the ruined room beyond, with a long tubular object across his shoulder.

"RPG!" Encizo roared.

The men of Phoenix Force threw themselves down as the rocket whooshed from its tube and sailed across the open. The rocket trailed smoke and fire as it flew into the room and slammed into the back wall. Hawkins was instantly up and firing his grenade launcher in response. The grenade detonated in the darkness beyond the rubble of the cracked-open compound. A ragged war cry rose up from the enemy.

"Allah akhbar!"

More than a dozen of the sheikh's men charged through the rubble with their bayonets fixed and their AK47s spraying on full-auto.

"Phoenix Flight!" McCarter snarled across the link. "Immediate fire support! Anything in or east of the crater is hostile."

"Roger that, Phoenix One!" Grimaldi responded. "Keep your heads down!"

The war cries of the Saudis was drowned out by a sound like vast canvas sheet tearing as 30 mm cannon shells hammered down into the killing bowl of the mortar crater. Direct hits tore men in two and separated limbs from torsos. In almost the same instant the rounds continued to hit the ground and detonate. The high-explosive rounds ripped what remained into red mist.

The charge ended exactly two and a half seconds after it had begun. Smoking steel shell casings rained down, clattering across the killing field.

Phoenix Force rose and moved across the blasted earth of the courtyard. Hawkins stooped and picked up a human head. He took out his Palm Pilot and quickly began thumbing through file photos. Since their mission was against a known Saudi terrorist supporter they were on the lookout for terrorists who might be hiding out with the sheikh. "Thamud Fazran. Wanted for terrorist acts in Iraq. One of those guys who had a hard-on for beheading people." Hawkins grunted with black humor at the head. "Positively ironic."

He tossed the head into a shell crater and Phoenix moved on, sweeping from room to room. The irony grew deeper as they came to a room that was empty except for a video camera on a tripod, a black banner on the wall and a mattress with butcher knife lying atop it. Someone had dropped a dime on the sheikh, telling him he was going to have visitors, and Phoenix Force knew the room had been set up for them. They passed a sumptuously appointed room that was obviously the sheikh's master bedroom.

McCarter frowned as he looked at the carpet-lined walls and silk divans and couches. They were running out of compound. "All right, I'm betting a strong room or spider hole. Tear the place apart."

It took only moments. Encizo ripped up the carpet and found a hatch in the corner of the room. McCarter squatted on his heels. The hatch was a square, white-painted steel plate. A recessed handle pulled up to open it and the screen of a touch pad electronic lock blinked up at them. The

Cuban sighed. "Gary's our demo guy, but I'm betting that hatch is rigged to blow."

"Rip up the floor around it."

The men of Phoenix Force put their bayonets to work and pried up the wooden floor. The top of the tunnel was just below the floor and it appeared to be a concrete tube. McCarter lined up his compass with the six feet of exposed concrete. He smiled as he sighted down it. The tunnel appeared to be heading due west of the compound, toward rock formations that would provide cover for an escape. McCarter thumbed his mike. "Phoenix Four, you should be expecting company presently."

DIRT RAINED DOWN as Jaspari heaved open the hatch. He was sweating from his stooped-over flight down the dark concrete tube and he wheezed from the effort of opening the hatch against the sand and dirt that covered it. He pulled his bulk up into the sunlight, shakily waving his carbine around in a covering circle and, with profound relief, found himself alone in the rocks. He sat by the hatch trying to catch his breath. Smoke rose eastward from the blasted oasis. It was impossible, yet here, in the kingdom, in his very own place of strength, the Yankee crusaders had come for him. Five men on camels had brazenly attacked him, and pulled forth a gunship from only God knew where. Truly the Great Satan helped them.

Jaspari was a man of great faith, but in many ways he was also a very practical man, and he knew that the Great Satan, like God, most often helped those who helped themselves.

He would have to help himself now. How the infidels had accomplished this was thought for another time.

The Americans had a gunship, and he couldn't run from it. However, a Mach 2 Saudi Arabian fighter jet from Prince

Sultan Air Force base could arrive in twenty-five minutes. With all the troubles in the Middle East several flights of F-15E fighter-bombers were always on standby. Gunships and helicopter transports from Red Sea bases could arrive well within the hour. All that was required would be a member of the royal family calling on the royal family emergency frequency saying his oasis was being attacked by Israeli commandoes.

Harith smiled. All he had to do was to make a phone call and stay hidden in the rocks for a few minutes. The sheikh took out his cell phone and flipped it open.

A voice spoke from the rocks behind him. "Excuse me, Your Excellency. Lose the phone."

Jaspari spun, firing his AKSU carbine. Bullets whined and sparked off the rocks. His Russian carbine suddenly locked open as the 30-round magazine exhausted itself on full-auto.

A man rose up out of the rocks. He was big, dressed in desert camouflage and festooned with weapons. The sheikh's most immediate concern was the long black rifle with the powerful telescopic sight the man held loosely in his hands. "Lose the phone," he repeated. "And lose the weapon." The big Westerner smiled and nodded in a congenial fashion. "I promise you that you'll be fairly treated."

Jaspari dropped the cell phone and the empty carbine.

The man nodded. "Thank you, Your Excellency. Now if you'll—"

"*Allah Akhbar!*" the sheikh screamed. His dagger hissed from its sheath. He raised it overhead and charged forward, intent on martyring himself.

As the curved blade flashed down for the kill, Manning sidestepped and dropped to one knee. He swung his thirteen-pound rifle around in a low lazy arc and cracked the twenty-eight-inch, stainless-steel barrel across the sheikh's shins. The man screamed in agony as white fire shot up his legs and his feet went numb. His legs collapsed beneath him and the dagger went flying as he fell into the dirt.

"American pig!" the sheikh howled.

The big man sighed. "I'm Canadian."

"Bastard!" The sheikh clawed for his fallen dagger, and Manning kicked it away. The sheikh screamed in renewed outrage and lost his English as the big Canadian sat on him and began speaking into his radio.

"Phoenix One, this is Phoenix Four. Package is secure."

McCarter's voice came back over the receiver. "Roger, Phoenix Four. Phoenix Flight will make pickup while we finish mopping up the compound."

"Affirmative, Phoenix One. Phoenix Four sitting tight and awaiting extraction." Manning sat on the squirming man as the sun beat down on them. He sipped lukewarm water from a tube that stretched around from his camel-back water pouch as *Dragonslayer* thundered toward him. "Yo, Jack, where the hell is Able Team again?"

"Last I heard they're in the Antilles, living in the lap of luxury, picking up Dutch girls gone wild, and drinking Jamaican beer."

Manning heaved a heavy sigh.

It was a line that often blurred, but Able Team tended to get the American local sphere actions while Phoenix Force took the more international missions. By Manning's reckoning, that meant that whenever a mission called for going to vacation destinations such as the Cayman Islands, Hawaii or the Mexican Riviera, Able Team got the job. On the other hand, for example, if the mission called for riding giant stinky beasts across sun-blasted desert, street fighting in the rain in Dushanbe, Tajikistan, or for perhaps running hither and thither naked through Greenland's frozen tundra, Phoenix Force was going to get the nod.

"The Dutch Antilles." Manning drank body-temperature water that tasted like plastic. "Assholes..."

CHAPTER FIFTEEN

Bonaire, Dutch Antilles

"Well, looky here."

Akira Tokaido looked up from his laptop. "What?"

Tino Tenari was sitting with his chair backward a few feet from the open window, watching the violated financial institution up on the hill through a spotting scope. "There's someone new coming into Infinite Financial."

"Oh?"

Tenari grinned. "Dude, you need to check out the geek seductress."

"What?" Tokaido rose reluctantly from his laptop and peered through the scope. "Wow."

She was hot. He watched as she took off her suit jacket in the tropical heat and threw it back in the limo. Her red hair was plaited into a single braid down her back. The sweat plastering her blouse to her body accentuated her curves. "Wow."

"Uh-huh." Tenari nodded happily. "I dig the little square-frame-black-glasses action."

Tokaido took his eyes off the woman and looked at her two companions. He noted the black T-shirts, ponytails and complexions of people who rarely saw the sun. All three were carrying laptop cases, computer gear bags slung across their shoulders. "Those guys are geeks."

"Yeah, Eurotrash geeks," Tenari agreed. "What she's doing with those pencil dicks is beyond me."

"They're a cybernetic team."

Carl Lyons walked into the room. Bonaire was a very small island with very little to do other than party and soak up sun. They were on standby to anywhere, so partying was out. Lyons had established surveillance on Infinite Financial for lack of anything better to do. "What have you got?"

Tenari raised his bulk out of his chair. "You got a new group arriving at Infinite. Akira has them pegged as cyber-geeks."

Lyons squinted through the scope, checking the legs on the redhead. "Nice." He took a long look at her two companions as they entered the gutted bank. "Police already investigated. Bank officials already came and investigated. So, the question is, what do these geeks want?"

Lyons turned and stared hard at Tokaido. "Did you get detected?"

"Uh-uh." He was adamant. "No way."

Lyons turned to the massive blacksuit. "T?"

"I don't know from computers, Chief, but I watched the kid at work." Tenari shrugged. "And he was slick, man. Like shit through a goose."

Lyons frowned and jerked his head back at the bank. "So what are you telling me?"

"If I had to bet, I'd say they're suspicious." Tokaido squirmed under the Ironman's gaze. "And..."

"And what?"

"And I don't think it's from me and T's angle."

Lyons would've been irritated except that Akira was so embarrassed he couldn't meet his eyes. "All right. So the enemy sent a cybernetic team. What can they find?"

"Nothing. I mean...I think. I mean, I was the ghost in the machine. I wasn't even a whisper."

"T?"

"Crime-scenewise, we didn't leave a trace. I ran a full sweep on entry and exit. Unless they have portable infrared equipment that can detect that Akira's ass was on that office chair thirty-six hours ago, they got nothing."

Lyons calculated the odds. "Akira's right. The robbery sent up a red flag. We'll have to assume they've alerted all parties concerned. T, get Pol and Gadgets off the beach and ready to roll. Akira, get hold of Barbara and tell her that Phoenix should expect heightened security if not some kind of welcoming committee in Saudi."

Lyons's phone rang. He checked the number and his worst suspicions began confirming themselves. "Yeah."

"Señor Blondie? It is Rafa."

Rafa was a Bonaire street urchin. Lyons had given him and a gang of his confederates a hundred gilders and a cell phone to play soccer in the field across the street from the hotel and alert him of anything suspicious.

"What have you got, Rafa?"

"A dozen men have gotten out of two vans. They are all wearing long coats and walking toward the hotel. Some are going around the back." Rafa paused. "I think they have guns."

"Thanks, kid. I live through this, you got another hundred coming." Lyons punched a button and Schwarz answered the phone.

"Yeah?"

"We're getting hit, here at the hotel. Dozen men, long coats, front and back. I need you and Pol, pronto." Lyons kept the line on as he held out his hand. "Tino!"

Tenari reached into a bag and pulled out a pair of Mossberg M-9200 A-1 semiautomatic shotguns and tossed one to Lyons. In years past the weapon had become a favorite of Special Forces operatives on drug interdiction missions in Central America and picked up the nickname of the "Jungle Gun." The big ex-Air Policeman had become intimately familiar with the weapon before taking a job with the Farm.

Tokaido stared in trepidation. "What's happen—"

Lyons unlocked the folding stock of the brutally short-ened shotgun and racked the bolt on a three-inch Magnum shell. He caught the bandolier of ammo Tenari tossed him and slung it over his shoulder. "We're gonna get hit. Cowboy up, kid."

Tokaido drew his Walther PPK uncertainly.

"T, you wear Akira like underwear. Back me from the doorway."

Lyons strode out into the hallway. The hotel was Dutch-Colonial architecture, tall and narrow, and Able Team occupied two of the four rooms on the third floor. Lyons phone peeped at him and he pushed a button. "What is it, Rafa?"

"I followed the men inside. They're going up the elevator."

"How many men?"

"Six."

"Anyone with them?"

"No, they shoved a lady out. Two men are watching the stairs."

The ornate doors of the elevator rattled and the needle above climbed from 1 to 2. "Thanks, Rafa." Lyons punched a button. "Pol, what's your ETA?"

"Ninety seconds, Ironman."

The floor indicator needle came to rest on 3.

Lyons raised his shotgun to his shoulder. "The party will be starting without you."

"Affirmative."

The elevator bell pinged and the door rattled open. For a split second six men in long coats gaped in horror down the muzzle of the 12-gauge. Lyons could see each man low-holding some kind of silenced automatic weapon with the stock folded. The lead man flinched and tried to bring up his weapon. "Che—!"

The Jungle Gun thundered in the Ironman's hands.

The range was five feet. The magnum buckshot loads had no time to spread as they left the barrel. All twelve double-aught buckshot struck their target in a pattern the size of a human fist. The lead assassin flew back into his fellows as his sternum disintegrated. Lyons swung the front sight of his shotgun to his next target. The elevator car and the men inside it were sprayed with bone, brain and blood as Lyons's second load of buckshot all but beheaded his opponent.

Lyons jerked back out of the doorway as men screamed in Spanish and began spraying lead. The Ironman took two steps back and dropped to one knee. One of the killers shoved his weapon around the elevator frame. The silenced weapon coughed on full-auto as he blindly sprayed the hallway, searching for Lyons. A line of bullets stitched the stucco of the far wall. The Ironman put his sight on the weapon three feet from his face and fired. The Jungle Gun punched back brutally against his shoulder. The enemy sub-machine gun flew down the hall as did most of the hand holding it. The assassin reeled out of the elevator clutching his spurting stump and another killer leaped out with him.

The Able Team leader folded Stumpy in two with a

blast of buckshot. The man behind him raised his weapon but he didn't see Tino Tenari lean out of the doorway down the hall. The blacksuit's weapon detonated and the assassin lurched forward as he took the pattern of buck between the shoulder blades. The killer's feet flew out from under him like he'd been clotheslined as the Ironman's blast took him beneath the clavicles.

The elevator pinged as one of the two living men within hit the down button and the doors started to rattle closed. Lyons shoved the barrel of his rifle between the closing doors and fired his last round. He dropped the spent shotgun and stepped back. Dozens of answering rounds from the silenced machine guns cratered the wall across from the elevator. Lyons drew his .357 Magnum Colt Python revolver as the elevator doors banged against the fallen shotgun. He cocked back the hammer and sighted at the Jungle Gun as the doors tried to close. A foot snapped forward to kick the shotgun out of the doors and Lyons fired. He was rewarded by a scream as the tip of the dress shoe disappeared in a splatter. The shotgun slid across the floor and the doors pinged closed.

"You all right?" Tenari boomed.

"Two hostiles still in the elevator, heading down. You?"

"Yeah." Tenari glanced at Tokaido. "What's happening on our six?"

"I…" Tokaido suddenly turned to the window as he heard steel rattle. "I think someone's coming up the fire escape." He ran to the window and looked down. A half dozen men in long coats were pounding up the narrow metal gantry. "They're coming up the fire escape!"

"Shoot 'em!" Tenari roared.

The lead man raised his submachine gun like a giant pistol. Tokaido shoved his Walther PPK in front of him in a two-handed Weaver stance. As he squeezed the grips, the Crimson Trace laser sight winked into life. It was daytime, but the back of the hotel was shaded and a ruby-red dot appeared like magic in the middle of the killer's forehead. John "Cowboy" Kissinger's words rang in Tokaido's head.

Shoot them until they fall down, kid.

The little Walther's report was little more than a pop compared to the cataclysmic reports of the short-barreled shotguns, but Akira squeezed the trigger and the PPK began rapidly *pop-pop-popping!* in his hands. The killer's forehead smeared and he collapsed back into his fellows.

Tokaido flinched as the weapon suddenly stopped shooting and smoke oozed from the empty chamber. He fumbled for the spare magazine in his pocket as one of the men farther down the fire escape leaned out and aimed his weapon.

"Reload!" Tenari's hand clamped on Tokaido's collar and yanked him back into the room. Bullets spattered against the window frame and ceiling as the man below fired upward. Tenari shoved his shotgun out the window and it began to boom like an automatic cannon. Sparks shrieked along the guardrails and steel steps of the fire escape as the big Samoan sent sixty buckshot pellets down the stairs in less than five seconds. The killers jammed into the fire escape's narrow confines shuddered and died.

Tenari's shotgun racked open on empty. One survivor leaped to the street. The big man dropped his shotgun and went for his pistol. The fleeing assassin landed badly and came up limping as he bolted for freedom.

He stopped short as Rosario Blancanales appeared in the back alley, blocking his flight with his Government Model .45 in his hand.

The assassin stood, leaning on his good leg with his

hands white-knuckled around his automatic weapon. Blancanales's voice was friendly but his eyes were as hard as the East L.A. streets he'd been raised upon. "Don't do it, friend," he said in Spanish.

The killer's brows bunched, eyes flicking, calculating. He locked gazes with Blancanales, glowering and growling gutter Spanish to screw up his courage as they stood, weapons leveled in a Mexican standoff.

The man moved and the Able Team commando's .45 barked in rapid fire in his hands. The heavy, flat-head slugs hammered the hired killer backward. His weapon chipped brick on the back alley wall and then fell to the cobblestones in a clatter. The assassin fell a second later.

Blancanales slapped in a fresh magazine and swung up his Colt to cover the fire escape. His bull-like shoulders sagged slightly. He'd wanted a prisoner.

"T! You all right?"

"Yeah, we still got two coming down the elevator and there are two more inside watching the stairwell!"

Blancanales clicked open his phone and hit the Able Team conference call button. "Gadgets, you got two more coming down the elevator, I'm coming in through the back."

"Roger that."

Blancanales kicked open the back door of the hotel and ran through the small kitchen. The staff gasped and cowered behind crates of produce as he rolled through with his smoking .45 in his hand. Guests and staff were screaming throughout the building. He moved into the dining room and fresh screaming broke out as Schwarz's .40-caliber Beretta Elite began firing in rapid double taps in the lobby. A man in a long coat, bleeding from the arm and shoulder, staggered through the double doors. Blancanales put his front sight on the man's chest dead to rights.

"Freeze!"

The man struggled to bring up his gun. *"Puto—"*

Blancanales's Colt boomed three times in rapid succession and sent the man falling back through the swing doors. Schwarz crouched in the lobby, using the front desk for cover. His pistol pointed unwaveringly at the elevator. Two men lay unmoving in pools of blood.

Blancanales stayed in the dining room door frame. "What have you got, Gadgets?"

"One guy's still in the car. He's got a wounded foot, but he's still salty."

Lyons spoke over the conferenced phones. "Did you say a wounded foot?"

"Yeah, he came limping out of the elevator and when I started firing he thought better of it and limped back in."

There was a moment of silence. The screaming had died down and Pol and the two men could hear the gunner in the elevator car gasping. Lyons spoke after a moment's reflection. "Pol, these guys speak Spanish?"

"Two of them did. The one in the alley was Argentine. I could tell by the way he swore."

"Pol, would you be so kind as to tell the asshole in the elevator that if he doesn't surrender in three seconds I'm going to drop a grenade down that shaft and send him to hell so he can rejoin his toe."

"Ah." Blancanales sighed with pleasure at the metaphor. Somewhere beneath the Ironman's stony exterior lurked the soul of a poet. He called out happily. The threat sounded even more beautiful in Spanish.

The man in the elevator began moaning and mumbling.

"What's he say?" Lyons inquired.

The wounded man was mumbling in Portuguese but he'd clearly gotten the message. "He's talking to himself, mostly, and God and Jesus and Mary. I think he's about ready to crack."

"Start counting."

"Uno!" Blancanales called out. *"Dos!"*

The man in the car moaned.

"Tre—"

"No!" The word was a shriek.

"Throw out your weapon!" Blancanales snarled. "And speak English!"

A submachine gun slid from the elevator into the middle of the lobby. "Don't shoot! Please! Don't shoot!"

"Come out slow! Hands in the air!"

"Don't shoot!" The killer was a heavyset man with thick black curls cut tight against his skull. He was sweating with fear and pain. He limped out, using only the heel of his right foot. The leather toe of his shoe was bloody and shredded. Schwarz came out from cover, and threw him to the floor and began hog-tying him.

They had a live one.

CHAPTER SIXTEEN

The Desert

"Your excellency?" David McCarter took a seat in front of the sheikh. "We have a problem."

The sheikh was sweating. He sat in a small room with a single shuttered window, handcuffed to a folding chair. On a platter beside him was some pita bread, goat cheese and zartar spice. A small pot of mint tea sat cooling beside the food. The sheikh had refused to eat. He glared at McCarter with as much dignity as he could muster. "You have detained me illegally. I demand to be released immediately."

McCarter ignored the comment. "The problem is this. There seem to be some Russian nuclear devices missing and the money trail, sir, leads to you."

"I do not know what you are talking about. I am a Saudi citizen and a member of the royal family. I am a victim of foreign aggression on Saudi sovereign soil. You American—"

Manning sighed off to the side. "I told you, I'm Canadian."

"And I'm English, then, aren't I?" McCarter suggested helpfully.

"Slave states." The sheikh spit. "Sending your soldiers wherever the Great Satan tells you."

"Your Excellency—" McCarter pulled his chair closer to the sheikh "—as I've told you, we have nuclear devices missing."

The sheikh lifted his chin and stared down his nose at McCarter. "This means nothing to me."

"What it means to you is this. I'm out of time. I can't send you to Guantanamo Bay." The sheikh flinched at the name of the U.S. military base in Cuba where they often sent suspected terrorists. "Nor," McCarter continued, "do I have seventy-two hours to engage in standard field interrogation protocols."

"I have no idea what you mean, you—"

"It means we are going to have to use more direct methods to obtain the information."

The sheikh paled as he stared into McCarter's eyes. "You would not dare."

"No, Your Excellency. I wouldn't do it. It isn't who I am, or the sort of thing we do."

"Then you will release me at once and—"

"But I know people who do, indeed, do that sort of thing." McCarter jerked his head at the sheikh, letting his anger deliberately kindle. "Get him bloody up, then."

"What? You—"

Manning and Hawkins stalked forward. Food flew and crockery broke as Hawkins kicked the food and tea out of the way and the two men yanked the sheikh up by the elbows. McCarter stormed over to the window and ripped the shutters open. "Bring him over here."

Hawkins and Manning marched Jaspari to the window.

The Briton cuffed the sheikh's headdress from his head, grabbed him by the hair and thrust the man's head out the window. "Do you know where you are, Sunshine? Take a look. Take a real good look."

The sheikh grimaced. The sun was beginning to set. The helicopter in which he had spent a long, blindfolded ride sat in a flattened area a few dozen meters away. Nearby was parked an old Jeep and a fuel truck. Beyond that rolling desert surrounded the little house on all sides. A dusty, one-track road leading south.

"The Nafud," the sheikh declared. "How dare you behave so in the kingdom! I will—"

"No, you're not in the bloody Nafud." McCarter grinned unpleasantly. "You're in the Negev."

The blood drained from the sheikh's face.

"Oh, that's right." McCarter nodded. "You're in Israel."

"I…" The man trembled slightly as the sum of all his fears unfolded in front of his eyes.

McCarter cocked his head slightly. "I have it on very good authority that you, personally, last year, offered one thousand U.S. dollars to the families of Palestinian homicide bombers for every Israeli citizen they managed to kill."

The Saudi began to shake uncontrollably.

McCarter forcibly craned the man's head around to look past the corner of the house. In the distance the lights of a town were beginning to shimmer on. "That's the city of Eilat. The Mishmar Hagvul maintains a brigade there, as I recall."

Jaspari flinched as McCarter invoked the infamous Israeli border guard. They were made up mostly of Druse Arabs and Bedouin trackers with full Israeli citizenship. Druse and Bedouin Israelis were excused National Service, which meant those in the border guards were all volunteers. They despised "urban" and "oil rich Arabs" and the terrorists they sponsored. Palestinian terrorists infiltrating Israel far preferred to be captured by regular Israeli Defense Force or police personnel.

"The Mossad also has a sizable station in Eilat, as well, and they'd just love to have a crack at you, wouldn't they, then?" McCarter yanked the man back. "Sit him back down!"

Manning and Hawkins manhandled Jaspari back to his seat. McCarter went to a small writing table in the corner and took out a piece of paper, a marker and a stapler. He began reciting out loud as he wrote in large letters, Hello, my name is Sheikh Harith Jaspari.

"That should do, then." He rose from the writing table. "Hold him."

Manning and Hawkins held the sheikh in place by the shoulders. He shrieked in outrage as McCarter stapled the four corners of the note to his robe. The Briton nodded to himself. "Lovely. Now drive him into Eilat and drop him off outside Mishmar Hagvul headquarters. Then drop a dime on the Mossad station. Let them know what the border guards have."

Encizo nodded. "How do you want me to phrase it?"

"Tell them the situation is Broken Arrow. Russian origin. Target unknown. Sheikh Jaspari is involved. Tell them we need all data extracted within the hour."

Hawkins stared down sadly at the sheikh. "You are so fucked."

McCarter stared unblinkingly at Jaspari. "Tell them to use whatever means necessary."

The sheikh was a big man, but his voice ripped out of him in a near squeak. "No!"

McCarter shoved his face into the sheikh's. "Sunshine? You are going to talk to me."

Computer Room, Stony Man Farm, Virginia

KURTZMAN SIPPED COFFEE that would strip paint and read Carl Lyon's after-action report. Akira had been in a gunfight, and according to the report he'd given a good account of himself. After Able Team had hit the bank someone figured out it wasn't a local affair, and they had the wherewithal to find the most likely foreigners on the island and sent a squad of hitters to take them out. Lyons's group would undoubtedly stand out.

Part of Kurtzman was angry as hell that his protégé had been exposed. Another part of him was secretly proud of the boy. Akira had broken Infinite Financial Antilles's defenses like a matchstick, and when the shit had hit the fan, he'd stood and fought. Regardless, Kurtzman decided he was going to chew Lyons out for getting Akira shot at when he got back. He grunted as he read the last part of the report. "So what can you tell me about Nine Toes?"

Barbara Price flipped through a dossier. "Able dropped him off at Guantanamo and the CIA was able to work up his info pretty quick. His name is Hugo Carlinho. Brazilian national. He was in the First Special Forces Battalion and reached the rank of sergeant. Honorably discharged in 1998 and went into private security."

"Who does he work for now?"

"That's where things start to get shady. Last the CIA can establish he worked for the Circulado Corp. It's a Brazilian textile and mining concern. Carlinho was on the Circulado security section payroll. His official job was VIP protection. Unofficially the rumor is he was one of the go-to guys when Circulado was having problems with local indigenous populations."

Kurtzman scowled. He'd read this kind of résumé

before. Circulado used Carlinho's jungle warfare skills to terrorize Indians into signing away their land. Given the nature of the attack on Able Team, he was also most likely one of the guys they sent to assassinate tribal union leaders. "Circulado didn't order Carlinho to the Antilles. Someone else did. Have Carmen dig up everything she can on Circulado. Pol says here he believes another one of the shooters was Argentine. My bet is they have larger, trans-South American ties."

"She's already on it." Price took a file that had been faxed from the Farm armory. "Meantime, the Cowboy sent us this on the weapon Able sent back."

Kurtzman looked at a spec sheet for the silenced sub-machine gun the hitters had used. It was a folding stock weapon with a large, disk-shaped clear plastic drum mounted on top. "MGV-176?"

"It's .22-caliber, the drum on top holds 176 rounds of ammo."

"Good heavens."

"Yeah, according to Cowboy, it's a remake of the old American 180 carbine. It caused a stir in the 1970s because it was the first weapon to have a laser designating sight."

Kurtzman looked at the sheet beneath it. The file had the specs for the 180. The seventies' era weapon had a full wooden stock and steel furniture. The new weapon had a folding wire stock and made extensive use of plastics. "So who's remaking it?"

"The Slovenes were."

"Really."

"Cowboy says Slovene Special Forces used them as assassination weapons during their war of independence from Yugoslavia. He says we can try to run a trace on them, but he's betting Slovenian military inventory will show them as lost or destroyed during the war."

It was interesting, but Kurtzman had to agree it seemed like a dead lead. "The question is what are exotic Slovenian submachine guns doing in the Antilles?"

Price shrugged. "As for Slovenian connection, we just don't have much, except that it's the most prosperous of the former Yugoslavian republics. Highest standard of living in post-Communist central and eastern Europe."

"Lots of foreign investment," Kurtzman concluded. He looked at the huge world map on the giant flat screen with red dots marking the recent action sights. "Casinos in Tajikistan. Dutch offshore banks in the Caribbean. Saudi royal family members. Slovenian submachine guns in the hands of South American corporate hitters."

Price saw where the Bear was going. "We're looking at a multinational with something very ugly in mind."

"We're looking at missing nuclear devices, the Russian *mafiya*, ties to Middle Eastern terrorists, and Phoenix Force was on its way to Germany before it got rerouted south to Saudi." He zoomed the screen in on Germany. "We're looking at Berlin, and we were looking at four German satellites over Moscow during the warehouse fight. We have to tie one of them into all of this, and I don't care how."

Carmen Delahunt burst into the room, her cheeks flushed from running. She was the prototypical vivacious redhead. She was emotional and liked to live large. Panic, however, wasn't part of her emotional acumen. She was old-line FBI.

But there was genuine fear in her eyes.

Kurtzman saw it and felt a twinge himself. It took a lot to rattle Delahunt. "Carm? What have you got?"

"I pulled some CIA contacts in the Russian navy. Akira

had it right. Admiral Sergei Beniaminov had oversight over special Soviet riverine naval forces whose missions included infiltrating the major European river and canal networks."

"Let me guess." Kurtzman felt his stomach sinking. "Nuclear demolition was part of their purview."

Delahunt nodded. "It gets worse. MI-6's contact reported they believed six weapons were stolen."

Price felt her own stomach start to sink. "Phoenix got back five. One is still loose. Right?"

Delahunt swallowed with difficulty. "We can't get anything more out of the Russians, but NSA has caught unconfirmed chatter at the highest levels of the Russian military and government. NSA can't confirm, but they recommend the missing nuclear demolition charge number be revised."

Kurtzman blinked. "Just how many devices does NSA think the Russians have missing?"

Delahunt took a long breath. "Thirty."

There was a moment of appalled silence in the War Room.

Price reined in her horror. "That's not counting what Phoenix recovered?"

"That's correct. Revised estimate is twenty-five devices unaccounted for."

Kurtzman put his head in his hands. "So what's the good news?"

"NSA came through on the German satellite survey."

"Who owns it?" Kurtzman asked.

"A multinational called the IESHEN Group."

"Carm, get me everything on the IESHEN Group. Top priority, cross-reference them with Infinite Financial Antilles and Circulado Corp. For that matter, find out what kind of business dealings they have in Slovenia."

"All U.S. Middle East assets are ready to assist them depending on where they need to deploy."

"The IESHEN Group is headquartered in Berlin, correct?" Price asked.

Delahunt glanced at one of her files. "That's correct."

"I'll have Able Team in Berlin within twenty-four hours, with full warloads and support in place when they get there."

Kurtzman frowned.

Price caught the look. "What is it?"

"Tell Akira his mission has been extended."

CHAPTER SEVENTEEN

Bonaire, Dutch Antilles

"Berlin?" Tokaido looked out the window onto the aching blue of the Caribbean Sea.

"Yeah." Carl Lyons stood with his arms folded across his chest. "That's where we're headed. I want you to come along."

"What's Bear going to say?"

"He already approved it before we got our marching orders. Question is, do you want to go?"

Tokaido let out a heavy sigh. "Honestly?"

"Yeah. Honestly."

"Carl, I don't know. I mean…" He struggled to put his feelings into words. "I mean, back at the Farm I'm always thinking about going out into the field. I guess almost every data specialist daydreams about it. But yesterday. I shot that guy."

"You've shot people before. We're proud of what you can do."

The young hacker flushed slightly. Lyons handed out

praise neither often nor lightly. "Yeah, but yesterday, I leaned out a window. I looked down into a guy's eyes." Tokaido shook his head. "I looked in his eyes and shot him three times in the face."

"And how do you feel?"

Tokaido searched for words and failed. "I don't feel anything."

"Good."

"Good? I killed a guy. Aren't I supposed to feel something?"

Lyons frowned. "Why would you?"

"Jeez…"

"Listen, kid, contrary to popular belief, I'm not made of iron. I have feelings."

The cyberwizard cocked his head warily. "Really?"

"Yeah. Really. Listen, I've killed more people than I can count. It comes down to perspective. I feel bad when people die because of my mistakes. I feel bad when innocents get caught in the crossfire, and I've dropped the hammer on people and wished to God it hadn't come to it."

"You're saying those guys had it coming."

"The one we got an ID on was a corporate thug who made big coin brutalizing indiginies for a South American strip-mining outfit. We're here trying to track down loose nuclear weapons and keep them out of some very bad hands. He came to stop us, Akira. He came to kill us. I'm not saying he deserved to die, but he made his choice. I'm not sweating him. Neither should you."

"I hear you. It's just pretty…sobering."

"That's exactly what it should be." Lyons cracked a rare smile. "There might be hope for you yet.

"So, you want to go to Berlin? The Bear says if we're

going to rip off the IESHEN Group's most sensitive data, we're going to have to do it on site."

"Same as the bank?"

"Nah, Gadgets gets us in past security quietly, then you hack the mainframe. In and out, undetected on both fronts, with luck. Our next move after that will probably depend on what kind of data you extract."

"Is Tino coming?" Tokaido had always been a little intimidated by the huge blacksuit, but the man's massive strength and good humor were very comforting in a "situation."

"Oh, yeah, as an Air Policeman he was stationed in Germany for a few years. He speaks the lingo, and he's got your back the whole way." Lyons nodded. "And if the shit actually does come down? I'll be standing in front of you. That, I promise."

Tokaido took in the ocean breeze. It occurred to him that he spent a little too much time beneath the earth in the Computer Room. "Berlin, huh?"

"Yeah, Berlin."

He thought a moment about the firefight and shot Lyons a sly look. "Can I have a bigger gun?"

One corner of Lyon's mouth quirked against his will. "Anything you say, Tex."

Berlin, Germany

LAURENTIUS DEYN CONSIDERED the impossible. Franka's instincts had been correct. The incident at Infinite Financial Antilles had been much more than a mere robbery attempt. The subsequent slaughter at the hotel had proved that the enemy was using Special Forces operatives against them. Strangely, however, they didn't behave like any Special

Forces men Deyn had ever known. Neither the U.S. Navy SEALs nor the British SAS behaved in such loose, almost cavalier fashion. His opponents appeared to be running the operation by the seat of their pants, almost making it up as they went along. This was something Laurentius Deyn didn't care for. The fact was, if the British or U.S. intelligence communities were on to his activities and acting against him, he would know about it.

The whole situation smacked of black operations.

Independent operatives, deniable assets. Deyn shook his head. It was all the sort of James Bond bullshit that he had very little use for. The situation did have advantages. For one, it narrowed things down. Only three countries had the wherewithal and the resources to engage in these Mickey Mouse kinds of games. Deyn appraised them in reverse order of possibility. French intelligence was famous for its rogue activities. They engaged in Byzantine international operations, often getting in over their head and resolving the situation by killing everyone involved. Deyn doubted he had attracted French attention. Another very real threat was the Israelis. They, too, engaged in fast and loose intelligence operations, but almost always against their Arab opponents. Anyone else they considered a threat they usually just assassinated.

That left the Americans, and, oh, how they loved their cowboy games.

U.S. intelligence was arguably the best and most capable in the world. The fact that Navy SEALs hadn't come knocking on his door in the middle of the night told Deyn that while U.S. intelligence might somehow suspect some aspect of the IESHEN Group was involved in some missing nukes, they had little else to go on.

Thus the cowboys probed, looking for clues.

The nice thing about black operations was that the operatives were generally considered expendable in the name of national security. Their actions were almost always illegal, and a team that was slaughtered would be denied. Then whatever dark corner of the U.S. government that was controlling the operation would have to face internal review, and only then, slowly and painfully try to rebuild their operation.

Long before that could happen, investigating Laurentius Deyn would be the least of the United States' problems.

It came down to one thing.

A group of cowboys needed killing.

Deyn pushed a button on his desk and a moment later three men walked into the room. One was the size and build of a sumo wrestler. Everything about him was rough-hewn and blunt. From his brow and jaw to his catcher's-mitt-size hands. Johan Mahke was Deyn's personal director of security in Germany. Beside Mahke stood the ex-Navy SEAL Clay Forbes and the Russian Spetsnaz officer Alexsandr Zabyshny.

"Gentlemen, you are aware of the situation in the Antilles?"

Three very dangerous men nodded.

"And you have received the report from our Saudi Arabian assets?"

All three men had read it. The snatch of Sheikh Jaspari was an absolute worst-case scenario.

"Gentlemen, we have a Yankee problem." Deyn tilted his head at Forbes. "No offense, Clay."

"None taken." Forbes grinned. "I'm a citizen of the world."

"Then let me be plain. The Americans are coming and I want them dead."

Computer Room, Stony Man Farm, Virginia

"GIVE ME EVERYTHING you've got." Hal Brognola slouched back into his chair.

Kurtzman handed him a file. "Suspect number one, IESHEN Group International."

"IESHEN Group? Jesus, Bear, you told me to invest in them!"

"I know." Kurtzman grinned. "How'd you do last week?"

"The stock split." Brognola shot a rare smile. "And I bought more. So I want you to give me some goddamn good reasons why I want to screw up my stock portfolio."

"IESHEN Group is a German-based multinational. They started off as a merger between the IES Technology Company in Bonn and HEN Light Industries in the late 1980s and they have steadily grown. They also diversified and have become the umbrella corporation for some very wide ranging endeavors.

Brognola peered at the file. "Like Infinite Financial Antilles?"

"They've put money there before, and while we can't prove it, we believe IESHEN Group has controlling interest. Hunt is on it."

"Uh-huh." The big Fed grunted. "And Circulado Corp?"

"Hunt already nailed that one down. There are two cutout corporations in between. Legally, IESHEN Group could deny all knowledge of Circulado's activities but at the end of the day we're saying IESHEN Group owns them outright."

"Okay." Brognola flipped through file pages. "So give me Sheikh Jaspari."

"That's where we lucked out. He just happens to warm a chair on the board of directors of Treibstoff-Chemikalie von Bonn."

Brognola flexed his rusty German. "Bonn Petrol-Chemical."

"Right. HEN Light Industries was getting into oil exploration in the late 1980s. When they merged with IES they bought into Bonn Petro-Chemical. IES was working on specialized technology for finding oil with new kinds of ground penetrating radar and satellite geothermal imaging. Some of their undersea geothermal exploration was nothing short of spectacular. They also put a lot of work into going to known oil reserves that were considered too difficult and expensive to exploit, buying the drilling rights cheap and turning a profit. The money they made on that in the 1990s gave them the financial base to expand into all sorts of new areas. Jaspari has been a significant investor and sits on the board. We believe he was the money conduit to Admiral Beniaminov."

"Straight answer, can you put Sheikh Jaspari in bed with IESHEN Group."

"Not at the moment. Remember, IESHEN Group is a multinational. They can always claim that one of their subsidiaries has gone rogue, and for that matter, they could be telling the truth."

"But they own our most likely satellite?"

"That one they can't squirm away from. That satellite has IESHEN Group stamped on the side in bold letters. There's a picture of it on their Web site. On a minor note, Bonn Petro-Chemical has been heavily involved in developing Slovenia's natural gas deposits. So I think we have a good guess on where those submachine guns came from in the Antilles."

Brognola stared hard at the file. They had a lot of intriguing data, but nothing conclusive. Snatching a sheikh out of his oasis and faking a bank heist was one thing. Going to war with one of the world's leading corporations based in one of the United States' closest allies was another. "I gather you have a strategy?"

Barbara Price spoke for the first time. "Able Team is in Berlin. All CIA and NSA German assets have been diverted. We suggest sending them in."

"Into the IESHEN Group's central headquarters."

"That is where are all current data threads leads. As I said, CIA and NSA assets are working up a solution to get Able inside the building undetected. Once inside, Gadgets overcomes their internal security and Akira overcomes their computers. We extract the data that can tie this all together. With luck we find the nukes either on site or at least information that can lead us to their location. Phoenix Force is sitting tight and can be anywhere on the planet in twelve hours or less. Able extracts the info and Phoenix moves. All we need is word go from the President."

"So how are you going to get Able in?"

Huntington "Hunt" Wethers walked into the conference room. The black man moved and spoke with the dignity of the university professor he was. He held a computer disk in his hand. "I believe I've found the in we need at IESHEN Group headquarters."

Kurtzman nodded. "You ran a survey on the IESHEN Group board of directors?"

"I did." Wethers slid in the disk and pictures of old men began to flash upon the screen. Some were obviously newspaper and magazine photos. Others were taken from ID cards and file photos. "Twelve men sit on the IESHEN Group board of directors, and a more uptight group of German industrialists you've never seen. However, what any of these men would want with thirty thermonuclear devices is hard to imagine, other than sheer greed for the profit they could make with them."

Brognola grimaced as he looked at twelve of the wealthiest men in Germany arrayed on the screen. "That was the CIA's assessment, as well."

"Well, we're not the CIA." Wethers allowed himself a smile. "So I called in some favors."

"My initial hypothesis is this. Looking at the members of the IESHEN Group board, I find it unlikely that any of them would want to traffic in nuclear weapons, much less desire access to them for 'personal' reasons. This leads us back to the rogue element scenario. It is not unlikely that some lower level element of the corporation has gone rogue and blackmailed one of the directors into assisting them. These are some very greedy German multimillionaires. They didn't get where they were without getting their hands dirty."

Brognola scratched his chin. "You dug up dirt on some of the directors."

Wethers frowned with distaste. "On the contrary, I found the one man of honor among them. The one man among them, who, if shown our findings and Able and Phoenix's after-action reports, redacted of course, would be suitably appalled and possibly willing to assist us."

Brognola raised a disbelieving eyebrow. "So who is this iron man of honor?"

Wethers pressed a couple of keys and one man's face came to dominate the screen.

Both of Hal's eyebrows rose as personal data began scrolling down the screen. "German Naval Combat Swimmer, 1955-65…Jesus! He was GSG-9?"

Wethers nodded. The GSG-9 was the German equivalent of Delta Force, formed after the massacre of Israeli athletes at the 1972 Olympic Games in Munich. They were some of the most highly capable operatives in the world. The Farm had worked closely with GSG-9 on a number of occasions. "A lot of his file is sealed on the German side, but according to NSA files he worked very closely with United States operatives on several missions in East Germany during the cold war. He's a patriot and his bravery, his loyalty and his mission record are impeccable."

Brognola nodded. "Bear, this is the break we've been looking for. I'm taking a meeting with the President in half an hour. Barbara, put everything in place, assume Able is a go. Get a hold of the NSA's best German liaison officer and get me a flight to Berlin."

For once things seemed to be going right. "Laurentius Deyn is our ticket in."

CHAPTER EIGHTEEN

Berlin, Germany

"Skorpion machine pistol." Carl Lyons stood at the ten-meter line of the German border patrol's indoor firing range. He held up a short, stubby, brutal-looking implement that was too big to be a handgun and too small to be a submachine gun. Lyons and Tokaido had the range to themselves. "The Cowboy sent it out special, just for you, kid. It's .32-caliber, just like the PPK he gave you, but this bad boy rocks and rolls at 850 rounds per minute and has a 20-round magazine."

Lyons suddenly shoved the Skorpion out at arm's length. Tokaido jumped as the little weapon ripped into life. A diagonal line of twenty ragged holes buzz-sawed up from the crotch of the silhouette target to the head. Lyons reloaded and slapped the twin wire struts along the top of the weapon, and the folding stock snapped down into place. "This is your shoulder stock. You get better accuracy and control with it deployed." He shouldered the weapon and pulsed off three quick 5-round bursts to the belly, heart and head of the ravaged target. "Use it whenever possible."

"Shoulder stock," Tokaido noted. "Got it."

The Able Team leader handed over the weapon. "It's a little underpowered for my tastes, but I've bet my life on Czech steel before. They know something about gun design. It's lightweight, concealable, and its gonna fit in one of your laptop cases. Like I said, a little underpowered, but it's going to send out those little .32s in swarms. You burn a burst into somebody's chest with this bad boy and you might as well have caught them with a pattern of double-aught buck."

Tokaido held the smoking Skorpion machine pistol. Again he felt conflicting emotions. But after burning through two mags of ammo under Lyon's tutelage, he'd achieved a solid degree of accuracy. He was ready.

"So, Herr...Brognola?" Laurentius Deyn sat back in his chair. "You wish me to betray my company and quite possibly give away technological secrets important to German national security."

Brognola measured the man in front of him. In person his body language and bearing read like his résumé. "Mr. Deyn, national security is exactly what we're talking about."

"*Ja.*" Deyn shook his head slowly at the file Brognola had given him. "It is bad enough that you tell me Circulado Corp is hiring assassins and Treibstoff-Chemikalie von Bonn is in bed with known supporters of terrorists, but Herr Brognola, twenty-five nuclear bombs? This I find hard to swallow."

"Thermonuclear demolition charges," Brognola corrected.

"*Ja,* nuclear devices, not bombs. I do understand the difference, I assure you, and I do realize, as well, that potentially millions of people could die if these devices fall into the wrong hands." Deyn sighed. "But this still leaves the question of why. Many of my fellow directors are ruthless men, Herr Brognola. The activities of the Circulado Corp proves that, and while I find this disturbing, and I give you my word, it shall be rectified, it does not lead me to conclude that any member or members of the board are nuclear terrorists."

"You're forgetting Sheikh Jaspari." Brognola countered.

"I forget nothing." Deyn locked eyes with Brognola and neither man flinched. "But Sheikh Jaspari is a member of the Saudi royal family. You will find a member of the royal family sitting on the board of every foreign company conducting business in the kingdom. It is the way business is done."

"What if it's not one of the board member's personal agenda? What if it's being forced upon them?"

"You mean, blackmail."

The big Fed let it hang between them.

"Herr Brognola, every member of the board is person-ally worth tens of millions of Euros, some of us vastly more than that. That kind of money can make blackmail go away. I know for a fact that two of the members of the board are homosexuals. They are 'closeted,' as you Americans put it, and would be embarrassed if such information were to be revealed, but again, I know both men and simply do not believe the threat of disclosure could drive them to acts of nuclear terrorism."

"What about a threat, a credible one, to them or their families?"

"That is a much more logical line of thought." Deyn smiled slightly. "However, I assure you, if any of the members of the board felt they or their families were in danger, they would come to me. The fact that you are here means you have investigated my background. I still have the kind of connections that could make a threat to a board member disappear."

"Your satellite."

Deyn blinked. "Which satellite?"

"IESHEN-SAT-135, your North Star high-intensity imaging/ground-mapping satellite, currently in geosynchronous orbit. Mr. Deyn, there was an operation in Moscow three days ago. The operators involved were almost instantly counterattacked. Intelligence shows that there were no observers in the air or within range on the ground. We believe your satellite guided the ambush."

Deyn steepled his fingers. "Herr Brognola, the North Star satellite is part of a satellite 'constellation.' As its name implies, it is the dominant satellite in the group and directs and coordinates the activities of the others in lower orbit. North Star 135, as you have pointed out, is in a high, geosynchronous orbit. It is looking at the entire northeastern hemisphere."

"But it is still powerful enough to pinpoint and track men moving on the ground."

"How do you know this?"

Brognola didn't, for sure, but kept his poker face. "We know, and as part of a satellite constellation whose main functions are exploring for signs of underground deposits of oil and natural gas, both North Star and in particular two of its lower orbit constellation satellites would have been in excellent position to track movements and direct an ambush in Saudi Arabia."

"Herr Brognola, literally hundreds of satellites owned by dozens of countries could have done the same."

"Herr Deyn, every scrap of evidence we have leads to Germany and all of it points to at least some aspect of the IESHEN Group being involved."

"The political rumor is that Sheikh Jaspari was kidnapped by Israeli commandoes." Deyn arched an eyebrow. "I gather you have him."

Brognola said nothing.

"What I find particularly troubling about these allegations is that satellite tasking is part of my purview at IESHEN Group."

"We know that," Brognola acknowledged. "We also know that during the timetable of our operations you were on a hunting trip in the Black Forest."

Deyn's features went cold with anger. "You are implying that IESHEN Group security and satellite assets could be tasked and used in illegal, indeed, terrorist operations behind my back."

"Herr Deyn, I have seen elements of U.S. Intelligence go rogue, with the assistance of powerful corporations and even high-ranking members of the United States government. If our suspicions are correct, then of all the board members you would be most likely to take swift and decisive action if such a plot were discovered. There is a saying, keep your friends close and your enemies closer."

"You are implying such activities would be easier to perpetrate under my nose rather than at a distance."

"That is how I would do it, Herr Deyn."

"You realize if your suspicions are confirmed, IESHEN Group is finished. Untold billions of dollars and thousands of jobs lost. Many smaller nations will reel from the loss of our investiture."

"I believe the same losses will be incurred at a thousand-fold, not counting the loss of human life, if twenty-five thermonuclear devices are detonated."

"You wish me to give you access to the IESHEN Group data core."

"I want an in into the building," Brognola told him. "Friends will do the rest. Any further assistance would be considered a bonus."

Deyn regarded Brognola dryly. "I assume if I do not assist you, you will attempt to break into the data core by other means."

"Most assuredly." Brognola shook his head. "One other thing you should think about, Herr Deyn. The Russians are aware that they are missing twenty-five thermonuclear devices."

Deyn's face lost all traces of amusement. "Are you threatening me, Herr Brognola?"

"I'm stating fact, Herr Deyn. The Russians do not know that the trail leads to IESHEN Group. The U.S. hasn't shared that information with them, nor do we intend to. But you must assume that Russian intelligence is working feverishly on the problem. As you well know, the Russians still have extensive intelligence assets left over from former Eastern German Democratic Republic. They are fully capable of carrying out clandestine operations in your country. Should it come to their attention that the IESHEN Group has the devices or was involved in their theft and transfer, you can only assume they'll move with total ruthlessness against the board. I can quite easily foresee the kidnap and torture of the board members and their families. You were a member of GSG-9, Herr Deyn. You know the Russians will stop at nothing to retrieve the devices and prevent the knowledge of their theft from becoming public."

"And if no evidence is found?"

Brognola shrugged. "Then I will owe you an apology."

"And if your 'friends' are caught and my collusion with your efforts at breaking into the IESHEN Group data corps discovered?"

"I suspect you'll be ruined." Brognola regarded the German frankly. "As I said, any further assistance would be considered a bonus."

Deyn's shoulder slumped. For a moment he lost the veneer of an ageless corporate giant and looked very much like weary man on the razor's edge of seventy.

Brognola drove the dagger home. "Everything I read about you leads me to believe you are a man of honor, and a patriot."

"Very well." Deyn gave Brognola a wry smile. "I will assist you."

CHAPTER NINETEEN

"Should be simple." Lyons stared down at the building schematic. "For once it looks like we caught a break."

Schwarz looked at the plans askance. "Simple makes me nervous."

"Why?" Akira Tokaido asked.

"Because nothing in life is simple."

Tino Tenari nodded. "Nothing's ever been simple that I've seen."

"Simple, not so simple." Blancanales shrugged. "Twenty-five nukes, amigos. We don't have a choice."

"Gadgets, go over it again," Lyons suggested.

"We go in soft." Schwarz fanned five plastic ID necklaces and five magnetic key cards like a dealer in Vegas. "The badges get us in as technicians. The key cards get us into places we aren't supposed to be. Any kind of security we don't know about, I'll deal with. The only thing we hit hard is the main security suite. There should be two men inside but with luck they'll never see us coming. Carl and I hit that and take control of the situation from there. Once we've taken over, Pol will bring in the helicopter while Carl, T and Akira head to the main computer network. Akira cracks the data core and goes hunting. According to Hal, we have a four-hour window, which should afford Akira enough time to get some serious digging done. If it looks like a no-go, then we extract exactly the same way we went in." Schwarz glanced up at the Able Team leader. "Carl?"

Lyons opened a case containing four black automatic pistols. The SOCOM pistols were big, large even for a .45. The tubes of their sound suppressors were attached and on the accessory rail beneath the slide of each pistol hung a module containing a tactical light, a laser pointer and a cassette holding the twin probes of an X-26 Taser gun. "Like Gadgets said, we're going in soft. Except for the two men in the security suite, everyone is a friendly, and even the guards we're handling nice." Lyons picked up a pistol and tapped the Taser mounted to it. "If you have to shoot, light them up with the juice. Though I'd prefer a nice stalk and hog-tie if you detect someone someplace they shouldn't be. Anyone we might run into is just some slob working late. The security guys are just doing their jobs, and so are any cops we happen to meet during extraction. We're at zero tolerance for friendly casualties."

Akira looked at his own laptop case full of weapons. "What about me?"

Lyons shrugged. "Bring the whole candy store if you want, but you don't shoot anything unless I tell you. You up for this?"

"I am down with the sickness," Tokaido declared.

"Jesus." Tenari snorted. "One bank heist and he thinks he's Jesse James."

Lyons nodded to himself as the rest of Able Team laughed. They were in good humor and ready for the mission. "All right, we're go in four hours. Check your gear, get some sleep."

Landwehrkanal

HAL BROGNOLA SAT in a communications van by the canal. A block down, the vast glass monolith of IESHEN Group corporate headquarters reflected the lights of the Berlin skyline. Laurentius Deyn sat next to him along with an immense security man named Mahke and two of his men armed with Heckler & Koch MP-5 submachine guns. Two more men stood outside. A woman named Franka was operating the remote security suite. Brognola watched through night-vision binoculars as Able Team pulled past in an unmarked car and headed for the building.

"I hope you know what you are doing, Herr Brognola."

Mahke shifted his bulk. "We could have done this, Herr Deyn." Brognola could feel the German juggernaut's eyes burning into his back with hostility. "We did not need to bring in…Americans."

"Perhaps." The big Fed kept his gaze on Able Team as it approached. "But if your own security had gone snooping around, it would most likely be detected by whoever is on the inside in all of this. This way is safest. It will look like corporate espionage."

Deyn gazed long upon his place of employment. "You think your men can break through Herr Mahke's security, Franka's cybernetic protocols, and then get away undetected?"

Mahke shifted angrily in his chair again. Franka Marx raised a bemused eyebrow. "Team is descending into underground parking lot."

Brognola watched Able Team disappear beneath

IESHEN Group corporate headquarters. "Those men are experts, and the very best in their fields. In the event that the unlikely, or God help us, the unthinkable should happen, both those men and their actions will be untraceable to you and the United States government." The big Fed lowered his binoculars. "Your ass is covered, Mr. Deyn. It's ours that are hanging out in the breeze."

"I appreciate your candor, Herr Brognola." Deyn smiled. "But I assure you, we are all risking much."

Marx clicked keys on her board and watched her screen. "The team has passed the security gate. The gate guard has logged them in and IESHEN Group security net has accepted their identification and itinerary." The computer expert leaned back in her chair. "They are in."

ABLE TEAM ASCENDED IESHEN Group headquarters via the service elevator. The four men wore white coveralls with matching caps. So far the paucity of German speakers wasn't hurting them, but their greatest asset was that it was 2:47 a.m. and hardly anyone was around. Tenari's German was limited but a grunted *"Guten morgen"* and a flash of their badges had gotten them past the gate guard and into the service area. The elevator gave a chime each time they passed a floor as it accelerated up into the Berlin skyline.

Able Team tensed as the elevator pinged and gently came to a stop on the twenty-fifth floor. The door hissed open and a weary-looking young man in a suit stood holding a cup full of coffee. He smiled tiredly and began to speak in German.

Lyons spoke out of the corner of his mouth. "T, what's he talking about?"

"He wants to know about this evening's soccer scores." The man cocked his head in confusion.

Lyons smiled at the young office worker. "T."

The big Samoan buried his fist in the young man's guts. His eyes bugged as the air gasped out of his lungs and he folded to his knees. Tenari dragged him inside and began tying him with plastic strip restraints. Schwarz pressed the up button and Able Team resumed its assent.

Schwarz scowled as Tino gagged the hapless office worker with duct tape. "If he was working with someone, this may cut into our time window."

"Bound to happen." Lyons shrugged fatalistically. "Let's do this."

The elevator pinged onto the thirtieth floor. Tenari threw their captive over his shoulder like a sack of potatoes and the four of them marched down the bleak gray access corridor to main security. A camera above the steel door swiveled to peer at them, but Schwarz marched straight to the door and swiped his magnetic card through the electronic lock. A fat, red-faced man in a black uniform blazer half stood from behind his bank of video monitors. His hand reached down to his control board. Lyons raised his silenced SOCOM .45. The guard stopped reaching for the alarm and desperately clawed at the leather flap of the holster on his hip.

The Taser unit beneath Lyons's barrel chuffed and the twin probes flew out trailing their wires. The barbs hit the guard's center body mass and Lyons hit the juice. As the current raced through the guard's body, he jerked and shuddered, going to his knees, his pistol clunking to the carpet. Lyons cut the juice, and Tenari dropped the office worker and jumped on the guard. Schwarz slid behind the security console. "Carl, there's two chairs here. We're missing a guard."

Lyons ejected his Taser's spent cassette and snapped in a new one. "Is he on screen?"

Schwarz swiftly hit keys and the video monitors flicked

from camera to camera throughout IESHEN Group corporate area. "I don't see him, but these two guys are supposed to be on the buddy system here in main security. He's supposed to stay close."

"There won't be any cameras in the toilets. Find me the closest."

Schwarz pulled up a schematic of the thirtieth floor. "There's one right down this access corridor and to the left."

Tenari loomed up from the bound guard. "You want me to get him?"

"You never leave his side." Lyons pointed at Tokaido. "I got this one."

Lyons trotted down the corridor and found the men's room. He silently opened the door and entered. The soft crepe soles of his boots made no noise as he crept in. A radio was playing and all the stall doors were open except one. He stepped up to the stall and kicked in the metal door. A young man wearing a black security blazer jerked up in horror from the German sports page he was reading.

"Up!" Lyons roared. *"Schnell!"*

The guard dropped his paper and grabbed for his pants. Lyons let him pull them up but not fasten them. A man holding up his pants wasn't in a position to resist and even if he dropped them it was an instant hobble. Lyons grabbed the guard by his lapels and swung him out of the stall. He slammed his palm between the man's shoulder blades and propelled him forward. *"Schnell! Schnell! Schnell!"*

Lyons marched the pleading guard back to main security. "Tino, tie him up and put him with his friend. Gadgets, what have you got, did the translator software work?"

Schwarz and Tokaido pushed away from the console.

"The computer controlling internal security is pretty simple and not tied to the main system," Schwarz stated.

"It just collates the security logs and coordinates the cameras, alarms, fire suppression and sends out signals to local police and fire. Those two jokers don't get relieved until 6:00 a.m. We own the building."

"Does this place have lockdown?"

Schwarz pointed at a big red button. "Oh, yeah."

Lyons thumbed his com link. "Control, this is Ironman. The building is secure. Proceeding to target."

Hal Brognola's voice came across the link. "Affirmative, Ironman."

Lyons jerked his head at Tokaido and Tenari. "Let's do it."

The Able Team leader directed his men back to the elevator. IESHEN Group's corporate mainframe was located on the floor just below the executive offices of the directors on the seventeenth floor. The elevator came to a halt on the sixty-ninth. The service elevators didn't reach the executive suites. They walked down the service corridor and entered the sixty-ninth floor. The stark gray corridor gave way to office hallways of plush carpet, teakwood walls and priceless art objects.

Schwarz spoke from the security suite. "Corporate mainframe is at the end of the hall. I have you on camera."

"Roger that," Lyons confirmed. At the end of the hall the expensive hardwoods of the office entries gave way to the cold steel of a double security door. Lyons took out his master magnetic card and swiped it. A red light blinked on the control panel and an electronic chime peeped unhappily. The door remained resolutely shut.

Schwarz came across the line instantly. "Ironman, you just set off an unauthorized access alarm. I suppressed it. Try again."

"Affirmative." Lyons swiped the card and nothing happened. "What's happening?"

"Hold on."

Schwarz thumbed his com link. "Control, this is Able Two. Key codes are not working."

In the remote communications van, Hal swiveled in his chair. "Mr. Deyn?"

Laurentius Deyn glanced at Franka Marx. The computer expert sighed and shook her head. "We did not give them the access codes, Herr Deyn. We gave the Americans the electronic algorithms of the lock system. From that they designed their own master keys. If the door does not open, the error has to be on their end."

Brognola's brows drew down. He'd known Gadgets Schwarz for a very long time. He'd met systems that had tested his limits. A lock whose electronic guts he'd already examined wasn't one of them. "I find that difficult to accept."

Deyn shook his head slowly. "I find it difficult to accept that this mission may have been compromised, but it is a possibility we may be forced to accept. Perhaps your men should abort. Have them withdraw the same way they went in."

Brognola punched his link. "Ironman, this is control. There's a possibility that the operation has been compromised. Our allies suggest you abort."

Carl Lyons stood in front of the steel doors. His blue eyes bore into them as he weighed his options. "No way. We own the building. I'm going in hard. Tell our allies that we may need tech support on the inside. Get Pol and the chopper here now. If you detect movement on the police bands, we'll lockdown and keep crunching on the computer until the last second and then extract by air."

Brognola turned to Deyn. "You heard the man."

Deyn sat back in his seat and looked at his security man. Mahke's voice rumbled like braking slate. "Risky."

"Your call, Ironman," Brognola stated.

Lyons faced the door. He thought for a moment before hitting his com link. "Gadgets, how many people are in the building?"

"Not counting us, security logs show 115 including IESHEN employees, private security and cleaning services. You want a breakdown by floors?"

"Negative." Lyons pulled a length of flexible charge out of his coverall. "Gadgets, I need the fire alarm suppressed on the sixty-ninth floor, we're going in hard."

"Affirmative, fire alarms are off."

Lyons pulled the safety strip off of the triangular cable of explosive to reveal its adhesive side. He pressed the five-foot length against the seam between the two steel doors and pushed in a detonator pin. Lyons took out his cell phone and pressed the star three times to arm the detonator. His team stepped back as he pressed the pound key.

"Fire in the hole."

Fire spit along the five-foot cable and the charge hissed like an enraged rattlesnake as the shaped charge burned through the steel. The blackened doors fell open to reveal a Spartanly furnished room. Banks of rack-mounted servers took up a full wall with familiar green LED lights blinking and the whir of cooling fans. A table with three chairs faced three sets of monitors and keyboards. Tokaido took the central seat.

Lyons peered over his shoulder. "What've you got?"

"It's big, but it's a pretty straightforward business system. They're running a very large Oracle database on top of Linux servers."

"How're you going to hack it?"

"Hacking a computer is a series of steps. The good news is you putting me physically in front of the target allows me to circumvent about ninety percent of them. We have two choices as I see it. One is, I can use cracking software. We push our way in through brute force. The software will generate millions of passwords based on number, letter and word sequences until we crack their security codes."

"Pros and cons?"

"Pro? This is the safest route, detection-wise. Once we're done I can easily convince the computer we were never here and the millions of code sequences were never run."

"Con?" Lyons probed.

"The problem is that the process is like trying every possible combination on a lock. It can take time. Also, while most business systems operate in English, IESHEN Group is running their data core in German. I'll have to use German language cracking software. It's good, but not as comprehensive as my English language software. If I'd had more time, I could have expanded it."

"Time's at a premium. What's our other choice?"

Tokaido smiled slyly and pulled out a gold-colored CD. "This."

Lyon's arctic blue eyes narrowed. "What's that?"

"Why, it's a bootable distro of a LINUX Operating System on CD."

"Lose the geek-speak."

The young hacker sighed patiently. "It's pretty simple. Most of the time when you're hacking you're creeping around in someone else's operating system trying not to get caught."

"And?"

"I'm going to reboot the server with my own, customized Linux Operating System to bypass the IESHEN Group's regular Linux and their built-in security levels entirely."

"You'll own their computers."

"Like Able owns this building." Tokaido grinned. "I can go anywhere I want and do anything I want."

"Yeah? So what's the downside?"

"Tomorrow they'll know their system was rebooted."

"What does that mean?"

Tokaido shrugged. "Exactly that. In the morning some-one is going to see that the computer rebooted during the night. Of course, computers can reboot for lots of reasons, bugs in the system, power surges. They might get suspicious, but with luck they'll never know we were here."

Lyons gazed back at the blackened security doors. "Tomorrow? They're gonna know we were here."

"Oh. Right."

"The reboot is quicker. Do it."

Tokaido paused. "See if you can get me linked with the remote van."

"Why?"

"Like I said, all the data is in German. The Bear's trans-lation software is the best there is, but no translation is perfect. A native operator could speed things up by getting me past anything the software doesn't recognize."

Lyons thumbed his mike. "Control, this is Ironman. We are going to install our own operating system. Requesting native translation support on your end."

"Hold on, Ironman." In the control van, Hal Brognola turned to Deyn and arched a questioning eyebrow.

Laurentius Deyn steepled his fingers. The plan had been to get the enemy into corporate headquarters. Once the Americans had found themselves unable to open the door to the corporate main computer complex, they would extract back down through the parking garage and find themselves face-to-face with a platoon of heavily armed men.

Deyn hadn't counted on the Americans bringing a flexible shaped charge with them.

Deyn slid his gaze to Mahke. The big security man had

been busily text-messaging on his cell phone and redistributing the teams for an assault on the building. He held up five fingers behind Brognola's head. He needed five more minutes to position the teams. Deyn nodded. "Very well, Herr Brognola. Franka, establish a link with their computer man and give him whatever language support he needs."

"Establishing link." Marx clicked a few keys and a real-time video window appeared in the top corner of her monitor. "I am ready to assist you."

Tokaido's face went blank as he stared at the video window on his end. "Uh... One moment control." He squelched his mike. "Carl, T."

The two men looked over. "What have you got?"

"Tell me I'm hallucinating."

Tenari reared to his full height. "Jesus! It's the cyberhottie!"

Lyon's blood ran cold. He flicked a dial on his com link so that only Able Team and Brognola could hear him. "This is a trap. Pol, we need helicopter extraction immediately. Gadgets, on my call, give me lockdown on the building. Hal...get out of there."

CHAPTER TWENTY

"Herr Deyn, I do not know what is happening. The Americans have turned off their microphone," Franka Marx said, frowning.

Deyn's hand drifted underneath his coat. "Mr. Brognola?"

"I don't know." The big Fed shrugged and tapped his earpiece. "I can't hear anything, either. Maybe you should—" The man from Justice slapped leather for his .40-caliber Glock. One of Mahke's men whipped up his weapon and the ruby beam of his laser sight gleamed into life. Brognola's Glock roared three times in rapid succession and the .40-caliber flat-head bullets caved in the security man's cranium. The second security guard swung his weapon in line with Brognola's head. He slid down out of his seat as the submachine gun snarled and punched a line of holes in the side of the van. The Glock boomed as its trigger was double tapped. The two bullets punched through the guard's throat and Marx screamed as she and her computer display were slopped with arterial spray.

Brognola whipped his weapon around to bring down Deyn, but Mahke's huge hand clamped around his wrist like a vise. Brognola was a big man but Mahke was huge. His size-seventeen shoe thudded into the Justice man's chest and pinned him against the side of the van like an insect. His hand went numb as Mahke squeezed.

"Drop it," the German ordered.

The big Fed struggled to bring his pistol to bear. Mahke pressed his thumb into Brognola's ulnar nerve just below his hand and his fist opened of its own accord. The pistol clattered to the floor of the van. Laurentius Deyn leaned forward in his chair and pressed the cold muzzle of a Walther P-5 into the American's temple.

The back door of the van flew open and the two guards leveled their weapons.

"Cease your struggling Herr Brognola. It is futile."

"Able, I'm compromised!" the big Fed snarled. "Lockdown and extrac—"

Brognola's vision went white as Mahke seized his jaw and squeezed both mandible hinges, stopping just short of popping his jaw from its moorings to his skull. Deyn leaned back in his chair and spoke into his microphone. "Forbes. Zabyshny." Deyn pulled up his schematics of IESHEN Group corporate headquarters. "Full assault."

ALARMS RANG throughout the building as Schwarz initiated lockdown. All the doors on the ground floor instantly locked and steel-mesh security gates began lowering across them. Heavy iron bars began descended down over the entrance to the underground parking. All of the elevators froze on the floors they were on. Lyons, Tenari and Tokaido ran for the roof. "Pol! What's your ETA!"

"I am inbound! ETA three minutes!"

"Gadgets!" Lyons ripped open the door to the stairs leading to the sixtieth floor. "Sitrep!"

"We have men with guns inside the building! Some of the cleaning people and after-hour executives were plants! We should expect assault teams any second!"

"Gadgets, what are you going to do?"

"It's thirty floors up to link up with you! I got armed men on the floors in between us! I think I'm going to head down. They won't expect that!" Schwarz's voice went cold. "Maybe I'll go see how Hal is doing. They won't expect that, either."

"Keep your com link open!"

"Roger that." Schwarz glanced around at his screens. There wasn't much else he could do from here. He took the guard's P-7 K-3 pistols and their spare magazine from their flap holsters. The little .380 automatics were dreadfully underpowered in Schwarz's view of the world, but they beat a sack full of rocks, and he only had one spare magazine for his .45. He stopped a moment and stared at the smaller of the two bound and gagged guards. The wicked curve of his Emerson Tactical Persian folding knife snapped open with a flick of his wrist. "You."

CARL LYONS BURST into the executive suite. It was blissfully empty of enemies. Blancanales's voice crackled across the com link. "Ironman! You have two helicopters landing on the roof! Armed and armored men deploying! Squad strength! I— Goddamn it! I'm taking fire! I've got company!"

"Affirmative, Able Flight! Get the hell out of here!"

"Ironman! What about you—"

"I'm going to commandeer one of their helicopters!" Lyons roared. "Get out of here!"

"Affirmative, Ironman! Able Flight—"

The ceiling above the executive suite shuddered and concrete, ceiling lights and rebar blasted downward from a five-foot hole in the roof of IESHEN Group corporate headquarters. The breaching charge filled the executive suite with smoke and gray dust. Lyons roared above the ringing in his ears. "Grenade!"

He overturned a table and Tenari ripped up a computer desk and tipped it over as a pair of black, soda-pop-can-size cylinders dropped down through the hole. Lyons squeezed his eyes shut and covered his ears. The flash-stun grenades detonated like thunderclaps and blasts of white light highlighted the veins behind his eyelids. He blinked and rose with his SOCOM pistol in a two-handed hold. The overpressure of the stun grenades whipped the dust and smoke into curling maelstroms. Most of the overhead lighting was gone and in the gloom the stun grenades' after-blast pyrotechnic effect left thousands of sparks whirling and blinking like berserk fireflies. The fire suppression unit came on and sprinklers descended to spray the landscape. The broken mains over the hole in the roof spilled their water like garden hoses.

A man in full riot armor repelled through the hole. As his boots hit the carpet, he brought up is G-36 short assault rifle. Lyons's silenced .45 cycled in his hand as he shot the man in his face shield. His helmet and armor were rated against bullets. His visor was made to stop bricks and bottles. The Plexiglas punched inward and went opaque with blood as the man fell bonelessly to the floor.

A second man dropped down through the hole as two of Tenari's bullets cored both legs before he even hit the floor.

Lyons snarled across the link. "T! Get his rifle and grenades! Akira, covering fire!"

The two men leaped over their cover. Tokaido rose with the folding stock of his Skorpion machine pistol firmly against his shoulder. A third man repelled down and the

Skorpion snarled on full-auto. The attacker twisted and lost purchase on the rope as he took the burst. The young hacker raised his aim and sprayed the rest of the magazine up the smoking hole.

Lyons grabbed the body of the first man down and heaved him back behind cover. Tenari picked up his man and hurled him over the top of the overturned computer desk. Tokaido sprayed a second magazine up the hole. He ducked as bullets sprayed back and ripped wood chips from the table.

Lyons stripped the dead man of his G-36 and pulled a flash-stun from his web belt. "T! They're going to hit us again! Duck and cover, after the grenades go off, hit 'em back with the same!"

"Affirmative, Ironman! I— Grenades!"

The grenades detonated with a whipcrack rather than thunder, and shrapnel sprayed the executive suite. A second rope snaked down the hole and armored men slid down both. Lyons and Tenari flung their flash-stuns and covered their ears. Twin thunderclaps rocked the room and twin lightning flashes lit up everything in incandescent white. The Able Team leader rose with his assault rifle spraying on full-auto. Tenari's joined his a second later and the assault team was put in a killing cross fire.

"T, we gotta get upstairs. Grab every grenade and all the ammo on that body!" Lyons pulled the grenades from his man's web gear. There were two flash-stuns and two frags. Lyons shoved spare mags into his pockets and looped his rifle sling around his neck. Tenari rose with both mitts full of grenades. Lyons looped a frag through the hole in the roof and hurled a flash-stun after it. His partner tossed up two more from the opposite side and up on the roof thunder boomed and fragmentation cracked in counterpoint.

Through the din, screams pealed forth on the roof. Lyons threw his last flash-stun and retained his last frag. "T! I need a boost!"

The blacksuit dragged the fallen desk over and jumped on top. He pulled the pins on his last two grenades and tossed them up through the hole. "One! Two! Three!" The hole above lit up with white and yellow flashes. "Go!"

The desk creaked as it took their weight. Lyons crawled up the massive Samoan like a ladder. Lyons put a hand on the man's head and pushed himself up. He stood on the big man's shoulders and found the top third of his body out in the Berlin night.

Fallen men lay in a circle around the blackened hole. Some moaned and writhed, clutching shrapnel wounds. Others lay unmoving. A civilian Augusta/Bell AB.109 helicopter sat on the pad with its rotors turning. The chopper was first priority. Lyons shouldered his rifle and put his front sight on the pilot side of the cockpit. The G-36 rifle rattled off twenty rounds. The windscreen pocked and turned opaque with bullet hits. The whine of the engines died as the dead pilot released the throttle. Lyons heaved himself up onto the roof. "T! Get Akira up here!"

Tenari yanked the younger man up onto the desk and heaved him upward. "Carl, Akira says he heard something!"

Lyons reached down and grabbed Akira's hand. "They're on this floor!" Tokaido shouted. "I think they're in the stairwell—"

"Jesus!" Lyons groaned as he suddenly took all of Akira's weight one-handed. Black-armored forms were dog-piling onto Tenari below. Tokaido flailed in midair. "Carl!"

He slid through Lyons's wet hand. "Carl!"

Lyons threw himself backward as a pair of rifles firing

on full automatic sent tracers streaking up through the hole. "Akira! Akira!"

The copilot had leaped from the helicopter. His handgun chipped roofing inches from Lyons's feet. The Able Team leader rolled behind a ventilating unit and clawed for a fresh mag. "Akira!"

THE YOUNG COMPUTER WHIZ fell through space. Almost instantly the air blasted out of his lungs as he hit the desktop. Water from the broken sprinkler main poured into his face. He groaned and flopped to the floor. "That's their IT guy!" A voice boomed. "Herr Deyn wants him alive!"

Tokaido blinked and gasped as a man in a black raid suit leaped on top of him and knee-rammed his chest. A hand grabbed for his gun. He twisted his wrist and by accident the muzzle of the Skorpion machine pistol flicked up under his assailant's face shield. Tokaido desperately squeezed the trigger. The Skorpion sprayed and the interior of the visor went red as all twenty rounds ricocheted inside the bulletproof helmet, churning the interior into chum.

Tokaido pushed the man off and struggled to his hands and knees. His machine pistol was empty, he was out of mags and he couldn't seem to get any air into his lungs. He looked up dazedly and saw Tino Tenari under siege.

The big man's rifle was gone. He pressed an armored opponent up over his head and bodily hurled him into a desk. Another man lay at his feet with his head flopped at a horrible angle. Two more armored men slammed into Tenari from both sides and wrestled his arms to his sides. A big man stalked forward. His face was dark beneath his visor, and the young hacker recognized him from Phoenix Force's after-action file as Clay Forbes. The ex-Navy SEAL held a huge revolver in his hand. He pressed the muzzle into Tenari's chest as he struggled between the two security men, and pulled the trigger. The Magnum revolver's roar was deafening. Tokaido started with shock as the bullet burst out of the blacksuit's back. He went limp between the two men and fell to the floor.

Tokaido's Walther PPK filled his hand without thought. The laser sight printed a ruby dot on Forbes's chest. His voice rose to a scream of hatred "Tino!"

Forbes took an involuntary step back as the young man printed a fist-size pattern of seven holes over his heart. Forbes's teeth flashed beneath his visor in a snarl of outrage. "You little prick!" Tokaido remembered too late that his opponent was armored, and desperately reached for his spare magazine. Forbes stalked forward and kicked the pistol out of his hand. Tokaido started to go for his concealed Beretta when the bottom of Forbes's boot came down and the world ended. Two more armored men stepped in and boots began falling on the young computer genius like rain. His vision went white with agony as one of the men connected with his kidney. The stomping seemed to go on forever.

"That's enough! We want him alive! Harte! Jup! Get his narrow ass out of here." Forbes looked up at the sound of gunfire upstairs. "Alexsandr! This is Forbes! We have one hostile still active on the roof and—"

Jup fell, clutching his hands under his face shield, thrashing and screaming. Harte had straightened. The blood drained from his face and spurted between the fingers he held against his throat. Forbes was appalled.

The IT geek had a third gun.

The tiny .25 rose toward Forbes's face. Through the mask of blood and swelling, stone-cold rage burned in the young man's eyes. Forbes brought his .357 down in an ugly arc and chopped it into the young man's wrist. The kid yelped in pain, and the hideaway gun went flying. Forbes's backhand blow left him sprawled in the rain from the sprinkler system. The former Navy SEAL seized the front of his opponent's shirt and yanked him up, cocking back his hand for another blow. "You ever been pistol-whipped, punk? Well, you're gonna be, but good."

Tokaido's eyes flicked from the stainless-steel bludgeon to somewhere over Forbes's shoulder.

Forbes whirled.

Tino Tenari's right hand flew forward. His fist plowed through Forbes's Plexiglas face shield like a train wreck. Forbes staggered backward, spitting teeth.

The Samoan ex-Air Policeman shambled unsteadily after his opponent. The entire front of his white coverall was wet with blood. His face was as pale as death. His voice came out in a beleaguered groan. "Get out of here, kid."

Tenari's left hand hit Forbes in the chest like a battering ram. The force of it slammed the ex-SEAL back against the far wall. Despite his body armor Forbes bounced and fell gasping to one knee. The blacksuit came in. Forbes spit blood and raised his revolver. Tenari lumbered straight at the gun with his right hand cocked back for the kill. Flame eclipsed the muzzle of Forbes's snub-nosed .357 Magnum revolver as it roared four times in rapid succession. Tino Tenari fell to the floor at Forbes's feet. The .357 Magnum hollowpoint rounds had left five fist-size exit wounds in the big man's back.

"Now…" Forbes gasped. "You." He rose and stalked back to his prey. The beaten and bloody young man was trying to crawl away. He grabbed him by his hair and yanked him to his knees. "You are coming with me and— Mother!"

Razor-sharp steel cut through Forbes's black tactical

raid suit and burned across his forearm. He chopped the trigger guard of his pistol into the side of Tokaido's neck. He clouted him once in the temple for good measure and the young man went limp.

Voices shouted from the stairwell. "Herr Forbes!"

Forbes wiped his revolver on his pant leg and reloaded. "Clear!"

A six-man strike team pounded in with their rifles leveled. Their eyes went wide beneath their visors at the carnage littering the floor. Forbes wiped blood from his mouth and spoke into his mike. "Alexsandr, we still have one on the roof, and one on the loose somewhere around main security."

"We have the stairs covered, the elevators are inoperable."

Forbes's eyes narrowed to slits. "Alexsandr, he's got thirty floors to climb. This son of a bitch knows he's cut off. I think he's coming down. I think he's coming straight down at you."

"We will be ready."

Another six men charged into the room.

Forbes glanced at his squad. "You two, put the hole in a cross fire. Kill anything that comes down. You two, take the prisoner down to the assembly point in the garage. The rest of you are with me, we're going topside."

"Akira!" Lyons bellowed into his com link. "T!"

No response. Lyons ignored the man across the roof with the pistol and charged back to the hole. A bullet whined past his ear as he ran, and gunfire erupted below as he snatched a look down. He emptied his magazine and jumped back. He had seen enough. Tino Tenari lay on his face. His back was cratered with exit wounds. There was at least a squad of armed men below. Akira was nowhere in sight. TNT was KIA. Brognola was a POW and Akira was MIA.

The mission was FUBAR.

Lyons tasted bitter rage. He had failed the Bear. He'd promised to keep Akira safe. Tino had died trying to keep that promise. The copilot took another shot at Lyons as he crouched. Rage turned the world into a red haze around him. Carl Lyons shoved his last magazine into his stolen rifle and stood. He was just going to jump down that hole and kill every son of a bitch in the building.

The Ironman's berserker mode broke as a pair of grenades looped up out of the hole and clanked down on the rooftop. He hurled himself back behind the ventilator as the grenades flashed yellow, and razor-sharp bits of shrapnel hissed and rattled against the ventilator housing.

Down the hole someone was shouting with the unmistakable authority of command. *"Schnell! Schnell! Schnell!"*

The enemy was coming up in squad strength. Another two grenades clattered to the roof to keep him pinned. Riflemen below were ready to rip him apart from all sides if he jumped down. There were two stairwells on either side of the roof. In seconds they would have him in a cross fire. There was only one course of action left.

Lyons charged.

The copilot shouted in alarm and fired as the Ironman bore down on him. Lyons heard the supersonic crack of the bullets ripping past him. He held his rifle in the hip-assault position and sprayed on full-auto. The copilot ducked back behind his helicopter. Sparks and bits of glass caromed off the cockpit as Lyons closed the distance. The copilot looked up from reloading his handgun in horror as the Able Team leader rounded the helicopter. The smoking, empty G-36 short assault rifle spun in his hand like a drum major's baton. He raised the rifle overhead by the forestock and swung it down like the Grim Reaper's scythe. The six and a half pound assault weapon crunched into the copilot's skull with grim finality.

Lyons grabbed the dead man's gun, racked the slide on a fresh round and leaped into the copilot's seat. He had no choice but to try to fly the chopper, hoping he remembered what Grimaldi had taught him. Doors flew open on either side of the roof and light beamed from the stairwells. Armed men spilled forth. Lyons rammed his throttles forward. The turbines whined and the rotors beat the air. The assault teams dropped to one knee and raised their rifles. All hell broke loose as eight automatic weapons opened up and began to chew the helicopter apart.

The besieged aircraft began to rise jerkily into the air. Bullets hit the fuselage like hail. Lyons ignored the carnage as he kicked his collective and concentrated on keeping the helicopter aloft. The chopper slew sideways two feet off the roof. The assault team to the left emptied their rifles and scattered as the aircraft scudded across the roof straight at them. Alarms rang and red lights flashed in the cockpit. A rifleman screamed and flapped like a ruptured bird against the glass as the chin of the chopper slammed into him and scooped him off the roof. IESHEN Group headquarters disappeared beneath Lyons's skids.

The men on the other side of the roof chased the chopper and continued to fire their weapons. Lyons snarled and wrestled the stick as he suddenly began to lose power. He was falling like a stone. If IESHEN Group corporate headquarters didn't scrape the sky at seventy stories, he would already have hit the neighboring buildings. Bullets hit the chopper from above in bee swarms.

Lyons hit his throat mike for the Stony Man Farm uplink at the Berlin CIA substation as he lost hydraulic pressure. "Mayday! Mayday! This is Ironman! I am in enemy chopper and going down!" Something above Lyons's head began clanking with each turn of the rotors and the smell of burning oil filled the cockpit. "Hal, POW! Akira, presumed POW! Tenari, KIA! Gadgets's status, unknown!" The stick went dead in Lyons's hand and the helicopter began to autorotate and spin out of the sky. "I repeat! Mayday! Mayday! This is Ironman! I am— Shit!"

The burning helicopter's spinning plummet stopped, and Lyons's transmission ended as he hit the black water of the canal.

CHAPTER TWENTY-ONE

Gadgets Schwarz charged down the stairwell. A black-armored man leaned in through the security door and aimed his rifle at the Able Team commando. He shouted something, but Schwarz came on yelling, "Don't shoot" in German. The rifleman saw a man in IESHEN Group private security garb bleeding from the scalp and screaming. His hands were raised and his empty holster flapped with each step.

The rifleman shook his rifle and snarled something warningly. Schwarz screamed and collapsed on the landing. The rifleman spit German obscenities and grabbed Schwarz by his lapel. The Able Team warrior shoved his silencer into the man's neck and squeezed the trigger on his Taser. The probes plunged into the gunman's throat and he shivered and collapsed as the current racked his body. Schwarz shoved the shuddering man away and dropped his empty .45. He'd expended it getting away from security.

Schwarz ripped his two commandeered security pistols from his pockets as a second rifleman stuck his head through the door questioningly. The gunman jerked backward as he took hits and fell. Schwarz came out the doorway and found a third man pounding down the hallway. He had his legs shot out from under him and he fell into a clattering sprawl. Schwarz ejected his spent magazines and reloaded with the two spares. He ripped away the thrashing rifleman's tactical radio and hurled it against the wall, then yanked the man's weapon and hefted it with satisfaction. It was longer and heavier than the short assault weapons most of the attack teams had been using. The barrel was thicker, a bipod was attached and the twin drums of a 100-round C-MAG was clipped into the Heckler & Koch Light Support Weapon feed well.

Schwarz slid the sling of his new G-36 light machine gun over his shoulder and went back to the stairs. He had been eyeing the interior fire hoses in the main hallways. He figured them at fifty yards in length. Figuring ten yards to get to an outside window, each story roughly five yards in height.

He really needed to get to the fourth floor, and the third would be better.

Schwarz took the steps three at a time as he hurdled down the stairwell.

Voices echoed upward in German Schwarz could understand.

"Number six! He's on number six!"

The remote van had usurped control of the security suite and he was on camera. Schwarz ducked out of the stairwell onto the fifth floor. Men were coming down. Men were coming up, and he was in an ever-narrowing middle. He raced down the central corridor of the fifth floor and drove the butt of his LSW through the safety glass protecting the firehose. He swung out the heavy steel spool and grabbed the nozzle, unreeling hose as he ran. He didn't want to come out at the canal, so he broke into an office suite facing north.

Out the window the black patch of Berlin's Tiergarten Park formed a haven of darkness in the bright lights of Berlin. Schwarz picked up a chair and hurled it at the window. It bounced off the glass with a broken armrest. He grimaced and brought his light machine gun to his hip. The G-36 snarled and spit lead. The floor-to-ceiling office window shook in its frame and cratered like the moon under the full-auto assault. Brass shell casings flew as Schwarz held his trigger down and the ten-foot pane of glass suddenly spiderwebbed with cracks between the holes.

The G-36 clacked open on an empty chamber, its 100-round C-MAG exhausted.

The Able Team commando snarled and hurled the smoking machine gun through the crippled glass. An entire pane ruptured and broke apart into a rain of razor-sharp shards that fell to the pavement below. Schwarz threw the nozzle of the firehose after his fallen machine gun and heaved out length after length of hose. He yanked and suddenly the hose went taut. Glass crunched beneath his boots as he stepped into the empty window frame and kicked out into the night.

The rough canvas of the fire hose gave good purchase, and Schwarz swiftly descended the side of the IESHEN Group building. All too quickly his boots hit the bulge of the nozzle. He glanced down. He was out of hose, out of luck and still three stories off the ground. Schwarz hung for a moment and considered the two P-7 K-3 pistols tucked in his pockets. The .380 pocket pistol round they were chambered for was unlikely to get him through the industrial glass beneath his boots, and he still needed them for one last job.

Decorative linden trees lined the street along the building's north side. Schwarz bent his knees and kicked out from the window glass. He kicked once, twice, three times, taking him farther and farther out over the pavement. At the apogee of his fourth push Schwarz let go. Gravity enfolded him in its not-so-tender embrace, and the linden tree below seemed to rush up to meet him.

Schwarz fell through the tree and every branch took a whack at him on the way down. His fingers closed on the uppermost branches, but they ripped through his fingers. A major bough struck him a horrific blow to the chest and blasted the air from his body. Broken branches tore at his face. His hand closed around a bough that bent beneath his weight. The bough broke and stripped away from the trunk. He never saw the pavement. He just met it.

Schwarz lay on the sidewalk seeing stars that had nothing to do with the night sky above. He was dimly aware of Carl Lyons shouting into his earpiece, but it seemed very far away. Schwarz suddenly blinked into awareness.

Carl was shouting "Mayday!"

Schwarz could still feel gravity. It felt as if it wanted to suck him down through the pavement and pull him into his grave. He rolled over and pushed himself to his hands and knees. With a groan he pushed himself to his feet. God only knew how badly injured he was, but he could stand and he could breathe, and if he could do those to things he could shoot.

Gadgets Schwarz filled his hands with his pistols and began limping down the sidewalk.

POL BLANCANALES FLEW for his life. He was a fair pilot, but he wasn't the prodigy that Jack Grimaldi was, nor did he do it every day for a living. The pilot following him was better, and he had a pair of door gunners shooting from both sides of the fuselage. He also had a pair of engines. The AB.139 chasing Blancanales could carry fifteen passengers at 157 knots. The Able Team warrior's French Ecureuil helicopter was light and agile, but it had only one engine and despite his desperate wishes to the contrary, at the moment he didn't have a pair of United States soldiers hanging out the doors on chicken straps behind M-60 E-4 general-purpose machine guns.

Blancanales was out of luck and he knew it. All he could do was run, and as he streaked across the treed expanse of the Tiergarten, he knew all that meant was that he was going to die tired.

Carl Lyons's voice snarled over the open channel. Blancanales could hear the scream of rotor noise through his headset. "Mayday! Mayday! I am going down! Hal, POW! Akira, presumed POW! Tenari, KIA! Gadgets's status unknown!"

"Ironman!" Blancanales yanked on his stick as tracers streaked past aft. "Ironman!"

The channel went dead.

The Able Team commando was outpowered and outgunned. There was only one thing left to bet on.

Guts.

Blancanales dived for the deck. His helicopter scudded as his skids hit the treetops. He yanked back on the stick and clawed for a few yards of altitude. He kicked his collective and the little helicopter spun violently on its axis. His opponent had dived after him, but his superior skill had left him skimming inches above the trees. He had counted on that. He dipped his nose and rammed his throttles full forward into emergency power as he dove down into his opponent's path.

Blancanales wasn't playing chicken. It had gone way beyond that. He was full-on attempting to ram his opponent. He was just betting that the man in the other helicopter was good enough to avoid it...but not without cost.

The AB.139 tilted violently as the enemy pilot tried to turn out of Blancanales's attack, but he was still too close to the trees. His rotor blades chopped into the treetops. A composite blade snapped off as it struck something too thick to chop through. The Able Team commando zoomed over the stricken aircraft and his chopper lurched as it took a hammer blow to its side. Glass flew like shrapnel through the cockpit. Blancanales fought for control as outside air rushed into the cabin in a maelstrom. The copilot's door was staved in, and a four-foot length of rotor blade was imbedded in the frame. His skids ripped through the trees once more. He heaved back on the stick with all of his strength, and his helicopter rose above the Tiergarten.

Red lights blinked across his board. There was a short somewhere in the electrical system and his fuel tank was ruptured, but the aircraft still obeyed his will. The enemy chopper lay on its side, cracked open and smoking in the parkland behind him. Blancanales banked the helicopter south toward the gleaming tower of IESHEN Group.

He had a bone to pick.

LAURENTIUS DEYN WATCHED the AB.139 helicopter slide off the top of his skyscraper and come tilting crazily out of the sky. Muzzle-flashes winked at the top of the building like fireflies as his men continued to shoot into the stricken craft. The helicopter began spinning like a Tilt-A-Whirl as control was lost. Deyn smiled with cold satisfaction as the chopper boomeranged to the ground.

"Herr Brognola, your team is magnificent, but it is over."

The big Fed was sitting back in his chair. His .40-caliber Glock, his snub-nosed .44 Special Charter Arms Bulldog ankle gun and his com link sat three feet away on a foldout desk. They might as well have been a million miles out in space. Johan Mahke sat in front of Brognola with his foot on the man's chest and his pistol in his face. Mahke was smiling, too.

"Let me give your team's status," Deyn continued. "The big man? He is confirmed dead. The blond man? The team leader? He was in that helicopter that just went down. Your IT man?" Deyn pointed to a pair of panel vans pulling out of the underground parking. "We have him. He is in one of those vans."

Brognola's stomach sank.

"There is one man in your helicopter, currently being pursued. There is still one man loose in the building." Deyn's head tilted in mock empathy. "Oh, and we have you, Herr Brognola. Tell your remaining men to surrender."

The Justice man clenched his teeth and said nothing.

Deyn nodded. His sympathy was almost genuine. "I understand your dilemma, and I believe we understand each other, so I will not promise you decent treatment. We both know that would be a lie. I will find out every single thing about you, your men, and how much your government knows or suspects. So I will not make promises about what I will not do. Instead, let me promise you what I will do. I will torture every scrap of information out of your IT man. I will do it in front of you, and I will deliberately use the crudest of methods. When he has given up every secret he has, I will continue to have him tortured, to death, in a long and protracted fashion while you watch. I have some former East German security men who I keep on the payroll for just such occasions."

Brognola's jaw flexed. Deyn caught the reaction and smiled. Mahke caught it, too, and hoped the man would try something stupid so he could hit him.

"Tell your men to surrender," Deyn repeated. "There

will still be interrogations, but your cooperation will be taken into consideration when I deliberate upon your demise." Deyn's lips formed a hard line. All mirth left his voice. "Herr Brognola, I am not bluffing, and I will only make this offer once."

The big Fed understood with crystal clarity that rest of his life was going to be measured in hours marked by unendurable agony.

"Fuck you."

"An unfortunate decision." Deyn motioned to Franka Marx. "What is the situation?"

Marx chewed her lower lip. "Forbes says he is no longer in contact with Helicopter One."

Mahke scowled. "Their helicopter had no weapons, how could they—"

"They're resourceful."

Brognola's chest seemed to collapse as Mahke leaned in with his foot and made a real attempt to make his spine and sternum meet.

Deyn raised a restraining hand. "Enough. You may continue once we have relocated." He motioned to his driver. "I see no reason to remain here. Klaus, get Sylvan and Dieter into the van and proceed to the assembly point. Franka, tell Forbes and Zabyshny to finish the one still in the building quickly and extract. The two prisoners we have are more than enough. Send in the other two helicopters."

"Herr Deyn!" Klaus pointed to an IESHEN Group security man staggering down the street. As he stepped under a streetlight, they could see blood all over his uniform.

"Have Sylvan and Dieter collect him, we must hurry from here."

Marx spoke into her mike and Sylvan and Dieter trotted toward the injured security guard. The guard lifted a pair of pistols and shot Sylvan and Dieter point-blank. The two men fell and the guard turned his attention to the van. The small-caliber pistols popped, and Klaus screamed and threw himself down behind the dashboard as bullets punched through the windshield and ripped apart his headrest.

"Go! Go! Go!" Deyn roared.

Klaus blindly rammed the van into reverse and stepped on the gas. The van lurched backward, tires squealing as bullets struck it. The driver rose in his seat and ripped the parking brake up and yanked the wheel. The van spun in a respectable bootlegger's turn and he put the pedal down. Tires screamed as the van surged forward.

"Scheisse!" Klaus screamed in unison with his tires.

A mud-blackened, bloody blond thing had risen up out of the canal. One arm hung limp by its side. The other raised a pistol.

"Scheisse!" Klaus screamed again. The van almost stood on its front tires as he rammed on the brakes. The pistol spit fire and bullets ripped through van. Franka Marx screamed. Klaus stomped on the accelerator and took the van into a tight turn.

Mahke snarled as a bullet struck him. The pressure on Brognola's chest eased. Marx screamed again as the big Fed lunged, seizing Mahke's massive calf and upending him out of his seat. The man from Justice threw himself across the van and his hand curled around the rosewood grips of his Bulldog revolver. He whipped the .44 around, aiming for Laurentius Deyn's head.

The P-5 pistol in Deyn's hand began blasting in rapid semiauto. Bullet after bullet hammered into Brognola's chest. He fell back against the van's rear door. Deyn knew the man was wearing armor but kept shooting him in the chest anyway.

He wanted the big Fed alive.

Deyn's pistol clacked open on empty. Brognola raised his revolver shakily and the .44 boomed. A monitor by Deyn's side burst into a shower of sparks. Deyn sat in his chair and reloaded. Brognola took a moment to cock his pistol and steady his aim.

Johan Mahke's all too familiar size-seventeen shoe slammed the Justice man against the back of the van. His huge hand enclosed both Brognola's hand and his gun and shoved the muzzle skyward. The big Fed squeezed the trigger. Mahke roared as flame from the cylinder flashed between his fingers. Hal struggled to pull the trigger again, but even severely burned, the German giant held the pistol in a viselike grip that would not let the cylinder turn.

Mahke's right hand exploded into the side of Brognola's head.

His vision stretched and narrowed to a dark tunnel. It was lit at the edges with pulsing purple pinpricks of light. A very distant part of the big Fed's mind remained lucid, and he threw his elbow back against the door handle behind him. The twin rear doors unlatched and suddenly fell open under his weight. Brognola fell backward. His weight was too much for the German to hold with a single burned hand. The American and his pistol ripped free as they tumbled out of the moving van.

The van fishtailed on. Gadgets Schwarz stood in its path. He dropped his spent pistols and bent to pick up one of the security men's fallen submachine guns. The van didn't try to take evasive action. It bore down on Schwarz like a battering ram. The Able Team commando grit his teeth and held his ground as he held down the trigger. Bullets sprayed the front of the van. He lurched aside at the last moment but the injured member of Able Team was too slow. The corner of the van clipped him and spun him to the ground.

Schwarz lay in the street as the van tore around the corner and disappeared from sight.

Brognola gasped for air. Lyons crouched beside him. "Hal, you gotta get up. Do you understand? You have to get up. I can't carry you."

A hand grabbed Brognola's shoulder and hauled him to his feet. "My com link's toast from the crash." Lyons's good hand patted down the big Fed's jacket. "They took yours. Figures." The two of them limped over to Schwarz, who didn't look good.

Lyons pulled his throat mike and earpiece. "Able Flight, this is Ironman. What is your situation?"

Blancanales's voice came through loud and clear. "I am over IESHEN Group headquarters. I have you in sight, Ironman."

"We're looking for a van. They have—"

"Ironman, I have convoys of vans heading out in three directions. What do you want me to do?"

"They have more choppers inbound." Brognola groaned.

The big Fed slumped to the ground.

Carl Lyons looked at the shattered remnants of his team. He could hear sirens a few blocks away. He knew their descriptions had been circulated to the police, and they had been described as armed and extremely dangerous. He also knew that Laurentius Deyn had the power to arrange it so that they wouldn't last the night in custody, much less the time it would take for the Farm to take any kind of action to retrieve them.

Lyons looked down at his broken arm. He tossed his empty pistol back into the canal. His resources were used up and his priorities were clear. Bitterness filled the Able Team leader's soul as he spoke into the link. "Pol, we need medevac. We need it now."

CHAPTER TWENTY-TWO

Computer Room, Stony Man Farm, Virginia

Aaron Kurtzman sat in front of a blank screen. He held his head in his hands and sorrow was etched deeply in his face. Sending Akira into the field had gone against his better instincts. From past experience he'd known it always went badly. Having Hal go to Berlin and take point command alongside the Germans had also run against the grain. Still, he'd gone along with it, and now Aaron Kurtzman's every misgiving had given birth to nightmare.

Akira was MIA. Tino Tenari was dead. Able Team had been crushed.

Barbara Price put a hand on his shoulder. "Aaron…"

Kurtzman shook his head and held up a silencing hand. It wasn't unreasonable to assume that within the next twenty-four hours every aspect of Stony Man Farm and its operations would be compromised. Which meant that the next twenty-four hours of Akira's life would be spent in agony.

It was likely that in forty-eight hours Akira Tokaido would be dead.

"Aaron, we have to—"

Kurtzman punched a button and his screen lit up. The face of Laurentius Deyn filled the screen. The computer genius gazed long and hard on the man who had become his greatest nemesis on Earth. "Barbara, Deyn was a combat swimmer for the German navy. I'm going after his military records. All of them."

"Aaron—"

"He was also GSG-9, a Special Forces operative. I want his mission records, and not the redacted ones the German government will give us. I want fitness reports, after-action briefings, psych evaluations, everything."

"You're talking about hacking the top-secret military databases of a U.S. ally. Hal will need to contact—"

"Hal's in the Berlin Embassy with a concussion."

"There are protocols for you to—"

"Barbara, we don't have time. Deyn was willing to shoot up IESHEN Group corporate and walk away. Do you understand? He's walking away from a vast personal fortune, his whole life and career, and he doesn't care. In a day or two the German government's investigations will reveal that he's dirty. He knows that, and he doesn't seem to care about that, either. You want to know why? Because by then it's going to be a moot point. Whatever Deyn is up to involves twenty-five nukes, and it's already in motion."

"All right. The President wants a briefing. The Joint Chiefs are highly agitated about the Berlin fiasco. The reports rolling in just keep getting worse and worse. They're calling it a goatscrew of monumental proportions, and they're looking for someone to blame."

"Hal will make sure the President gets a full report. We also need a report on every single business endeavor we can connect to IESHEN Group."

"Bear, we've already—"

"Do it again. Bring in NSA and the FBI. Deyn's cut and run and no longer has access to his regular IESHEN Group assets. He'll be relying on personal, undeclared fortunes and hidden cutouts in the corporate structure. Somewhere there has to be a clue about what he's up to. Work it up. Make it happen."

"All right. I'm on it."

Kurtzman stared up at Laurentius Deyn and began bending the weapon of his mighty intellect against his enemy. Deyn was a cutting-edge industrialist, a patriot and a highly decorated Special Forces soldier. Kurtzman shoved his emotions aside. Deyn wasn't his enemy. He was a problem to be solved, and Aaron Kurtzman was a man who had let his MENSA membership dues lapse because the membership bored him.

"Larry?" Kurtzman steepled his fingers, his eyes stared unblinkingly as he addressed the enigma on the giant flat screen in front of him. 'What is motivating you?"

Berlin, Germany

AKIRA TOKAIDO SLOWLY and painfully clambered out of a very dark hole into consciousness. When consciousness turned to lucidity he wanted to crawl back into oblivion's dark embrace. Every inch of his body ached. He flinched as he was spoken to.

"Ah, Herr Tokaido! You have returned to the living!"

The young hacker tried to look around but pain flared like white light whenever he tried to turn his head. He was in a reclined chair. His wrists and ankles were restrained. He looked at the curved roof and stared up into the recessed overhead lighting. His tongue slid across his split lip.

Several very important things were screaming for his immediate attention but he couldn't seem to focus.

"I…" Tokaido suddenly became aware. "I'm on a plane."

"Very good!" Laurentius Deyn's head eclipsed the overhead light. Tokaido pressed himself back down into his chair with instinctive fear as Clay Forbes's face swam into view. Fear was a great focuser. His stomach sank in new sudden terror.

They knew his name.

Deyn smiled as he read the young man's body language. "Ah, well, Herr Tokaido, you…babbled, a bit, during your sleep." Deyn's smile became sharklike. "We administered some sodium Pentothal, to help you rest."

Tokaido couldn't keep the fear off of his face. Clay Forbes laughed unpleasantly. "Man, you said all kinds of shit. Farms, bears, politicians?" Forbes poked the young hacker painfully in the forehead with his finger. "I swear it's like the goddamn Wizard of Oz in your melon, kid."

Tokaido glared back into Forbes's grinning face and spoke with steel he didn't know he had. "My boys are going to take you out, Forbes."

Forbes kept smiling. "Oh, really."

"We know your name, and we have assets you can't even imagine." Tokaido's anger burned through eyes swimming in broken blood vessels as he slid his gaze to Deyn. "So why don't you and Hitler here go find a cave in Afghanistan, get comfortable and kiss your asses goodbye. The boys will be coming along directly."

Forbes threw back his head and roared with laughter. "You know something? I've been a SEAL and a black op for…what, fifteen years? And I've never been shot. I've been shot at, but shot, no way. But you? You shot me seven times last night. Then you goddamn knifed me, and no one,

I mean no one, ever got the drop on me with a blade before. You'd think that would earn you some respect."

Forbes's hand shot out and clamped around Tokaido's trachea. The young hacker's eyes bugged as his breathing tube came just short of cracking. His tormentor's voice dropped to a dangerous snarl. "But that's where your punk ass would be wrong. All you did was piss me off and make me look bad in front of my boss. All your ass has earned is pain, blues and agony."

Tokaido's vision began to darken as Forbes's fingers pressed down into his carotid arteries.

"You aren't in Kansas anymore, punk. Me strangling you into unconsciousness? This is as good as it's ever going to get in what little remains of your life. No one knows where you are. No one knows where you're going. And where you wake up? That will be your final destination. When you get there? You're going to have a nice, long talk with Mr. Deyn, and I'm going to be there to make sure you tell the truth, the whole truth and nothing but truth, so help you God." Forbes pressed his face into Akira's. "I got three words for you before you pass out. Jumper cables, blowtorches and pliers."

Tokaido slipped back down the long black hole and kept on falling. Forbes released him as he went limp.

"Sweet dreams."

CARL LYONS GLARED at the cast on his right forearm. The ulna was cracked, and a steel pin had been required to hang his thumb back onto his hand. He popped a pair of painkillers and took a long pull on his bottle of beer. He had been dreading the ass-chewing he was going to receive at Kurtzman's hands. Now it would almost be a benediction. There had been no ass reaming. The computer expert wasn't blaming Lyons for what happened. He was blaming himself.

Blancanales entered the safehouse's living room and flopped into a chair wearily. On the TV Argentina was playing Germany in soccer, but Lyons was glaring sightlessly into middle distance unheeding. Soccer fanatic that Blancanales was, he couldn't bring himself to care.

Lyons's voice was little more than a distracted grunt. "How's Gadgets?"

"Bad. Broken ribs, separated shoulder, he's peeing blood and the doctor thinks it's his kidney." Blancanales sighed heavily. "But for a guy who fell three stories and was run over by a van, he's doing okay. He's awake and lucid. I brought him a laptop and when I left him he was in communication with the Farm."

"And Hal?"

"Well, they beat the hell out of him, and then he fell out of a moving vehicle. That big German asshole really teed off on him. Nearly took his jaw off his head. They suspect a concussion. He had a CAT scan about forty-five minutes ago, and they're going to keep him overnight for observation. So much for his appealing to Deyno Boy, did we back the wrong horse."

Lyons grunted and resumed glaring at nothing.

Blancanales ran his eye over Lyons's cast and the stitches over his eyebrow. Wounds were nothing to brag about, and scars were simply proof that you had zigged when you should have zagged rather than medals of honor, but Able Team had been decimated, and Blancanales still felt twinges of shame that he had come through it unscathed.

Lyons red eyes focused on the armchair in the corner. Tenari's Jungle Gun lay propped up against it. Empty beer cans and a half-eaten bratwurst lay on the table next to it. "Damn Samoan slob."

Blancanales sighed. He had already grieved for Tenari.

Lyons was living up to his nickname and internalizing everything, including the blame. Any feelings he was willing to show would be expressed through anger or brooding silence.

"There's a shitstorm brewing in D.C. I think we're going to be recalled."

Lyons rose and walked over to Tenari's chair. He scooped up the shotgun and awkwardly snapped out the folding stock. He held the shotgun like a giant pistol in his left hand with the stock against his inner elbow. "Cowboy needs to send me a folding stock with an arm brace. He can probably steal one off a SPAS-12 and jury rig it."

"Carl…"

Lyons refolded the stock and threw the shotgun into his gear bag along with his .357 Python revolver. "Give me a call if you hear anything."

"Where're you going?"

"The shooting range." Lyons stalked out the door. "I need to put in some practice shooting left-handed."

Tel Aviv, CIA Station

"IS IT TRUE?" Gary Manning and the rest of Phoenix Force looked up as David McCarter came into the conference room. He'd been gone for an hour. The Briton didn't come back smiling.

"Able got ambushed in Berlin. They were set up, straight from the get-go. Gadgets and Hal are in hospital, Carl's got a broken gun hand. The mission failed. We don't know where the nukes are, and our suspects made a clean extraction."

Calvin James shook his head. "Damn it."

"It gets worse. Akira was in the field. He's a prisoner."

Every man at the table sat up.

McCarter nodded ruefully. "We must assume that within

the next twenty-four hours or less all of our identities and our current mission profile will be compromised. We have to get out of Israel ASAP before the enemy can launch a strike against us. Aaron suggested we head to CIA Cairo Station. He'll have full war loads and a jet waiting for us. From there we'll deploy as the situation develops. I want to be out of here within the hour."

James was the first to say what each man was thinking. "What's the situation on a rescue mission?"

"None. We don't know where Akira is. Like I said, as soon as we're out of Israel we're on standby for rapid deployment to anywhere, but finding the nukes is still our number-one priority."

Manning scowled. "There's got to be something we can do."

"With any luck, finding Akira and the weapons will end up being the same mission. Rescue is definitely part of the mission profile."

"And if it isn't?"

Anger crept into the Briton's voice. "Then it's bloody search and destroy."

CHAPTER TWENTY-THREE

Berlin, Germany

Thunder rolled across the indoor range. German border patrol officers lowered their 9 mm pistols and stared in awe as Lyons shot. It was the third time he'd been to the range in twenty-four hours. The Germans on the range had all admired his stainless-steel Colt Python revolver. They gazed on in awe as the Able Team leader cut loose with his shotgun. He held out the brutally shortened 12-gauge semiautomatic like a huge handgun. An hour earlier an overnight package had arrived for Lyons from the Farm, and within was a replacement for the Jungle Gun's standard folding stock. It was an ugly, phosphate-finished, abbreviated piece of skeletonized sheet steel. Beneath the stock was a blunt, U-shaped, swing-out padded hook. The principle was simple. The steel stock braced along the forearm, the hook swung up and under to cradle the firer's triceps, allowing the operator to fire the shotgun one-handed. The concept had been tried on several combat shotguns. Most knowledgeable gun experts eschewed the technique as impractical. It wasn't that it didn't work.

It just required a shooting animal of a higher order.

The Jungle Gun roared like the biggest beast on the range it was as Carl Lyons bent the weapon to his will. He was on his tenth silhouette target at ten meters. The first nine were a carpet of confetti on the range floor. Bruises were already blossoming unnoticed on the Ironman's left arm where the steel had slammed him.

Blancanales walked onto the range. Lyons lowered the smoking shotgun. "Don't even tell me we're being recalled."

"From everything Gadgets and I could pick up, that's the way it looked like it was headed."

Lyons set down his weapon. "Was?"

"Well, probably still is, but I pulled a fast one."

Hearts and minds were Blancanales's specialty and he could manipulate allies as easily as enemies. He wasn't nicknamed "The Politician" for nothing. "What did you do?"

"I made a phone call."

"Who'd you call?"

He shrugged. "The cavalry."

Stony Man Farm, Virginia

AARON KURTZMAN had barely moved in twenty-four hours. Hacking German top secret military records was proving harder than expected. With the firefight in Berlin, the German military and police were on a terror attack footing, and they were angry as hell at the rumor of American operations gone awry to the point of firefights in the streets of Berlin and helicopters falling out of the sky. The President himself had authorized the hack but had told Kurtzman in no uncertain terms that being detected would prove disastrous. Kurtzman was certain Akira could have done it with his eyes closed. Hunt and Carmen were good, but the young man was a genius in his field. Kurtzman himself wasn't bad, but his true genius lay in extrapolating data and coming up with answers rather than breaking systems.

Laurentius Deyn was eluding him.

There had to be something. Some key that was— Kurtzman lurched up in his chair and realized to his chagrin that Mack Bolan could have been standing behind him for an hour for all he knew. "You shouldn't sneak up on a guy like that, Mack."

Bolan smiled. "Sorry, but you looked so intent I didn't want to disturb your train of thought."

Kurtzman sighed. It was quite possible Bolan *had* been standing there for an hour. He had the patience of a saint. The computer whiz grinned back. No, he had the patience of a trained sniper. He could outwait a rock and then blur into a killing whirlwind with the speed of a buzz saw. There was hardly a place on Earth he hadn't been and hardly anything he hadn't done.

"I came as soon as I got word, Bear."

"Barbara called you."

"No, Pol did. Then I called Barb and told her I was coming in," Bolan said. "So what do you have on this end?"

"Actually, I'd appreciate your input. I just can't figure this guy out."

"I read the dossier Carmen worked up him on the chopper. I think I have him figured out."

Kurtzman simply stared. "Really."

"He's a hero, Bear. A soldier and a patriot."

"Well, that we know. But we can't find any sympathetic terrorist leanings in his past. We've tried working the closet Nazi angle but it just doesn't figure. Neither do any residual East German Communist leanings. The money or power angles don't work, either. He could assassinate his fellow board members at IESHEN Group, take over the whole multinational corporation and probably get away with it. But why? The man is a millionaire. We're talking hundreds of millions, and that's just what you can see on paper. What does a man like him want with twenty-five nuclear demolition devices?"

Bolan raised his eyes to the man on the monitor. "He wants revenge."

Kurtzman blinked. "How do you figure that?"

"I told you. I read his résumé." Bolan's cobalt-blue eyes bore into the computer expert's. "Then I looked in the mirror."

Bolan's disarming smile suddenly flashed across his face. "The question is, revenge for what? You figure that out, Bear, and you've got this guy pegged."

Kurtzman sat up, intrigued with the new logic thread. "And here I was trying to work the megalomaniac angle."

"He's that, too," Bolan agreed. "That's why in his mind he's going to call it justice. No matter what the collateral damage is."

"Well, hell, I'm glad you stopped by." Kurtzman suddenly cocked his head. "So what are you going to do?"

"Hal and Gadgets are in the hospital, Akira's been captured and rumor is Able may get pulled."

Kurtzman shook his head. "That's the way the wind seems to be blowing."

"You pull Carl at this juncture and he's liable to go rogue."

"The thought had crossed my mind."

"So I'm on a plane."

Kurtzman raised an eyebrow. "You're going to take over Able and keep Carl on a leash?"

"No, Able is Carl's team." Bolan grinned again. "I'm going to back his play, to the hilt."

"I knew you were going to say that."

"I've got a flight to Berlin in two hours. Tell the President." Bolan strode out of the Computer Room and stopped in the doorway. "Revenge, Bear. That's the key to taking this guy down."

AKIRA TOKAIDO WOKE UP in the hurt locker. He was hanging by his hands in a room with a steel floor and corrugated iron walls. Clay Forbes had administered what he described as a "leisurely, introductory beating" and then left him to hang awhile to think about his misdeeds and his short, unpleasant future.

He was startled when the door to his cell opened and the cyberhottie walked in. Two large men with automatic weapons flanked the door. One of them closed the door behind her and locked it from the outside. The woman stared, appalled as she took in Akira's bloody, bound form. "Mr....Tokaido."

It took the young hacker several moments to work up enough saliva so that he could croak out an answer. "Yeah."

She held up his laptop. "This is a remarkable piece of engineering."

Able Team's and Phoenix Force's after-action reports made for spine-tingling reading. Tokaido had read every single one he could get his hands on. Members of Able and Phoenix had been on both sides of interrogations. Akira was surprised to find that in his beaten and probably drugged condition he was able to recognize the good cop/bad cop routine. Again, he found himself speaking with mettle he didn't know he had.

"Fuck you, Franka."

Marx stared. "How do you know my—"

"We had passive listening in the van. That, and you had your name in your video conferencing window."

"Ah." Marx flushed slightly. "I had not factored in direct communication with your entry team."

"The communication was a closed loop. It's a small error when you look at it that way. Besides, you were planning on betraying us anyway."

The redhead flinched at the word betrayal. "I betrayed no one, you are Americans trying to—"

"Save the world." Tokaido couldn't believe he was talking like this, but it kept rolling out of his mouth. "But what do you care?"

"Save the world?" Marx shook her head in disgust. "Corporate espionage is not—"

"Corporate espionage? You ca—" Tokaido suddenly bit back his retort. Several things occurred to the young man at once. One, it occurred to him that the conversation was very likely being monitored. Two, he couldn't be sure whether the woman knew what was really going on or not, but if she didn't, then there might be one very slim card he could play. He turned his head and glared at the wall. "You can go to hell."

The young woman straightened and adopted a professional tone. "I am having difficulties breaking into your hard drive."

Tokaido snorted and felt congealed blood move down his throat. "Of course you are."

"My employer wishes every bit of information on this computer. You will give it to me."

"Or what?"

The redhead suddenly couldn't meet his eyes. She was clearly uncomfortable with the situation. "I am told Mr. Forbes and Mr. Mahke will extract it for me."

Tokaido's stomach clenched. He had zero doubts about that, and the fact was, Clay Forbes absolutely terrified him.

The young hacker knew something else from his work on the Farm. He had heard that once you gave the enemy something during an interrogation it became easier and easier for them to extract more, like pulling bricks out of a wall until it collapsed. Then again, Forbes's words kept ringing in his throbbing head.

Jumper cables, blowtorches and pliers.

Tokaido had surprised himself since his capture, but he held no doubts that any tough-guy pretenses he had left would collapse like a house of cards when Forbes began applying everything in Hardware Aisle B to his flesh and bones.

His guts churned. The fact was, it was going to happen. No matter how much he cooperated, in the end they would butcher him up like a Thanksgiving turkey to make sure he had given up every last scrap of information. Speed was the question. They wanted him willing, so that they might learn everything they could so that they could modify their defenses.

The fact was there was a part of himself that he had so far barely kept in check. One that it had taken every ounce of will not to give in to, and it was the one part that held any chance of anything good coming out of this situation. He thought of his family that he would never see again, and his friends at the Farm. He found he didn't need to act. A man hanging naked and bloody in chains had little need to pretend at despair. His throat tightened and his swollen eyes stung.

"Please…"

Marx's hand crept to her chest as tears spilled down Tokaido's cheeks.

"Don't…don't let Forbes hurt me anymore."

The woman watched in pity and revulsion as the young man begged for his life.

"I'll do anything you want. Please, just, no more, please, just, no more..."

Marx rapped twice on the door. The two security men came in and one of them unlocked Tokaido's manacles. He collapsed to the metal floor and clutched himself in a fetal ball. Shame and terror racked him. The security men pulled over a little metal folding table and a chair, and shoved him in it. Marx placed his laptop in front of him and then set a second one beside it.

"First you will download a copy of your hard drive into my computer." She connected the two laptops together and powered them up. "Do not do anything foolish."

Tokaido brought his bruised, torn and trembling hands to his keyboard. He wasn't connected to the Internet. The two guards looming behind him would beat him into paste if he tried to contact the outside world. The only thing he had was his connection with Marx's laptop.

His laptop was a creature of his own design. It looked like a normal laptop the same way *Dragonslayer* could appear to be a normal civilian helicopter, and in its own way was every bit as dangerous. His laptop had been in communication with Franka Marx for a few moments back in Berlin. He brought up a window and began typing in code.

Marx's eyes narrowed at the few sparse lines of letters, numbers and symbols. "What are you doing?"

One of the guards clamped a hand on Tokaido's shoulder. He flinched and stopped. "I'm typing in the access codes."

Marx scanned the screen again. "You are lying."

There was no time to finish. It would have to do. Tokaido's hands flicked out and he punched Return.

The guard yanked him backward out of his seat by the hair and hurled him to the floor. Inside of Tokaido's laptop there was a distinct tick and hiss noise. Marx gave a little shriek as the one-half ounce of plastic explosive buried in the hard drive snapped like a firecracker as the battery pulsed electrically and detonated it. Number and letter keys flew up from the keyboard and the high-definition screen went black. Wisps of smoke oozed out of the firewire and USB ports.

Tokaido summoned the last vestige of his courage as he stared up at Marx from the floor. "Screw you."

The woman pulled out her cell phone and punched a key. "Mr. Forbes? The subject has chosen not to cooperate."

Tokaido struggled as the guards descended on him, but the big men manhandled him with ease back into the hanging manacles. Marx unplugged her computer from the ruins of Akira's laptop. She shook her head and walked out the door.

Tokaido wondered how often Marx checked her instant messaging. His speculation turned to stark terror as he heard Forbes's voice down the hallway.

CHAPTER TWENTY-FOUR

Stony Man Farm, Virginia

"I'm sending you the files now, Aaron."

Hunt Wethers sent the decrypted German intelligence files to Aaron Kurtzman's workstation. Translation software had converted the files, memos and reports into English. Kurtzman leaned forward, his fingers flying as he briefly scanned document after document. Just as there were two Koreas, there had once been two Germanys and during the height of the twentieth century's cold war they had been split as decisively by ideology as they had been by the concrete wall, barbed wire, mines and machine gun towers that had split them geographically. The two Germanys had engaged in a decades-long clandestine war every bit as bloody and ruthless as that between the Koreas.

It appeared that Laurentius Deyn had been in the absolute thick of it.

File after file scrolled in front of Kurtzman's eyes, telling tales of undercover operations, kidnapping and assassination and desperate battles on both sides of the Berlin

Wall that the rest of the world had never known. It was information the German government would never want known. History perceived West Germany as the good guy in the cold war, but their hands were far from clean. It made for fascinating reading. Kurtzman pieced through stories of betrayal and blackmail, double and triple agents, and the willing sacrifice of assets on both sides as pawns in the greater game. Mack Bolan's words rang in Aaron Kurtzman's head.

Revenge, Bear. That's the key to taking this guy down.

But revenge for what? The West had won the cold war. The Soviet Union had collapsed. The Berlin Wall had fallen and there was now a relatively peaceful, unified Germany. In many ways the eastern portion of Germany was still the poor cousin. They were still playing catch-up from almost half a century of Communist inefficiency and infrastructure. Where in all this did Laurentius Deyn's thirst for vengeance lay?

Nothing leaped out.

They would have to work up each file piece by piece and pray they found some sort of link. Every second at this point was very likely an eternity of anguish for Akira, and Kurtzman's every instinct clamored that he was missing something. He brought up Deyn's personal file again. He was sixty-eight and a widower. His wife had died of stroke-related complications five years ago. He had lost his two sons in a tragic boating accident decades ago. Plenty of reasons for a man to grow bitter in his old age, but Kurtzman just couldn't see vengeance on a thermonuclear level, much less who the target might be.

"Could the wife have been murdered, Hunt?"

"We have the doctors' files. She had a stroke and lived with the complications for about a year before another stroke killed her. We have a copy of the autopsy. No sign of foul play. No police reports. Nothing attached to Deyn's fitness or psych reports indicate anything out of the ordinary about his relationship with his wife or her demise."

"And his sons?"

"Both died in a boating accident, on holiday among the North Frisian Islands. It was fully investigated. We have the police reports."

Kurtzman contemplated the enigma of Laurentius Deyn for the thousandth time. "They were both in the military?"

"They both served in the German navy. They were both combat swimmers and were both honorably discharged."

"Hack their records."

"We did." Wethers swiveled at his workstation. "We have their military records and the police reports."

"We hacked the German Office of Intelligence of the Armed Services." Kurtzman called up the service ID photos of the two deceased young Deyns. "I want to hack the BND."

"The BND?" Wethers was appalled. "That's German Federal Intelligence Service, Bear. That's their CIA and NSA all rolled up into one. If we get caught hacking old, cold war documents from the proceeding century they'll be upset, but if we get caught hacking current BND files that's technically an act of war."

"Do it. The President said the thermonuclear devices must be located and retrieved at any and all costs. I think that covers all the bases."

"What are you thinking?"

"Something that Mack said. He said this guy wants revenge."

"Yeah, but revenge for what? A boating accident?"

Kurtzman turned away from the screen. His instincts were speaking to him loud and clear. "You know what they say the worst thing on earth is?"

Wethers nodded soberly. "For a parent to bury their child."

"Deyn buried both of them. His line is ended. He wants revenge." Kurtzman turned back to the screen. "And his sons didn't die in any boating accident."

LAURENTIUS DEYN looked out over the water thinking of his sons when the office intercom buzzed and Clay Forbes's voice came over the speaker. "It's Forbes, boss."

Deyn shoved his anger back down to the dark place within himself where it festered it and grew. "Come in."

Forbes's mass took up most of the little metal room. His tailored suit jacket and silk shirt were gone. He had stripped to his sleeveless T-shirt and removed his watch and rings. His T-shirt and hands were stained with blood.

Deyn offered Forbes a chair. "So how is our guest?"

"Tougher than I thought," Forbes acknowledged. "Mahke wants your permission to go hardcore on him."

"One attracts more bees with honey, I believe the saying goes."

"Normally I'd agree with you, but his guy knows he's dead meat. He pulled a last act of defiance and fried his computer." Forbes scowled at one bloodstained fist. "Now he's gone salty. He's just holding on as long possible on the outside hope that his friends will come and rescue him."

"That is on a very low order of probability."

Forbes grinned. "That is a fact."

"What is his medical condition?"

Forbes scowled. "He's had the bejesus beaten out him. The medic says he has a concussion, as well as cracked ribs and contusions and other minor-to-significant injuries too numerous to count."

"The bottom line?"

"The doc strongly recommends we don't hit him in the

head anymore." Forbes shrugged. "Your boy Mahke wants to start cutting, starting with the toes and then working up toward intimacy."

"And what do you think, Clay?"

"I think he took too many hits in Berlin. His body is all busted up, but his will is still intact. I think if we go hardcore or electrical on him he might just vapor lock on us before we can extract anything useful. As much as I'd love to do it, I suppose after all we should save the hardcore shit for the last resort. What's our timetable?"

Deyn checked his Omega Seamaster watch. "We are on schedule for seventy-two hours. Past that time any information you can extract will be superfluous. I gather you wish to use chemical interrogation methods?"

"The punk has proved he can take a punch, but he's tech-ops, not a field agent. I want to hit him with sodium Pentothal again and then administer 400 micrograms of LSD-25. We give him a couple of hours to let it sink in and then hit him with lights, sound and suggestion, take him to the places where the bad dreams are. I predict within twenty-four hours I can have that boy babbling like a brook."

"And should those methods fail?"

"Then Mahke starts cutting lunch meat."

Deyn smiled. "I do enjoy your metaphors, Clay. Tell me, did you observe Franka during the initial interrogation?"

"We caught it all on camera, she clearly is unhappy about torture, but so far all she suspects is beatings." Forbes looked at Deyn pointedly. "I know she's a highly valuable asset, but just how much does she know?"

"She knows we are engaged in something illegal. However, she believes it involves technological espionage against the United States on a grand scale. She is not aware of the end game, and I intend to keep it that way until the last moment."

FRANKA MARX STARED at the screen of her laptop in shock. Her instant messaging window informed her that she had an unread message. The message was from Akira Tokaido. Franka swiftly disconnected her laptop from her docking station. Her first instinct was that Tokaido had downloaded a virus into her computer, hoping to infect her entire system. She knew her number-one priority should be to close the laptop and take it directly to Herr Deyn.

Marx began furiously chewing on a pencil.

There was zero chance of Tokaido infecting the computer system. He would know that she would isolate the laptop before opening the message. Perhaps he just wanted to destroy her laptop in revenge, but she had four of them onsite and all information was backed up in a variety of formats. Even if he had managed to ruin the operating system on this one laptop it was a tiny, spiteful act of revenge and she could not imagine it was worth the beating he had received for it. Marx shuddered as she thought of the bloody, beaten young man hanging in chains. He had shown immense bravery, and the only logical conclusion was that Tokaido was trying to communicate with her, and without Deyn or Forbes knowing about it.

Fear and curiosity twisted in the woman's stomach. Her pencil snapped in two in her hand. Her finger seemed to move with a will of its own as she clicked her cursor on the message.

The two and half lines of code she had seen the young man type on the screen appeared in the window. It appeared to be a simple cipher, with letters, numbers and symbols substituted for other letters, numbers and symbols, though it was impressive that he could type in code from memory, particularly in his present circumstances. Franka Marx broke code for living. She broke code in her spare time for fun. She pulled a disk of cipher breaking software she had personally designed out of a drawer in her workstation and loaded it.

If Tokaido was indeed trying to communicate with her, the cipher would be deliberately easy to break. He would only have used the code to give himself the few vital seconds to sneak it past his captors. She told the software to assume the cipher was in the English language, and it instantly began to attack the code. The software looked for repetition and matches in the most commonly used consonants and then began trying to match them with the most common vowel pairings to build words and then sentences. Lines of code scrolled down Marx's screen as the software crunched the two and half lines of code at tens of thousands of combinations per second.

It took her software exactly one minute and seventeen seconds to break Tokaido's cipher. It informed her that it believed the literal translation was accurate to ninety-nine percent. It then asked her if she wanted it to assume the translated words themselves were a word-for-word code and continue attacking.

There was no need. Marx simply stared at the two and a half lines the man had typed and transmitted before she had interrupted him and the beatings had resumed.

DEYN HAS TWENTY-FIVE NUCLEAR WEAPONS
HE PLANS TO USE THEM
HELP ME STOP

Franka Marx was far more than a genius at number crunching. She was a hacker who did battle across the worldwide datum plane for IESHEN Group. Her instincts were as sharp as her intellect. Against her will, her mind instantly began sorting the orders, directives and actions she'd received and coordinated over the past six months. She read the three sparse lines again.

Franka Marx felt her world spinning out of control.

She jumped out her chair as the intercom buzzed and Laurentius Deyn's voice spoke. "Franka, I need you, now. Come immediately."

CHAPTER TWENTY-FIVE

Akira Tokaido twisted, screaming his throat raw as rats ate out his eyes. Two hours ago they had injected him with something. It had begun pleasantly enough. He had learned to recognize the relaxing effect of the sodium Pentothal, but there had been two needles. As the drugs began working on the 5-HT2 serotonin receptors in his brain and spinal chord, his pain had backed away to a much more endurable background of aching and throbbing. Despite his situation he felt a general sense of euphoria and well-being. When he began to see trails of pretty colors when he moved his head, he had suddenly realized he was on an acid trip. They had given him a full ninety minutes to let the LSD-25 settle into his cerebral cortex and coil around his centers of mood cognition and perception. At the same time the drug had invaded his locus ceruleus, the brain region that received sensory signals from all areas of the body. At ninety minutes the real fun began.

They had started with noise, hitting him with the piped sounds of gunfire, the moans of the dying and the screams of horses being killed, all at horrific decibels. At the same time they had played with the lights, alternately strobing them and then plunging him into darkness. In a phenomenon known as synesthesia Tokaido "heard" colors and "saw" sounds, and the colors were all blood and fire and the sounds formed the shapes of utter nightmare. LSD users often reported mental transitions so rapid they seemed to experience multiple emotions at the same time. His emotional landscape was blind terror and crushing despair. Any good hippie knew that on one's first LSD trip it was best to have a "guide" or experienced hallucinogenic drug abuser to help the first timer "safely" through the rapid emotional shifts and altered perceptions.

Tokaido's guide was Clay Forbes, and the former SEAL was intent on deliberately leading the young man into a bad trip rather than away from one, and to personally insure that the bad trip Akira was on was a Halloween horror show of epic proportions. Forbes had turned the lights off and spent half an hour hurling the young man around the cell while wearing night-vision goggles. He'd blasted him with a fire hose, hung him upside down and shook him in the blackness, shouting words like bear, farm and politician in his ears. The former SEAL had finished the initial session by stringing the computer hacker back up in his chains, turning the lights off again, ramming his thumbs against his eyeballs and informing him that rats were eating his eyes.

Tokaido hung in his shackles in the dark and screamed like the damned in hell.

Computer Room, Stony Man Farm, Virginia

"FRISIAN ISLANDS, HELL." Aaron Kurtzman shook his head in disgust as he examined the hacked German BND file. "Steffan and Karl Deyn died during a clandestine operation off the North Korean Peninsula."

The file kept getting worse and worse. The operation had been concluded under the command of United States Special Operations Command. West German intelligence had found out about a secret rocket engine technology transfer between East Germany and North Korea. The ball had already gone into play, but the Germans had known the identity and probable route of the courier. U.S. Intelligence assets in North Korea had discovered his entry point. It was the late 1980s and no one wanted North Korea's SCUD missiles upgraded. However, West Germany and the U.S. were behind the timetable, and an amphibious intercept dangerously near the coast of North Korea was deemed the only option. The team had engaged in a high-altitude, low-opening jump. The submarine USS *Los Angeles* would make the pickup. Steffan and Karl Deyn had represented West Germany in the special operations team that had deployed that night into the Korean Bay.

The operation had gone wrong. The seas had been rough, and whether through an intelligence leak or a bad combat drop, the insertion had been detected. The assault team had just reached the target when the North Korean gunboats arrived, spraying the surf with their heavy machine guns and hurling grenades into the water like depth charges to kill the team as its members dived for the retrieval sub. Two United States Navy SEALs and Ensign Steffan Deyn had died in the onslaught. The North Koreans had pulled Petty Officer Karl Deyn out of the water severely wounded. According to intelligence assets, Karl Deyn had died under interrogation by the North Korean Secret Police. Kurtzman sat back in his wheelchair with a sigh. Bolan had been right.

Laurentius Deyn wanted revenge, and he had been waiting for his chance for twenty years. Deyn's motive and weapon of choice were established. The question now was where and how he intended to wreak his revenge.

"There should be a file on this operation on the U.S. end, so why don't we have it?"

"This one was run under U.S. auspices. We ran it, commanded it and screwed the pooch, hard. Everyone wanted this one covered up. West Germany and the U.S. both. I bet Deyn didn't know the particulars of his sons' deaths for years until an old navy buddy or someone in German intelligence leaked it to him."

"We need the U.S. file on the op and then we need to go back and cross-reference Clay Forbes's service record with it. See if he knew anybody on that raid. I also want to know who was in command of the operation. That's where we're going to find our answers."

"I've already got it. Forbes was supposed to go on that mission but a knee injury sidelined him. He had done liaison training in Germany before the mission. From what little I can dig up it appears he was good friends with the Deyn brothers. Forbes is the one who flew to Germany to tell Deyn Karl and Steffan were dead. Forbes himself was an orphan and got into a lot of trouble before joining the Navy. I think Deyn and Forbes sort of adopted each other."

"I need the name of the man in command of that mission."

"We're ripping open old wounds. No one is going to like this."

"Go straight to the President if you have to, but SOCOM has to give up that file, ASAP." Kurtzman looked up at the file photos of the two dead young men. "We're running out of time."

AKIRA TOKAIDO SAT in a shuddering, fetal ball in the corner of his cell. He was rocking and crying and he couldn't stop.

The hellish hallucinations had passed, but they had left him with the agonizing reality of his beaten, shackled body. Far worse than the state of his flesh was the state of his mind. He blinked and moaned.

The Farm would have changed all access codes within an hour of his capture and gone on highest alert status. However, the intelligence agencies of every nation hostile to the U.S. would pay vast sums for the personnel and mission data Akira Tokaido had in his brain, and that Clay Forbes now owned. He had revealed everything.

The young man cried out in fear as the door to his cell opened. He collapsed as Franka Marx quickly entered and closed the door behind her. She was carrying a duffel bag and she looked at him grimly. "Are you all right?"

He was far from all right, but he no longer had the wherewithal for snappy comebacks. The woman knelt beside him, and Akira couldn't prevent himself from recoiling and trying to crush himself farther into the corner.

Marx chewed her lip at the state of the young man in front of her. "You must listen to me. We do not have much time. You were administered LSD-25 twelve hours ago. I have done research on the Web. You have had a 'bad trip.' The drugs will have worn off by now, but there can be devastating psychological aftereffects. You are undoubtedly suffering severe anxiety and mental depression."

Tokaido was one hairbreadth away from a psychotic episode and knew it.

Marx reached into her duffelbag and he shrieked as she pulled out a syringe. Marx glanced desperately back at the door. "Listen! This is morphine! For pain! I stole it from medical! We do not have much time!"

"You're…going to help me?"

"Yes." Marx flicked the head of the syringe with her finger and spritzed out a small amount. "Give me your arm."

"I…can't." Tokaido shuddered and closed his eyes in fear at the needle. "I'm sorry, I can't, I just—" He yelped as Marx stabbed the needle into his right buttock. He just couldn't take any more. Any more of anything. He felt the screams rising up as he officially lost it. The scream suddenly died in his throat as a warm, fuzzy, loving blanket seemed to enfold every inch of his brutalized body and smother his pain. He relaxed back against the wall with a sigh. "Oh…man."

"No! I cannot have you fall asleep!" Marx shook two green capsules out of a brown prescription bottle. She pushed the pills into his mouth and cracked open a plastic bottle of water.

Tokaido smiled and swallowed. His pain was gone. As if by magic. The nightmares had receded to a very distant corner of his mind and taken the crushing anxiety and terror with them. Whatever the woman wanted was fine with him. He mumbled around the water bottle. "What are those?"

"Military amphetamines. I believe in the United States military they are called Green Hornets. They should take effect in a minute or two. I need you pain-free enough to walk and awake enough to function. As I said, we do not have much time."

"Better living through chemistry," the young hacker agreed sleepily. "So, you got my e-mail?"

"Yes. I was unable to verify your claims. However, I found far more than enough anomalous IESHEN Group activities to make me believe that you were right and that Herr Deyn plans to do something terrible."

Tokaido was suddenly desperately thirsty and he chugged the bottle of water almost without swallowing. "You've come to rescue me?"

"I cannot rescue you." Marx looked at Akira very steadily. "I believe that the best I can do is get out a message. I will need your help, and I do not believe either of us will survive the attempt. I think you and I will both be dead very shortly."

"Okay." For some reason this didn't seem to bother him very much. "But tell me why."

Marx pulled a blue warm-up suit that looked a size too large out of the bag, and Akira's running shoes. She also pulled out his switchblade and a compact pistol he didn't recognize. "I found your guns, but they were empty, so I stole this one." She smiled sheepishly. "I have spent the last four hours stealing things."

"I can see that." Tokaido pulled on the sweat suit and runners. The slide of the pistol said Mauser M2. It was bigger than the PPK that Kissinger had given him, but most of the controls were all in the same place. He checked the pistol as he had been taught and found the magazine was full and there was a round in the chamber. He pocketed the pistol and the knife. "You still haven't told me why."

"I have done many illegal things for Herr Deyn, and willingly, but I will not be a party to mass murder."

Tokaido took a deep breath. Saving the world was still on the table. He felt better. He was also starting to feel very wide awake. His fatigue was falling away, and everything around him was coming into sharp focus again. His thoughts felt jangled and jumpy, but he found he could think fairly clearly. He wasn't afraid anymore. The young hacker surprised himself by smiling. Opiates and amphetamines made for a very heady cocktail. Just what every torture victim reeling from LSD withdrawal needed.

Marx nodded. "You are better?"

"Yeah, I feel better. Thanks."

"Listen to me. You have been exposed to very powerful drugs in a very short period of time. You may feel better now, but soon you will crash, and not just physically but I fear mentally and emotionally. When you come down it will not be pleasant."

Tokaido pushed himself to his feet. He fell against the wall as a massive head rush washed colors across his vision. He took deep breaths and steadied himself. "If this is a suicide mission, then I don't want to come down. Just keep me going until we've done what we have to do."

Marx handed him the bottle and a second syringe. "This should get you through."

He suddenly straightened as his mind began kicking into gear. "Why do you need my help to get out a message?"

"We have gone dark. No outgoing messages can be sent via computer without protocols that only Herr Deyn, Forbes and Mahke have access to. All personal communication devices have been confiscated except for key personnel, myself included. Local radio transmissions are being jammed across all frequencies."

"Well, how about an escape attempt? We can send out a message once we're clear."

"Can you pilot a helicopter, Herr Tokaido?"

"Uh…no."

"Neither can I, and we are in the middle of the ocean."

Tokaido's stomach sank. "Okay, so how do you want to play it?"

"As I see it, we have only one option. I must disable the communications security protocols and get out a message. I have to do this from the control room, and I doubt I can do it without being discovered, given the current security situation."

The young man took a very long breath and let it out.

He felt the weight of the pistol and the knife in his pockets. "You're saying you'll need a diversion."

"Yes," Marx agreed. "I will need a diversion."

CHAPTER TWENTY-NINE

"Damn it." Akira Tokaido sighed as he peered out the porthole and stared across the blue ocean and couldn't see any land. He was on an offshore platform. "What ocean are we on?"

"I don't know." Marx frowned. "Our exact location is on a need-to-know basis. We flew for twelve hours out of Germany. I do not know which direction. We landed on a private airstrip in the night and then took a helicopter for several hours to come here."

Tokaido stared vainly at the chopper on the pad. Grimaldi had offered to teach him how to fly, as he had the other Stony Man personnel, but he'd always been too busy with his computers to take the pilot up on the offer. He regretted it bitterly now. "What about a boat? Can't we steal a boat?"

"And go where? Which direction? We would be swiftly overtaken, and the radio frequencies are being jammed." Marx gripped his arm tightly. "We must send out a message from the control room."

"You're right." He gazed out across the ocean again. "We stick to the plan."

"Good." Marx peered at him hopefully. "So what is the plan?"

Tokaido had been thinking about that, and no option was looking good. The woman had broken into the security suite and fed a ten-minute video loop of him lying on the floor, shaking. He doubted anyone was monitoring the feed, and it would fool a cursory look. Marx had taken a crash course on controlled substances. LSD trips, she'd informed him generally lasted nine to twelve hours depending on the dosage. Forbes had been timing the drug's onset, so he was also probably timing when they'd be wearing off. They had to hope Forbes was waiting the full twelve hours so that Tokaido would be lucid for the second part of the interrogation. It was a huge if, but if so, according to Marx's timetable they had about twenty minutes before the witching hour and Forbes came for his pound of Akira's flesh.

Tokaido pulled the pistol out of his pocket. "I could shoot Forbes."

A smile ghosted across Marx's face. "That is the amphetamines talking."

She was right. Despite the beatings and the psychological torture, at the moment he felt pretty unstoppable. However, he was lucid enough to know that only morphine was keeping crippling pain at bay. The amphetamines were giving him borrowed strength, as well as chemically induced courage and clarity. "Yeah, but it's still not a bad plan. I could go back to my cell, strip down, curl myself in the corner around the gun, and then shoot Forbes and anyone with him when they walk in. He'll never expect it."

"Yes, but can you beat him? Forbes and the medic? And any assistants he has with him? And the two security men who will be stationed outside during interrogation?"

"Yes! I mean no!" Tokaido's fists clenched in sudden anger. "I don't know!" He glanced around the access corridor they were hiding in helplessly. "Jesus, Franka! I'm a tech guy! Not a field operative! What do you want me to do? Huh? Tell me and I'll goddamn do it! Okay? But just don't…"

Tokaido's voice trailed off. Marx was crying. She was tech, as well. She had never bargained on betraying everyone and everything she had ever cared about, much less face torture and death at their hands, and she didn't have luxury of Green Hornets and morphine to take the edge off certain annihilation. "Listen, Franka, I'm sorry, we're both in over our heads. I—"

Marx fell weeping into his arms. The young computer genius stood with a beautiful German redhead in one hand and German steel filling the other. He was on an oil platform with a hot babe facing impossible odds and a nuclear countdown. His ultimate fantasy of being out on field ops made real. Despite the amphetamines, he suddenly felt like throwing up. Instead he steeled himself for what was to come. "Franka, what do you want me to do?"

She looked up and smiled tremulously. "I'd like you to make love to me, but I don't think we have time."

He looked at the woman he held in his arms. "Damn it."

"I know. So what I need you to do instead is to clear the control room, at least as much as possible."

"I attack." Tokaido nodded. "And make them chase me."

"Yes, and in the confusion, I will try to send a message to the outside."

"All right, how much time do you need to get there?"

The woman wiped her eyes and squared her shoulders. "Give me five minutes, and then do whatever you can think of."

Command Shack

"HERR DEYN."

Laurentius Deyn turned from looking out to sea. Johan Mahke was gazing intently at the security suite. One monitor in particular seemed to hold his attention. Clay Forbes leaned over the giant German's shoulder. "What have you got, Johan?"

Franka Marx walked into the control room with her laptop under her arm. "What is happening?"

Everyone gather around the monitor. It was the video feed from the holding cell. Akira Tokaido lay naked, shivering and sniveling incoherently in the corner. Deyn frowned. "You have really done a number on him, Clay. I hope you did not ruin him."

"Nah, that's still the LSD messing with him. His body should finish metabolizing the drug…" Forbes checked his watch "—about ten minutes ago, and that's on the outside envelope. I got distracted with some operational details."

"That is not the problem." Mahke's voice rumbled low in his chest. "We have an anomaly."

Deyn's face became a steely mask. "What kind of anomaly?"

Mahke held up a thick finger, his eyes still intent on the screen. "Wait…wait…there!" A black line twitched through the screen for an eyeblink and then the feed resumed. "I have seen it twice now."

Marx's stomach dropped. The jig was up, all she could do was try to play it for a few more seconds. She stabbed her finger at the screen. "Someone has looped the security feed! That is a recording!"

Deyn drew his pistol. "Forbes! Take four men and get to

the holding cell now! Mahke, you are with me! I want the boats, submersibles and the helicopter secured immediately!"

Gunshots rang out and three rapid smacking sounds rattled the windows of the control shack. Forbes shoved Marx to the floor. The heavy steel storm shutters were open but the bulletproof glass had resisted the attack. Three bullets had cratered and cracked the observation window. Outside, a thin figure in a blue tracksuit was running away across the central platform with a pistol in his hand and his ponytail flying.

Forbes drew his magnum. "Why, that little piece of—"

Mahke punched the alarm button and Klaxons began to roar. The German hit the intercom and his voice roared over every inch of the rig. "Intruder alert! I repeat, intruder alert. Armed and dangerous! Asian, in blue IESHEN Group tracksuit!"

Mahke turned to Deyn. "You want him alive?"

Deyn's eyes glinted with steely anger. "Oh, indeed, I want him alive. I want to know how he got out, how he managed to compromise security, and most of all, who helped him. Franka, run a diagnostic on the security suite and find out how it was compromised." Deyn turned to one of his techs. "Jurgen, scan all communication frequencies. I want to know if Mr. Tokaido is somehow in contact with someone. Everyone else, you have your orders." Deyn snapped open his phone and began speaking in Russian as he and the armed men left the control shack.

Jurgen put in his earphone and ordered his computer to start scanning frequencies. "How can this have happened?"

"I don't know." Marx sat and began to think furiously. She really needed Jurgen's workstation. "Let me see the communications logs of the past twenty-four hours."

"What? Why?" Jurgen grew agitated, but he never

looked up from his screen. "I would have known about any communications! There are no open lines! We have been dark for twenty-four hours! Work the security suite like Herr Deyn said! I will check the logs!"

"As you say." Marx searched for a weapon. Jurgen wasn't the physical specimen that Forbes, Mahke or even Deyn was, but he was still a man and outweighed her by thirty pounds. She wasn't going to win a wrestling match with the communications officer. The control shack consisted of monitors, metal tables and chairs. Marx picked up a metal chair and folded it. "Pull up the last hour."

"There were no communications in the last hour!"

"The security computer was fooled. Your computer might have been fooled, as well. I have an idea."

"What idea?" Jurgen didn't sound convinced but his fingers rapidly pecked keys. He looked up as he pulled up the log. "What idea— Franka!"

The top of the chair back hit Jurgen's head edge-on. He screamed and fell out of his chair, clutching his split scalp. Marx raised the chair and slammed it down, bending it across Jurgen's upper back and skull. He went to his hands and knees still screaming. Panic swept through the woman. She raised the chair and swung again. Jurgen put up a hand and partially blocked the blow. His fingers curled around the chair frame. Marx heaved, but Jurgen wouldn't let go. He got a foot underneath him and grabbed the chair with both hands. "You bitch! You dirty bitch! I'll—" Jurgen suddenly got his priorities straight and began shouting at the top of his lungs as they played tug-of-war with the chair. "Help! Help me!"

Marx let go of the chair and Jurgen toppled backward. She ran for the door and stopped. There was nowhere to go and she still had to get a message out. She yanked the fire extinguisher off of the wall rack and advanced on Jurgen. The communications man rose shakily to his feet. He held the chair in one hand and pushed at the blood streaming into his eyes with the other. "Help me! Hel—"

Marx swung the fire extinguisher like an Olympic hammer thrower. The metal rang dully against Jurgen's skull, and he dropped to the floor. Setting the extinguisher on the communications desk, Marx sat shuddering with adrenaline reaction. Her hands shook as she began over-riding the "gone dark" security communication protocols.

Her first instinct was to contact German intelligence, but the BND would take time to verify her identity, then they'd take days to investigate before they took any action. For that matter she had no idea where she was or whether Germany had any assets deployable. Even contacting the CIA or U.S. military intelligence would waste valuable time. Akira's words came back to her. Stick to the plan. He swore his organization could act within hours if they could locate the platform. With Akira's capture they would have changed their codes, but they would still have cutouts monitoring for traffic on the old ones for some time.

Marx hammered keys.

She didn't have a phone, and taking one from Forbes or Mahke would be problematic. A computer communication would be almost impossible for Akira's people to trace back without attacking security, and she didn't have time for that. An open radio communication would have to serve, and she prayed she could keep the line open long enough for Akira's friends to triangulate.

Marx's hands flew as she overcame Jurgen's protocols and unlocked the radio control and turned off the jammer.

"What are you doing?"

Marx jumped in her seat. She hadn't heard the door

being unlocked or opened. She hadn't heard Alexsandr Zabyshny walk up behind her. She frantically kept working. "The prisoner! He was here!"

"The prisoner?" Zabyshny lowered his machine pistol slightly. "Here? In control?"

"Yes, he and Jurgen fought! Jurgen was hurt, and I hit the prisoner with a chair when he got on the computer!"

Zabyshny took in the bent folding chair and Jurgen's bleeding and unconscious body. "What are you doing now?"

"Trying to assess what kind of damage the prisoner has done. I do not believe he was able to communicate."

"Good." Zabyshny flipped open his phone and glanced out the window. "Mr. Deyn, we have a—"

Marx swung the fire extinguisher into the back of the Russian's head, and he sprawled to the floor. She scrambled for his fallen phone. She could hear Herr Deyn shouting on the other end of the line. Marx clicked it shut and rapidly punched in the phone number Akira had given her. A woman's voice answered on the first ring.

"Hello, how may I direct your call?"

"My name is Franka Marx! I am with Akira Tokaido! We are on an oil platform! I do not know which ocean. Laurentius Deyn is here! You must trace this call!"

"Stay on the line."

A frantic moment passed and then a man answered. "Miss Marx, where is Akira Tokaido?"

"I helped him escape from his cell. He is creating a diversion so I can make this call."

"Are the nuclear devices on the platform?"

"I—"

Zabyshny popped to his feet. Marx swung the extinguisher one-handed, but he caught the blow in his palm with ease. The Russian moved with liquid speed. The woman didn't even see his fist move before he buried it into her gut. Every ounce of air blasted out of her lungs. The fire extinguisher fell from her hand with a clang as her knees turned to mush. The Russian took the phone from her palsied hand and killed the call. He punched in another.

"Mr. Deyn?" The security man watched bemusedly as Marx pushed herself, wheezing and gasping, back to her feet and reached for the folding chair. He took a step forward and backhanded her over the communications console. "Mr. Deyn, as I was saying, we have a problem."

Stony Man Farm, Virginia

"WE GOT THAT!" Aaron Kurtzman bellowed. "Tell me we got that!"

The Computer Room was a frenzy of activity. Computers crunched while high above in space NSA communication, command and control satellites dissected the phone transmission and tried to find its router and vector its source. Hunt Wethers grimly watched his monitor. "It was short, Aaron."

"Give me anything, Hunt." Akira was alive. That was all that mattered. The game was still on and the oil platform confirmed Kurtzman's worst suspicions.

"Carmen, I need a map with every offshore oil platform on earth. I need it now. Hunt?"

"We got a partial. We have the initial router. It's in the western hemisphere."

"Cut that list by half, Carmen."

Wethers looked up from his screen. "This could be a feint, Aaron, or a trap. Hell, it could be a nuclear Trojan horse. We haven't faced anyone this slick in a while. I'm not putting anything past them."

Kurtzman nodded. Despite his excitement all of that had occurred to him, as well. "Carmen?"

"She was breathing hard, but she sounded professional, and scared. Of course if someone put a gun to her head you could get the same reaction."

"Gut instinct."

"I think she's for real."

"Send the tape to NSA for voice analysis, but we're operating as if this is gold until proved otherwise. Have Able and Phoenix prepare for amphibious operations."

Kurtzman turned back to his workstation. Akira was alive, and on the loose.

CHAPTER TWENTY-SEVEN

Tokaido ran for his life. There weren't a lot of places to hide on an offshore platform, and he was running out of them. He squatted breathlessly between two pallets of fuel drums. Armed men were running back and forth across the platform while others scrambled up and down ladders. They were all shouting at one another.

"Crews quarters, secure!"

"Boat landing, secure!"

The helicopter pad was ten yards from where Tokaido crouched. The helicopter sat on it, guarded by two men with automatic rifles.

"Command and control, clear!"

The young computer genius popped the magazine in his pistol. He had six rounds in the clip and one in the pipe. He shoved the magazine back in and considered the end game. He was dead, and he knew it. He gazed hard at the helicopter. He couldn't fly it, but disabling the aircraft might actually slow whatever the bad guys were up to. Hell, if he could just start it up and get it a foot off the ground, God only knew the damage he could wreak on the platform. He glanced at the communications array at the top of the platform tower. For that matter, the helicopter would have a radio, and Franka just might have disabled the radio jammer by now.

It was a poor plan, but it was a plan, and it beat hell out of being the last man out in an armed game of hide-and-seek.

Tokaido stood and aimed the Mauser with both hands. He put the white dot of the front sight between the farthest guard's shoulder blades and fired. The M-2 barked three times in his hands. The man slammed forward against the fuselage of the helicopter and smeared it crimson as he slid down. The second man whirled. Tokaido turned his body like a turret the way Kissinger had taught him. The M-2 barked and cycled, and the guard's rifle snarled off a burst. The young man flinched as the sonic cracks of the rifle rounds passed by his head. The guard fell face-first to the deck.

The Stony Man hacker shoved his smoking pistol in his pocket and grabbed a fallen rifle. He yanked open the cabin door and leaped up into the aircraft. As he climbed into the cockpit, he could see armed men running out of the crew's quarters toward him. Akira sat in the pilot's seat and gazed across the instrument board. There was no keyboard or mouse. It was all gauges, switches and lights labeled with terse acronyms that didn't mean anything to him. There was no key or ignition and he saw no immediate way to start the aircraft up.

So much for crashing the helicopter into the command shack.

The computer genius shoved the muzzle of the G-36 rifle against the instrument board and held down the trigger. Instrument glass and black plastic exploded in all directions and brass sprayed the interior of the cockpit. The chin window raddled with cracks and holes as he fired off the entire magazine. The rifle locked open on empty and he dropped it to the cabin floor. Tokaido smiled to himself. If he couldn't use the helicopter, then neither would the enemy. It was time for Plan B, and he did have the basic knowledge of how to operate a radio.

He put on the headset and tuned to the Stony Man Farm radio frequency. "Mayday! Mayday! Mayday! This is Akira Tokaido! Repeat, Akira Tokaido! I am on an offshore oil platform! Location unknown! Deyn, Forbes and Mahke are here! Location of packages unknown!"

The young man sagged with relief as Barbara Price's voice came back instantly. "Akira! This is Control! Received telephone communication from Marx! We are trying to triangulate your location! Keep this frequency open as long as possible!"

"Copy, Control!" He watched as half a dozen men formed a ring around the helicopter and leveled automatic rifles. The young man stared into his firing squad. "Uh, Control, I'm—"

He jerked and clawed at the headset as static blasted into his ear. The frequency jammer was back in business. Tokaido pulled the M-2 from his pocket as Forbes came out onto the platform with another four men behind him. The big man pointed an accusing finger. "You have no idea what I am going to do to your punk ass!"

Tokaido was pleased to find that he was angry rather than afraid. He checked his pistol. The magazine was empty and there was one round left in the chamber. He considered trying to shoot Forbes, but the distance was twenty yards and he didn't know if the bullet would be deflected by the crashproof cockpit glass or whether it would even go through it.

His best option became very clear to him.

They had Franka, they had him, and this was the end. In his young life Akira had never contemplated suicide. It was something he would never have the strength to do on his own, but the amphetamines jangling in his bloodstream bolstered his courage and he was feeling no pain. He made up his mind. They wouldn't get any more information out of him. He would atone for giving up information about the Farm, and he would be good and goddamned if he let Deyn and his pet goons get their paws on him again. He locked eyes with Forbes, waggled his eyebrows, grinned and pressed the muzzle of the M-2 against his temple.

He was pleased to see Forbes's eyes widen in shock.

"Herr Tokaido." The radio crackled and Laurentius Deyn's voice spoke with steely calm. "I have someone here who would like to say something to you. Franka, say something nice to Herr Tokaido."

Tokaido had never heard another human being scream in agony, much less a woman, and the sound of it made his whole body clench like a fist.

"Herr Tokaido, in Berlin, I offered your superior, Herr Brognola, a deal. I will offer you the same. Franka has betrayed me, but she has no information that I need to extract from her. Surrender now and I will not have her tortured to death."

The young man's pistol dropped down from his temple. He felt like he'd been kicked in the stomach. Forbes held a finger to the earpiece he was wearing. He was listening to the exchange and grinning from ear to ear.

"Herr Tokaido," Deyn continued, "there are over fifty men on this platform. If you do not surrender, they will take turns violating every opening in Franka's body, and when they tire of that they will take knives and flay her alive while you watch. Do not doubt me."

He didn't doubt it at all. "And if I comply?"

"You will not be tortured anymore. These last few moments have convinced me that the threat of torturing Franka will be far more effective in making you talk. You and I will have a discussion about your associates, their likely courses of action, and you will confirm the information you have already given Herr Forbes. Assuming I believe you, you and Franka will be killed humanely, with a single bullet each. This is the best deal you are going to get."

"I don't believe you. My friends will be coming, and you're going to keep me as a hostage."

"Indeed, you are correct," Deyn conceded. "But that is neither here nor there. The only thing that concerns you at the moment is that the rape and living dismemberment of Franka will happen, whether you commit suicide or not, and whether your associates come or not. There is only thing that will stop it, and that is your immediate surrender and compliance."

Tokaido's knuckles went white around his pistol.

"Very well, but remember, Herr Tokaido, you can stop this. You can stop it at any time." The door to the command shack opened and Franka Marx tumbled outside in a bloody heap. A lanky man Akira didn't recognize stepped over her and opened a folding knife.

Deyn's voice crackled over the radio. "Proceed, Alexsandr."

Marx screamed as the Russian took a knee beside her and yanked her up by the hair. She screamed again as the shining blade pressed down against her neckline.

"Stop!" The word ripped out of Tokaido's mouth of its own will.

The knife froze, poised between Marx's collarbones.

"The pistol, Herr Tokaido," Deyn prompted.

The M-2 clanked to the floor of the cockpit.

"The knife!" Forbes boomed. "And the knife!"

Tokaido numbly pulled out his switchblade and dropped it.

"Herr Forbes." Deyn's voice oozed the cold pleasure of a reptile. "Collect our guest."

Clay Forbes's eyes never left Tokaido's as he strode to the helicopter. The smile on his face was sickening.

Stony Man Farm, Virginia

"WE'VE LOST CONTACT!" Barbara Price furiously worked dials on her board. "Akira's signal is being jammed."

Kurtzman nodded. "Hunt, do we have a triangulation on the radio signal?"

Wethers's eyes were glued to his screen. "Oh, yeah, but we don't need the signal. The radio jammer is shining like a beacon. The coordinates are coming now. It's…" His voice trailed off. "It's close. Good Lord! It is very, very close."

"Close to what?"

"Close to here." Wethers shook his head. "Less than four hundred miles. South, just off the Mid-Atlantic Seaboard."

Price pressed a button on the intercom. "David, we have incoming information. What's the status of Phoenix and Able?"

"We're fully armed and ready," McCarter replied. "Two helicopters on the pad warmed up and ready to deploy on go."

"Stand by, David." Price frowned as she swiftly scanned their list of offshore oil platforms and called it up on the world map. "Both the Marx woman and Akira said they were on an offshore oil platform." No oil rigs were evident near the signal source. "Do we even have any oil platforms out there?"

"No." Wethers hit a few keys and overlaid a political

map on the screen with the radio signal's location. "The signal is just off Cape Hatteras. That's national seashore. No one's allowed to drill there."

"No..." A very chill wind began to blow through Kurtzman's bones. "It's a research station. Remember, a great deal of IESHEN Group's early work was in undersea research and exploration."

Wethers's fingers hammered keys. The cybernetic systems in the Computer Room were the most powerful search engines on Earth. "Bingo! Hatteras Ridge Research station." The cybergenius smiled thinly. "No doubt made possible by a grant from the IESHEN Group."

"This is almost a best-case scenario. Able and Phoenix can assault the platform in less than two hours. SEAL Team Six is on standby in Virginia Beach. They could hit in under an hour."

Wethers let out a long breath. "For that matter we have warships and planes that can launch cruise missile strikes almost immediately once given the coordinates."

Everyone in the Computer Room was quiet for a moment. They all knew Wethers was right, and they all knew that the plan condemned Akira to certain death. "I don't like the idea of launching an attack with Akira on the platform. I love that kid, but an overwhelming cruise missile strike that instantly wipes that platform and everyone on it off the planet is probably our best option. It is very likely Deyn would never even detect the strike before it hit. All information we have has indicated that Deyn has been collecting weapons but hasn't deployed them stateside. If we've caught a break and the devices are on the platform, then there's a good chance he'll never get to detonate."

Carmen Delahunt didn't like it. "This guy's nuts, but he's

smart. We have to assume if he has the devices on the platform he'll have them on a deadman's switch for insurance."

Price was thinking the same. "All right, let's assume it. All twenty-five thermonuclear demolition charges are on the platform and each device has been dialed to the maximum ten kilotons and is on a deadman's switch. We either assault the platform or hit it with a strike and the devices detonate. What's the worst-case scenario?" Price cocked her head. "Bear?"

Kurtzman was furiously typing. "What? Oh." He looked up distractedly and swiftly did the math. "Two hundred and fifty kilotons, given dead simultaneous detonations, or twenty-six kilotons, given a low-order detonation due to the missile strike." He overlaid weather patterns on the map. "Since the detonations will take place out to sea, there'll be little if any fallout except for insignificant bits of the platform itself. At twenty-six kilotons, damage from the blast itself would be fairly minimal. However, you would get a tsunami that would flood Cape Hatteras itself. The Cape natives would stand to take a significant dose of radiation, but by the same token the Cape Hatteras National Seashore would take the brunt of it. Take it to maximum, Cape Hatteras takes a horrible beating but damage to the continental United States would be minimal to nonexistent. The Cape acts as a buffer."

He resumed his speed-reading and scrolling.

Price heaved a sight of relief. There was a glimmer of hope. "Deyn has to have those same figures, too. I'm willing to advise the President to negotiate for the surrender of the platform and the devices. Failing negotiation, I will advise for the cruise missile strike against the platform. I will also advise the immediate evacuation of Cape Hatteras."

Wethers shook his head unhappily. "Deyn will be monitoring the situation by satellite. If he detects an evacuation, he may detonate."

Price had considered that. "That will be for the President to decide, but given the Bear's model, I believe those are the best options we can present."

Kurtzman stopped and looked up. His face had gone pale. "The model assumes that the nuclear devices are on the platform."

Price looked askance. "I know it's not solid, but we have nothing that indicates any of the devices have been transferred to the continental United States."

"No." He sighed. "I don't believe they have."

"Then where are they?"

Kurtzman opened up his file on the six-foot flat screen. Jaws began to drop around the room as the Stony Man cybernetic team read the file. Kurtzman nodded. "I believe at least some of them have been transferred to the Continental Shelf."

A light blinked over the radio at Price's station. It was still monitoring the frequency of Akira's last transmission. Price lunged for the button. "Akira!"

A voice spoke in a cold, clipped German accent. "My name is Laurentius Deyn. I wish to speak with Aaron Kurtzman, the man known as the Bear. When I am finished, I strongly suggest you speak with the President of the United States."

CHAPTER TWENTY-EIGHT

The Situation Room, the White House

Aaron Kurtzman tugged uncomfortably at his hand-painted Milanese tie. He couldn't remember the last time he'd worn a suit. He could hardly remember the last time he'd left the Farm. He'd worn the suit only once before, and that was for a wedding. A Farm blacksuit who had been volunteered to assist him held a sealed white plastic bucket. Because Hal Brognola was indisposed, Kurtzman was about to directly address the President and his chief advisers. The Man's secretary quietly picked up the phone, nodded and smiled.

"The President will see you now, Mr. Kurtzman."

One of a pair of Secret Servicemen flanking the entrance like stone Buddhas suddenly smiled and opened the door. Kurtzman wheeled himself into the crisis center. The President, his VP and several of the Joint Chiefs of Staff and cabinet members were arrayed around the room. The President made no introductions and got straight to the point. "I've been briefed on the radio conversation between you and Mr. Deyn. Frankly, it sounds a bit fantastic to me. I understand you have researched the situation and run some simulations. Is what he's threatening possible?"

Kurtzman collected his thoughts. "Perhaps a little history would be useful, Mr. President."

"Make it brief, Mr. Kurtzman, and make it pithy."

The computer genius had been given access to a computer and the main screen in the crisis center. He plugged in and pulled up a photo of a forbidding thousand-foot-high rock cliff. "Ladies and Gentlemen, that is Storegga, or the 'Big Edge' in Norway. Storegga looms on the edge of the European Continental shelf. Storegga didn't used to be a cliff. It used to be a peninsula. About eight thousand years ago the bottom of the shelf dropped out in an underwater landslide that was one of the greatest slides in Earth's history. More than a thousand cubic miles of sediment and rock rolled downhill in a solid wave. When it moved, the landslide made a hole in the ocean into which the sea rushed down, hit bottom and then bounced back up. This propagated a tsunami of gigantic proportions. Waves of twenty- to fifty-foot heights flooded the coasts of Scotland and Iceland. In Norway itself the narrow fjords may have channeled and crested waves sixty-five to seventy-five feet high. When all was said and done, where there was once a shelf, there is now the thousand-foot cliff you see on the screen."

General Jack Harper Hayes stared long and hard at the cliff. "What caused the slide?"

"You will have to forgive me, but this is the most direct way I know of demonstrating." Kurtzman rolled up his sleeve and pulled on a rubber glove. He nodded to the Farm security man. "Chuck?"

Chuck cracked the seal on the bucket and Kurtzman reached in. Everyone in the room gave a collective gasp of disgust as the overwhelming stench of rotting eggs filled the crisis center. Kurtzman held up what looked like a beslimed chunk of white-and-brown ice. "This is methane hydrate."

"Methane?" The President wrinkled his nose. "So, you have ice from cow gas."

"Close. But not ice, hydrate. I won't bore you with details. The simple explanation is this. Storegga is solid rock. The great landslide started beneath it, in a weak layer of porous sediment, around the middle of the Continental Shelf. That sediment was held to together by methane hydrate."

General Hayes nodded. "So the sediment beneath the rock was locked up in hydrate, making it solid."

"Exactly, General. However, approximately eleven thousand years ago, the Earth was in a warming cycle, and the last ice sheets retreated from Norway and the Norwegian Sea. Atlantic seawater flowed in and began warming the sea bottom by about nine degrees Fahrenheit. Now, it took about three thousand years for that warming to propagate down through the base of the hydrate stability zone. That's the level where the methane is always on the verge of becoming gas."

General Hayes sat back in his chair, his combat engineer's mind chewing the problem. "So, the methane hydrate warmed, went from solid to gas and bubbled up, leaving all the sediment with no support and billions of tons of rock on top of it."

"Indeed, General. It was most likely took a very long time, bits of the hydrate going gaseous in burps and belches, but, when enough of it escaped the shelf, the shelf collapsed and slid."

Kurtzman pulled up another picture. It was all dark blacks and grays and whites, like a black-and-white orbital photo of Mars pocked with valleys and craters. "These are underwater photos of the Continental Shelf just north of the Storegga headwall. Some of these cracks are three miles wide and fifty feet deep. Notice the pockmark-like cratering. Geologists believe that's where the methane went gaseous and escaped."

The Secretary of State gazed greenly at the chunk of hydrate in Chuck's hand. "Can that go back in the bucket now?"

"One last thing." Kurtzman nodded to his assistant. "Chuck?"

Chuck pulled out a lighter, chinked it open and lit it with a snap of his fingers. He waved the lighter beneath the chunk, and pale yellow flame instantly flared and licked upward around the gooey rock. "Methane hydrate burns at very low temperatures, and can melt and go gaseous at a thousand feet below the surface. Some scientists postulate that an earthquake actually started the slide, but no one questions the fact that the melting hydrates set up Storegga for the disaster."

The President of the United States watched as Chuck plunged the burning methane hydrate back into the bucket and sealed the lid. "And Deyn has embedded thermonuclear demolition charges into the methane hydrate ridge off Cape Hatteras."

"That's what he's claiming. As I've said, the circumstances that set up the Storegga slide took thousands of years, and the gas bubbled up and escaped in fits and starts. Some scientists think the slide took hours, others think it happened slowly over days or even weeks. Deyn has threatened to light off the entire Hatteras hydrate ridge like a firecracker, instantly, with twenty-five thermonuclear devices."

The President's face was stone. "Damage estimates?"

"I've only had an hour to run the simulations, but even best-case scenario, it's bad, Mr. President, very bad."

"Give me worst case."

"Very well." Kurtzman took a deep breath. "Even if he's only emplaced a few weapons, the fact is there is a very good chance that the entire hydrate ridge will catch fire. It has never been completely mapped, but it is extensive. Marine geologists caused quite a stir in the scientific community when they discovered cracks and pockmarks much like the ones off Norway at the edge of the Continental Shelf near Cape Hatteras."

"Damage, Mr. Kurtzman."

"If the Cape Hatteras shelf slides, the entire Mid-Atlantic seaboard will be submerged beneath vast tsunamis. As I mentioned before, the fjords in Norway made the Storegga tsunamis worse. Geographic features can funnel a wave like rapids in a river. An immense wave, and possibly a series of them, will roar up Chesapeake Bay, splitting and gaining size and velocity as they hit Point Lookout on the inland tip of Maryland. By the time the waves reach the mouth of the Potomac they could be one hundred feet high."

Everyone in the crisis center realized the room they sat in could be submerged at any moment.

"It should also be kept in mind that rather than a gradual escape of gas, this deluge will be caused by possibly twenty-five ten-kiloton nuclear devices. You will all recall during the South Asia tsunami large inland stretches of land at sea level were covered with mud and sediment. In this instance, much of that mud will be radioactive, underwater fallout if you will, and it will inundate the Mid-Atlantic soil and water table. Even in a best-case scenario, Mr. President, Laurentius Deyn has designed a nuclear and geological disaster of biblical proportions, and it could happen at any moment. After this briefing I strongly suggest you and the Joint Chiefs get into Air Force One and get off the ground immediately."

The crisis center sat stunned.

Kurtzman sighed. "I must also point out that IESHEN Group erected their research station off Cape Hatteras in 2002. I've been working on this problem for the past two hours. Mr. Deyn has had years to plan this situation to inflict absolute maximum damage."

"Mr. Kurtzman, this government, like every government before it, has maintained a policy of no negotiations with terrorists."

"I believe it would be useful in this situation, Mr. President, to remember that Laurentius Deyn is not a terrorist. He has no political agenda. He blames Washington for the screw-up that cost him his sons. The commander of the mission is a retired colonel. He lives on beachfront property on Chesapeake Bay. Deyn is a madman, bent on revenge. Stopping him is our only option. Any negotiations he may engage in will be feints or simple stalls for time."

"So, we hit the platform with a cruise missile strike, hope there's no deadman's switch and pray for a partial or low-order surface detonation."

The vice president didn't like it. "We still lose three towns on the Cape."

General Hayes closed his eyes, hating the words coming out of his mouth. "Considering the scope of the situation, I would have to advise that those are acceptable losses."

The President rubbed his temples. "I am very open to a Plan B."

Everyone in the crisis center stared at one another.

Kurtzman cleared his throat.

"Tell me you have a plan, Mr. Kurtzman."

Harebrained scheme was a more apt description. "We've had an idea, Mr. President, but we'll have to move fast."

Patuxent Naval Air Test Center, Maryland

"THERE YOU HAVE IT, GENTLEMEN." John "Cowboy" Kissinger and Gadgets Schwarz stood proudly in front of what they had wrought. Mack Bolan, Able Team and Phoenix Force stood at a table covered with maps and charts, staring past them at the hot-pink monstrosities hanging on the racks. Four massive, bulbous pressure suits half again the size of a man stood like giant cyclopean robots inside the hangar.

A highly perplexed looking naval officer stood with Barbara Price.

Schwarz was still heavily bandaged from his injuries in Berlin. They hadn't kept him from feverishly working with Kissinger. "These are Hardsuit 2000s, fully autonomous, anthropomorphic, atmospheric diving suits, or ADS. Capable of diving as deep as two thousand feet." Schwarz pointed to what looked like four electric fans anchored on the back and waist of the suits. "You have two 2.25 horsepower thruster modules, two directed vertically, two horizontally, which are controlled by footpads within the suit. These allow you to fly through the water or maintain station within a current."

McCarter stared at the monstrosities. "How do you move the bloody things?"

"Normally you couldn't. The suits weigh hundreds of pounds, but the arms and legs each have four hydraulically compensated rotary joints that will allow you to move the limbs. You'll find they're surprisingly flexible."

Calvin James had seen such suits before. "What's the duration of the life support?"

"Six hours without external resupply. That should be more than enough to get down to depth, do the job and get back up. You're bringing your own pressurized environment down with you, so decompression isn't a problem."

"None of us has any experience in one of these." James glanced at the naval officer. "Why don't trained Navy divers handle it?"

Commander Lloyd Cole was a short man who might as well have had the word "Diver" tattooed to his forehead. "That was my initial response, as well. However, I am informed that this will be a combat mission. My men who are trained on these suits are trained in submarine rescue and salvage. I'm told you men have a great deal of experience in unusual situations such as this. My job is to get you up to speed on these suits ASAP."

"Which brings us to armament options." Kissinger took a wooden pointer and indicated the ugly black implements that had been strapped on both arms of each suit. "We had exactly six hours to work these up, and we had to do it without degrading the suits' structural integrity, so it's all strapped on and operated with pulleys. On the right arm of each suit is a Russian APS underwater assault rifle. Most of you have fired one before. The bad news is, as you can see, the suits' hands are little more than pincers, so reloading isn't an option. You have twenty-six rounds in the magazine and that's it. Your trigger is a simple cable between your claw and the rifle's trigger housing. Turning your manipulator claw all the way down, like flexing your wrist, will pull the cable taut and fire the weapon. It will be slow, and getting on and off the trigger will be problematic. I give you no more than two bursts at best. That's the lightning."

Kissinger tapped the left arm of a suit and the pair of rails and cylinders strapped to it. "This is the thunder. Two Russian RKG-M antitank grenades just like you used in Moscow. The trigger is the same as the rifles. You crank the manipulator claw all the way to the right and it will pull the cable taut enough to trigger the first piston. The piston will shove the rail and the grenade mounted on it two feet forward of the suit's claw and at the same time pull the grenade pin. There's a magnetic ring on the edge of the grenade as well as waterproof adhesive. With a good seal you should get a proper detonation, and even if you don't, the effect should still be ugly at a short distance. Turning your manipulator claw all the way to the left will extend and fire the second charge."

James's mind was running the situation like the trained underwater warrior he was. "What kind of opposition are we expecting?"

Price picked up the ball. "We can't be sure. Deyn has stated if he hears any kind of approach above or below water he will detonate, so we have to assume he's got passive sonar as well as being able to ping if he wants. The submarine USS *Virginia* has been sitting and listening passively off station. As you've read in the dossiers, we've heard construction noises down on the ridge. Their computer has logged all sounds, and we have detected at least six different motor signatures that match the thrusting modules on the ADSs you see before you. So you have to expect men suited up the same as you. There have also been several different submersible noises. They don't match anything in the sonar sound catalog so we have to assume they are private craft developed by IESHEN Group. What kind of armament they have down there, we just don't know. If they're placing nukes, then you can expect them to have drills and other equipment that they could turn hostile pretty quickly. Regardless, you're all going to have to get very close to inflict any hurt on one another."

"Two shots on each arm." Blancanales wasn't happy. "And we're outnumbered?"

Kissinger shrugged. "Listen, the fact is I can't guarantee those weapons. They've never been tested to the depths you're going." He tapped the stainless-steel, serrated pincer of one of the suits. "The fact is, you may have to go claw-to-claw with these guys."

Blancanales sighed. "Pink?"

Price smiled. "You really want to be able to tell friend from foe down there. We don't know what color their suits are, but we're betting it's not baby-doll pink."

Grimaldi rose up and down on his toes and pointed at a sixteen-foot object that looked like a cross between a double-nosed fighter plane and a cockroach. Iron T-bars had been strapped, a pair each above and below the hull. "And that?"

"That, Jack," Schwarz stated, "is the U.S. naval evaluation prototype of the Deep Flight II submersible. And it's all yours."

Grimaldi grinned. "Cool."

"You've all been on board a submarine before. They pretty much float around the ocean operating exactly like blimps. The Deep Flights are designed to fly like a plane. The pilot is strapped in prone and can do any maneuver in water that a fighter plane can do in air—loops, barrel rolls, albeit a whole lot slower. You've got two manipulator arms. We'll be putting an RKG grenade in each one. Extend the arms fully straight and you'll pull the pins. You also have the option of dropping them if you need the claws for something else. The good news is that the Deep Flight has points for various external equipment fits. As you can see we've mounted two rifles beneath each wing and you'll have an electrical trigger to fire them."

Carl Lyons glowered at his broken hand. "There're only four suits."

Price took on his simmering wrath. "Carl, that's all we could get given the timetable."

Lyons glowered. He wanted payback and everyone knew it. "And what are the seating assignments on this flight?"

"Calvin is our most experienced diver. He's leading the mission. Rafe is next best, then David. Gary is our best demolition man. He's studied the captured nukes inside and out. If we have to diffuse anything down there, he's the man. That's our strike team. Jack is going to pilot the Deep Flight, of course, and Pol is going to operate the manipulator arms and weapons."

Lyons's brows dropped down dangerously.

"Your hand is broken, Carl. Besides, you hate pink."

Lyons was unconsoled.

"You couldn't operate the multiple right limb controls of an ADS suit even if we had one for you." Price met Lyons's eyes and didn't back down. "You'd be a liability, and you know it."

Lyons suppressed his rage, knowing Price was telling the truth and hating every second of it.

James's mind was all business. "How are we inserting?"

"A C-130 will fly in under their radar, all four suits and the Deep Flight will be strapped to a pallet. The pilot will slow just short of stalling speed and drogue chutes will deploy and pull you into the water. The straps will be within reach of the ADS manipulator arms. You should be able to cut through them with ease. The pallet will be made of aluminum and sink out from under you. The four divers will lock on to the Deep Flights' tow bars and Jack will make the descent. We know that Deyn will be listening with passive sonar so you will sink down to target. Jack will vector you in silently just using his diving planes to steer and his own passive sonar to locate the targets. When you are right on top of your targets, you switch on your lights and motors, attack with surprise and secure the nukes."

"What's the weather forecast?"

"That's the other good news. We're expecting rain, gusty winds and surface chop, so the sound of you hitting the water should be diffused."

Barbara turned her eye on Bolan. "You have something to add?"

"What about the platform?"

"What about it?"

"Akira is on it, so might some of the undeployed nukes. I say we take it."

"Washington has decided that assaulting the rig is too risky. The strike team will try to take out the threat to the hydrate ridge off Cape Hatteras. That is the number-one priority. We can't afford to have Deyn detonate the weapons he's already emplaced."

"He'll do that anyway, once he knows there's an attack going on downstairs."

"The President has authorized the *Virginia* to hit the platform with a full spread of cruise missiles once the strike team indicates they have the situation on the ridge under control or the mission has failed."

"That may not stop him in time, and for that matter, when the cruise missiles hit, you have a decent chance of one or more of the nukes still on the surface detonating low-order." Bolan's finger traced Cape Hatteras on the map. "With a surface detonation of one to ten kilotons you stand to lose the towns of Avon and Buxton, not to mention the ecological devastation of Pamlico Sound."

"The President and the Joint Chiefs are aware of that.

A direct assault on the rig has been deemed too risky. All psychological assessments indicate Deyn will detonate if he finds himself under attack. We can't risk an amphibious insertion or a combat drop against the rig. The possibility of detection is just too great."

"Not with a high-altitude, high-opening jump."

"We don't know how good the radars are on the rig. Deyn could detect the plane and push the button."

"No matter what kind of radars he has on that rig, I doubt he could detect a B-2 stealth bomber flying at ten thousand feet."

Price simply stared. "You're suggesting jumping out of the bomb bay of stealth, into a squall, at night."

"I'm not suggesting anything. Carl is going to lead the surface strike team and I'm volunteering to go with him."

Lyons nodded at the wisdom of the statement and both men turned to T.J. Hawkins, who rolled his eyes. "Oh, like you have to ask."

Bolan turned back to the satellite picture of the platform. "With any luck, at least one of us will manage to hit the rig undetected. We go in soft and poke around for any loose nukes. Failing that, we take the control room and hopefully anyone who's on a deadman switch. Once that's done, we locate and secure Akira and Franka Marx. Anyone who misses the platform and doesn't drown can swim to it and work their way up underneath from the boat dock and secure us extraction. The final option is still the same. If it looks like the situation has gone FUBAR, I'll call in the missile strike from the *Virginia* myself."

"I'll...have to clear this with the President." Price composed herself. "Meantime, Calvin, Commander Cole is going to take you and your team through ground school with the suits and Deep Flight. Then you and your team have four hours' practice time in the Potomac. Then there will be two hours while they are rechecked, reloaded, and recharged with fresh air and battery supplies. It's six o'clock now, we expect you airborne by midnight."

"You heard the lady." James grabbed a chair. "Commander Cole, we're all yours."

James's team assembled and the commander began explaining the finer points of atmospheric diving. Price pulled out her phone and handed it to Bolan. "Hal's still in the hospital."

"You want me to explain my plan to the President?"

"I don't think I can outline it in any way that doesn't sound like suicide."

CHAPTER TWENTY-NINE

Diamond Shoals, Atlantic

The Hercules vorticed up rooster tails of spume as it roared over the water ten feet off the deck. Calvin James lay in the cargo hold, strapped to a pallet and encased in an eight-foot-tall, pink carapace of titanium and carbon composite. It was eerily quiet inside the suit. What few sounds came through were muffled and distant. The stub wing of the Deep Flight II hung over him, the tow bar within easy reach. If he craned his head back, he could see the nose of the sub through the massively thick observation bubble encasing most of his head. James smiled. During the two-hour refuel and retrofit of the suits and the sub, Grimaldi had taken the opportunity to paint the Flying Tigers shark teeth insignia on the twin noses of the sub. Grimaldi loved his submersible.

The dive team hated the hard suits.

Any kind of fight was going to take place in slow motion. Moving the arms and legs was like moving through mud and there was distinct lag time between the human limb moving and the hydraulic joints of the suit following. It took a full second to crank the manipulator claws into the weapon-firing position and then off it. During firing practice in the Potomac River, nearly the entire team consistently fired off twenty of the twenty-six rounds in the magazine. McCarter had managed 15-round bursts, but in combat conditions under the sea James knew that anyone one of them would be lucky to get off the trigger before blowing the whole magazine. Grenade deployment was torturously slow. Again, it took a full second to pull the trigger, another second for the piston to extend, and that still left three seconds of fuse time. That would leave a lot of time for an opponent to try to break contact, and that was just practice in the Potomac. At nearly a thousand feet below the ocean, things would be even slower.

An air crewman knelt beside James, knocked on his helmet bubble and held up five fingers. Five minutes to go. James ran a final systems check on his air and electrical. All indicators were in the green. He craned his head back and could see Grimaldi grinning down from his cockpit. The pilot gave his teammate the thumbs-up. The air crewman went around tapping helmets and holding up one finger.

One minute to go.

James felt the vibration in the pallet beneath him as the Hercules's cargo ramp opened and air blasted at the straps. Water sprayed inward and misted his helmet. The air crewman stood over him and pumped the thumbs-up three times.

"Go! Go! Go!"

James lay on the pallet and watched as the rope to his right whipped like an angry snake as the drogue chute deployed out into the storm. The pallet jerked as the rope snapped tight. For a moment nothing happened. Then

James heard the groan and clank through his suit as the pallet began to move on its rollers. The air crewman saluted as he rolled past. James looked up and saw the tail of the Hercules and then the world ended.

His stomach lurched as the Hercules flew out from underneath him and well over a ton of armored suits and sub fell through space. The fall was mercifully brief. The pallet hit the Atlantic, and the shock of the hit was like being backhanded by God. Rain splattered James's helmet. A second later a wave sluiced over him, and he was submerged. All became rocking, bucking blackness. He ran a second quick check on air, electrical and motors and all lights blinked green. The rocking and rolling ceased as the entire pallet slid beneath the surface.

James's suit hydraulics gave a soft whine as he extended his right hand. He had practiced the maneuver twenty times on the ground. He reached out and opened his manipulator claw from memory. His manipulator claw was like a pair of needle-nose pliers with narrow tips, a few inches of serration inside for grip and shearing surfaces in the back. The tow bar was exactly where it was supposed to be. He closed his claw around the tow bar and locked it. He reached out with his right and felt resistance. The Phoenix Force warrior vised down, and the retaining strap parted beneath his claw.

The rest of the dive team cut their straps and the pallet slipped away.

James rotated his right arm so that he hung beneath the Deep Flight facing forward. They were in Grimaldi's hands now, running silent and dark as the pilot vectored them in just using his diving planes and passive sonar. The sea was silent and as pitch-black as the grave as they sank into the crushing depths.

CARL LYONS SAT in the belly of a Stealth bomber. Mack Bolan and T.J. Hawkins sat beside him. The jumpmaster was an extremely confused Air Commando. This model didn't have a pod. The bomb bay of the B-2 had never been designed for passengers. In fact, a man couldn't fully stand up inside it. The only compromises that had been made for passenger comfort were three folding aluminum beach chairs and oxygen bottles attached to the bomb racks above their heads. The crease of the bomb bay doors sat directly under Lyons's chair. Luckily it was a short hop to the drop zone. They were maintaining strict radio silence so the pilot was speaking to the jumpmaster through a cell phone. The Air Commando listened and then nodded to Lyons. "Five minutes, Jump Leader. We've reached the area of radio-jamming, so once you go out the door your tactical-communication gear will be nonfunctional."

"Roger, that," Lyons responded. The team rose to a crouch and stowed their chairs and checked one another's gear. Lyons gave Bolan's straps a yank. "Thanks, Mack."

They both knew that if Bolan hadn't spoken to the President himself, there would be no airborne mission, and Carl Lyons wouldn't be leading it. Bolan checked Lyons's straps. "You sure you'll be okay to jump with that busted paw of yours?"

"I'll be right behind you."

Bolan had known Carl Lyons a very long time, and he could read the Ironman like a book. "You know, I lost Akira once, too. We'll get him back."

Lyons's blue eyes were cold beneath his goggles. "The nukes are our number-one priority."

Bolan smiled under his oxygen mask. That was what he wanted to hear.

"One minute, Jump Leader!" the jumpmaster called. "Switch to bailout bottles!"

The team unhooked from the overhead oxygen and switched to the small bottles attached to their jump rigs. The jumpmaster passed by each member of the team and checked his gear a final time. He gave Lyons the thumbs-up. "Hook your men up!"

Lyons and his team hooked their static lines into the struts of the bomb racks overhead. Jumping out of a B-2 wasn't a skydiving best-case scenario. Luckily the engine intakes were on top of the plane so no one would get sucked into and food processed through the turbines. But the stalling speed of a B-2 was still around 120 knots. The jet wash would be fairly ugly, and there was a chance of being smashed against the fuselage on the way out. Static lines would insure that the chutes opened even if a man had been knocked unconscious or passed out because his oxygen bottle had been ripped off. Still they were jumping into a squall, and any man who hit the water unconscious or injured wasn't likely to live long.

"Green light!" the jumpmaster shouted. The Air Commando and the team grabbed the bomb racks and braced themselves. The bomb bay doors opened beneath them and wind roared up into the cramped weapons' compartment. At ten thousand feet the night was indescribably beautiful. There was a full moon, and it shone down on the clouds as if there were a carpet of cotton beneath them.

"We are over target area!" the jumpmaster called. "Go! Go! Go!"

Hawkins released the bomb rack above, bent his knees and fell out of the plane.

"Go! Go! Go!"

Bolan pushed out into the night.

Hawkins's static line went taut and then flapped and whipped as it released.

"Go! Go! Go!"

Bolan's line went tight.

Lyons dropped into emptiness. The wind whipped him away from the aircraft and the giant black bat-shape pulled away with a rumbling whine. His harness yanked against him as the static line ripped his chute from his pack, and then the straps tried to squeeze the life out of him as his chute deployed. He'd had a medic at Patuxent shoot up his hand with a local anesthetic. He couldn't feel his hand, but his first two fingers and thumb woodenly obeyed his will. Lyons grabbed his toggles and stabilized his flight. Bolan and Hawkins were clearly visible in his night-vision goggles. The air was thin, clear and stable, and their descent line toward the target was textbook despite the rough deployment. It was a High Altitude, High Opening jump so they had a few minutes of flight-tie on their chutes. They arced down toward the target in large lazy circles, guided by their compasses and the radio signal trackers strapped to their forearms. Lyons watched the carpet of clouds come up toward him. The wind was picking up.

Things were about to get interesting.

Hawkins disappeared into the clouds. Moments later Bolan was enveloped. Lyons flared his chute slightly as he hit the mist. The world became a wet, black, buffeting sponge. A second later it became hell on earth. Lyons was whipped 360 degrees around on his lines as the wind ripped at him and driving rain hammered his airfoil. The Ironman didn't fight; he powered through the circle and used the momentum to sling him straight again. Through the wind and the rain the platform was a bright beacon of light below him and to the east. The wind was in his favor, but it stood a good chance of flinging him past his target. Lyons worked his toggles, going with the gusts and arcing through them rather than fighting them and overcorrecting. He followed Bolan's lead, and Bolan followed Hawkins. Lyons's eyes flared beneath his goggles. Hawkins was making his approach. The platform was huge, but the ocean was vast and the winds were pushing them along with far too much velocity.

Hawkins flared his chute to slow down. The wind blasted up into his chute and ripped him around in a series of vicious circles, nearly collapsing his canopy. He finally managed to power through it and straighten out as Lyons had, but the damage was done. Modern airfoil parachutes made a jump much more like flying than falling, but in the end the only real direction was still down. The gust had braked Hawkins too hard and lost him too much speed. His approach was too low.

Their radios were being jammed and Lyons wouldn't have broken radio silence anyway, but he still shouted through his mask into the storm. "T.J.!"

Hawkins wasn't going to make it.

The black shadow of the platform eclipsed him as he sailed beneath it. Lyons judged Bolan's line with a practiced eye and could see his line was going to bring him down on top of the platform, so he stuck to Bolan's tail as much as the winds would let him. The Executioner flared his chute and the wind tried to rip him around, but his boots hit the platform. The chute filled with wind and tried to pull him back over the edge, but he hit his quick-release buckles and dropped into a crouch. The half-collapsed airfoil flew up into the night like a crazed ghost and danced away into the darkness borne upon the wind. Bolan scuttled to tarp-covered pallet of heavy machinery and glanced back.

Lyons flared his chute as the platform flew past beneath his boots, and his landing was perfect. The wind still wanted his airfoil and heaved at it. The Able Team Leader's anesthetized hand fat-fingered the right hand release. He was yanked off his feet, his oxygen bottle and mask ripping away as the chute dragged him face-first across the platform. Lyons grunted as a vast weight came down between his shoulder blades and pinned him. He saw the glitter of the knife that slashed his shrouds, and Bolan heaved him to his feet and yanked him back behind cover.

"You all right?"

Lyons spit blood and shouted over the howl of the wind. "Yeah! You see T.J. on your way in?"

"Saw him go under! He could have hit the boat dock or the drink!" Bolan unstrapped his Barrett rifle and grenade launcher. "Maybe he ate a pylon or got hung up in the supports! Either way we gotta assume he didn't make it! The nukes and Akira are probably downstairs, with luck we'll meet him coming up!"

Lyons unclipped his shotgun from his jump harness. He unfolded the stock and wrapped the hook under his elbow. The rain pounded into his face with the force of needles.

"Let's go."

CHAPTER THIRTY

Continental Shelf

Calvin James was distracted from his depth gauge inside his helmet by a dim glow in the black depths beneath him. The glow became a constellation of lights, like an upside down Little Dipper, which resolved into the work lights of an underwater construction site. Some of the lights moved as men in ADS suits floated around the rock shelf like men doing a space walk. The bulbous shapes of submersibles hovered over the work area. The light of a cutting torch flickered like a blue sun. The Phoenix Force commando counted eight men in suits and two submersibles. They were outnumbered two to one, but surprise was on their side. Their descent had gone undetected, and the enemy wasn't looking in their direction. The team had floated down over their targets like undersea angels of death.

Grimaldi blinked the running lights beneath the Deep Flight II's wings to signal the attack. James unlocked his claw and released the tow bar. He hit his thruster module and began flying toward his target under his own power.

He could feel rather than see or hear Blancanales flying wingman on his left. The Deep Flight slid forward like a slow-motion fighter plane as Grimaldi began his attack run. The enemy submersible looked like a goldfish bowl surrounded by a steel frame. Oxygen tanks and thrusters hung on its framework like afterthoughts. Four massive manipulator arms sprung from its chin like the steel tentacles of a squid. Two men in warm-up suits sat inside the glass bubble, their bodies looking miniature and distorted through the thick plastic. The submersible's manipulator arms held a pallet loaded with six sealed metal cylinders. James could only assume the thermonuclear demolition charges had been repackaged for deep ocean delivery. The two men inside the bubble looked up in shock as Grimaldi loomed in out of the gloom and slid to a stop. One of the Deep Flight's arms extended as the submersibles came almost nose-to-nose.

The two men in the submersible stared in horror at the RKG-M antitank grenade adhered to the side of their compartment. Grimaldi reversed his screws and backed away from the submersible. The men inside the sphere screamed and worked their controls. The submersible tilted as the nuke-laden pallet dropped, and a manipulator arm reached up with aching slowness to rip away the grenade.

The two screaming men were eclipsed with white fire as the shaped-charge warhead burned through the plastic bubble and filled the compartment with superheated gas and molten metal. The fire was instantly extinguished as the Atlantic Ocean's invisible hand closed around the compromised compartment like a fist and crushed it like an eggshell. The pallet of nukes continued its long slide down into the depths, and the slain submersible followed, trailing bubbles from its ruptured tanks and steam from its molten interior.

Calvin James closed on his target.

Four men in ADS suits hovered around a small platform mounted into the shelf. A drill the size of a Volkswagen slowly turned. A pair of the sealed cases sat on the platform. Nukes ready to be embedded. The three men had turned at the sound of the muffled explosion, but the Deep Flight had already peeled off back into the gloom. One of the men sensed something and slowly turned his suit around.

James closed to three feet and cranked his manipulator claw all the way to the left as he extended his arm. The piston strapped to his forearm spit bubbles and shoved the two-foot metal rail forward. The grenade's pin pulled and the cotter lever clicked away. In the syrup slowness of their underwater maneuvering James's warhead and the chest of his opponent's ADS suit coincided with a clank. James could hear a sound like bacon sizzling as the superheated jet burned through the chest of the ADS suit, the man inside and blasted out the back. The dark water around them flared orange in the glow and the ADS suit spasmed and crumpled in on itself like a tin can being crushed.

Blancanales's opponent never saw what hit him. The Able Team commando's grenade locked into the rounded silver hump of the hardsuit's atmosphere unit and fired. The back of the suit blew open as the oxygen tanks exploded and instantly flattened out, leaving slowly sinking remains like the aftermath of an underwater steamroller accident.

The third man on the platform lunged at James with a thruster-assisted hop. His claws were held in front of him defensively. The plierlike hands of the suit opened like mouths to rip at James's suit seals. The fourth man took the better part of valor and lifted off the platform in full flight.

The Phoenix Farm warrior leveled his arm and cranked his right claw all the way to the side and the APS underwater assault rifle rattled against its restraining straps. Yellow fire strobed as five-inch steel darts flew from the muzzle in a stream into the enemy hardsuit. James snarled inside his helmet as the darts deflected. It was as he suspected. At this depth the darts didn't have the velocity to penetrate a hardsuit. He raised his aim into his opponent's face.

His opponent got his arm underneath James's and shoved the assault rifle out of line. The man's claw opened like the mouth of a snake and the steel tips scraped sickeningly against James's face glass.

Blancanales's voice crackled over the hydrophone. "Hold him!"

James and his opponent jockeyed for position. The suits were incapable of turning their heads, but the men within got a fish-eye lens view to the sides from the curved glass. James's man caught a glimpse of Blancanales coming in and pushed away. He turned and hit his thrusters, lifting off and away from the shelf like a man wearing a rocket pack.

The Able Team warrior flew after him, straightening his right arm to aim. Darts hissed in bubbling streams from his APS rifle. The darts wouldn't penetrate the pressure body of the suit, but Blancanales had other ideas. His darts drew lines into the whirring propellers of his target's thrusting module. The fleeing man's hardsuit suddenly listed as his portside thrusters broke and jammed. Pol adjusted his aim and sent his last five darts into the two thrusters starboard. Sparks ticked as the system shorted. The man's flight into the open ocean slowed and stalled. Blancanales flew in for the kill.

With twenty-five thermonuclear time bombs ticking, there was neither room nor time for mercy in the Stygian depths. Blancanales hit his opponent from behind and drove him out and away from the shelf. The enemy hardsuit didn't have the mobility to reach backward. Blancanales drove him out a hundred feet away and dropped him.

The IESHEN Group terrorist had only one forward-firing thruster. He hit it for all it was worth as his adversary rose up and away, but all it did was push him in a slow circle as his suit tilted to the side. The crippled suit began a long, slow death spiral into the dark.

James had no time to contemplate the man's lonely fate. His own thrusters were whining at full power as he flew to the second battle scene. McCarter and Encizo were besieged. The two men were back-to-back and surrounded by enemies. Two crushed hardsuit husks lay on the undersea platform, evidence that the men of Phoenix Force had driven their shaped-charged warheads home. The enemy had learned the hard way and circled their prey, looking for the opening to pull McCarter and Encizo apart and kill them individually. One of the enemy ADS men held the stuttering, blinding blue light of a cutting torch in his claw. The enemy submersible hovered over the scene defensively. Grimaldi looped and rolled around it, looking for his own opening. One side of the enemy submersible's steel frame was blackened where he had gotten a near miss with his second grenade. Grimaldi was out of grenades, and his four automatic underwater rifles were useless against the enemy craft. He slowed his thrusters, manipulator arms extended to try to rip away tanks or propellers, but the enemy sub simply spun on its axis defensively, like a crab, presenting its four arms to the Stony Man pilot's two.

James caught light above and saw another enemy submersible descending. "Jack! Enemy sub on your six!"

Grimaldi hit his thrusters and squirted out from the closing jaws of the trap. McCarter and Encizo were not as lucky. Freed of its opponent, the first sub dropped like an octopus upon its prey. Its four arms reached out, seizing McCarter's arms while the other two dug into his thrusting modules, the stainless-steel jaws crushing and rending the plastic propellers and motor housings with ease. The submersible rose upward, plucking McCarter out of the fray.

The four enemy hardsuits descended on Encizo like a pack of wolves upon a stray dog.

The back of the Cuban's helmet blackened as the torch played across it. James plowed into the torch man like an aquatic fullback. Their hardsuits thudded and James drove him out of the melee. The former SEAL began to extend his last grenade for the kill, but the man hit his thrusters expertly and rose and spun at the same time. The piston slammed forward and extended the grenade. James tried to bring it back in line but he was too slow. The grenade flared like a sun as it detonated. With no target to lock against, the superheated jet of the shaped charge shoved him out into open water like a rocket. James blinked at the flashing lights in front of his eyes when something thudded hard into his suit. He tried to tear with his claws, but they slid along the smooth shifting surfaces of the enemy's suit.

He suddenly found himself face-to-face with Clay Forbes.

Their face shields clanked and James could hear Forbes's shout through the physical connection. "Gonna drop you, gray meat! Gonna drop you down deep!"

The left side of James's helmet glass blackened beneath the incandescent blue flame of the torch. The Phoenix Force commando got his right arm up and cranked his claw full right. Forbes's eyes flew wide as the APS underwater assault rifle spewed six darts into his face. The darts bent and broke, pinging against the glass and barely chipping it.

Forbes's voice roared over the hydrophone. "Not good enough! Gonna burn you open, bitch! Send your crushed ass down into the cold!"

The flame came forward inexorably toward James's face. He pulled the sacrifice play and let it come. He let his arm bend into his chest and the torch suddenly shoved forward. As it did, the nozzle of the torch came straight between his claw. The Phoenix Force commando's face plate blackened, but he ignored the flame and vised his claw down. He turned his hand and the claw rotated it 180 degrees, bending the nozzle all the way back at Forbes.

Forbes leered. There was still a foot between him and the fire. "Cute."

James clamped his claw down and snipped off the torch's nozzle.

A three-foot jet of fire enveloped Forbes's helmet. The tube of acetylene squirted out of his claw and corkscrewed away like a berserk rocket-propelled torpedo. James reversed his thrusters and backed away as contact was broken. He brought up his claws defensively, but the left hand wouldn't obey him. His manipulator claw had been caught in the acetylene blast and been soldered shut.

Forbes hovered back in. The right side of his helmet was blackened, but the big man's eyes were on James's claw, noting the damage. "What'ya think you're gonna do one-handed?" He rotated his claws, opening and closing them for his adversary's benefit as he looked for his opening. "Gonna have to open you up the old-fashioned way, rip your seals and let the ocean in and—"

Forbes's speech was cut short as the jagged line of a crack ran violently down the blackened side of his face-plate. Forbes went slack-jawed with horror. "Jesus, God…"

The big man screamed like a rabbit being killed. A

needle-thin stream of the Atlantic hissed into his helmet with a thousand pounds per square inch of force ripping through the flesh of his face like a laser. Forbes's head whipped back and forth in screaming agony. The stream widened and fanned into his face, ripping the flesh from the skull and blasting out his eyes like a hydraulic mining hose stripping a mountainside. His agony ended abruptly as his faceplate imploded and his stripped skull was crushed. His hardsuit spasmed like a puppet as the chest, arms and legs crumpled inward as all pressure integrity was lost.

The shattered ADS began its slow sink into the gloom, trailing what was left of Clay Forbes in a thin red ribbon of chum.

James wheeled and kicked his thrusters. His team was in a bad way. Grimaldi was in a stalemate dogfight with one of the submersibles. The second sub had pulled up out of the fight and taken McCarter with it. He hung suspended in its embrace, slowly flailing his limbs while the copilot tried to rip him open with the second pair of arms. His suit appeared to be intact, but two of his thrusters had been ripped away. Encizo and Blancanales were in an ADS dog pile on the platform. They were outnumbered two to one, and it would only be moments before their opponents got a good hold on their suit seals and opened them up to the Atlantic.

James chinned his hydrophone. "Jack! Come to me!"

The Deep Flight's main advantage was speed and maneuverability. Grimaldi pulled his sub into a tight loop and flew to James. His voice clearly said he didn't like leaving the fray. "Tell me you have a plan!"

"Pick me up! Drop me on top of one of the subs! Then ram the dog pile, break it up! We'll wing it from there!"

"Roger that!" Grimaldi arced around and slowed as he passed over James.

The Phoenix Force commando reached up with his good claw and clasped the tow bar. "I'm on!"

Grimaldi shoved his throttles forward and shot toward the fray. He flew straight at the sub holding McCarter and pulled up and over it. James released and powered his thrusters down, directly behind the submersible. He maneuvered underneath it. The manipulator arms had McCarter by two arms and one leg. He had his remaining leg jammed up against the sub's support frame, but he was nearly crucified, and the sub's fourth arm was blindly raking across his suit, trying to rip him open.

McCarter looked up in his struggles and saw his teammate.

Exterior hydraulic tubes would be crushed at this depth, so the arms on the submersibles were simply skeleton frames operated by cable pulleys.

The ex-SEAL reached up into the manipulator arm control assembly and began snipping cables with his remaining claw. The claws lost all strength, and McCarter fell free of the submersible's steely embrace.

Grimaldi came around in a tight circle and flew toward the struggling mob of hardsuits. He aimed the nose of his Deep Flight at the back of an ADS that wasn't pink and shoved his throttles full forward. His ceramic hull hummed and his six-thousand-pound submersible hit the mob at six knots. The hump of his main target's air and life support buckled, and the rest of the ADS followed suit in explosive decompression. The remaining five men were scattered, two of them being pushed off the platform.

James noted McCarter still had one grenade attached to his arm. He jerked his head toward the battle, and the Briton descended. His teammate clanked his claw against the submersible's chin. The two operators looked down at James. Both men wore suitably appalled expressions. The ex-SEAL chinned his hydrophone. "Are you receiving me?"

The two men nodded as a unit.

"Good, you are going to set this tub down on the platform." James opened his good claw and twirled it. "If you don't, I am going to cripple your motors, cut open your life support, and watch you take the slow train to crush depth. Do we understand one another?"

The two men nodded as a unit.

"Do it slow."

The pilot grabbed his joysticks and began slowly maneuvering the submersible to an octagonal pad on the platform with an "x" of lights marked on it.

James checked the battle below.

McCarter hovered over a blasted-open hardsuit. Encizo and Blancanales stood shoulder to shoulder forward of him. The two remaining men ADS men hovered in front of them. One began to move toward a rack of tools on the platform.

Grimaldi swung into view and flew straight toward him. The four automatic rifles stuttered fire beneath his stub wings, and 104 five-inch darts streamed into the man's faceplate. The glass gave beneath the onslaught of steel and his suit ruptured and crumpled. The remaining IESHEN Group hardsuited watched as the craft flew past a foot over his head and peeled off into the darkness doing a victory roll.

The man cut his thrusters, dropped to the platform, clamped his claws shut and put them up in surrender. The enemy sub set down on the pad, and Grimaldi swung back in and came to a hover in front of James. The hydrophone bounced sound against his helmet. "The other sub is ascending. I'm out of grenades and darts. You want me to pursue?"

"No, let him go. Surface ships will pick them up." James kicked his thrusters and floated in front of the prisoner. "Who are you?"

"Alexsandr Zabyshny."

James pointed his fused claw at the remnants of broken hardsuits littering the platform. "You want to die?"

The Russian glanced at the crushed carnage and then met James's gaze as he chinned his hydrophone. "Not today. Not down here."

"Where's the trigger?"

Zabyshny pointed at a thick cable. It lay near a heavy box. Cables stretched away from it in ten directions across the shelf. The first cable trailed up the Continental Shelf and disappeared into the darkness. "Eight weapons embedded. Mr. Deyn wanted ten minimum. Once we connect it, any attempt to cut it will trigger devices."

James dared to hope. "The circuit isn't connected yet?"

"Two more devices to emplace."

"What was your timetable?"

The Russian stared out at the second platform and the drill. "Finished in one hour."

Calvin did the math. Twenty-five devices. Six had spilled down into the abyss of the Hatteras Plain. Since they hadn't gone off, they had most likely been crushed inert. Eight had been embedded in the hydrate ridge around them. Two more were ready for placement on the other platform. That left ten thermonuclear demolition charges unaccounted for. "Where are the other ten?"

The Russian's eyes rolled to the surface far above. "Deyn has them."

"They've been modified and put into deepwater casings?"

"No, Deyn believed ten devices minimum for this project, sixteen for insurance. He decided the other ten would be earmarked for…other purposes. They are in original configuration."

James nodded. "You can lock on to that submersible and head for the surface. Naval helicopters will pick you up along with us." James kicked his suit around to the Deep Flight. "Jack, send up the retrieval beacon. We're done here."

Grimaldi punched a button, and a cone-shaped device released from the top of his sub in a stream of bubbles and shot toward the surface where tracking satellites would pick up its signal. James locked his claw on to the Deep Flight's tow bar as the rest of his team assembled.

The Mid-Atlantic Seaboard and Washington, D.C. had been saved.

But three little towns named Avon, Buxton and Hatteras had been deemed strategically acceptable losses. They still faced a one-hundred-kiloton blast at Deyn's hands in a last act of defiance. The only thing standing between them and annihilation were Carl Lyons, Mack Bolan, and T.J. Hawkins.

CHAPTER THIRTY-ONE

The Platform

"They have won." Johan Mahke leaned his bulk back in his chair in disgust.

Deyn's fists clenched. "What do you have on the sonar log?"

"There was a battle. The enemy consisted of four attackers in hardsuits like those our men were wearing, plus a submersible our sound catalog does not recognize. The battle lasted four minutes. There were sounds of explosions, violent decompressions, and what can only be cataloged as underwater gunfire."

"And?"

"And the sounds of battle have ceased, Herr Deyn. Submersible Number 1 fled to the surface during the battle and is currently calling for recall. Number 2 has dropped off sonar. I am assuming it has been destroyed. The enemy submersible and sub Number 3 are currently rising to the surface in formation."

"How has this happened?"

"I do not know. Sonar shows no surface ships in the area. I cannot imagine how they inserted."

"It was an airborne insertion."

"Airborne?" Mahke was incredulous. "With four ADS suits and a submersible?"

"Yes. I do not know how they did it, but they did."

Mahke pressed Play on the CD recorder. "And we have this."

The two Germans listened to a crackling, slightly garbled recording of the hydrophones as Calvin James demanded Alexsandr Zabyshny's surrender and the Russian capitulated. "Mr. Deyn, the construction crew was ahead of schedule. Eight devices are in place, but they failed to establish the link with them before they were attacked. We cannot detonate the devices from here."

"I am well aware of that." Deyn took a flat plastic box out of his windbreaker.

Mahke eyed the box in Deyn's hand as if it were a venomous snake.

Deyn smiled. "If the enemy is below, then I am willing to bet that they are here above, as well."

"How could they—"

"They are here. Sound the alarm. Prepare for evacuation." A muscle twitched beneath Deyn's eye. "And bring the prisoners to me."

LYONS MOVED toward the command shack. He and Bolan came to a stop in the shadow of a crane. Steel storm shutters had been drawn down over the shack windows, but narrow observation slits spilled out yellow light. The platform was buttoned up tight against the storm. Neither Lyons nor Bolan was fooled. Deyn would be on a war footing. Everyone on the platform above and below would be armed to the teeth and ready to repel boarders.

Bolan scanned the command shack and surrounding outbuildings with his rifle optics. "How do you want to play it, Carl?"

The two men hunched as every light on the platform clicked on, lighting up the structure like a Christmas tree. Klaxons began to sound. Armed men began spilling out of the buildings.

"Lets just play it by ear."

Bolan raised his weapon. The door to the barracks flew open and two men with rifles leaped out with more behind them. The Executioner put them both down with a burst and then squeezed the trigger on his M-203. The grenade looped through the barracks door, smashing one man off of his feet and detonating to send more screaming, jerking and torn to the ground.

Bullets from above smashed out the windows of the crane operator's box. Lyons extended his arm like a fencer, the folding stock of the shotgun locked around his arm and began to fire up at the observation tower. Buckshot rounds blasted out the windows, and the rifleman folded around the rail and fell end-over-end into space. His ruptured body hit the ground level of the platform with a hideous thump.

"Rocket!" Bolan's hand slammed down on Lyons's shoulder. "Move!"

A hissing line of fire and smoke streaked across the platform. The Stony Man warrior dived behind a bulkhead as the rocket grenade slammed into the crane and blew the operator box to flying shreds. Cables broke, and the crane boom collapsed and fell with a horrendous clang over the bulkhead. Bolan ducked as the two-ton boom bounced against the bulkhead, then slid past just over his head in a shower of sparks. The boom hit the platform with a final clang.

Lyons rose up, his shotgun extended. The IESHEN Group rocketeer was reloading with the help of his crewman. The Jungle Gun roared, printing a pattern of buckshot in the rocket man's upper chest and head. His rocket tube fell to the roof and the dead man fell nearly headless to the platform. The loader screamed and dropped his rocket as a pattern of buck ripped his legs out from beneath him and a second blast rolled him off the roof.

Other than the yammering of the Klaxon, the howling of the wind and the ceaseless drumming of rain on corrugated iron, it was suddenly very quiet.

"They're waiting for us," Bolan suggested.

Lyons shucked fresh shells into his shotgun, his eyes fixed on the command shack. "We could go knock on the door."

"They're waiting for that."

The two of them crouched behind the bulkhead as the rain sheeted down on them. The storm was picking up. "I'm open to suggestion."

"Well...I could pull a Santa Claus."

Lyons flashed a rare smile. "The rocket launcher."

"If you haven't blasted it to shit."

"Do it. I'll do the front door."

"Cover me." The Executioner slung his rifle and burst from cover. He made for the shack at a dead sprint and leaped, grabbing the dripping eaves, pulling himself up and flinging a leg over the top. He rolled across the roof and came up in a crouch, unslinging his rifle and shouldering it one movement. He scanned the platform for targets and saw nothing moving. Bolan raised a hand and waved Lyons in while he covered.

Lyons ran to the shack and pressed himself against the

wall by the door. He pulled out a length of shaped-charge adhesive and pressed it against the seam of the shack's steel door. He took out his detonator box and clutched it in the two functioning fingers and thumb of his right hand. The Able Team leader raised the muzzle of the Mossberg over the eaves and waved it to signal he was ready.

Bolan slung his rifle and examined his prize. It was a Panzerfaust 3 light antitank weapon system. Lyons's buckshot had blown out the optical sight and the tube had some dings and lead smears on it, but the weapon seemed serviceable. He picked up the fallen rocket, which vaguely resembled a football on a stick with a long probe sticking out the front. Large yellow letters on the side of the warhead read BASTEG. Bolan nodded. A Barricade and Street Encounter Grenade would fill the bill nicely. He shoved the rocket motor down the tube and it clicked into place.

The problem was minimum range. He needed room for the rocket motor to ignite and the warhead to arm.

Bolan squinted into the squall and examined the radio antenna tower as it teetered in the wind. He took the thirty-pound weapon across his shoulder and began to climb. The antenna groaned beneath his weight. He reached the top and figured he had the minimum twenty yards. At the top the little tower swayed sickeningly in the gale. The soldier pointed the tube down at the roof and shouted over the wind. "Fire in the hole!"

The rocket hissed down into the roof. The BASTEG was a tandem warhead weapon. The extended probe in the nose of the warhead hit the roof and detonated the shaped-charge warhead, cutting a hole. The second warhead was a high-explosive grenade encased in preformed metal fragments. It instantly launched behind the shape charge and flew into the shack.

Steel shutters rattled on either side of Lyons's head. The glass within shattered and flame and smoke squirted out the observation slits. He hit his detonator box. "Fire in the hole!" The cutting charge slashed down the door frame in a hissing line. Lyons put his boot to the door and it flew off its hinges. He came in, shotgun at the ready. The interior of the shack was in ruins. Four men with rifles lay blasted and dead. Laurentius Deyn and Johan Mahke were nowhere in sight. Lyons called up through the smoking hole in the roof. "Clear!"

Lyons kept his eye on the door at the back of the shack. Bolan appeared a moment later with the reloaded Panzerfaust across his shoulder and another rocket thrust through his belt. He thumbed his throat mike and frowned. "Radio signals are still being jammed. There has to be a secondary command and control."

The Able Team leader scanned the torn and blackened control panels. He flipped a switch and the Klaxons ceased their honking. Lyons pressed a button on the panel and was pleased to see the public-address system had survived. He picked up the mike and clicked Send. His voice reverberated throughout the platform.

"Surrender the weapons. Surrender the prisoners. I'm only going to ask once."

"No." Laurentius Deyn's voice came back. "You will disarm, go to the helicopter pad and kneel with your hands behind your heads, or I will detonate the Hatteras Ridge."

"If you could do it, you would've done it already. We've secured the ridge, and you know it. Have your men disarm and go to the pad. Surrender any remaining devices you have. Surrender the prisoners."

"I have nine weapons on this platform, each set for the maximum ten-kiloton yield. I have detected no evacuation of Cape Hatteras on satellite. You will be unable to secure the devices. The casings are tamper-proofed to detonate if they are molested. If you come for the devices, the Cape towns will be slaughtered. If you come for the prisoners, so will they." Deyn's voice went reptilian. "But come, come anyway."

Lyons clicked off. "You know something? I think the psycho son of a bitch still thinks he's getting out of this."

"I agree. He has an out."

"He doesn't have shit." Lyons's lips skinned back from his teeth. "He isn't leaving this platform alive."

T. J. HAWKINS AWOKE to the sound of gunfire. At first he was startled to find that all he could see was green static. He spit blood out of his mouth and reached up to his face. He ran his fingers over his night-vision goggles and found the lenses were cracked. He pushed them up onto his forehead and winced when he found a lump the size of an egg in the way. He pulled off the goggles and glanced around groggily. The first thing he noticed was the massive concrete pylon three feet in front of him. A Rorschach inkblot of blood stained it directly in front of his face. Hawkins peered upward and saw his parafoil wrapped up around rebar and struts. He was hanging sixty-five feet above the ocean by his straps. Hawkins remembered sailing beneath the platform. He remembered the pylon rushing toward him. He remembered trying to steer around it. He did not remember eating the pylon, but the math was pretty clear. His nose was broken. His front teeth felt loose. His vision kept blurring. He wondered if he had a concussion.

The Phoenix Force commando glanced down and saw a dock at the bottom of the platform. An open-frame elevator shaft as well as a steel staircase led up to the main platform. A number of concrete berths surrounded the dock. Three were empty. One contained the long dark cigar shape of a submarine. The sub looked small, like a diesel-electric coastal patroller. Hawkins wasn't enough of a naval nut to identify what international inventory it had come from, but Laurentius Deyn was a billionaire with the ability to sift and manipulate the funds of a multinational corporation. If he wanted to buy a small, obsolete patrol sub from North Korea, China or Russia quietly, he had the money to make it happen.

That answered another question.

Deyn himself might be willing to go down with the Continental Shelf, but most of the men working for him wouldn't. They would want a ticket out before the aquatic Armageddon. Diesel-electric boats, no matter how obsolete, had one very distinct advantage over the latest nuclear-driven boats. They could be very, very quiet when they wanted to be, particularly when hugging the mud along a coastline, and Deyn would have had years to upgrade the boat with the latest acoustic tiling, listening devices and quiet propeller screw designs. Hawkins smiled and spit some more blood. One mystery solved. How he was going to get down and do something about it was the next one.

His ass was literally hanging in the breeze.

It was slightly calmer beneath the shelter of the platform's mass and there was no rain pelting him. There was really only one choice. Hawkins took a deep breath, hit his release buckles and dropped into space He tucked his knees into his chest in a cannonball as he fell sixty-five feet into the Atlantic, which hit him in the tailbone like a mallet. He gasped and swallowed ocean as the black water closed over his head. He instinctively began to kick. Ceramic armor inserts, assault rifles, pistols and grenades weren't exactly buoyancy bonuses. It took every ounce of his strength to claw his way to the surface and start to stroke. Every wave hit him like a hammer. The Atlantic lifted him up and dropped him back down, and he felt like he had drunk half of it. He felt nauseous and his limbs were going cold. All he could do was continue his enfeebled stroke, aiming desperately for the dock.

Hawkins's hands and feet hit metal. He crawled up the hull of the sub while the waves struggled to wash him back into the water. He got up onto relatively dry land behind the sail and spread out his arms and legs, clutching the hull and shaking like a dog that had been left out in the rain.

The Phoenix Force warrior took a deep breath and resumed his crawl up the hunched back of the sub to the sail. He rose to a crouch and peered over. Two men stood on the dock twenty feet away in slickers. They were smoking cigarettes and luckily peering off to the east. The howling wind and slapping waves had covered his approach. Hawkins reached for his silenced SOCOM pistol and found his sodden holster snapped open and empty.

So much for silence. Guns were going off upstairs anyway. Hawkins unclipped his Barrett and rested it on the lip of the sail. He blinked and yawned as his the crosshairs doubled skewed as he peered through the optical sight. He let his vision return to normal and put his sights on the farthest man's back. His hands were shaking uncontrollably.

Sparks shrieked off the railing by the guard's shoulder as he fired.

The two men jumped in alarm and spun, bringing their rifles to bear. Hawkins flicked his selector to full-auto as sparks whined off the sail next to his head. He squeezed the trigger and was rewarded as water sprayed from the chest of the guard's wet slicker and he crumpled. The second guard sprayed on full-auto, and bullets cracked overhead. A single bullet from Hawkins's 5-round burst snapped the guard's head back and dropped him.

The big ex-Ranger sagged against the sail and groaned. The gun blasts stabbed through his throbbing head like knives. His was definitely messed up. He was too weak, slow and cold to— The hatch in the sail clanked open and a man with a pistol shoved his head up and started shouting in German. Hawkins hosed the man back down the ladder with the rest of his magazine. Pistols barked back instantly from below. Hawkins pulled a fragmentation grenade, yanked the pin and tossed the bomb down the hatch.

The men in the sub shouted in alarm, Hawkins followed it with a white phosphorous. The submariners screamed as shrapnel whined around the narrow confines of the bridge. The screams ended as white-hot smoke and burning metal filled the interior. Hawkins leaned back as streamers of white fire rose up out of the sail. He reloaded his rifle and tottered along the hull, leaping for the dock and nearly missing.

The Phoenix Force commando put his hands on his knees to catch his breath and woozily contemplated the stairs and the elevator. The elevator car was currently up top. It was a wide, steel freight elevator, made to take heavy loads from the bottom to the top. It made only two stops. Hawkins pulled a length of flexible charge from his fanny pack, leaned inside the open girder shaft and wrapped it around the pair of thick cables in a figure eight. He pushed in a detonator pin and stepped back.

"Going down!" Hawkins flicked the arming switch on his detonator box and pushed the button. The flexible charge hissed yellow fire in a halo around the cables and they suddenly came free, snapping and thrashing like angry snakes. Upstairs something made a very unhappy "clank!" and the elevator car dropped free.

"Oh, shit!" Hawkins threw himself behind the stairwell as the car hurtled down toward the dock. It hit bottom like a train wreck. The car was little more than a metal cage, and sections of it scythed across the dock in all directions. Several large size pieces slammed into the stairwell and rang it like a gong. Hawkins rose from cover and surveyed the mangled metal cage, then glanced back at the burning sub. He may have missed his landing, but he was doing a fine job of making mayhem from the ground up. Hawkins looked up at the mass of the platform overhead. He wasn't looking forward to walking up sixty-five feet of stairs, but if the enemy decided to bolt, they were going to have to come through him.

He put an exhausted foot on the first step and began his ascent.

CHAPTER THIRTY-TWO

The Platform

"Clear!" Lyons moved out of the dispensary and down the narrow corridor. They had cleared the barracks and the generator room and were working their way down. The Stony Man warriors had left a trail of death and destruction behind them, but by now the enemy knew they were just two men and had ceased their fighting retreat. Lyons and Bolan had broken two ambushes, mostly with the help of the Panzerfaust. Now they were fresh out of rockets.

Lyons stopped and held up a fist. Bolan crouched ten yards behind, covering the corridor with his rifle. At the end of the corridor a door was hanging open very suspiciously. "How many more do you figure?"

"Hard to say. Enough to keep us honest."

Lyons nodded. There was no way to go except forward.

The serrated lump of a fragmentation grenade sailed out the door and clattered across the floor. "Grenade!" Lyons shoved his arm out to full extension. The 12-gauge Jungle Gun roared, and the soft lead buckshot slammed into the iron casing of the grenade and sent it spinning back the way it had come. He fired a second and third time, and the grenade rolled back through the door and a man screamed as it detonated. Lyons crept forward. He took a quick peek through the door and nearly had his head taken off by gunfire.

The interior was a hangar. Massive steel frame racks stood empty where they would hold ADS suits and submersibles. A huge steel hatch had been cut into the floor and winches and cranes ringed it to lower divers and subs into the sea. Benches, compressors and equipment for servicing the deep diving gear was everywhere. Plenty of good solid cover for the bad guys.

Laurentius Deyn's voice rang out. "I would be very careful about throwing grenades into this room. You might hurt someone you care about. Isn't that right, Mr. Tokaido?"

The young hacker groaned with sudden pain.

"Carl!" Bolan shouted.

Lyons had burst into the hangar. Pistols and automatic rifles reverberated in the space. The Able Team leader rolled behind a massive winch and emptied his shotgun over the top.

Bolan ran forward, hurling his last flash-stun grenade in front of him. It detonated in harmless thunder in the middle of the hangar, but the sound and light allowed him to leap behind a compressor large enough to pump up a submarine. The echoes of the grenade reverberated away.

"Foolish," Deyn declared. "Throw down your weapons."

Lyons shoved fresh shells into his shotgun. Ammo was running low. He shot a glance over to Bolan. The Executioner had set down his rifle and filled his hands with a .50-caliber Desert Eagle in one hand and a Beretta 93-R machine pistol in the other. It would have been a Butch and Sundance situation except for the nuclear devices and a hostaged friend.

"Throw down your weapons," Deyn reiterated.

"Not gonna happen!" Lyons snarled.

"How can I convince you?" Deyn mockingly queried. A woman screamed. Johan Mahke rose up from behind an overturned steel worktable and bodily flung Franka Marx into the middle of the hangar. He quickly dropped his bulk behind cover again. Lyons's eyes narrowed. The German woman was a bloody mess and her clothes were torn, but it looked to be little more than a beating so far.

"Throw down your weapons!"

The knuckles of Lyons's good hand went white around the grips of his shotgun.

"Very well…Lars!"

A man popped up from cover in the corner of the hanger. His MP-5 submachine gun barked off a single shot.

Franka Marx screamed as the bullet blasted into the back of her leg and burst out the front.

"No!" Tokaido screamed.

"Carl!" Bolan shouted.

Lyons didn't need the admonition. He knew all about the sniper's draw. They would keep wounding Franka Marx until he and Bolan were forced to attack, and when they did they would have to rush across the open hangar into a cross fire, and Deyn still had Akira as his ace in the hole.

"Throw down your weapons!"

Marx lay on the giant steel door clutching her leg and weeping helplessly.

"Lars!" Deyn shouted.

Lyons swung his shotgun around, but it wasn't Lars who popped up. Mahke snaked his pistol out from cover and fired.

Marx screamed in agony as his bullet smashed through her shoulder.

Bolan looked over at Lyons and mouthed two words. *Your call.*

Lyons nodded.

Hawkins's voice roared from the back of the hangar. "Go! Go! Go!"

A pair of flash-stuns went off, filling the hangar with thunder, lighting and dancing pyrotechnic fireflies. Lyons and Bolan rose. The Executioner's Barrett boomed on rapid semiauto, and his armor-piercing bullets punched holes in Mahke's steel cover. The big man reared up bleeding and bellowing. He and Bolan exchanged fire. The soldier's ceramic armor took the 9 mm rounds. Johan Mahke's massive frame had to take the .50-caliber bullets as they tore through his Kevlar and ripped out his back, and the big man toppled like an oak.

Lars rose up, but Marx was no longer his target. Lyons's Jungle Gun roared like the King of the Beasts it was and buckshot hammered Lars's head into red ruin. Marx screamed again, not with the agony of another bullet but the panicked scream of a trapped animal.

Somewhere across the hangar Tokaido was screaming. "Franka! Franka!"

Mahke had thrown her onto the submersible deployment doors. Whoever had the controls had pressed Open. She tried to get away, but her gunshot wounds reduced her movement to a crippled crawl. The clamshell door opened beneath her and Franka Marx slid down the smooth steel, screaming as she fell into empty air.

Mack Bolan didn't hesitate. He tossed away has pistols and took a running leap. He did a jackknife over the doors and arrowed straight down into the dark after her. Lyons kept moving forward. Two of Deyn's men charged forward in full raid armor. The Ironman cut their knees out from under them, then mercilessly shot open their face shields at point-blank range.

Lyons crouched behind a rolling tool bin as everything went quiet. "Deyn!"

"He's in the corner!" Hawkins called.

"How many men?"

"One!"

Lyons had been expecting a lot more. Hawkins had to have taken care of some things down below. "Give it up, Deyn! Don't make me come get you!"

"You will surrender," Deyn replied, "or I will activate the devices. Then I will begin shooting your friend Akira apart a piece at a time."

"Kill his ass!" Tokaido shouted. "Just kill his—" The young man's call was cut off.

Lyons stalked forward like biblical retribution. He saw Hawkins moving forward along the far wall and gave him a single nod. The man nodded back. Lyons's directive was clear.

If you see the shot, take it.

"That is far enough," Deyn declared.

The German stood in front of a diving cage. Inside was a pallet holding the thermonuclear demolition charges. In front of the cage a pair of aluminum suitcases lay open to expose sophisticated communications equipment. Tokaido stood handcuffed in front of Deyn. Lyons's eyes went arctic. The kid looked like death warmed over. There wasn't an inch of exposed flesh that wasn't pulped. It was his eyes that were the worst. The young man stared out of the sea of broken blood vessels. He saw Lyons but from some terrible middle distance. Deyn's right arm was snaked under his hostage's arm, the muzzle of a Walther P-5 pressed firmly under his chin. Deyn held a black detonator box in his left hand. His smile was beatific. It was clear that he was absolutely insane.

It was a lose-lose situation. Everyone was going to die.

Lyons smiled back. If Deyn had had anything left of his tiny little mind, the smile would have sent him running to hide under the bed. "You're going to do it anyway."

"Drop the shotgun."

Lyons dropped the Mossberg.

Tokaido sagged in Deyn's grip. "Jesus, Carl, just—" He grimaced as the pistol jammed up against his jaw and shut it.

Deyn lifted a bemused eyebrow at the silenced SOCOM strapped to Lyons's thigh. "The pistol, with two fingers."

Lyons fumbled the snaps with his broken right hand. He pulled out the heavy pistol and dropped it to the floor. Tokaido's eyes rolled with utter despair. He was getting more of his friends killed.

"Tell your man to drop his rifle and pull back."

"T.J., drop the rifle. Pull back."

"Carl!" Hawkins was appalled. "We—"

"Do it!" Lyons snarled. A rifle clattered to the floor back by the far wall. Lyons lost the berserker smile. "Let him go."

Deyn's eyes flew wide with sadistic delight. "Let him go?" Deyn waved the detonator box like a magic wand. "Why—"

Lyons moved. He wasn't the best shot at Stony Man Farm or the most accurate, but perhaps second only to Bolan, Lyons never hesitated. He was beyond fast. Lyons was sudden. He was facing Deyn, and the German couldn't see the Colt Python where it rested in a small-of-the-back holster. Lyons was right-handed but he had spent hour after hour at the BUD firing range and then more at the Farm during the mission lull practicing his weak hand draw and emptying the Colt into a target at ten feet. His body detonated into the movement he had burned into his muscle memory.

The Big Snake struck in a blur of stainless steel.

The first .357 Magnum hollowpoint round burst apart Deyn's left hand and the detonator box it held. The German's eyes went blank with shock as he regarded the remaining shreds of his hand. Lyons had no time for Deyn's discomfort.

Lyons shot Tokaido through the left thigh.

The young man gasped and buckled. Deyn's right arm had to take the young man's body weight. Deyn's pistol scraped out from underneath Akira's jaw and fired into empty air. He struggled to bring the weapon up, but his embrace around Akira's handcuffed body encumbered him. He stared down the barrel of the Python, his pupils dialing down to pinholes of insane, thwarted rage.

"No—!"

The 125-grain jacketed hollowpoint round punched through the bridge of Deyn's nose and blew out the back of his head.

He and Tokaido fell to a tangle on the floor.

"T.J.! Medic kit! ASAP!"

Hawkins charged forward as Lyons pulled Tokaido free and applied pressure to his wounded leg. A .357 round made an ugly wound. The computer wizard already looked to have gone through hell, and he was slipping straight into shock. Hawkins skidded to a stop and ripped field dressings out of his web gear. His jaw dropped as he looked at Tokaido. "Jesus…"

Lyons took the bandages and eyed Hawkins. The former Delta Force commando's eyes looked out from textbook raccoon bruising. His nose was clearly broken. "You all right?"

"I think I have a concussion."

"Mmm." Lyons nodded. "That's got to be the radio jammer. Cut it and get on the horn."

"Carl..."

Lyons turned his head toward the cage. The casings were making a slight whirring noise. They all simultaneously made a sharp click, and their exposed dials all rotated a notch. Lyons stared at Laurentius Deyn's shattered skull.

Deadman's switch.

Tokaido bled through the first field dressing and Lyons applied another. "Can you see the timer?"

Hawkins strained his arm through the bars. "I can't reach the access panel!"

Lyons applied a third dressing. "How the hell were they going to get out of here in twenty minutes?"

"Oh." Hawkins yawned and shook his head. "They have a sub."

"A sub?"

"Yeah, but...I fragged it."

"You fragged it." Lyons took a long hard look at the man. He didn't look too good. "That would've been our only way out."

Hawkins blinked. "I ate a pylon. I have a concussion."

"See if you can cut the jammer."

Hawkins knelt by the communications gear and began flipping switches. "Jamming is off. We have tactical."

Lyons thumbed his mike. "Control, this is Ironman."

Barbara Price's voice came back instantly. "Sitrep, Ironman."

"Akira secured. Deyn dead. Striker and Franka Marx MIA."

Bolan's voice came back over the sound of the howling wind. "I have Marx."

"What is the status of the devices, Ironman?"

"They are active and on a countdown."

"How long?"

"We don't know. I am out of explosives and the devices are tamper-proofed and secured in a cage. I can neither access nor defuse. I have wounded. Can you extract us?"

"Negative, Ironman. Not in time. Helicopter resources are extracting the dive team. The hardsuits have to be extracted by sling and they took a prisoner as well as the crews of two submersibles. Extraction resources are at their limit." Price was clearly trying to control her emotions. "They secured the ridge. Primary mission is a success."

"Well, that's good news." Lyons let out a long sigh. Tokaido had slipped into unconsciousness. It would be a blessing to leave him that way. "Call in the strike, Control."

"Carl…"

"Call in the strike. With any luck it'll be a ten-kiloton blast or less rather than a hundred."

"Stand by, Ironman."

Bolan's voice came across the link. "Carl, I'm coming up."

"You're clear, Mack. Come ahead."

The wind moaned up through the open deployment doors while they waited. Bolan came up out the stairwell soaked with a bloody and bandaged Franka Marx unconscious in his arms. He placed her next to Akira. Bolan smiled with genuine warmth and stuck out his hand. "Nice knowing you guys."

Hawkins grinned. "It's been a privilege."

Lyons rare smile crept onto his face. "Hell of a ride."

Price's voice came back across the line. She and Bolan had been intimate and her voice was breaking. "The *Virginia* is about to fire. You could try…swimming, or—"

"You can't outswim one hundred kilotons, Barbara. Much less a hundred."

Lyons gazed down at Tokaido. "I told the Bear I'd stick with Akira no matter what."

Hawkins sighed. "I have a headache."

"We're just going to stay here, Barb. Tell everyone else…well, tell them, and tell Calvin good job."

Lyons cocked his head. "Tell the sub to belay the missile strike."

The line was silent for several shocked moments. "Carl…"

Bolan had seen that look on Lyons's face before. Many of the operators were meticulous planners. Others flew by the seat of their pants. The Ironman often operated on what could only be described as divine madness.

Price was flabbergasted. "Carl, I don't have the authority to—"

"Barb, can you put the sub's captain on the line?"

"Stand by."

Moments went by and then the line clicked. "Ironman, this is Captain Laswell. How may I be of assistance?"

"Can you sink the platform?"

"Sink it?"

"Yeah, rather than blowing it up with missiles and detonating the weapons on the surface, how about you sink it with torpedoes?"

"Ironman, the water will absorb the heat and radiation, but you'll still be blasted sky-high when the weapons go off."

"Yeah," Lyons admitted. "But like you said, the ocean will absorb the heat and radiation. It will be just like a one-hundred-kiloton depth charge. Except for some high water, Cape Hatteras won't take the hit."

The line went silent.

"Carl?"

"Yeah, Mack?"

"You're amazing."

Lyons glanced at his watch and thumbed his mike. "Barb?"

"Stand by."

Moments passed as Kurtzman, the Joint Chiefs and the President of the United States were consulted.

Captain Laswell of the USS *Virginia* came on the line. "Fish in the water, Ironman. ETA two minutes."

"Affirmative, *Virginia*."

Bolan rose. "Let's go up top."

Hawkins sighed wearily where he sat against the wall. "Why?"

Bolan picked up Marx. "In here we drown. Up top we float until the blast. It'll be quicker."

Lyons pushed himself to his feet and gathered up Tokaido. "Roger that."

The three of them made their way up to the platform. The wind and rain lashed against them. Hawkins dug life jackets out of the barracks lockers. Lyons checked his watch as they lashed themselves together with the slings from their weapons. "Ten seconds—"

The entire platform shuddered as if an earthquake had struck. The steel superstructure moaned like a wounded beast with a sound that vibrated their bones. The four Mark 48 Advanced Capability torpedoes were at the limit of their range. They had cut their guide wires tens of thousands of feet back and gone into search mode. The massive support pylons of the platform were the only game in town. Their warheads were large enough to sink a Russian cruiser. The platform's support pylons were massive steel girders encased in concrete. The torpedoes didn't have the power to blow the platform's legs off, but the entire structure shuddered as it was knee-capped.

Lyons took hold of Tokaido in a death grip. "Here we go!"

Stomachs dropped and everything unsecured slid as the entire platform tilted. The team went with the lean, taking short running steps until the wall of the command shack was beneath their boots and was no longer a wall but a floor. Pallets tumbled and broke open. The fuselage of the crippled helicopter tumbled across the deck, and the broken crane boom scraped by showering sparks once more. The metal girders ceased their moaning and screamed as they tore and snapped. The platform was no longer leaning. It was falling. It went dark as the platform lights went out.

The world fell out from under the team's boots.

Lyons took a deep breath.

The Atlantic Ocean hit him like a fist to jaw.

The sea closed over his head and didn't stop. The platform was a huge mass of concrete and steel, and as it hit the water it made a hole. The ocean rushed in to reclaim its space and pulled the team down with it. Lyons's ears pounded and lights pulsed behind his eyes as he was sucked down into the black.

Unlike the million-ton mass of the platform, Lyons and his team were wearing life jackets. They were buoyant, and at a certain point the water equalized and they popped back up like corks. The surface was little better. It was as black as below but with driving wind, rain and waves slapping them forehand and back.

"You all right!"

"Yeah!" Bolan shouted back. "You?"

"Yeah! T.J.?" Lyons bellowed over the wind. "T.J.!"

Hawkins made a noise like a bear being impaled as he retched up the Atlantic. "Let's do it again!"

Bolan laughed. It was a strange sound in the howling, freezing dark, but in open ocean facing certain death, the sound was strangely infectious. The Ironman found himself laughing. He threw back his head and laughed so hard his ribs ached. Hawkins made strangled, barking noises of amusement between retching.

The laughing soldiers pulled themselves into a circle and waited for death. They had cheated it so many times they had earned the right to laugh in its face. Lyons grabbed Hawkins by the hair. "Try to keep your head above water!"

"No!" Hawkins heaved a bit more. "No, I hear something."

Lyons shoved his head under the water and his eyes flew wide despite the salt sting. A very distinctive *tung-tung-tung* noise was hammering through the water below the surface.

The bow sonar of the USS *Virginia* had gone active.

Lyons pulled his head up and spat. "We're being pinged!"

Bolan's voice shouted in the dark. "You still got a piece? I dumped mine!"

Lyons unsnapped the Big Snake from its holster. He hadn't reloaded, but he still had three rounds in the chamber. He drew the pistol and held it under water. Lyons methodically pulled the trigger once, twice and three times. They were five bodies bobbing on the surface in a storm. Not much for even active sonar to detect. But in the acoustic world of the *Virginia*'s main sonar array the hammer of the Magnum's blast was like a triple flare in the darkness.

Lyons and his team bobbed in the storm and waited for one hundred kilotons of released energy to blast them into the sky. "How's Franka?"

"Breathing!" Bolan shouted. "I can't tell, but she's got to be bleeding again. Akira, too!" Bolan paused. "T.J.'s unconscious!"

That was bad with a concussion, but—

"Carl!"

Lyons didn't need to be told. Out across the waves a searchlight was playing across the rolling surface.

"You got any more ammo!"

Lyons tried to break open his Python but his fingers were numb. "Try T.J.!"

A second later the darkness flashed yellow as Hawkins's 9 mm SIG went off in Bolan's hand. The soldier began to squeeze off a shot in the air every three seconds. The searchlight swung in their direction and played over them as a waves lifted them up. Aching moments passed, but the light stayed fixed on their position. The waves churned and the dark mass of the USS *Virginia* plowed toward them. Sailors with a gaff leaned out and Lyons seized the hook.

The team was pulled up against the hull and more men grabbed them and manhandled the scrum of humanity onto the sub. A midshipman shouted down the hatch as seamen cut apart their lashings. "We have them!"

"Get them down and button up! Engines full!"

Marx, Tokaido and Hawkins were lowered down. Lyons and Bolan slid down the ladder and the last sailor sealed the hatch behind them. The *Virginia*'s hull throbbed as her S9G nuclear reactor rods were pulled out to full and her turbines steamed to full emergency war power.

Blankets were thrown over Lyons's and Bolan's shoulders, and hot coffee mugs shoved in their hands. The three wounded disappeared down a corridor toward the infirmary. Lyons and Bolan were ushered to the bridge. A tall, dark-haired man in a captain's uniform regarded them. "Evening, gentleman. Worth a man's life to go out swimming tonight."

Lyons shook his head. "Captain?"

"Yes?"

"All due respect, but you're an idiot."

"Yeah, well, maybe." Captain Laswell shrugged. "But I figure a man who called down a cruise missile strike and full spread of torpedoes on himself on the same day deserved a fighting chance."

"We'll be blown sky-high."

Laswell stood proudly on his bridge. "Mister, this is the USS *Virginia*, lead ship of the Virginia-class line. Besides, you got me thinking when you compared the detonation to a one-hundred-kiloton depth charge. We're doing over thirty knots out of the blast area and we're on the surface." The captain looked over at his XO. "We can take the hit, can't we, Tom?"

The commanding officer regarded his captain leerily. "Well…"

"Of course we can." The captain grinned winningly.

Submarining was the most dangerous and stressful form of sailing known to man. It took a special form of sailor to navigate the dark depths playing hide-and-seek with the navies of the other superpowers, and a man didn't rise to captain the flagship of the U.S. Navy's new line of attack submarines without a bucketload of skill, balls and daring.

Lyons held up the shreds of his cast. "Thanks."

Laswell wrapped one of his mitts gingerly around the Ironman's broken hand. "Not a problem. I know you Special Forces types have a thing about no one left behind. Well, this is the Navy, and we have a policy about not leaving anybody bobbing."

Lyons well knew that in both services those policies were unofficial, particularly when it came to risking an attack submarine and her entire crew by sailing it into a nuclear blast zone to save five people. Laswell was going to have a lot of answering to do if they lived.

The sonar operator's speakers screamed feedback and blew out as the BQQ-10 bow sonar array received the loudest noise it had ever encountered. The hull rumbled like distant thunder. The XO grabbed a microphone and his voice boomed over the shipwide intercom. "All hands brace for impact! Repeat, all hands brace—"

Lyons had been on subs under attack before and felt the Godlike slap of depth charges trying to crack a hull, but this was different.

God snuck up behind the *Virginia* and tried to shove her off the planet.

The Atlantic Ocean had swallowed Deyn's platform down to the bottom, but it hurled up the *Virginia* as if it didn't want it. The steersman's hands were white on his controls. "Oh...my...God..."

The depth gauge slammed at zero because it couldn't go into negative numbers. The *Virginia* needed an altimeter as all 7,800 tons of her left the surface. The deck beneath their feet rolled sickeningly. The ocean might not have wanted the *Virginia,* but gravity did. She fell back to Earth like a four-hundred-foot leviathan. Lyons left his feet as the *Virginia* hit the unyielding surface, and everything not bolted down went flying. The lights went out and his face met something made of steel. Lyons saw stars and the air was smashed from his lungs as he landed on the deck and rolled. He came to a stop against the bulkhead.

Red bathed the bridge as the emergency generators clicked on. Water sprayed from a broken main above. Numerous alarms were peeping and howling. Lyons took stock of his surroundings and realized that the floor was tilted at a seventy-five-degree angle.

"Full stop!" The captain clung to a rail with his head split open. "Damage report!"

The XO managed to climb to a console and get on the horn with the rest of the sub. "Captain, reactor rods are out of alignment. The chief engineer has ordered the evacuation of the engine room."

"Any radiation leakage?"

"No, sir. Leakage is confined to the engine room and it's

being sealed off. We've lost the aft stabilizer. Numerous injuries reported on all decks. Mostly broken bones."

"Are we taking on water?"

"No, sir." The XO shook his head wonderingly. "The pressure hulls are intact."

"See?" The captain glanced over Lyons. His teeth flashed out of the blood masking his face. "Told you we could take the hit."

EPILOGUE

Stony Man Farm, Virginia

"Check it out!" Akira Tokaido popped a wheelie in his wheelchair. "Wait for it! Wait for it…" The young man rocked the chair from side to side and suddenly leaned and tipped. "One-wheel wheelie!" He held the position for several seconds, then let the chair slam back down. He grinned, and waved at Bolan and then turned back to his workstation.

Bolan smiled. "They say he'll be on crutches in a week, and walking again in about a month."

The smile on Lyons's face died the moment the young man turned away. "Yeah, but I was supposed to take care of him. I got him captured instead. Hell, I had to shoot him to retrieve him."

"Yeah, and he won't shut up about it, either. He's going to wear that scar like a badge of honor."

"I've spoken to the doctors. What he isn't talking about is the nightmares and the clinical depression. He's been grinning and bearing it, and only because they have him on a severe regimen of antidepressants."

"The body heals. So does the mind. It just takes longer." Bolan looked pointedly at Lyons. "That goes for you, too, Carl. The Bear's already forgiven you. Akira sees nothing to forgive. He looks up to you like God on high. The person you've got to forgive here is yourself."

The Ironman locked eyes with the Executioner. "You try to hug me, I'll snap your goddamn neck."

"Wouldn't dream of it. But I know you, Carl. Known you for too long. You feel guilty and you want to make things right. Walking around with tombstone face and spending eight hours a day shooting left-handed at the range isn't going to help."

Lyons slowly shook his head. "I'm not going to therapy."

"Okay, then let's make something right."

Lyons glared suspiciously. "What do you mean?"

"Captain Laswell's been put behind a desk pending review of his actions during the crisis."

"I've already written my report. I recommended putting him up for a Navy Cross."

"Yeah, but that isn't up to us."

"So what are you recommending?"

"I've done some research on the good captain."

"And?"

Bolan grinned. "He's a single-malt man."

Lyons smiled despite himself. "Well, let's go buy the man a drink."

James Axler
Outlanders®

CLOSING THE COSMIC EYE

Rumors of an ancient doomsday device come to the attention of the Cerberus rebels when it's stolen by an old enemy, Gilgamesh Bates. The pre-Dark mogul who engineered his own survival has now set his sights on a controlling share of the cosmic pie. Kane, Grant, Brigid and Domi ally themselves with Bates's retired personal army, a time-trawled force of American commandos ready to take the battle back to Bates himself, wherever he's hiding in the galaxy, before the entire universe disappears in the blink of an eye.

Available February 2007 wherever books are sold.

Or order your copy now by sending your name, address, zip or postal code, along with a check or money order (please do not send cash) for $6.50 for each book ordered ($7.99 in Canada), plus 75¢ postage and handling ($1.00 in Canada), payable to Gold Eagle Books, to:

In the U.S.	**In Canada**
Gold Eagle Books	Gold Eagle Books
3010 Walden Avenue	P.O. Box 636
P.O. Box 9077	Fort Erie, Ontario
Buffalo, NY 14269-9077	L2A 5X3

Please specify book title with your order.
Canadian residents add applicable federal and provincial taxes.

GOLD EAGLE®

GOUT40

TAKE 'EM FREE
2 action-packed novels plus a mystery bonus
NO RISK
NO OBLIGATION TO BUY